BOOK
OF
FORBIDDEN
WORDS

Also by Louise Fein

Daughter of the Reich
The Hidden Child
The London Bookshop Affair

BOOK OF FORBIDDEN WORDS

A Novel

LOUISE FEIN

WILLIAM MORROW
An Imprint of HarperCollinsPublishers

BOOK OF FORBIDDEN WORDS. Copyright © 2026 by Louise Fein. All rights reserved. Printed in the United States of America. No part of this book may be used or reproduced in any manner whatsoever without written permission except in the case of brief quotations embodied in critical articles and reviews. For information, address HarperCollins Publishers, 195 Broadway, New York, NY 10007.

HarperCollins books may be purchased for educational, business, or sales promotional use. For information, please email the Special Markets Department at SPsales@harpercollins.com.

FIRST EDITION

Interior text design by Diahann Sturge-Campbell

Title page book illustration © ~Bitter~/Stock.Adobe.com

Library of Congress Cataloging-in-Publication Data has been applied for.

ISBN 978-0-06-341143-2

$PrintCode

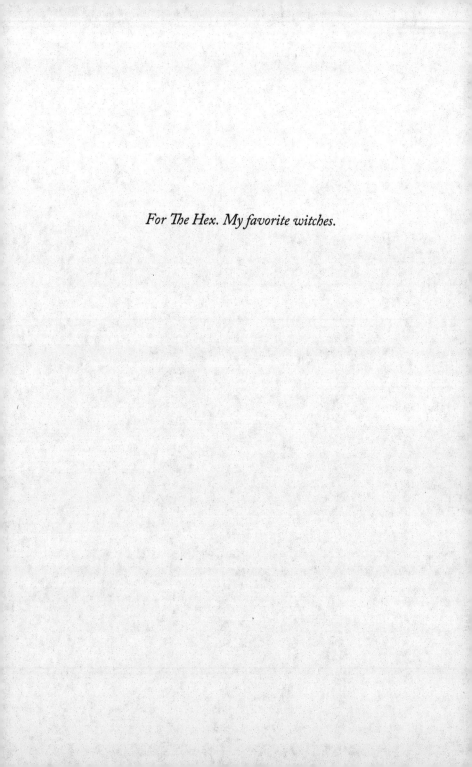

For The Hex. My favorite witches.

"He who destroys a good book kills reason itself."
—JOHN MILTON

"If all printers were determined not to print anything till they were sure it would offend nobody, there would be very little printed."
—BENJAMIN FRANKLIN

Historical Note

In the little German town of Mainz, sometime around the mid-1400s, Johannes Gutenberg came up with an idea that would change the world forever: the printing press.

What was to follow would revolutionize the Western world, taking it out of the feudal Middle Ages and into the Modern era. Printing meant the common man (and a few women), at least those who were literate, could spread ideas far and wide, for good or bad. News and false news could be circulated with, compared to previous times, lightning speed. The era of mass media had been born.

Information was no longer solely in the hands of those who held the power—the church and the state. This was a seismic change. Amazingly, not long after, the first feminist pamphlets began to be published, advocating ideas of respect and equality for women.

In 1517, this time in the town of Wittenberg, Germany, another man, a monk, named Martin Luther, published a document containing ninety-five ideas about Christianity he invited discussion on. This was a time when there was no such concept as secularism, and everyone believed in God and the afterlife. Luther's questioning of the status quo exploded a bomb into Europe, and many years of violent religious wars were to follow in what became known as the Protestant Reformation.

Today, the violent storm that blew up over whether the Bible could be translated from Latin into other languages, or whether salvation for a person's soul could be gained through payments to the church, is hard to understand. But, boiled down, the violence that erupted was over the challenge to the authority and wealth of the church and those who ruled, and who would gain from the shift. Those fearing these new ideas would result in the end of the world clung desperately to the existing order, and they hunted with increasing ferocity the "heretics" who sought change.

BOOK
OF
FORBIDDEN
WORDS

Prologue

Paris, July 1552

The moon hung low in a cloudless night sky.

She paused a moment to stare at it, wondering what magic held it there, suspended like a specter in the dark, round as a freshly minted coin, pale as buttermilk.

But this was no time to linger, and, pulling the hood of her cloak farther over her head to be sure the fair band of her hair was fully covered, she crept, quiet as a cat in her indoor slippers, the cobbles hard and rough against the soles of her feet, toward the gate that led into the Cemetery of the Innocents at the heart of Les Halles. She turned and checked behind her before entering the graveyard.

For it was the living, not the dead, who filled her with trepidation..

All was quiet and still.

She heaved a long, slow breath to gather herself, then, head down, she hurried on, recalling the route in daylight yesterday. The distance was short. The manuscript was safe. And, with good fortune, by the time the sun rose, she'd have secured its future too.

She turned right onto Rue Saint Denis, St. Catherine, before her, keeping to the shadows of the walls of the hospital, left, then right again, passing the hulking shape of the church in the square, then winding down toward the river. She could smell it now, sharp in her nostrils, raw and earthy. She glanced east and fancied there was a lightening of the sky over Paris, but perhaps it was just the glow of the moon, still shining bright as a polished pearl button.

She was at the edge of the bridge now, *Le Pont Notre-Dame*, and hesitated. There she would be at her most vulnerable. The bridge ran straight and true across this stretch of the river, on to the island at its center where the great church of the *Notre-Dame de Paris* dominated the surrounding buildings. But with the houses densely packed side by side along the bridge, if she were pursued, there would be no escape. No alley to dart down, no wall to hide behind. Her fingers found the tender flesh at her wrist. Her head still ached and her ribs were bruised, but she would not cry. Enough tears had been shed already, and they were useless.

She could see the Notre-Dame cathedral from where she stood, its tall steeple dense against the paler sky, rising like a long, tapering finger toward the heavens. It felt like a message. *God will not abandon you in this, your hour of need.*

A soft breath of wind from the river stroked her skin. She listened. No sound on the cobbles, just the rush of water beneath the bridge and she was moving again, tripping in her haste, her breath shallow, heart beating like a drum. Eyes fixed on the far end of the bridge, she didn't look back, didn't dare. At last she was on solid ground, the walls of the Convent of the Blessed Heart rising before her and she almost cried with relief.

All she needed to do now was follow the wall to the end of the street, turn left, and the woman would be waiting.

A tiny stone, no bigger than a silver penny skittered beside her left heel. The sound of it echoed off the tall stone wall, too loud, too unnatural, and a dart of red-hot fear shot through her. She whirled around. The figure of a man loomed but three feet behind her, hooded, swathed in black. She stumbled back, attempted to run, but her legs turned to liquid.

There was a beat of time as her mind tripped. *Where had he come from? How did she not hear him?*

A viselike grip on her arm, and she was spun around as if she were but a feather tossed on the wind. She glimpsed his face beneath the shadow of his hood, the set of his jaw, shape of his chin. The shock of recognition.

"Please—"

But her words, her sob, her struggle against his grip, were stopped as he pulled her flat to his chest, her throat tight with terror, his large, solid arm pinning her to him.

Silver flashed in his other hand.

There was no more time for thought or words as a roar filled her ears and a searing pain like none she had ever known tore at her throat.

Chapter 1

Milly

Levittown, Long Island, New York, November 1952

The library squats low in one corner of South Village Green. Utilitarian and plain, it crouches beneath a flat, brown roof. Its ugliness belies the beauty of what harbors inside its bland walls. It's Milly's favorite haunt, with or without the children. The shelves of books, the smell of them, evocative of knowledge and worlds other than her own, transport her right back to a very different library. That one, as soaring and beautiful outside as in, was steeped in history and privilege. It was there that she spent many delicious hours before the war, engrossed in her studies. Before her dream of a life in academia was stubbed out, like a cigarette ground into the dirt beneath a soldier's boot.

Before George. Before Edward and Olive. Before everything.

The morning is damp and raw, the threat of snow hanging in the air like a bad mood. Milly hesitates at the door. She should go straight home, use the precious time before she must collect Olive to clean the house, wash the clothes, iron George's shirts, prepare a tasty meal like a good wife would. No, that can wait. She'll make a game of it all with Olive later. Perhaps she should take the advice of the Coven, otherwise known as the mothers from Abbey Lane Elementary School, and get some help at home. But the thought of having someone in her house that she must make polite chitchat with, give orders to, makes her feel sick.

She steps inside the bright warmth of the library and tension flows out of her, a long exhale. Milly rolls her shoulders and finds herself drawn, as usual, to the small section, right at the back, *Classical Greece and Rome*.

She stares at the spines, *The Greek Myths*, *The Iliad*, *The Odyssey*. The collection is basic, but better than nothing. She lifts Herodotus's *Histories* off the shelf, wondering if it is permitted under library rules to take it out again, seeing as she only returned it two days ago. A distraction from the discomfort that still sits in her belly from this morning's encounter with Doris Sykes and the Coven at the monthly PTA Tuesday morning coffee.

It was George who suggested she should go. *I know it's hard for you, Milly-Moo, but we've been here six months now. Look at the children! They're making friends and fitting in. Make an effort with the other mothers. Spend time with them, get to know them. And while you have coffee, the children can play with their little friends. You just need to fit in.*

Fit in? This morning, she fit in like a mongrel at a pedigree dog show. The blur of names, their elegant clothes, the perfectly pinned curls, painted nails, and rouged lips. The look in their eyes as they took in her patched-up coat, straight hair, lack of makeup. She might lack fashion sense but there is nothing wrong with her ears and she heard all right their sniggers over *tweed* and *those shoes* as they assessed her shapeless skirt once the offending coat had been removed.

"This is Millicent Bennett," Doris crooned, placing an arm around Milly's shoulders and pulling her into the heart of the Coven. "She and her husband, George, came over from London—"

"It's Milly. And it was Oxford."

"Oxford, England, just six weeks ago, and—"

"Months. It was six months ago. But we stayed with George's

parents early on, in Kentucky, while he looked for a job and found this house. Lucky it wasn't *too* long because I think we outstayed our welcome. George's mother, Patricia, well, she and I didn't rub along too well, and I think, honestly, she prefers horses to people, which I can understand, but it was awful really, she didn't want the children breaking anything and I felt like I was walking on eggshells . . ." Everyone was staring and she knew she should stop but she couldn't now she'd started. "George was gone for a month at least, and everything I did seemed to be wrong, especially my cooking. I mean who doesn't like bubble and squeak or toad-in-the-hole?"

"Coffee?"

"I prefer tea. Milk, one sugar." She'd caught the look exchanged between Doris and Sissy Friedland. "Please."

While Doris was in the kitchen, Sissy asked what brought them to America. Milly was so nervous by then, everything got muddled and came out in the wrong order.

"Poor George, after the war he struggled to find work in England. I mean, he'd been in Germany—he was in the air force for a bit after we were married—well, he went back and forth or how else would we have made the children?" Someone sniggered and she felt her face flush hot. "But then Mother got ill and he was de-mobbed and he wanted to come here, but we couldn't—because of Mother's cancer and being an only child, there was only me—and that's when he struggled to find work." She heaved in a breath. Plowed on. "He was so good with her, but she died of the cancer anyway, and England is so gray and clapped out and the rationing got to us, so we thought, better to come here where there are jobs and no rubble." *Shut up, Milly. Just. Stop. Talking.*

"I'm so sorry about your mother," someone said.

"Oh, well, thank you. That's why we stayed in Blighty so long, you see. She went downhill rather slowly, and I could hardly abandon her, could I? Not with my father gone already. Not that I was much use at the end. Couldn't face her pain. George was the one. The strong one. The better one."

Milly cringes now as she remembers her words and the way the other women had looked at one another. She'd sounded so callous and that wasn't it at all. Mother's absence left a giant hole inside her that nothing and nobody could fill, not even George. Mother understood her in the way nobody else in the entire world understood her. She and Father, while he had still been alive, had nurtured what even Milly could see was a bizarre obsession with everything Greek and Roman after she had read, at age five, a children's book of Greek and Roman myths. She'd badgered them for Latin lessons and later they paid a tutor for her to learn ancient Greek, which in the end had been the reason she'd landed her place at Somerville College studying those languages and the ancient world.

She places Herodotus back on the shelf. *Not today.*

She turns and walks purposefully toward the modern literature shelves. She needs to live in the present. There are the hair and the clothes that need to be tackled, but first she should immerse herself in American culture if she wants to fit in. She owes it to George and the children to try.

Milly walks slowly up each aisle, breathing in the musky scent of the library, scanning the books arranged in alphabetical order by authors' surname, *A* to *Z*. She reaches the end of *S* when someone clears their throat just behind her left ear, making her jump.

"Oops, I didn't mean to startle you." It's Miss Leeson, the librarian, who reads to the children during Story Hour. "Oh, Mrs. Bennett! I didn't realize it was you. Perhaps you need some help choosing a book?"

Milly takes an involuntary step back. The woman is so close, she can see the open pores on her nose and a ridge of tiny dark hairs on her upper lip. She reads the curly black writing on the badge Miss Leeson has pinned upside down on her chest, *Hi! I'm Susan and I'm here to help.*

"Goodness, Miss Leeson, you gave me a quite a fright."

"Oh dear. I always seem to be surprising people. I really don't mean to . . ."

"It's all right. I'm fully recovered."

"How are the little ones?"

"Oh, they're fine. Edward is in first grade, and little Olive is settling in nicely at kindergarten. She loves to be busy and is even starting to read and write all her letters."

"Goodness. She is a clever girl. You must bring her in to choose a book soon."

"I most definitely will."

Miss Leeson smiles and Milly thinks she catches a look of sadness in the older woman's eyes. Perhaps she wishes she were married and had had children? By now she might have had grandchildren to take to the park. Perhaps she *had* wanted to marry but never found the right man. Milly wonders why. She is pleasant enough. A little off-kilter perhaps, but genuine. And genuine is an undervalued attribute. Especially in women.

"Remember, story time is twice a day, ten a.m. and two p.m." She looks from Milly to the bookshelves beside her. "We have some swell romances over there, if you're looking for something for yourself." She points to a section by the far wall. "This, here, is the more serious fiction . . ." Milly must have given her quite the stare, for the woman's face reddens and she says, "Well, if you don't need any help, I'll leave you be."

Miss Leeson turns away from her, shoulders bowed. Perhaps

the librarian is simply lonely? An emotion Milly herself knows only too well.

"No, wait, Miss Leeson, I could do with some help. I'd like to read some American authors. Get a better sense of your history and culture. Before I was married and came to live here, and, well, before the war, I was at university. I studied Ancient Greek and Latin at Somerville College, Oxford." She pauses, and Miss Leeson blinks rapidly behind her glasses. *Too much*, Milly thinks. *Again.* "Not awfully useful to me now." She points to the line of books under *S*. "I was looking here for novels by John Steinbeck—*Of Mice and Men*, or perhaps *The Grapes of Wrath*? But I can't see any. Are they all out on loan?"

Miss Leeson blanches. "Oh!" she says, glancing behind her. "Oh dear."

"What is it?"

"I'm afraid we don't stock those books here, Mrs. Bennett." She draws closer to Milly and lowers her voice. "Nor any others of that ilk. I suppose being from abroad, perhaps you didn't know?"

"Didn't know what?"

The woman glances around the library again. There are a few other people scanning nearby shelves. It is deathly quiet, the only sounds being the soft thump of a book being placed on a table, the hum of the lights, and Milly's pulse in her ears.

Miss Leeson swallows. "Steinbeck is a . . ." Her face puckers, and she mouths the word *communist*. "Our library only stocks suitable books," she says a little louder. "Anyone borrowing from us can be confident they will not find anything unpatriotic, profane, explicit, or unsuitable." She speaks as though reeling off a well-rehearsed list.

Milly feels herself flash scarlet as the browsers turn to look. What on earth must these people think she has asked for? She can feel the judgy stares of the other librarygoers. She wouldn't have said a thing had she not been trying to be kind. Indignation throbs inside.

"I didn't mean to cause offense," she says through gritted teeth.

Miss Leeson takes a step closer. "Look," she whispers, "why don't we step into my office for a moment?"

The woman places a firm hand between Milly's shoulders and guides her between the bookcases toward a door at the back of the library.

Once they are seated on hardbacked chairs in the center of the small room that appears to serve as Miss Leeson's office, Milly's anger dissipates. Miss Leeson and her disheveled bun, heavy glasses, and soft cheeks is a creature to be pitied. This is the extent of her empire. This sad stack of books waiting to be stamped. Library cards to be written up and issued, catalogs to be gone through.

"I didn't mean to embarrass you out there, but I *had* to say all that if I want to keep my job."

"Miss Leeson, I really—"

"Susan, please. My dear, we've known each other long enough, and look here . . ." The nervous giggle again. "Now we are getting to know each other better still."

"Well, okay, Susan, then I suppose you must call me Milly, too, but I don't—"

"The thing is, Milly . . ." Susan jumps from her chair and scurries around behind the desk pressed into the corner of the room. She disappears as she crouches behind it. "There are lots of reasons this library has chosen not to stock certain volumes as I said—profanity, sexual deviance, communist ideals, blasphemy. The list is long." There is a sound of rummaging. "Mr. Sullivan, my boss, is very particular about that."

"I am sorry," Milly says, anxious now to escape this suffocating little room and being alone with Susan. "I really didn't mean to cause trouble, and hopefully there is no harm done, but I should be going now . . ."

"Oh, I won't keep you a moment . . ." Susan pops up again, waving a book in her hand and grinning. "Found it!" She dashes back around the desk and places the book with a sweep of triumph into Milly's hands.

Of Mice and Men, Milly reads. She glances up in surprise. Susan is smiling widely, teeth just a little too big for her mouth.

Milly glances back at the book in her hands. "I don't understand," she says slowly. "If this book is illegal, how come you have it?"

"It's not illegal as such, just banned from the area's libraries. Now, if you ever want a book that has, shall we say, a *controversial* subject matter, just ask me on the quiet. I keep a growing private collection of my own in here. For a select group of discerning customers only." She places her hands on her hips and surveys the room. "Mr. Sullivan *never* ventures into my lair, so it's quite safe."

"Goodness."

"Personally," Susan continues, "I think we should be able to read and discuss books freely. And you, being a college girl, I'm sure, would agree. Am I right?"

Milly finds herself smiling back. "You are."

"Now, I must be getting back to work. Just bring that in when you've finished it. Perhaps we can chat about what you think over coffee sometime?"

Milly tilts her head, seeing Susan in a new way. She is quite unlike the Coven. And to chat about a book rather than the laziness of home helpers, chipped fingernail polish, or whatever would be awfully refreshing. "I would love that."

"Oh, and one more thing. Keep this to yourself, will you? **Not** even your husband can know I've lent you this."

"Absolutely." Milly waves the book. "I assure you, Susan. **I am** very good at keeping secrets."

Later, Milly, the book clipped safely inside her handbag, **and** four-year-old Olive, full of tales from her morning at kindergarten, walk hand in hand down Old Oak Lane toward their **home** at number 26. It has been a meandering trip, there being no **need** to hurry. First, they stopped at the playground for Olive to **ride** on the merry-go-round and the seesaw, then Milly pushed her **for** a while on the swing. After that they visited the duck pond. The walk home from there took half an hour rather than the usual fifteen minutes as there were leaves to collect, stones to examine, and cats to stroke. At last, Olive professed to be hungry for lunch, so they sped up a little along the last stretch.

It is only as Milly reaches number 22 that she notices the **man** standing on her doorstep. She doesn't recognize him immediately, on account of the calf-length coat, the hat, and scarf half obscuring his face.

"Who is that man?" Olive asks pointing at him with one **small,** gloved finger.

Milly is about to reply that she has no idea, simultaneously **not**ing the twitch of the curtain at number 25 and Mrs. Humphries surreptitiously glancing over while apparently tending her rosebushes, when the man turns around.

"Oh my," Milly murmurs, stopping so abruptly, Olive almost trips.

"Mummy? Is he a bad man?" She leans in, gripping her mother's hand tighter.

"No." Milly lets out a breath. She lurches forward, tugging Olive so she must run to keep up. "He is a *good* man. The very best. Just one I never expected to see again."

Milly locks eyes with the man, and he raises his hand in greeting. All at once the years slide away and she is back in the hut in Buckinghamshire during the war, her eyes swollen and sore under the fierce glare of lights. There is dust in her throat and a cacophony of noise outside. She remembers being hunched over her desk in the intense summer heat and the numbing cold of winter. Long, long, tedious hours, fighting against sleep to concentrate because lives, so many lives, relied on it. And, between shifts, the glorious release of music and dancing, plays and performances, the chatter, the meals, the camaraderie. The laughter. The fact she, for perhaps the first and only time, really had fit in, made friends, and earned the respect of her superiors.

For the first and only time she had been part of something that really mattered.

And here, now, so unexpected and out of place, the man with the soft eyes who saw something in her that most people miss, because most people just see what they want to.

Milly is running up the garden path, her staccato breath snagging, like her memories of the past. She comes to a halt before him, barely aware of Olive's small hand still clasped tight in hers.

"Mr. Harvey-Jones," she says, the name a whisper on her breath. So strange to say it after all this time. He is a little grayer and more stooped than she remembers. But the kind, sloping eyes are unchanged. "How on earth did you find me?"

The man's face breaks into a lopsided smile and his shoulders move in a way that says *It's complicated* and *I'm sorry*. But he shouldn't be sorry at all.

It is only seeing him, here on her doorstep, that she understands, in spite of George, of the children, of her new life here, the extent of the gaping hole left since those extraordinary years at Bletchley Park when they managed, against all the odds, to break the unbreakable German Enigma code and help bring an end to World War Two.

Chapter 2

Charlotte

Rue St.-Jacques, Paris, July 1552

It was the tolling of the noon bells at the Church of Saint-Benoît calling the faithful to prayer, that marked the moment Charlotte Guillard's life shifted from the practical to the illuminated. The illumination was not, of course, immediate. That sort of instant clarity of vision was reserved only for the saints. In her case the Lord, perhaps considering her to need convincing, was to reveal his plan in increasingly distressing increments over several days. But still, the chiming of those bells would be a daily reminder of the moment that divided everything into the Before, and the After.

That July morning, until the ringing of the sext bells, her day progressed perfectly ordinarily. Rising at the cock's crow shortly before dawn, Charlotte washed, dressed, and made straight to the workshops where her journeymen and their apprentices were already hard at work at her six printing presses: setting the type, mixing the ink and spreading it, laying the paper. All of it watched over by Frédéric, her best corrector and editor to date. But still, even though she trusted him to pick up the smallest error of spelling or imperfection in a translation, her presence was necessary to remind her thirty-two print workers, as well as the booksellers in her bookshop, her illustrators, her bookkeepers, and her servants, that it was she, not he, or some other man, who was the head of this, her printing empire, and its sprawl of workshops, warehouses, shop, and living quarters that stretched along the *Grande Rue St.-Jacques* beneath the sign of the *Soleil d'Or*, the golden sun.

At six, Charlotte took her cup of wine and breakfast of eggs in the large dining room with her workers. Frédéric entered the room, a stack of paper tucked beneath one arm, and sat heavily beside her. He glanced at the journeymen, engrossed in their food, their tales of financial hardship, their women and cockfights, won and lost. He turned away from them and spoke to her in a low voice.

"I have tried every paper supplier in the city," he began, "and this is the best I can find."

Charlotte picked up a few sheets and held them to the light streaming through the long window behind, her gold rings glinting. There were terrible variations in the thickness. In some places the sheets were so thin they would surely tear at the folds and the edges.

She turned back to her editor. "This quality won't do. If we use this . . . *dung*, the pages will rip. The folios will not be able to lie flat. Within a few years, the books will disintegrate. I cannot risk my reputation on this."

"I know it. We cannot print *Corpus Juris Civilis* on this pigswill." They stared gloomily at the folio samples.

"But what is to be done?" Charlotte asked, the egg sitting like a stone in her belly. Visions of dissatisfied customers demanding their orders be reprinted or worse, their money returned, swam before her eyes. "I'll lose all future university business before vespers today, if the lawyers should see this."

"The paper suppliers mock us," Frédéric muttered. "They take advantage of the fact we cannot legally buy from anyone but them."

"I'll take them to court," Charlotte announced, almost before she'd processed the thought. "The Paper Guild cannot be permitted to fill their pockets while our profits shrivel. Yolande Bonhomme, of printing house Kerver, must be suffering too. We will act together."

"You cannot take on the guild . . ." Frédéric's eyes widened. "They are too powerful . . . They are *men*, Madame. Men who will not give way."

Charlotte huffed. "I'm well aware of that, Frédéric. But if we can get the court to agree to our sourcing *direct* from the paper mills, and not from the Paris Paper Guild, we can control the quality. It will be the best long-term solution."

"But, Madame . . ." Frédéric seemed for a moment at a loss for words. "It would be . . . Brave."

"You mean foolish."

"Well . . ."

"And you have a better idea?"

He shook his head.

"I've not lived these sixty years or more to let this bring me down."

"Madame, be careful. Should word that you will take them to court reach the ears of the guild . . . It could be dangerous."

Back in the workshop, Charlotte began leafing through the folios of the newly printed French edition of *The Apophthegmes of the Ancients*. The preface to the little collection of uplifting tales from the ancients written by Desiderius Erasmus, was missing.

She turned sharply to Nicolas. The typesetter stood behind her, arms crossed over his chest, rolling his eyes at the apprentice slouching beside him.

"You have omitted the preface, Nicolas. Why is it not here?" She glanced at the large pile of folios already completed. "Are they missing from all those too?"

"I didn't think it important, Madame. And I'm saving you the cost of one full sheet for such a small number of words . . . The man is dead, he cannot mind." The apprentice sniggered, and Charlotte silenced him with a glare.

Nicolas added, "Some would say publishing this man's work is an act of heresy . . . Madame."

"Let us be clear, Nicolas. It is *my* decision, and mine alone, what we print and where we save costs." Charlotte's heart ticked faster. But the man was not wrong about the last point. She walked an ever-thinner tightrope in this increasingly intolerant world, pushing her to more and more conservative decisions as to what to print, distribute, and sell. That tension, always, existed between what she felt was important to set free into the world and what the church, the King, the judges sitting in the *Parlement* court might ban, or worse.

Monsieur Riant, her lawyer, had strongly advised her this must be the last print run of Erasmus's work that Charlotte should produce. She remembered the furor over his *Colloquies*, the way he ridiculed greedy priests, phony rituals, and miracles and declared celibacy of the priesthood should be dropped in favor of married life. Parlement had ordered every copy be burned, and anyone found reading *Colloquies* should be executed. But even as Erasmus was hated by both Protestants and Catholics, the pope naming him as the leader of all heretics, Charlotte had known him to be a supporter of peace, liberty, and tolerance and outspoken in his criticism of burning books and heretics. Erasmus had been a friend of publishers everywhere.

Charlotte in her own quiet, determined way had vowed to continue to print his work for as long as she could. But she knew it was becoming too dangerous to continue.

Still, Nicolas was insubordinate. She took a deep breath to stem her rising anger. There was always one like him. A resentful young colt who considered it against the laws of natural order that an old mare like her should wield any power, especially over him.

"Erasmus would be turning in his grave to hear you speak so," she scolded. "As well as disrespecting the dead, you are ignorant of the fact that those wishing to purchase these volumes from the far corners of Europe do so *precisely* because they want this great man's work to live on forever through his words inked on this paper. That is the very point of what we do, here, in these print works." She took a breath. "And do not forget that if I wish to save cost, I may do so by cutting *your* salary, as well as that of your apprentice. There are plenty who would happily take your place." There was no sniggering now. "Set the type for those prefaces, and I will have Frédéric ensure they are correctly added to all of those." She pointed at the folios piled up awaiting their final binding.

Charlotte stepped away, chin raised, her workers' scowls burning into the back of her skull. They must not perceive so much as a whisper of weakness. She had been around long enough to understand how the world of men worked.

But her own words vocalized unsettling thoughts that had been smoldering in her mind these last months. Each day that passed brought her closer to her end. Who knew how much longer she had on this earth? The idea of leaving it brought with it the discomforting knowledge that, unlike Erasmus, she had nothing of real value to leave behind when she moved from this world to the next. Perhaps this yearning was born from the fact she had never had children. Or perhaps it was because she had spent a lifetime preserving into ink-on-paper the words of others. She took pride in this, of course, and to see her own printing mark on book after book still gave her a thrill, and yet, where was *she* in it?

Where was the essence of Charlotte Guillard?

The urge to do something, anything, which would leave some impression of *her* behind when she was gone, niggled at her like fleabites.

She continued her rounds, checking the typeset for the newly translated works of the Greek fathers into Latin she had been commissioned to print for her long-standing client, the Carthusian monk Godefroi Tilmann. All seemed in order. She was aware of the sun's heat building as the morning wore on, of an ache at the back of her eyes from staring at print in the low light, and of the tenderness in her lower back as she spent too many hours bending over the presses, the folios, the illustrators, and the bookkeepers.

Midway through the long morning, she allowed herself a short break for a cup of wine and her favorite snack of bread dipped in honey. Outside in the courtyard that lay between the workshops and Charlotte's living quarters, after weeks of no rain, the day was as dusty and dry as kindling ready for the fire. The air lay thick and heavy, a faint odor of sewage rising from the street beyond the buildings. As she made her way into the house, her mind snagged on the paper problem. She shall write to her lawyer, Monsieur Riant, and to Yolande Bonhomme, who she hoped would join her in a claim to the courts for freedom to purchase paper other than through the guild.

Her late first husband had built this house, close to the hallowed halls of the University of Paris. These days the university was a hotbed of Lutheran hunters, urged to be ever more voracious in their appetites to catch heretics by the chief inquisitor, Antoine de Mouchy. Knowing that madman sat in his lair but feet away made Charlotte shiver, despite the heat of the day. She crossed the yard, strewn with dishes and pots from breakfast waiting to be cleaned, and with carts of clothes and laundry ready to be taken to the *lavoir* by the maids. Stepping around them, she lowered her head to catch the sweet scent of orange, musk, and cloves from her pomander. In this intense heat, by late afternoon, the smell from the street would become intolerable.

Once in the sanctity of her study, Charlotte sank with a groan into the seat behind her desk. She leaned against the hard, lacquered back of the chair. A towering pile of correspondence awaited her attention. The air was too stuffy and hot, and sweat trickled down her back, pooled at her armpits. She opened the window in a futile attempt to let fresh air into the room. Frédéric's earlier words of warning rattled through her brain. *Madame, be careful. Should word that you will take them to court reach the ears of the guild . . . It could be dangerous.*

Frédéric was right.

Spies in Paris lurked in every echelon of society, from church and royalty to merchants and lawyers. From heresy hunters to those seeking business secrets and financial advantage. Charlotte silently thanked her dead second husband, Claude, for teaching her the skills of encoding.

She opened her desk drawer to take out some clean writing paper and, as she considered what she would say to her lawyer, Monsieur Riant, she lifted out the false back of the drawer to reveal its hidden secret compartment. Feeling her way inside, her fingers found the folded vellum sheet, thicker and more luxurious than paper. Unfolding it, she stared at the groups of letters and symbols that formed the cipher Claude had taught her, and that, in turn, she would use to communicate with Riant. He possessed a similar sheet with the key.

It was then that the sound of the noonday bells floated through the open window.

And as they did, a knock came at her study door. Flustered, she shoved the cipher back into its hiding place and quickly replaced the back of the drawer.

"Enter," she called, as she slid the drawer closed.

A visitor was shown in, a woman, a stranger.

The woman was tall and thin, and she wore the clothes of the gentrified class. Her face, unadorned and although not young, was so beautiful, it made Charlotte's breath catch. The visitor carried a high color on her pale cheeks, her eyes darting around the room as though in fear of finding danger lurking in its dark corners.

"Lysbette Angiers," announced the servant girl who showed her in. "She says she has traveled all the way to see you from Calais, Madame."

And with her entry into the room, Charlotte's senses were suddenly alight. The air shifted; a breeze rustled the papers on her desk.

And the heavens watched on.

Chapter 3

Lysbette

Chelsea village, outside London, November 1524

Lysbette Angiers stood, drenched to the bone and shivering violently, on the threshold of a vast kitchen in the grandest house she had ever set eyes on in her life. A house that was now to be her home. A fact young Lysbette, even in her exhausted, frozen state found exciting, and terrifying, in equal measure.

"For the love of God, someone stop that child from dripping all over my floor!" The bellowing woman, who must have been the cook, scowled at Lysbette from beneath her bonnet, jowls quivering ominously. She waved a flour-covered rolling pin above her head, as though the threat of it might stop the dripping. Behind her, Lysbette glimpsed a half-rolled mound of pastry atop a heavy oak table. Steam rose from a large pot beside it, and she caught the warm, rich aroma of freshly cooked stew. Her empty stomach growled with hunger.

The woman took two more steps toward Lysbette and swore under her breath as her slipper sloshed in the pool of water gathering around Lysbette's feet.

"Damnation! If I slip on the puddle she's makin' and crack me head open . . ." The cook's face reddened. "Then where'll you all be, eh?" She flapped her apron in Lysbette's direction as one might shoo away a stray dog.

A rough hand grabbed the neck of Lysbette's cloak, and she

was half lifted, half dragged toward the huge fireplace where a side of beef was roasting on a spit, fat popping and sizzling onto a giant tray beneath. Two hands now reached around her throat, unfastening the pins, peeling off the sodden cloak.

The kitchen door slammed, making Lysbette jump, shutting out the thundering rain. As they'd journeyed here through the interminable deluge, Lysbette had wondered if this was how England always was. She'd only ever heard bad things about the country. Terrible food, smelly people with bad manners, and awful weather. She felt so far from Bruges and its bustling waterways, its city squares, and stately buildings that she couldn't be sure she hadn't descended into hell. And suddenly she longed for home. The scent of freshly baked bread from the bakers on the corner of her street, the excited chatter of her friends as they gathered outside the convent school. The vision of her mother turning to greet her as she stepped through the door from the street. Her heart lurched and she hastily pulled her mind back into the present before the tears could come.

She crept a little closer to the roaring fire, reaching out with hands she could no longer feel, hoping the warmth would bring them back to life. As she did, she sensed two dark brown eyes staring up at her. They belonged to a small filthy boy crouched in the corner of the hearth. It was apparently his job to turn the spit, but before she could open her mouth to ask him if this was how it always was in England, the rough hands were on her shoulders once again, spinning her around to face a terrifying witch-woman who stared at her with button-black eyes. Beneath them sat a hideous, bulbous nose, and above, her forehead sloped dramatically beneath her hood and cap.

The maid with the rough hands who had done the spinning, poked Lysbette hard in the ribs, making her gasp. "This is *the mistress!*" she hissed.

Should she curtsy? Address her as *Madame* or *Lady More*, or something else she hadn't thought of? Terrified of making a mistake in this first, crucial meeting with the mistress, she remained mute, the silence stretching painfully as they stared at each other. And Lysbette couldn't help the cruel and unforgivable thought that crept into her head. *Why would the great Sir Thomas More choose this creature for a wife?*

"She's soaked through," the maid spoke instead, filling the void. "She'll need a full change of clothes before she can be taken to see his honor . . ." She peered closer, wrinkling her nose at Lysbette's mud-splattered front. "And her face scrubbed clean an' all . . ."

"Get it done then," the mistress ordered. "And get her out from under Cook's feet." Her eyes drifted toward the boy crouching in the corner. "There're enough waifs and strays in this house as it is. Heaven knows why Thomas thinks he needs an orphan *girl* to add to his collection. And, at this time in his life, just when he is rising in the King's favor." She sniffed. "Well, off you go, Mary, make her presentable. You've time, the master will be at prayer until dinner."

She swept away and out of the kitchen on her short legs, leaving Lysbette blessedly alone with the maid, the cook having returned to her pastry rolling.

"Do . . . you . . . speak . . . English?" Mary's lips formed exaggerated shapes as she spoke loudly and slowly.

"English, French, Latin, Flemish. A little Greek. Which would you prefer?"

The maid's eyes widened. "English will do," she said firmly. "But when you meet his honor, Master More, likely French. Let's go and get you cleaned up."

Lysbette suddenly felt so tired or anxious, or perhaps both, that her legs shook, and it took all her strength not to simply collapse in a heap on the floor next to the spit-boy. The journey to Beaufort House had taken three days, although it felt like half a year. The weather, the moment she had stepped off the ship at Dover, had been apocalyptic, the roads a quagmire of mud. She was weary, not only of body but also of mind, equally consumed with grief for her dead mother, who had only outlived her father by one year. A worry-filled year as the full, devastating details of her father's secret indebtedness had come to light. A worry that had killed her mother, or at least, that's what everyone had whispered and tutted when they discussed it as though Lysbette wasn't there at all. And now, not only was she an orphan, but she was without a penny to her name.

The maid, carrying a jug and with a cloth slung over her arm, led Lysbette through a covered passage toward the main part of the house. A boy of perhaps thirteen or fourteen emerged from a door at the other end of the passage and tore toward them at a fast run, doublet unfastened and flapping at his sides. He slowed as he reached them, a sheepish grin breaking out on his face, cheeks high with color.

"Forgotten something again, John Haydon?" Mary tutted, but there was warmth in her voice, as though this lovable rogue would be forgiven any misdemeanor.

"You know me too well, Mary." He winked at them both as he passed, rich hazelnut-colored eyes resting for a moment on Lysbette.

"John is a ward of the master, like you," she said as they continued on their way. "Been here since he was seven years old. One of the family now. Sent by some distant cousin of the mistress, from Northumberland. One day, he'll inherit a peerage and a fortune."

They climbed the steep back stairs and walked the length of a long, dark corridor. Right at the far end, the maid opened a door and they entered a small, simply furnished room, three stories up. A window overlooked the extensive gardens at the back of the house.

Mary placed the jug and cloth on the dressing table, tutted at the unlit fire in the bare grate, hands on hips. "Remove those wet garments and wash your face and hands," she ordered. "Now, you'll need dry clothes, but your trunk is yet to arrive . . ." She bit her lip and surveyed Lysbette. "You are much smaller than I was expecting . . . How old are you?"

"Ten years."

"Hmm . . . I'll have to see what we have in the house to dress you in."

Alone in the room, Lysbette surveyed the gloomy view from the window, the grounds blurred and indistinct behind the curtain of driving rain. She turned away and stripped off her skirt and bodice. Shivering in her thin shift, she washed quickly, wishing the fire had been lit, her stomach clenching as she remembered how Mistress More clearly had no wish for her to be here, poor, orphaned, and female as she was. The vast house and sodden grounds suddenly felt menacing and not welcoming at all.

Mary returned with another maid who lit the fire while Mary produced dry linen undergarments, a kirtle and simple skirt and bodice. She helped Lysbette into all of it, tidying Lysbette's hair beneath a cap.

"Now child," Mary said, standing back to appraise her appearance. "I think you are ready to meet the master."

"What's he like," Lysbette asked, "Sir Thomas More?"

Mary stared at her. "I thought you knew him?" She shook her head "Why else would he take in a scrap of a thing like you?"

"I have met him . . . But I don't remember. I was perhaps two or three years of age. My father knew him during his time in Leuven and Calais. They became good friends. But my father died, and then when Mother became ill last year, she wrote to Sir Thomas, pleading with him to take me in. Apart from a half-drunk uncle who my mother disliked, there was nobody else to care for me."

"Well then," Mary said with a sharp nod. "What manner of man do you think he might be, to take in a stray orphan child and care for her like his own daughter?"

Sir Thomas stood before Lysbette, a man of great bulk and height. Beneath the intensity of his gaze, she felt as though her legs were filled with air, not flesh and bone, and that they might buckle under her weight at any moment. She put out a hand to touch the wall and steady herself.

"Welcome, child, to Beaufort House." he said.

"Thank you for taking me in, sir."

He nodded. The fire crackled and spat as they solemnly regarded each other.

"I shan't be any trouble." Her voice came out in a whisper, and he had to lean down to hear her words.

"I don't doubt it." He grunted and straightened. "This house . . ." He waved his arms expansively and Lysbette stole a look around the room. Floor-to-ceiling bookshelves stretched across one wall, filled with books. Heavy velvet curtains, the color of red wine, were drawn across the windows and so many candles sat in cups upon the walls and atop the vast desk alongside the roaring fire, that the room was lit as though by warm sunshine. ". . . Is very large and must be filled with life and young people. Nothing gives me more pleasure than to give sanctuary to those who need it. Just as our Lord bade us do." His eyes rested again on hers.

"Your mother told me you are clever." He paused. "I am sorry about your mother, and father. I heard of his downturn in fortunes, before his untimely end." He shook his head. "What a terrible business. But these are changing times, Lysbette. Where once there was order and stability, now there is discord and the threat of anarchy." He fell silent for a few moments, deep in thought. He was the first man not to tut and blame her father for his own misfortune, and it made her chest hurt.

"I promised your mother I would do my best for you, and I shall honor that promise," he continued. "I planned to adopt you, as I did Mercy—Margaret—who you shall meet, but Alice thought it best not." He sighed. "No matter, you'll remain under my care until a suitable husband is found. Well . . ." He beamed, rubbing his hands together, the gold ring on his left forefinger glinting in the candlelight. "We need not worry about all that yet. These days, I am very busy with the King's business, but Alice will make you feel at home, and you must ask her for anything you need."

"Yes, Sir Thomas." She thought of Alice's fierce eyes and doubted she would ever ask her for anything.

"And tomorrow, you will meet Mr. Roberts, the tutor I've engaged to run my school here at Beaufort House. You shall join the other students. They are mostly girls. I do think girls should be taught, like boys, for they are just as clever. Sometimes more so." He smiled. "Now, I'm sure you are hungry, and we must not be late for any meal the Lord has seen in his wisdom to provide . . . through the King's money, of course." He chuckled. "Shall we?"

He led Lysbette along the passageway, past vast, high-ceilinged rooms, around corners, downstairs. As they walked, Sir Thomas told her he had commissioned this house to be built to maximize the household's study, prayer, and quietude. Finally, they arrived at the dining hall.

"This," he said, casting his eyes around, "however, is a room for entertaining. For welcoming family, friends, guests. It is for sharing my good fortune in life and for the healthy exchange of ideas. One day I hope, young Lysbette, you shall meet many of my excellent friends, including my best of all friends, Desiderius Erasmus."

Lysbette gazed at the ornately etched wall paneling; heavy drapes the color of juniper fell ceiling to floor beside the windows; vast vases were filled with dried flowers and in the center, a long, heavy oak table set for twelve or more, brightly lit with candelabras that sent the edges of the room into flickering shadow. A dizzying array of meats, bread, and pies were laid upon the table. There were healthy fires at both ends of the room. Sir Thomas introduced Lysbette to his family in a blur of faces and names. *My daughter, Margaret, and her husband, William Roper. My other daughters, Elizabeth and Cecily; my son, John;, my wife, Alice; and my father, also John. Here is Mercy, and here are my other wards, another John—John Haydon, Anne, and Margaret . . . Now sit, sit.*

So many Johns and Margarets, but she recognized the running boy from earlier, his pleasing face and winning smile. There was a tremendous scraping of chairs and banging of cutlery, of calling for wine and beer, the rising clamor of conversation and then silence as Sir Thomas said grace. "Let us eat in the name of the Lord and satisfy our bodies temporally with such meats as he hath sent . . ."

My new home, Lysbette thought. *Please, Lord, let me be happy here.*

Chapter 4

Milly

Milly, Olive, and Winton Harvey-Jones stare at one another on the doorstep of Milly's home. From the corner of her eye, Milly can see the bulky outline of Mrs. Humphries next door standing straight, any pretense at rose pruning forgotten. Mrs. Cross will be watching, too, from behind the lace curtains at her window, across the road at number 25. Before the day is out, the entire street will know that Milly Bennett had an unknown male visitor. It doesn't matter that he is old enough to be her father. They already know her own father is dead, that she has no family in the vicinity, and her in-laws never come by. They know the awkward little Englishwoman has no friends to speak of and yet, here one is. Gossip will soon be unfurling from house to house as swift as toxic gas.

"Miss Featherington . . ." Mr. Harvey-Jones removes his hat, gives Milly a little half bow.

"It's Mrs. Bennett now."

"Of course it is. I apologize. Old habits."

"No need. It's been a long time. Please, call me Milly."

"Quite right. To hell with formalities, we aren't at Bletchley now, and I'm no longer your boss. Winton, at your service." He smiles.

"How did you find me?" she asks again. "We're a long way from

Buckinghamshire."

He threads the brim of his hat through his fingers, turning it in slow circles. "I remembered you were engaged to an American chap, Eighth Air Force. Stationed at High Wickham." She nods. "Spoke to some contacts . . . Once I had your new name, it didn't take long. People aren't so hard to track down as they might like to think."

"I hope I'm not in trouble."

"Oh!" Winton laughs. "No, no. Nothing like that. He glances around. Clocks Mrs. Humphries still staring, pruning shears aloft. "Could I come in? Just for a few minutes. It's not bad news, I promise. I have a little favor to ask, that's all."

"Of course! Sorry. Always forgetting my manners." She skirts around him, dropping Olive's hand to fumble in her handbag for her door key, Olive pressing herself between her mother and the front door.

Stepping through the entrance, she ushers Mr. Harvey-Jones—Winton—into the small entrance hall.

"I'm sorry I didn't write first and let you know I was coming," he says, following her into the kitchen at the back of the house. "Vanessa, my wife, told me I should, but I thought my request might come across . . . odd and out of the blue, in a letter . . ."

"And turning up after seven years of silence on my doorstep in a different continent, isn't?"

He flinches. She hadn't meant to be sharp. "Sorry, I didn't mean—"

"No, quite right. I deserved that." He sighed. "I was worried you'd write back and say you weren't interested. And besides, I have an aversion to doing what I'm told. The doctor told me to lay off the cigars and the port, but that only makes me have double." He gives a throaty laugh. "Vanessa says my contrariness will be the death of me."

"Vanessa is probably right. For the record, I would never have said I wasn't interested in seeing you."

He glances away. "It was only . . . After what happened . . . I thought you might not remember me in the best light."

Milly's throat swells and her eyes grow hot. She shakes her head.

"Don't be silly. I know all that was outside of your control."

Olive is clinging to Milly's leg, staring at Winton as they all stand in the kitchen. Milly gently peels her daughter away and crouches to her level, looking into her huge blue eyes. "Mr. Harvey-Jones and I worked together during the war. Say a polite hello, and then you can play with your dolls while I make you a sandwich and Mr. Harvey-Jones and I can talk grown-up things. How does that sound?"

Olive considers this for a moment then nods her solemn consent.

"How do you do," Olive says obediently. She thrusts her right hand toward Winton and they shake. "Are you my grandpa?"

Milly laughs. "Oh, Olive, you know your grandfather from England is dead."

"Yes, but maybe *he* could be my English grandpa instead? I only have an American one."

"It would be my honor," Winton says, giving her a bow.

"Yippee!" Olive laughs with glee, all shyness vanishing.

Milly makes the sandwich and places it on a plate. She spoons tea into the pot, pours in the boiling water, and pops it under the tea cozy to wait for it to brew. Winton tells her he is in New York for an auction of rare books. Collecting became his passion, he tells her, since retiring a couple of years after the war.

"And how is it, living here? Rather a change . . . after Bletchley," Winton says, joining Milly at the kitchen window; together they stare out over the soggy, leaf-strewn back garden.

Deep in her chest is the old ache of loss for the place. For the sense of being useful, doing something that made a difference. When all around her were on the same side and it didn't matter that she didn't have the social airs and graces that seem to come so naturally to everyone else because it was her language skills and her latent ability to see patterns and solve puzzles that mattered to them. Of course, there had been thousands of them there, working on breaking German and Japanese coded messages, so their success was a collective one. But it was only after it was over that it began to dawn on her that so much of her value was tied up in her contribution to that almighty effort. She recalls Winton's rarely bestowed words of praise when she had decoded a particularly difficult message that made her breathless, as though she had been dancing the jitterbug all night.

Winton is staring at her expectantly.

"It's wonderful," she says finally. "A dream come true."

"It's a nice little place you have," Winton says, turning to look around the fitted kitchen with all its modern appliances. The shiny worktops, laminate flooring, and floor-to-ceiling cupboards. The large refrigerator, the oven and stove, the central heating and overhead lighting. If he was to look in the small utility room off the kitchen, he would find the Hoover, the twin tub washer, the dryer and iron with the ironing board propped against one wall. This house has absolutely everything a discerning housewife and mother could want, small sized, but perfect. Three bedrooms, dining room, sitting room, and a kitchen looking out onto the backyard so Mommy can cook while watching the kiddies play.

"Small but perfectly formed," she says with a laugh and a flourish.

Milly recalls the day George returned to his parents' place with good news about the marketing job he'd successfully secured at Cooke's National Bank, and about the house in Levittown, Long Island. *It's going to be like living in a modern Utopia, Milly-Moo.* He'd picked her up and twirled her around. *A beautiful new house with everything you and the children could want or need just a short walk away! Parks, churches, stores, swimming pools, playing fields, great schools.* A Utopia indeed, if only the people living there didn't ruin the dream.

Milly carries Olive's sandwich and glass of milk through to the sitting room, turning on the television so she can watch a cartoon.

"Special treat," she says with a wink, placing the tray on the coffee table. "Don't tell Edward or Daddy or they'll be jealous."

Back in the kitchen, Milly pours the tea and she and Winton sit opposite each other at the table.

Milly clears her throat. "It's really good to see you, Winton. How have you been?"

He smiles. "As I said, I'm retired now. The services weren't interested in keeping on an old chap like me after the war. I'd done my time, and there were new, younger fellows chomping at the bit to take my place. Only fair I stepped aside . . . I keep busy. Golf, a bit of gardening with Vanessa to keep the old muscles from seizing up entirely. But my library is my passion. Old books. I've always loved them. First editions and rare volumes."

Milly smiles.

He lifts his cup and saucer and takes a drink. "Best cup of tea since I arrived," he says, and she laughs.

Milly hasn't thought of Hut 6, where she was stationed at Bletchley, in years. But now, with Winton sitting here in his customary bright yellow waistcoat, bow tie, and beloved old-fashioned fob watch, it all floods back. The smell of the hut: sweat, wet wool, tobacco smoke. The telephone ringing as the Wrens on the Bombe machines called through with a possible key to try. The building sense of excitement as they set the machine with the key, tapping in the letters from messages gathered from the Watch, noting down the lighted letter from the machine that came up. Nonsense in, German out, one letter at a time. Once they had enough to make a "menu," they would telephone that through to Eastcote Outstation so that as many messages as possible could be unencrypted. The Germans really thought their double encryption method of coded words disguised by a supposedly unbreakable cipher meant their messages could never be understood. But they reckoned without the multitude of extraordinary minds at Bletchley. At midnight each night, the Germans changed their ciphers, and the whole process began again.

Milly was sworn to secrecy under the Official Secrets Act, so nobody knew or would ever know of the work she had done during the war. As per instruction, she had told George when they first met, that she was a secretary at a local mental asylum. She'd insinuated they had men there suffering from shell shock from the Great War, as well as this one. Because of that, the institution was run by the War Office, so she was subject to the Act. He'd never once asked her about her job, for which she was grateful. Milly hated that she had to lie, so the less said the better. But sometimes, when George had regaled her or the children with stories of his forays across the Channel, she wished she could say something of her experience, her contribution. But of course, she never did.

Winton clears his throat, bringing her back into the room.

"I'm sure you are wondering what I'm doing here," he begins.

"I am rather intrigued."

"But first. I owe you an apology."

She stares at her hands folded in her lap. Swallows hard against the lump in her throat.

"No, you don't need—"

"I really did try when, after the war, you asked if I could get you a good position in the Secret Intelligence Services," he says and there is a crack in his voice. "But they weren't interested in a woman. No matter how bright, how capable. You were the only female I put forward. I told them how exceptional you were but . . ." He sighed. "There were more men than positions. Men who desperately needed jobs, to support their families. They said you would only go and marry anyway–"

"It's okay . . ."

"I was a coward. I should have told you."

She remembers the weeks stretching to months that went by as she'd waited for news from him, while George, then her fiancé, was in Germany with the air force. She had nothing to do but housework and reading because, as a woman with no secretarial skills, there were no decent jobs. Each morning she'd rush to the letter box whenever she heard the postman. How she had missed the work she'd been doing and the camaraderie, plus she and her mother desperately needed the money. But as the months passed, hope faded and she realized Winton had either tried, and failed, or hadn't put her name forward at all. She had felt such shame and embarrassment that she had ever had the audacity to ask. "But by then," he was saying, "I knew they wanted to push me out, too, and I wasn't in a good place. I'm sorry I let you down, I—"

"Winton. Stop." She looks up at him and smiles. "They were right, see? I *am* married, with two children. And I don't even live in Blighty anymore. I would have been an awful prospect. Now I know you did your best for me, that's all that matters. I appreciate it. Thank you."

His face relaxes. "I thought you would be angry."

"Of course not. So much water under the bridge."

He nods. "What did you do, after the war?"

"I went back home to live with Mother. George was in Germany for a while before he applied to be demobbed. So I passed the time writing. It started out as a silly thing. A friend I had made at Somerville, Helen, married and had a baby. She asked me to be godmother to her young daughter. I thought a unique and fun present for her christening would be a little book of Greek myths. I wrote them, shortened and simplified, and had them bound. It turned out her husband worked at Penguin Books and, well, to cut a long story short, the publisher commissioned a short series of Little Books. So there was *The Little Book of Greek Myths*, *The Little Book of Greek Philosophy*, *The Little Book of Greek Gods*, and so on. There were five books in all, over a couple of years. But sales were poor, and they didn't want any more. So that was the end of that. It was fun while it lasted. They aren't even in print anymore."

"I'm sorry to hear that."

Milly shrugs. "As I said, all water under the bridge."

She reboils the kettle.

"I hate to be a bore, Winton, but it won't be long before I must collect my son from school . . ."

"Quite right. I should get to the point. I'm here," he says, bending down to pick up the briefcase, "because I'm hoping you can help me with something. You were one of the brightest sparks I had the privilege of working with at Bletchley. Stubborn, too. Never one for giving up." He chuckles.

"Oh, but it's been a long time. I'm out of practice."

"Nonsense. It's like riding a bike. You never forget." Winton slides a leather-bound book, a little taller, wider and thicker than a modern hardback, from his briefcase. He hands it to her.

The book is heavy in her hands. Its cover is cracked and mottled with age, the pages are thick and sit unevenly between the covers. "What's this?"

"It's called the Van Hal manuscript," Winton explains. "It's believed to be around four hundred years old, and it's encrypted. I came upon it by accident, at an obscure antique sale in Gloucestershire not long after I retired in 1947. It belonged to a German collector named Van Hal, and after his death, his wife sold it, having no idea, clearly, of its potential value. Not sure how it ended up in the British countryside but perhaps, having been in the possession of a German, that helped keep the price down. I got it for a song." He drank some tea, then continued.

"It's something I've been working on ever since. But, five years on, I'm getting nowhere. Van Hal failed to decrypt it, and his wife put his notes in with the auction lot. According to the notes, the manuscript was found, long forgotten, on a shelf in the library of a monastery in Northern Italy. I've shown it to some ex-colleagues, even Alan Turing, as well as some academic experts, but so far, nobody has succeeded." He pauses. "Word has gotten about, and now it seems there is considerable interest in this manuscript. Not only from other collectors, but also from the British Museum Library, Oxford and Cambridge Universities, and other prestigious universities around the world, including Yale, Princeton, and others. If we can crack its code and uncover the secrets it holds within, it could shed extraordinary new light on the times in which it was written." He nods at it. "Whatever is in there, Milly, could be academic and historic dynamite. And because of that, worth *a lot* of money."

Milly looks from Winton's animated expression to the book lying heavy as a rock in her hands. Carefully, as though it may ignite, Milly places the possibly priceless book on the table.

"That . . . That all sounds very exciting, Winton, and I wish **you** every success, but what on earth has this to do with me?"

"Ah. Well. After studying the manuscript very carefully, **and,** of course, consulting with others, I have concluded three things. First, I am convinced, unlike some, that this is the genuine article and not a hoax. Second, that the underlying language is Latin, and third, that it has been written by a woman, or women. **And** that is where you come in. I need someone with excellent knowledge of Latin, a code breaker *extraordinaire*, and someone **who** thinks like a woman. Well, *is* a woman. And I need someone who is both competent and discreet whom I can trust completely. There was only one person I could think of who fulfills all those requirements. In short, Milly, I need you."

Winton nods once more at the book and says, "Now please, I've brought it all this way. Please look inside."

Milly hesitates, then takes a deep breath and opens the book.

Chapter 5

Milly

Levittown, Long Island, New York, November 1952

The manuscript is exquisite. Bulky, bound in ancient, cracked leather, its pages thick and stained with time and the grease of countless, long-dead fingers. Up close, the faint pattern of calfskin can be made out under the full glare of the overhead light, for the pages are vellum, not paper.

But its real beauty lies in the illustrations and the lines of undecipherable words, composed in some sort of unknown language or code, painstakingly etched by hand, page after page of them, the ink now faded like autumn leaves into a dull, rust brown.

Between the paragraphs, delicate birds flap their inky wings, snakes slither and twist about the words, and strange plants curl and loop in the margins. Unlike the words, the illustrations, despite the long passage of time, are rich in vibrant color. Deep reds, greens, blues, and ochre shimmer, while curious creatures leap from the page with vibrant energy.

There is a beat to this book, a heartbeat, faint but discernible, a metronome buried deep within its pages, pulsing away time until its mysterious contents can be revealed. It is as though the manuscript is a creature of immense importance, waiting patiently, all but forgotten for countless years, somehow knowing its time will come.

And now, here it is on her kitchen table, as though poised for the peeling back, for the unveiling.

Milly tears her eyes away and back to Winton who is watching her closely.

"Another reason for my visit to America," he says, "was to take it to the University of Chicago, to have it carbon dated, before coming to visit you."

"Carbon dated?"

"A new method proven to be fairly accurate in aging objects that were once alive. This vellum, once upon a time, was a calf. Or to be more accurate, several calves. Now we can't prove when the ink was applied, as ink is much harder to date, but the estimate is that the vellum itself dates to the early sixteenth century. This is plus or minus around fifty years." Winton continues. "Although we can't age the ink, I managed to get the composition tested, and the best estimate is that it was ink mixed prior to the 1800s when soluble blue was added to iron-gall ink." He takes a breath. "This leads me to two thoughts. First, the age of the ink and the vellum makes it highly unlikely this is a fake. Second, use of vellum in the sixteenth century would have been unusual. Paper was widely available by then. So why use this much more expensive and harder-to-come-by material?"

They lapse into silence as they contemplate the manuscript. The high-pitched voices of the cartoon Olive is watching drift through the door from the lounge, jarring and uncouth as a soundtrack to this priceless beauty before Milly. She stares at the lines of coded words, her mind sluggish, out of practice. She shakes her head.

"Winton, I'm flattered you should think me capable, but I can't take this on. I'm just a housewife. How could I possibly untangle this mystery, when *real* experts cannot?" Milly pours more tea into their cups, adds a splash of milk, and pushes the sugar bowl in Winton's direction.

"Thank you." Winton purses his lips, drums his fingers on the table. "I thought you might say as much. But hear me out. Everyone I have consulted has a different opinion about what this might be, and I think—"

"That the manuscript was written by a woman."

He nods.

"So you said, but based on what? The chances are, that's unlikely."

"Milly, have you ever heard of the Nüshu?"

"No."

"Nüshu was a language spoken and written only by women in a small area of southern China. I believe it is now an extinct language, but the reason it developed was so that women could communicate with one another, without any danger of men understanding them."

Winton leans forward and carefully turns a few pages.

"You see," he continues, "if you look at the illustrations, where there are any figures, they are almost all women. Women carrying out all manner of daily activities, women of various ages and stages of life." He points out some of the pictures. "Here, some pregnant women, floating in a lake. Here, women spinning. Here, a woman surrounded by her family. And others where women are reading, sewing, speaking to a crowd. Whatever they are doing, they are front and center of the story, and I believe that is the key."

Milly says nothing, but she studies some of the illustrations that adorn the pages. There are women dancing in fields littered with wildflowers or sitting close to one another as though deep in conversation beneath a starlit night sky. They have been drawn with exquisite care.

"So why has nobody else thought of that?"

"Quite a few experts, unable to solve the mystery, have concluded it's an elaborate hoax. Others think the illustrations are a decoy." Winton points to the painted images of absurd tubular plants, fantastical creatures, bizarre buildings, and nonsensical topography in the background. "Either way, nobody has so far seen the presence of the women as in any way significant, other than the suggestion that this could be some sort of male fantasy world." He pauses. "In the early sixteenth century, very few women were literate or would have had the means, time, and capacity for putting together something like this. That narrows things down greatly. Other than religious writing, and that of royal or aristocratic women, there is almost nothing. This, if it *is* what I think it is, could be historical gold in shedding some sort of light on women's inner worlds. And, perhaps even more intriguingly, why the contents of a two-hundred-and-forty-page manuscript have been so successfully hidden and disguised for four hundred years."

"If you are right."

"My hunches often are." He smiles.

"And the hunch that Latin is the underlying language?"

"That part is more than a hunch. See here," Winton says, pointing to some areas of text. These are Latin letters and numerals." Milly looks closely at the neat text. He is right, but the letters are combined with symbols, and nothing makes sense. "The construct," Winton continues, "the style, the context. In sixteenth-century Europe—if this is a code, the underlying language *is* most likely to have been Latin."

"That is a lot of ifs, hunches, and suppositions." Milly glances at the kitchen clock.

"Winton, I'm sorry, but I need to collect Edward. I don't really know what to say." She pauses, staring at the manuscript. She can feel the pull of it. The stirrings of desire to unravel its mysteries. Her pulse quickens at the set of the challenges to solve this puzzle, old and familiar, just like she used to experience at Bletchley. When she felt fully alive. But this is much too big, too important for someone like her. She isn't at Bletchley now. She is a house-wife, a mother. Those things are her priority. She cannot possibly take on something like this. What would she say to George?

"Of course," Winton is saying. "And I must be getting the train back into the city. Say you will give it a shot and make an old man happy?"

"Oh, Winton, I want to help. Really, I do. But I can't. You overestimate my abilities. And I'm a mother. I haven't the time or resources to work on this before you go home."

"That is why I propose leaving the manuscript with you until I return to New York in the spring. And you don't need any re-sources, Milly. All you need is in here." He taps his temple.

"You couldn't leave such a priceless thing with me for that long. The scholarly world would be horrified!"

Winton snorts. "Like I said, I rarely do as I'm told. If I'd given in to their pressure, I'd already have handed it over for their safe-keeping. Over my dead body are they having it. At least, not until we've unlocked this manuscript, and we fully understand its his-toric value. Then they can pay a fair price for it and acknowledge who broke the code. Indeed, it's less about the money, more about the challenge and the recognition." He leans toward her across the table. "We can never be valued or credited for what we did at Bletchley, Milly, but this . . . This is a different matter. If you suc-ceed, I'll make sure you get the credit and the spoils you deserve. It would be the least I can do, after letting you down before."

Milly chews her lip. The clock ticks. The manuscript sits, tan-talizing. She really must leave now, or she will be late for Edward. What would George think if she says yes? He might be pleased that she has a little project of her own. Or he could think it a terrible idea. He knows how she can be when she gets her teeth into something. An obsessiveness in her soul that was perfect for Bletchley but a weakness in daily life. And besides, how would she fit such work around the children? What if she became so engrossed in it that she forgot to feed them, or collect them from school, or they were to have a terrible accident while she was working? Or what if the manuscript got lost, or damaged?

She can feel the weight of Winton's expectation as his eyes rest on her.

The clock ticks louder, faster.

"How about," she finds herself saying, "I just spend a few days taking a closer look. You come back before your boat leaves for Southampton next week. By then I'll have a better notion as to whether I think I can help. And if I don't think I can, then you must take the manuscript home with you."

His face breaks into a wide smile. "That sounds fair," he says, standing and reaching for his coat. "Until next week then."

After Winton has gone, Milly picks up the manuscript. She feels a little sick and shaky, like she has drunk too much coffee. She needs to keep this book safe and out of reach of the children. She carries it up to her bedroom and opens her side of the double wardrobe she shares with George. On the top shelf is a shoebox in which she keeps a few pieces of memorabilia from her mother. She removes them and places the manuscript carefully inside. She replaces the lid and, standing on tiptoes, pushes it to the back of the shelf. She puts the assorted photos, letters, and a notebook from her mother into her bedside cabinet.

As she and Olive hurry toward the school, Milly wonders what she should tell George about the manuscript. If she does tell him, it will result in all sorts of awkward questions about Winton, how she knows him and why he thinks she, an ordinary housewife and former lowly secretary, can break a seemingly unbreakable code. In any event, it is so unlikely that she will make any progress with it that she very much doubts the manuscript will still be in her possession this time next week.

George, she decides, doesn't need to know anything about it at all.

Snow arrives in the evening, large flakes spinning their slow descent outside the window. The children, ready for bed, fling the back door open and spill outside, dancing in the light spilling from the kitchen. They turn their faces toward the sky, mouths open for the flakes to fall into, arms spread as though they might take flight. Milly watches them, leaning against the doorframe, putting off the moment she must tell them it's bedtime. How wonderful to be a child, to live only for that moment, to see joy and wonder in the simple things, while adults dwell too much in the dungeons of their own minds, hollowed out and weighed down.

The front door bangs shut, footsteps sound across the hallway, and strong arms wind themselves around her waist. George plants a kiss on her cheek.

Milly sinks against him, breathing in his familiar scent. Tobacco. Damp wool. Newspaper, with faint hints of citrus and sandalwood from the cologne he applied many hours before.

"Hello, you," he says. He rests his chin on the top of her head. "Shouldn't those kids be in bed?" He lifts his wrist, checks his watch. "It's almost eight thirty. What's bedtime again?"

"Seven."

"Okay . . ."

"But it's snowing, George! What's the point of being a child if you can't play in the snow?"

"I guess. But they have school tomorrow . . ."

"They'll be fine. Sleep is overrated. And so is school."

She can feel him smile into her hair.

The first time Milly met George, back in 1943, she had been reluctant. Her father's sister, Aunt Tabatha, who lived in Scotland, had written saying that the nephew of an old friend of Father's from America was stationed at an air base near Milly, and it would be very nice if she could meet up with him for tea and cake and make him feel welcome in Blighty, seeing as he was one of the brave young men who had come over to help our chaps. The aunt, of course, had no idea of the real work Milly herself was doing. Aunt Tabatha, in suggesting she meet the airman, had assumed Milly would welcome a break from the monotony of typing. She was sure poor Milly was still getting over the death of her father after his sudden heart attack. She must need a break from worrying about her bereaved mother, and meeting a nice young chap would do her a world of good.

Milly, awkward around the opposite sex, didn't relish wasting her limited and precious free time, but she was an obedient girl and had gone to do her duty. She would find excuses if Aunt Tabatha pressed her to go again.

When Milly arrived at the tea shop, she could see from her reflection in the window that her hair was in disarray from the windy five-mile cycle from her billet to the village. She'd not bothered with her clothes, choosing her most practical of dresses and sensible cycling shoes. Now that she was here and could see the airman already seated at a table waiting for her, she regretted her lack of effort. The young man was so engrossed in the pages of P. G. Wodehouse's *Very Good, Jeeves* that she almost lost the courage to intrude. He had a kind-looking face and laughter lines around his eyes. Just as she was having second thoughts, he looked up and smiled at her watching him.

"George Bennett," he said, rising to greet her. She noticed his sandy hair was thinning a little on top, and he wasn't awfully tall but when he shook her hand his grasp was firm, his eyes bright and warm, and his smile wide.

"Millicent Featherington . . . Milly . . . It's awfully nice to meet you," she said, realizing with surprise that she meant it.

"Did you encounter a hurricane on your way here?" he asked, head tilted to one side, eyes ranging over her hair. If anyone else had said that she'd have died of shame but somehow, the way George said it, a lopsided grin on his face, made her laugh.

"I prefer the thrill of going fast down hills," she told him, "to the effort of maintaining a fancy hairdo."

"Then you sound like my kind of girl."

The afternoon passed quickly after that. There was no awkwardness between them, no attempts to impress. Just tea, followed by a stroll beside the river. Conversation flowed in a way she'd never experienced before. They talked about books and her studies at Oxford, how he would have loved to have gone to university, but never got the chance. He told her about Kentucky, where he was from, his parents' horse farm there, his favorite music and films. They covered the difference between English and American muffins and whether dogs were, in fact, preferable to people. Which, they agreed, they probably were.

When he asked to see her again, all thoughts of excuses to Aunt Tabatha evaporated because Milly had said yes before her mouth had connected with her brain.

After that, they met regularly. George never seemed to notice her frumpy shoes or that her hair was a mess. Instead, he always told her how lovely she looked, and for the first time in her life, she felt beautiful.

Now, as they stand together watching the children whoop and twirl on the rapidly whitening lawn, those days feel so long ago, it could be another lifetime. In the intervening years, the war ended, she lost her mother, they moved to America and, best of all, together they'd made these two perfect, tiny humans, Edward and Olive, who nestle inside her heart like precious pearls in an oyster shell.

"Tough day at the coalface?" he asks.

"Made it through another day. You?"

He sighs. "Fine, fine. Oiling the wheels of high finance. I didn't think I'd catch these two rug rats before they went to bed. So . . . This is nice."

"Well, I'm happy you're home." She gives his arms a squeeze. "I made casserole tonight." She catches George's grimace. "With mashed potato."

"It smells good! And perfect for a night like this. I'll fetch us a drink."

He leaves the room, and Milly reluctantly calls the children inside. They fill the kitchen with wet boots, sodden nightclothes, and happy, shining eyes. She rubs them dry with a towel and they giggle at each other's mussed hair.

George returns with two glasses of whiskey, which he tops up with soda, handing one to her, taking a gulp from the other.

"You'll need dry nightclothes," he tells the children. "Look at you both! Damp scamps." They laugh and thunder upstairs to change into dry pajamas.

"You are happy here, aren't you, Milly-Moo?" George asks suddenly, leaning back on his heels to look at her, searching her eyes.

Milly shifts, uncomfortable beneath his pleading look, and

glances away, taking a gulp from her glass. She savors the burn as the whiskey hits the back of her throat.

"Of course I am, why do you ask?" She busies herself with the oven gloves, opening the oven to check the casserole.

"I know you've found it hard, but it's getting easier, right? Look how well the children are doing. That's all down to you." Her heart fractures a little. Oh George.

"Moving here was the very best decision."

He leans down and kisses her, his lips still cold. She can taste the whiskey on his tongue.

"I'm so proud of you," he murmurs.

"And I love you, George. You and the children . . . You're everything."

He hugs her a little tighter, his kisses deeper, as Edward and Olive reappear, crying, "Yuck, not kissing!" He releases her, and they all laugh, George pretending to kiss her more, puckering his lips and making the children clutch their stomachs in disgust.

"All right, you two," he says finally. "Time for a story. Quick now upstairs and into bed. I'm mighty hungry and if I don't eat what your mother has been cooking, I might have to take a bite out of one of you instead."

"No, Daddy!" they cry and jostle and race up the stairs again.

"I'll be up in two minutes!"

Milly fetches the potato masher, adds some butter, and slops in the milk. George leans against the kitchen counter, regaling her with some tale about work. She tunes out as she pummels the potatoes. She's quite pleased with the results. Not too many lumps although perhaps she added too much milk as the end result is a little on the runny side.

Olive's voice floats down the stairs, "My English grandpa came to see Mummy today."

"Don't be silly, Olive," Edward replies. "We don't have an English grandpa."

Milly freezes. *Why didn't she tell Olive not to speak of Winton's visit!*

"Well, he might not be *your* grandpa, but he promised he'd be *mine*." Olive calls from the top of the stairs, "He did say that, didn't he, Mummy?"

George looks at Milly and she feels her face flush hot.

"He did," she calls back as she makes herself look straight into George's eyes, no hesitation, no break in eye contact. "A distant cousin of mine, Winton Harvey-Jones, visited today. He happened to be passing through New York."

"Winton." George's brow furrows. "I don't remember you mentioning that name before."

"I've not seen him in years. There wasn't really any need to mention him."

"You should have invited him to stay for dinner."

"I didn't think of it. And besides, it might have been awkward. You know. Relatives can be strange beasts. He might have found my cooking unpalatable."

"That's quite likely." George peers over at the soupy potatoes. Milly pokes him in the ribs.

The children appear back in the kitchen. Olive's nightdress is on inside-out.

"But, Mummy, you said you used to work with him." *Damn it, Olive!*

"Well, I didn't exactly. He got me that secretarial job at the asylum, through his work at the War Office, that's all."

"I see." George put his drink down, looking like he really didn't see at all. "What did he do in the War Office?"

"Oh goodness. I can't remember. I'm not sure I ever knew.

Something high up and probably a bit hush-hush . . . Look, the children really need to be in bed now. Do hurry, or there shan't be time for any story."

George disappears up the stairs with the children and Milly covers the mash to keep it warm. There was a moment, just a moment, after Olive first spoke that Milly could have told the truth. The back of her neck prickles. But how could she? If she had mentioned the manuscript and how she really knew Winton, she would have had to explain about Bletchley and she couldn't do that. She thinks back to the beginning of her time there, when the two officers had sat her down and explained the implications of signing the Official Secrets Act. The penalties if she were ever to disclose the work she was to do, the place in which she was to do it, would be severe. Terrifying words were used. *Espionage. Treason. Fourteen years in prison per offense.* She could receive any number of fourteen-year sentences and spend the rest of her life locked up. After the war, when their time at Bletchley was over, those warnings were reiterated in no uncertain terms. They must never, ever speak of Bletchley's existence or the work they did there. In this new, cold war era, the need for secrecy was greater than ever.

So, much as Milly hates to lie to George, she has no choice.

It's just a tiny white lie. And really, what harm can it do?

Chapter 6

Charlotte

Rue St.-Jacques, Paris, July 1552

Charlotte observed her visitor, Lysbette Angiers, from behind the large desk in her study.

"What can I do for you, Madame Angiers?" Charlotte began.

"I'm sorry to intrude without an appointment, but I'm hoping you will be able to help me, Madame Guillard."

Madame Angiers's delicate frame was swamped by the generous upholstery of the armchair in which she sat. She was uncommonly thin, and Charlotte wondered if the woman carried ill humors. She noted a wedding band glinting on the woman's pale finger, yet there was no sign of any husband. Despite her beauty, on closer inspection, her skin appeared to have an unnatural sheen, the area around her eyes a little puffy. Her fingers fussed at her sleeves, tugging at the lace as though afraid her wrists might be revealed. She stared at Charlotte with wide-set eyes of the palest blue, like a freshly rinsed sky.

Could this woman have a sickness of the mind?

Charlotte admonished herself. Men had accused her many times over the years of being of unsound mind. They were prone to make such accusations, she observed, when she disagreed with them.

But there was something unsettling about the woman, although she couldn't discern what it was. Suddenly, Charlotte longed for her husbands. Someone with whom she could consult. Someone whose opinion she could trust.

It was here, in this room, more than in any other place in her *hôtel* that she felt the presence of her long-dead husbands. Perhaps it was the wall hangings, depicting scenes from ancient Rome and of the gods of antiquity, that conjured her first husband, Berthold. He had chosen the subjects carefully for this, his study, the hub of the business and the place he had taught her so much about the printing trade. *Charlotte*, he would say, *do not forget, the secret of success in printing is first and foremost, distribution. If we cannot get our books to readers, we will fail.* She hadn't forgotten, nor any of his other snippets of value. *Befriend the professors at the university. Students read. A lot. Find the learned among the monasteries, the aristocracy, the lawyers, the intellectuals. All good business is built on relationships and trust. Show yourself to be reliable, honorable, always turn out a high-quality product on time, and good fortune will follow.*

Much easier said than done, Berthold, but good advice. Charlotte had always known that, should he go before her, in the absence of a strict printing guild, she as his childless wife, would be able to continue to run the thriving business in her own right. She'd been as involved in the business as he had been. They were a partnership.

The desk and the bookshelves, now filled with over two hundred books printed by Soleil d'Or, had belonged to Claude. Dear Claude, who'd married her after she had carried on the business alone for months once Berthold had departed for his place in heaven. Claude had known, as there were no children with Berthold, there would likely be none for him, either, but he had married her anyway. They'd been a good team and despite the many years since she had lost him as well, a wave of grief washed over her. She shook her head and addressed her visitor again.

"I assume the help you seek is of a printing nature?"

The woman nodded, opened her mouth to speak, but paused as Sophie, Charlotte's maid, entered with a tray of wine, sugared almonds, and candied fruit, setting it on the desk.

Charlotte poured them both a goblet of wine and pushed the tray of delicacies toward her visitor. "Please, drink. Eat. You must be tired and hungry after your long journey. Have you just arrived in Paris?"

The woman accepted the proffered wine, bringing it to her lips and drinking deeply.

"We arrived yesterday after a three-day journey. I am a little tired." She eyed the tray of delicacies. "You are most kind."

Charlotte watched the woman's hand tremble as she raised the wine again to her lips.

Lysbette wore an English-style cap, but she had spoken in French, rather than English or Flemish, the lingua franca of the Pale of Calais, a remote part of England now for over two hundred years. Surveying her clothes, Charlotte noticed her lace cuffs were somewhat frayed, the silk of her gown carried the sheen of the well-worn. She suspected the garment had been reworked from something previously altogether grander. Her hair was pulled in tight beneath her cap and hood, and she wore a single string of pearls from which a heavy gold cross hung at her chest. She was otherwise unadorned with ruff, jewelry, lace, or finery. There was no frippery in her hairstyle, no whitening of her skin or rouge on her cheeks. Charlotte placed her in the minor noble or merchant class, fallen upon hard times.

"The printing commission, Madame?" Charlotte prompted.

The woman cleared her throat, shuffled forward an inch in her chair. She glanced over her shoulder at the closed door.

"It is delicate."

Charlotte sighed heavily. "Madame, I hope you have not traveled all this way in vain. I have a large backlog of work and only very rarely take on small, personal commissions. Most of my publications are of a religious nature, and my clients range from monasteries to the University of Paris. Printing is an expensive business, and if I am to take the risk on the cost, I need to know there is a market for such—"

"Oh no. There would be no financial risk. Do not be deceived by my"—she looked down at herself with apparent dismay, as though she were covered in filth from the street—"poor dress. I have money and will pay the full cost."

Charlotte hesitated, and anticipation pulsed between them. Lysbette Angiers did not blink, and Charlotte found herself mesmerized by the woman's steady gaze. Those eyes. Her face, like a fine, fine painting.

"May I ask," Charlotte inquired, "why you did not engage a printer in London? The journey surely must be faster and without the complication of crossing the border." She helped herself to a handful of sugared almonds, popping them into her mouth one by one.

"London printers are smaller, their quality inferior. You have an excellent reputation."

Charlotte thought of her own terrible paper quality and stifled an ironic laugh.

Something crashed in the yard outside, accompanied by shouts of, "Attention!" Madame Angiers shot up from her seat as though it was on fire, her face blanching as if the very devil himself hovered on the other side of the window.

Charlotte turned to look outside, craning her neck to see that a ladder had fallen and the contents of a bucket were strewn across the yard. The men had been repairing a hole in the roof above the warehouse. She swore under her breath at the broken tiles that would need replacing. No bodies, though, thanks be to God.

She turned back to her guest who seemed frozen in shock.

"You are ill at ease, Madame."

Madame Angiers gripped the edge of the desk as though she might fall if she let go.

She took up the wineglass again and swallowed down another large mouthful, which seemed to calm her.

"The truth is," she said finally, "I believe my life is in danger."

"*Dieu!*" Charlotte started at that. Was this woman deranged? Or worse, could it be true? Had she brought danger to *her* door? "But why?"

Madame Angiers swallowed. "The religious temperature in England is dangerous for us practicing Catholics." She stopped, staring into the middle distance as though lost in some uncomfortable past. It was true, France was full of English exiles, run from their country in fear for their lives. But this did not sound like something Charlotte wanted to get drawn into.

"Look," Charlotte said, a prickle of irritation rising. "I am a busy woman, Madame Angiers, and—"

"I was once a nun," Madame Angiers interrupted. "Until my abbey was dismantled by the old King, some years ago."

"I'm sorry . . ." Charlotte drew the sign of the cross over her chest.

"After leaving the abbey, I married a cloth merchant. I didn't have any other options, you understand. Being skilled at languages, I help him with his contract negotiations. We live in Calais but travel regularly to Paris and around Europe to source the best materials to sell to the aristocracy of England. Currently, my husband is at Les Halles, negotiating the price of cloth with his suppliers." She lowered her voice. "I was able to slip away because his negotiations were being conducted in a tavern where I was not welcome to go with the men. That suited me, as it gave me the opportunity to pay you a visit, alone. My husband does not know I'm here."

"Why not?"

Lysbette gave a small laugh. "Books are not where his interests lie. But I have for so long wanted to come to the house of the famous Charlotte Guillard, beneath the sign of the Soleil d'Or. It has been my dream for you to print my work." She stopped, staring at Charlotte as if she was afraid to go on.

Charlotte drew a deep breath. "Madame, I'm flattered, of course, but you must enlighten me—what is the nature of the work you hope to print? Is it a religious text? Or a translation? And I still do not understand why you fear for your life."

The woman fixed her once more with her exquisite eyes, now bearing a radiance, as though kindling had been lit behind them. "I know well the beauty of your religious texts. I curated several volumes that bore your mark at Barking Abbey."

Charlotte sat up a little straighter.

"Your life, Madame. You fear it is in danger?"

"Yes . . ." The woman swallowed. "Madame Guillard, I have been writing my life's work these past ten and more years. The content of it is a fantasy, a notion dreamed up by my imagination. But at the same time, it is a truth. And as such, there are those who would consider it a dangerous text."

"A dangerous text in what sense?"

Madame Angiers gaze was steady now. "Heresy, sedition, sorcery. The work of the devil, some might call it."

Lord have mercy.

"But I thought," Madame Angiers continued, "I could print it under a pseudonym, and without your print mark to preserve your anonymity. I would fear, too, for you, should it become known you had printed it."

Charlotte fancied she could see Antoine de Mouchy's ears twitching from his lair at the Sorbonne. His spies were everywhere. For all she knew, one could be hiding right here, listening at the keyhole. She was likely already under scrutiny for printing the works of Erasmus (God rest his soul). And she, as a printer and distributor of his books, at least in the eyes of de Mouchy, was as guilty and worthy of burning as the books themselves.

"Madame," she said, lowering her voice, thinking of ears and keyholes, "I cannot possibly consider printing such a work. Anonymity offers no protection. Do you know how many men it takes to print one pamphlet? Anyone involved in a project can talk. Even if they mean no harm. Idle chatter spreads. I cannot help you."

"Please," Madame Angiers eyes widened, her voice dropping to a whisper. She leaned forward in her seat. "I beg you! I know you to be a woman who values the new learning. Who understands that the power of words and ideas can make our earthly realm a better one."

"How can you possibly know that of me?"

"Through the works you print. Aside from religion and law, you have printed those of science, poetry, philosophy. And of course, Erasmus." She sits back in her seat. "I knew him, once. And I know *you* to have been a friend of his. That says a great deal about you, Madame Guillard."

Charlotte regarded her with astonishment. She opened her mouth to speak. Then shut it again, allowing her thoughts to settle. She had underestimated this woman. But this woman was overestimating her and the risks she was prepared to take. She thought of Erasmus's words being inked onto folios at this very moment in her workshop, and her blood thudded harder in her veins.

It would be madness to take on this unknown, possibly even lunatic, woman's work.

Charlotte studied her. The woman had an intriguing tale. And she had courage coming here. And if there was one thing Charlotte admired, it was a woman with pluck. They were, after all, two women trying to make their mark in a man's harsh world.

She sighed. She could not welcome any risk or danger into her home. "I cannot help you," she said again.

Above them, a floorboard creaked, and Lysbette Angiers flinched. Outside, the sound of hooves and the clanking of cartwheels over cobbles was followed by muffled voices and a peal of laughter. The woman's eyes swiveled to the window, then back to Charlotte.

"I know I ask much of you, when I am a stranger. But if you see my work, I know you won't turn me away."

"A bold claim indeed. You come empty-handed. Where is this manuscript?"

"I delivered it before coming here to a place of safety. Madame Guillard, there are those who would have it destroyed, which is why I must have it in print. One copy is easy to destroy. But surely not tens of copies, or hundreds. A few could be hidden and escape the flames should it be so condemned. And . . ." She leaned forward, dropping her voice again, "I fear soon my own life will be snuffed out so I may not write another word."

Charlotte should call for Luc, her manservant, and have him throw this woman out. Every instinct told her it would be foolish to ignore the threat of the heretic hunters. Fear crept through the Paris streets like bad air, floating under doorways, seeping through the walls, infecting men's minds until half the population were mad with it.

But then Charlotte remembered that nagging urge to do something extraordinary. To leave her mark, here, in the corporeal world. She regarded the woman sitting before her in a new light.

The woman had been a nun, until evil powers had stripped her of that highest calling. Had God himself sent her to Charlotte's door? If he had, she could not turn her away.

"Where, exactly, is this document?"

Madame Angiers' eyes grew big as saucers. "It is in the care of my old friend, Dame Agnes, at the Convent of the Blessed Heart beside the church of Notre-Dame. Meet me there tomorrow morning, as dawn breaks. Once you have seen it, you will understand." Sweat was beading at her hairline. "And then, after you have heard my story, seen what is contained within, I am certain you will agree to print. But if you don't, I swear to you, I won't bother you again."

They stared at each other across the desk. Charlotte tried to read what was behind this woman's eyes. She could discern neither hostility nor madness. Only the pleading look of a desperate woman. The words of the parable of the Good Samaritan clattered through her mind. Here before her was a traveler in need of help.

"Fine," Charlotte found herself saying. "I will look at your manuscript, and you will tell me everything. But I make no promises. And even if we were to print, that is no guarantee the book will not be banned, rounded up, and burned."

Madame Angiers exhaled, her cheeks high with color. Something approximating a smile of relief flashed across her face.

"I know the risks," she said. "All I ask is that you see it, and listen . . . I'll meet you outside the main convent gates as the lauds bell chimes. I trust you will not regret it."

Chapter 7

Lysbette

Chelsea, England, February 1527

T his is the one," John Haydon exclaimed, snatching a slim volume off the library shelf.

"Shhh, or Mistress Alice will hear," whispered Lysbette. "Then she'll have a reason to have me locked in my room for the afternoon."

"Not if you're with me. She adores me." John tossed his head in the manner of a proud pony. On other boys, this self-assurance could tip over into arrogance. But not John. He wore his confidence like his ready smile. Warm, genuine, masking no malice or unease. And besides, it was true. Alice *did* adore him.

"I'll bring her round," he continued, "should she pick on you. But she won't, because the library is the last place she'd come. I don't think I've ever seen her with a book in her hand, other than her Book of Hours. "Now come, you need to read this."

But talk of Alice always set Lysbette's stomach roiling. The woman's dislike of her seemed to swell by the day, however hard Lysbette tried to please her. The woman's sole objective in life was to ensure that the fortunes of the many More family members rose higher and higher toward the shining light that was King Henry of England. As a poor orphan, Lysbette was of no use to her scheming. Alice also seemed irked by Lysbette's friendship with John. If she ever caught them together, she would find one reason or another to break them apart. An errand for John here, a task for Lysbette there.

"It is high time you were betrothed," she had proclaimed loudly to John last evening at supper. "Now that you shall soon be starting a career in the law, it won't be long before you will be in need of a wife." She'd glared at Lysbette, and John had caught Lysbette's eye across the table, the tips of his ears red, a bloom on his cheeks.

At thirteen now, Lysbette was also of marriageable age. But Alice harked on about her fourteen-year-old niece who would bring John a vast estate in Yorkshire. "A perfect match, and she is quite the beauty," she had pronounced with a sly sideways glance at Lysbette. "Don't you agree, Thomas?" Which of course he had, because he agreed with everything his wife said, particularly on the subject of marriage.

Now, as John clasped Lysbette's hand and drew her to the window seat where they squashed in side by side, backs against the wood, her body pressed up against his bigger, warmer one, she pretended that conversation never happened. He handed her the little book. *On the Best State of a Republic and On the Island of Utopia*, she read.

"What is this?"

"Sir Thomas wrote it," John said. "A few years ago now, but he was already in the service of our King. Not Speaker of the Commons or Chancellor as he is now, but I think you will find it an odd sort of tale for one so pious, one so committed to our prince and to upholding the law." John was leaning over her, his breath warm against her cheek. It sent shivers down her spine. She wondered if he could feel them, sitting as close as they were. It was hopeless, of course. She, thirteen years old, penniless, and stupid with love for a sixteen-year-old member of the noble classes. He would never, *could* never notice her or think of her in *that* way. For him, she was just a fellow ward. Friend, at best. She gave herself an internal shake.

"*Island of Utopia*," she said. "In Greek that means, *Island of Nowhere*. What an odd name."

"Here . . ." John turned the book over and opened the back of it. He pointed to the addendum, where Sir Thomas had written, in Latin, *not the Island of Nowhere, but the Good Place, the place of felicity . . .*

"This imagined place of Utopia is nowhere, because it doesn't exist, but if it did, it would be the happiest place on earth," John said, his voice smooth like warm cream. "In the book, the story of the island is told to Sir Thomas himself by this fictional character, Raphael, who lived there, with the Utopians, for years. It is a jape, Lysbette. Sir Thomas says he wrote it for amusement while he was away from England on business in Bruges and he was bored."

"So, while he was sitting through interminable negotiations about this or that tariff," John continued, "he must have been dreaming of the explorers traveling west and finding strange lands full of savages. I suppose he must have thought, why not an imagined land that couldn't possibly exist? Or could it? And that, Lysbette, is the beauty of it." He flipped the book over again and ran a hand over the cover. "Of *him*, of Sir Thomas." His voice carried a hint of reverence, as was the case with many who knew the man. "Perhaps, behind the humor and the jesting, he was being more serious than he lets on. Perhaps he hoped, or even thought, that *maybe* a place like this *could* exist." He turned to look at Lysbette. His eyes were glittering, full of something that made her heart hop.

She carefully opened the book and inside the front cover she found a beautiful map of *Utopia*, complete with towns, countryside, mountains, rivers, people, and ships floating upon the ocean around it. On the page beside it, a group of incomprehensible letter-like symbols were placed beneath Latin letters and phrases. She peered closer.

"And this?"

"That's the Utopian language."

"What!" She laughed.

"Yes, he even made up a whole language to give authenticity to his imagined place."

Lysbette smiled. That was so like him. Attention to detail. Nobody she had ever met worked as hard as Sir Thomas.

"Tell me about it," Lysbette said, hugging the book to her chest and leaning her head against John's shoulder. Through the diamond panes of glass in the window, she could see the garden's perfect circle of rosebushes, its topiary and brick walls and the straight, wide gravel path cutting through the middle that led down to the river Thames. In that moment, sitting here, with her body pressed against John's, she thought she might never be happier. Warm and safe, he trusted her, and only her, with his innermost thoughts. Her insides were dancing a jig.

"You can read it yourself." John laughed, giving her a little nudge with his shoulder. "Your Latin is better than mine now. You know you are our tutor's prize pupil, with your excellent mathematics and vastly superior Greek and Latin."

"No, I'm not!" But she felt pride swelling like a blooming bud deep in her chest.

John sighed. Then he said softly, "The best brains *and* beguiling beauty. It's an unfair combination, Lysbette. What am I to do?"

She froze, not daring to breathe. Their faces were but inches apart and for a moment she thought he might press his lips to hers, but he smiled then and the spell broke, leaving behind it a whisper of hope that, like the first rays of sun breaking through a morning mist, the feelings would grow stronger until all doubt was burned away.

He touched the book still clutched but forgotten against her chest. "Let's meet again tomorrow after classes and you can tell me what you think. *I* find it strange that the man who wrote this, a book that advocates religious tolerance"—he taps the book's cover again—"is ordering the burning of books he calls *pestiferous works sent to this realm to pervert the people from the true faith of Christ. Or to stir sedition against their princes.*"

"And the same man who calls his best friend that heretic, Erasmus?" John added. "So many inconsistencies, Lysbette. Why? That is what *I* want to know."

With thoughts of John making sleep utterly impossible, Lysbette lit a candle, placing it beside her bed to read the little book *Utopia*. Silence had descended over the house like the thick fog that rolled up the Thames from the sea. Soon it absorbed her so completely that she temporarily forgot John and the promise of what she hoped may develop between them. By the time she had finished the book, it was well into the night and, as she blew out the flickering flame, she fancied she heard a door creak open and shut, and footsteps shuffle along the corridor outside her room. It must be two o'clock, the hour Sir Thomas rose, devoting the time until the prime bells sounded at six o'clock to prayer and his own writings.

Lysbette closed her eyes, prickly and sore from straining to read by the poor light of the candle. In her head she could *see* that island, *Utopia*. Its mountains and valleys, rivers, and the deep blue ocean around its shores. She could visualize its golden fields of swaying wheat, where the benign weather never brought storms or droughts so that harvests were rich every year and nobody starved. She could see the contented people who all dressed the same because there were no laws about who could wear what, and there was only one class of people because nobody could own any property. She wondered what the houses would look like in the towns because everyone was given an identical one by the fair king. Big and comfortable enough for each family. She saw the mothers and fathers who were not too tired because they only worked for six hours a day and spent eight hours a night sleeping.

How would life be in a land where there was no thieving because nobody needed to? Where there was enough time for leisure besides work, and where learning and reading was a pleasure enjoyed by all, boys and girls, just like in Sir Thomas's house. It was a land where *every* person could read and write. And like her, nobody had a penny to their name but they, unlike her, didn't care because it was a place where gold and silver, where money itself, had no value at all. A place where her prospects wouldn't be limited to a lowly marriage or life as a nun.

Lysbette turned onto her side and squeezed her eyes more tightly shut in the hope that sleep would come. But her head was too full of images and thoughts from the book. In *Utopia*, she could marry John. In *Utopia*, nobody cared what religion you had. You could believe in God and the immortal soul of man, or the sun or moon or anything else, and nobody punished you for it. People of all beliefs lived side by side without any accusations of heresy or arrest or burning. And if anyone did commit a crime in *Utopia*, which seemed to Lysbette unlikely as everyone had everything they needed, they became a slave as punishment, rather than going to jail or being tortured or facing execution. The slaves were given the worst jobs, like the killing of the beasts, because that brought unhappiness on those who had to do it.

The ideas in the book made her skin prickle and her nerves jangle just like they did when John suggested they creep through the kitchen when Cook wasn't there to raid the larder for gingerbread. And between every word in the book, there was Sir Thomas, with his clever mind and bawdy humor. She could almost see him, sitting in his study in the early hours of the morning when the whole household but him was fast asleep, his quill scratching on the parchment, chuckling to himself as he wrote that in *Utopia*, men and women should get to see each other naked before they married. How the very implausibility and outrageousness of it all made it seem, well, somehow possible too.

She did not know a book could do this. Could make her *feel* like this. That by reading its words, she would never again see the world in quite the same way. It was as though a secret room, until now shrouded in darkness, was suddenly lit by the rays of the sun, illuminating its hidden treasures for all to see. Now she had read *Utopia*, she was more alive with ideas and notions and questions than she had ever been before. It was all so hard to fathom that her head began to swirl until, finally, like a silent, swooping bird, sleep took her.

It felt but moments later that Mary held her roughly by the shoulder, shaking sleep away. The flickering light of a reed lamp in her face made Lysbette wince as she prized open her eyes.

"Whatever is the matter, Miss Lysbette?" Mary cried. "Why are you not up and dressed? Did you not hear the bell? You shall be late for class!" She tutted then leaned closer, alarm widening her lake-green eyes, and placed a cool hand on Lysbette's brow.

"You're not sickening for something?"

"No, no, I'm well, Mary. I simply read too late, that is all."

Mary spotted the burnt-down candle stub on the bedside table and shook her head.

"Don't you start adopting the night-working habits of the master," she warned. "Hurry now or you'll earn yourself a caning from Mr. Roberts for being late."

Minutes later, Lysbette was on the galleried landing with the dozen or so other students, mostly girls, from the village. She looked around for John, but there was no sign of him. The chapel bell chimed six and the door swung wide as Mr. Roberts appeared and ushered the pupils inside the schoolroom. Each carried his or her own candle and parchment paper on which to write. The younger ones clasped their hornbooks with the Lord's prayer and the alphabet pinned to the front. Inside, the tutor took his place at the front of the classroom, giving the students time to organize themselves before he began the first lesson of the day. Lysbette sat beside John's empty desk. Had he overslept too?

By evening, John had still not appeared and Lysbette was sick with worry. "Where is John?" Lysbette finally asked Mary as she helped her dress for supper.

"He left for London first thing this morning to take his place at the Inner Temple," Mary said, lacing Lysbette's bodice tightly from behind. "Following in the master's footsteps to train in the law."

Lysbette whipped around, pulling the laces from Mary's hands making her curse.

"He can't have!" she cried, her eyes awash with tears. "What do you mean, he's *gone*?" Terror gripped her like hands about her throat. "But he is coming back? He would never have gone without . . . Oh, but I overslept!"

Mary shook her head. "He'll be living in London now." The maid's voice was gentler. "You must have known he'd be gone soon enough. At sixteen, he needs to be out in the world, building a life of his own. You'll miss him. I know the two of you are close." She turned Lysbette around again with firm hands and continued lacing.

"But why did he not tell me he was leaving?" Did he care so little for her that he didn't think to mention it yesterday? She let out a sob of utter misery. How could he do that? Give her such hope of his affection, then simply leave without a word?

"He didn't know himself," Mary said. "The mistress arranged it that way. Less time to worry about leaving, I suppose."

Lysbette stood, silent tears coursing down her cheeks while Mary finished with the laces. Rage stirred inside. Alice must have done this on purpose. To spite Lysbette, she was sure of it. The prospect of life here in Chelsea without John was so desolate, she couldn't think how she would bear it.

Who else could she talk to? Mercy was kind enough toward her, but she was much older, and they rarely crossed paths. Sir Thomas himself was so busy, always, on the business of the King or Parliament that Lysbette caught only brief glimpses of his rich red traveling cloak and heavy furs as he passed in and out of the house. King Henry, appointed only a few years ago by the pope as Defender of the Faith, was incensed at the steady stream of that monk, the *agent of the demons*, Martin Luther's works pouring into England. It was an act of heresy to be caught with any of Luther's writings. All those found had been thrown into a great bonfire at St Paul's with a crowd of thirty thousand looking on. But still the books came, and it was Sir Thomas's job to stop them. Lysbette would watch from the window as he walked, stooped shouldered, down to the boathouse beside the river where the waiting barge would take him from Chelsea to Greenwich or Richmond, or to Parliament at Westminster. When he was home, he spent his time praying in the chapel or writing or receiving important guests. It was no wonder he had little time for anyone, let alone Lysbette.

Without John, who would shield her from Alice's vicious tongue? And now, she never would get her chance to discuss *Utopia*. Never get her chance to become closer to him. She'd always known it was a hopeless dream but yesterday, she felt sure John returned her affections, and that had given her hope that somehow, some way, they might find a path to be together.

She squeezed her eyes shut and bunched her fists to stop the tears.

"Hush now," Mary said, turning Lysbette to face her. The tears rolled freely once more at the sight of Mary's kind, sad eyes. John had been her favorite, too, and out of anyone, she would understand Lysbette's loss most keenly. "It's not like you'll never see the boy again," she said. "He'll be back visiting before you know it. And besides, you can write him a letter, can't you?"

She *could* write to him. Of course she could.

"Oh, Mary, yes! But . . . The mistress wouldn't like it, would she?"

"She need never know," Mary replied, with a wink.

Chapter 8

Milly

Levittown, Long Island, New York, November 1952

With December just around the corner, the children are wrapped against the cold like fat Christmas parcels in woolen coats, hats, gloves, and scarves until only the pink of their cheeks reveal that there are, in fact, small humans beneath the layers. They are late leaving for school, and Milly is so hot and bothered after all the bundling that she is not in the mood to be kind when Mrs. Humphries calls to her, almost slipping over in her haste to get to Milly.

"Oh, Milly," she says, "I'm so glad I caught you." She's shuffling fast along the snow-dusted pavement to catch up with Milly. Milly grips the children's hands tighter and doesn't stop.

"Good morning, Mrs. Humphries," she finally concedes over her shoulder. "Sorry but we're already a little late for school."

"I don't want to hold you up, but . . ." She's alongside now, her breath puffing in clouds like a slow-moving steam train.

Milly sighs, and in a show of defeat, stops and turns to face her neighbor, painting on a smile.

Mrs. Humphries has been offering for weeks to mind the children, should she ever need it, her own brood having fled the nest. *I just love babies*, she'd told Milly as they stood outside the baker's one morning, eyeing Milly's flat midriff with some disappointment. *Yours are just adorable. I'd be happy to have them anytime, should you ever need a little break, Mrs. Bennett. You only have to ask.* She'd whittered on about having too much time on her hands, what with Hank away for months at a time with the military, *it can be awful lonely, you know?*

"I'm getting a puppy," she says now, making the children squeal, and they both tug on Milly's arms pleading for a puppy too.

"Well, that is nice," Milly grants her neighbor another smile, wondering why this should have anything to do with her.

"Perhaps the children might like to come visit when he arrives?" They chorus yes.

"I'm collecting him a week from tomorrow. A golden retriever. It'll be like an early Christmas present." She beams.

"Lovely." Milly moves to continue on their way. "Now, I'm sorry, but we really must go. The children are going to be horribly late for school, Mrs. Humphries."

"Mrs. Cross and I were so glad to see you had a visitor yesterday," Mrs. Humphries calls out, stopping Milly in her tracks.

Milly turns, unable to stop herself, and says, "Why should you notice or care whether I have visitors?"

Mrs. Humphries's cheeks swell scarlet. She twists her hands, squeezing one inside the other. "It's neighborly to care, isn't it? We know how it is to feel all alone, some place new. We want you to feel at home here in our beautiful town. Mrs. Cross and I, we understand only too well what it is like to have a husband in the military, the kiddies tiny. A person can feel quite desperate."

"George isn't in the military. At least, not anymore. And I'm not desperate. Not in the least."

"I know that, but he's working all hours at that bank in the city. You only get to see him properly at the weekends."

"It's not the same though, is it?" Milly is irritated but ashamed all at once. They only gained the house in Levittown because

George had been in the air force. Almost all the residents have some link, past or present, to the military. Demand for houses everywhere is so high that in Levittown, priority for a new house is always given to those who had fought for America. "I'm sorry, Mrs. Humphries, I know so many of the wives here have husbands out fighting in Korea. I hope you aren't thinking I don't care, or I'm not grateful . . ."

"No! Of course not. We want to make you feel right at home here. That's why Mrs. Cross and I were so happy to see you had company yesterday. New friend, was it?"

And there it is.

"No, not new. Just a distant relative of mine from England," Milly says airily.

"I see." Mrs. Humphries's shoulders visibly slump. Not much gossip to report back there. "Well, that's nice . . . Say, how would you like to come along to one of our military wives' lunches, or our weekly knitting afternoons?"

"Oh no." Milly laughs, beginning to walk again. "I can't knit for toffee, I'm afraid, and I'm far too busy to lunch during the week. Goodbye, Mrs. Humphries!"

After dropping the children at school, half an hour late, and with only a minor scolding from Edward's teacher, Milly rushes home. The house looks tidy enough to warrant no housework, and happily George has a dinner tonight at Sardi's in Manhattan so she is off the hook for cooking and can eat sandwiches with the children.

She lifts the manuscript from its hiding place, carrying it carefully to the kitchen table. First, she examines the spine and cover, then the pages. They carry holes, smudges, blotches, and on one, a water mark as though someone once knocked over a glass and it spilled across the folio. The vellum is soft, as though it has been well leafed, and Milly wonders if the fingers that touched and bent its pages belonged to its original writers, or curious scholars down the ages. Some of the pages can be unfolded, extending to four times their original size, all filled with illustrations and text. Four of them reveal what look like illustrations of the heavens, but although they are exquisitely drawn, these planets and stars bear little resemblance to the known universe.

Focusing purely on the illustrations, Milly can see they are arranged into groups, or categories. She writes them in a notebook. Horticulture, astronomy, medicinal, childbirth and women's health, government, industry, agriculture. She calls the last one miscellaneous, as it seems to encompass a number of different topics in one. She thinks about Winton's hunch that this was written by a woman, or women, like the Nüshu, to keep its contents safe from the eyes of men. Or perhaps he was wrong, and this was men's work, an imagined erotic male fantasy, given the number of naked women appearing in the illustrations. She is no expert on erotica, but the women cavorting about in blue pools look to her much more like they are having fun for themselves, than acting out titillating male dreams.

She returns to studying the holes and marks and concludes they are from previous fixings. She frowns at the cover. Although its leather is mottled and worn, she suspects it isn't as old as the pages themselves. It wouldn't be surprising, she supposes, for a book this age to be re-covered. This cover is stitched, whereas the holes give the impression it was previously bound with leather straps or clasps, which would tally with the marks. It is perfectly possible, therefore, that although the order of the book appears to make sense from the illustrations, it could have been incorrectly reassembled, accidentally, or purposefully to confuse the viewer, in the wrong order.

Next, Milly turns her attention to the text. It would take her some considerable time to look at every character or symbol and try to figure out frequency rates, where they appear together and if any might represent whole words or syllables, vowels or places/names.

Instead, she looks carefully at the formation of all the letters. At first glance, the writing throughout the manuscript looks so similar that it is easy to conclude it must have been done by one person. But on closer inspection, she sees small variations. She picks a few of the less often occurring characters and tracks them through the book. Comparing them throughout, she can see the inconsistencies. A tail with a more pronounced flick, bigger or smaller loops, a deeper slant, a shorter foot. These differences re-cur through the pages. But they are *the same* differences. Milly becomes engrossed hunting for them. It begins to feel like a game, and she is enjoying herself. She finds three different telltale styles. She suspects, therefore, three different authors of this work.

She yawns, stretches, looks at the clock. Another hour and it will be time to collect Olive. She boils the kettle, makes tea. She helps herself to a biscuit from the tin. Takes another. It was clever of Winton to leave this with her for a short time. He knew the task would grip her. That once she got her teeth into it, she wouldn't want to let go. And it is far more enjoyable than PTA meetings or knitting parties.

Carefully, and a good distance away from the manuscript, she pours herself a cup of strong tea, adds a splash of milk. Whoever put this manuscript together has managed to avoid its contents being disclosed for hundreds of years. Being handwritten, even with three authors, it must have taken years to complete. The encryption is highly sophisticated, the artistry exquisite. It has layers of decoy. Whoever made this must have been well educated, wealthy, and had the time and wherewithal to produce it. And, most intriguing of all, they must have had good reason to go to all this effort. If Winton was right, if this was the work of a woman, or women, in the early 1500s, only a very few had the ability to produce something like this.

The early 1500s, Milly recalls from her school days, was the time of the Protestant Reformation and terrible religious wars that followed. It was when Henry VIII was on the throne, when he formed the Church of England to split from Rome in order to divorce Katherine of Aragon and marry Anne Boleyn. Milly resolves to visit the library soon and see what they have about sixteenth-century Europe. But first she will finish *Of Mice and Men*, so that Susan won't think she is wasting her precious, illicit books on someone who isn't going to read them.

Milly finishes her tea and returns to the manuscript, slowly turning the pages, admiring the workmanship (or workwomanship) and studying the illustrations. Her eye is drawn again to the four pages she has come to think of as the astrology pages. On each one there is a spectacular wheel, divided into sections by spokes, writing, and illustrations spanning the outer circles. It reminds her a little of a Caesar cipher disk, but she dismisses that idea as being too simple. In its center is a blazing sun with a face, rays radiating outward, sprays of stars strewn between them. It's this sun that claims her attention. She stares at it transfixed. Somewhere in the depth of her mind a memory stirs. This image is familiar. She has seen it before; she is sure of it.

If only she can remember where.

Outside Abbey Lane Elementary School, mothers stand in strung-out closed circles, a few stragglers and nonconformists hovering between the groups. The flat-roofed school, like the library, stretches long and single storied beside Gardiner's Avenue. The temperature hasn't risen above freezing all day, and a thin layer of snow crunches underfoot. Milly slows her pace, joins the stragglers, willing the large double doors to be pulled wide for the mothers to stream in and collect their offspring. Chatter rises and falls like a morning chorus of robins, the sound sharpened in frost-stiffened air.

Olive tugs hard at Milly's hand. "Mummy, look! There's Betty—can we go wait with her?" She points toward the densest crowd closest to the entrance of the school.

"Who?" Milly is distracted, searching for a spot on the pavement to stand, away from anyone she may have to make small talk with.

"My best friend, Betty." Olive rolls her eyes. "I *told* you."

"But you change your best friend every week, Olive, I've lost track."

"Betty Sykes will be my best friend forever."

Olive pulls Milly along the pavement until they catch up with Doris Sykes and the other PTA mothers. Of all the children in her class, of course Olive has to pick Betty to be her bosom buddy. The two girls greet each other like long-lost friends, while Milly hovers at the edge of the Coven. Milly feels a twist of envy as she watches her daughter's animated conversation with Betty. They clasp hands and begin a skipping game at the edge of the circle of mothers. Olive has an effortless way with other children, making friends as easily as a signet gliding into water. Poor Edward is more like her. Goose, not swan.

"It is just not okay," Doris is opining loudly to her bevy of eager listeners. "I suppose it is to be expected, given the man's background. *Not Christian.*" She taps her nose. She turns and clocks Milly.

Milly nods and mouths *hello*.

Doris's painted red lips stretch to a smile.

"Milly!" she exclaims in her bright, high voice. "Come join us, won't you? Isn't it just lovely how Betty is getting along with Olive? She really is such a bighearted kid, welcoming Olive like this. Your two have found it so hard to settle . . . Well, it must be such a big thing, moving to another country. Especially for the little ones."

"Oh, no, they're fine. They've slotted right in. Easy as anything . . . Not like me. I'm less easy to slot. Like a rusty old key." Milly laughs.

Everyone stares. Self-deprecation doesn't seem to go down so well here. She notes that one not to repeat for the future. Like the others she is stacking up in her mental notes to self. Pants are not underwear. Do not use the Lord's name in vain. Sarcasm isn't funny. It's okay to turn up unannounced. Prettiness, not brains, in a woman is a key attribute.

Well, that last one is universal.

Olive and Betty now stand facing each other, clapping hands and saying a rhyme.

"We were just discussing the new superintendent of the Education Board, Mr. Hubert Goldstein," Doris tells Milly.

"Oh?"

"Right," agrees Sissy. "He needs to go."

There's a general tutting and murmuring around the circle.

"Why? What's wrong with him?"

"He wants to shake things up. *Modernize* our schools. Offer subjects like philosophy, ethics, science, religious studies," Doris explains.

Milly looks around at the faces of the other mothers. "Why, isn't that a good thing?"

Doris offers her an indulgent smile. "Our schools are perfectly fine as they are. Traditional, solid, reliable. And for my part, I think religious education and ethics should come from the church minister, don't you?"

"Well—"

"Not from a teacher who likely isn't even American or a God-fearing Christian." More murmurs of agreement around the circle.

Olive and Betty collapse into giggles, then start clapping again.

"Jimmy has been asking us about the fairness of the New Deal and whether racial segregation is morally acceptable," Sissy says, lowering her voice. "He's not yet twelve years old!"

"And their English class is reading *Huckleberry Finn*," muttered someone else.

"Look, with the change of government, I'm sure we will have a sympathetic ear from our congressman. This won't be tolerated by President-Elect Eisenhower, mark my words. It's dangerous," Doris opines.

"Dangerous, how?" Milly asks, but nobody responds.

"I'm planning to write letters to our congressman," Doris is saying, "and to the school board, that we have concerns about national security and the corruption of young minds. We need names, so anyone supporting these ideas can be investigated. I'll alert the PTAs of other schools in the area, in case they are worried about teachers with communist leanings. Don't worry, Mr.

Goldstein will be on that list."

Milly has read the papers. The constant refrain of *beware-of-the-communist-in-our-midst* stories. Joseph McCarthy has been reelected and there is talk of communist spies in the CIA, and all levels of government. But in the heart of Levittown? In Abbey Lane Elementary School? She isn't sure whether to laugh or cry. Instead, she blurts out, *"It is the mark of an educated mind to be able to entertain a thought without accepting it."*

Everyone turns to look at her.

"That's Aristotle," she explains. "A modern education might not be as modern as you think. In a democracy, teachers *should* teach our children to think for themselves . . ."

"Well," Sissy huffs, "I don't know about Aristotle, but I want *my* kids to think like me. Not little communists."

"C'mon, ladies." Doris smiles sweetly at Milly. "Give her a break. She's new here. Let's make her feel welcome . . ."

Before anyone can say any more, there is a rattling of the doors. The bolts are drawn back, and the doors swing inward, the crowd of mothers lurching forward to collect their darlings, and the conversation is thankfully over.

Edward appears from the first-grade class, walking alone, fair head bowed behind a cluster of more wholesome boys. He looks small next to his classmates, bony knees, pale legs poking from beneath his short trousers, almost blue with the cold, so skinny they could be snapped like twigs. Her heart snags at the sight of him. He greets Milly solemn faced, as though the grave weight of the world rests on his narrow shoulders alone.

"Hey, soldier," she says, wanting to pull him into a hug, but holding back, knowing he wouldn't want that in front of the other kids. "How was school?"

"Fine."

She takes his hand, gives it a squeeze. At least he still lets her do that. She leads him and Olive outside.

"Can we go to Finny's for a soda?" Olive whines. "My legs are tired of walking."

"Well, I suppose . . . Edward, do you have homework?"

"Just some spellings but they're easy. Finny's do the best hot cocoa. With marshmallows. Please, Mum?" He looks up at her, the first hint of a smile.

"All right," she says. "Finny's it is!"

They turn and trail other mothers and children back toward South Village Green, past snow-frosted front yards glittering beneath a low, anemic sun. Back in England, on a day like this, fires would be lit, the air heavy with woodsmoke. In London, heavy smog would lie thick, yellow, and noxious for days at a time over the city, seeping beneath doors and through ill-fitting window frames into houses and innocent lungs. Here, away from the main roads, the air is fresh and clean, the pretty, neat rows of modern houses set back from the street surrounded by grass and trees and each equipped with central heating and insulated walls with no need for dirty fires. Everywhere, children can safely play. Shops and schools merely a healthy walk away. If a person living here didn't want to, they would never have to venture into the grimy reality of the big city. Here, cocooned in this Long Island, middle-class oasis of purity, one could almost pretend the outside world didn't exist.

A real-life Utopia.

Doris falls in beside Milly, and Olive squeals with delight at the sight of Betty again. Doris is a tall woman, and by physical necessity must look down on Milly. Milly suspects it is a metaphorical act too.

"Listen, Milly," she says, "I do hope the ladies didn't make you feel uncomfortable. I realize we might sometimes come over as a little . . . daunting? No harm done, I hope?"

"No, of course not."

"Well, that's swell because I was thinking, how about you and Olive come over for lunch one day after kindergarten? You can stay until it's time to pick the boys up."

"Oh." Milly looks up at her in surprise. Is this because of Betty and Olive suddenly becoming inseparable lovebirds? She doubts it is down to her plea for a liberal education. Doris has barely spared Milly a glance until now. She'd sized her up when they'd first arrived, and even when Milly joined the PTA at George's urging, Doris has always adopted an air of superiority, giving the impression she is far too important to speak to the likes of Milly.

"Thank you, Doris. We should like that very much."

At least George will be pleased.

Chapter 9

Milly

Two mornings later, Milly visits the library after dropping the children at school. Susan is stamping books at the counter and gives her a friendly wave. Milly has *Of Mice and Men* in her bag and is wondering how to return it to the librarian discreetly.

"Thank you for your help the other day," Milly begins, glancing around at the few people perusing the nearby shelves. "I, er, want to return . . ." She pats her hand against her bag.

"You finished it already?" Susan asks, eyes widening.

"I'm a fast reader," Milly explains. "And it's a short book."

"Say, how about we grab that coffee?" Susan asks, glancing up at the library clock. "My break is in forty minutes. Can you wait? You could choose some more books."

Milly thinks of the manuscript, of the time she won't be able to spend on it if she is with Susan. But Susan's face is hopeful, and she likes this woman. She did her a kindness, too, so the least she can do is have a coffee with her.

"Yes, that would be nice," she says and Susan almost claps her hands in glee. "I'd like to read more fiction," Milly adds, "but today I'm looking for books about Europe in the sixteenth century. Do you have anything?"

"Why, yes, of course we do. Once the scholar, always the scholar," Susan says with a tinkle of laughter and directs Milly to the right section. Milly flicks through some volumes on Luther and the Reformation, Henry VIII's England, Francis I of France, and Charles V, Holy Roman Emperor. She picks up *Monastic Life in Early Modern Europe* and as she skims through the book her eye is caught by a short section entitled *The Beguines of the Low Countries: Communal Living for Single Women.* Not nuns, but unmarried women who chose to live together in communities for safety and to give their lives to the service of God and other people. They were not part of the Catholic Church, but a semireligious group organized by women themselves.

Milly feels a kick of excitement that perhaps she is onto something, but then she sighs and replaces the book on the shelf. This is all conjecture. It won't help decipher the code.

Once Susan is released for her break, they go next door and find a free corner table in the window of Bel's Bakes.

Seeing Susan outside of her natural library habitat is strange. Today her badge, *Hi! I'm Susan and I'm here to help!*, is fixed the right way up on her sweater.

"Well! Isn't this nice!" Susan beams.

They order donuts and coffee and stare out over the village green. The early snow has melted, leaving behind it a landscape bleached of color. In place of brilliant white, dirty puddles now lie in dips and hollows.

Milly slides *Of Mice and Men* across the table and Susan drops it into her own bag.

"I'm sorry about the subterfuge," Susan says.

"Why should you apologize?" Milly asks. "It isn't your fault these books are banned from the library, is it?" She is glad they are straight into a meaty topic, skipping the usual opening talk.

Susan snorts. "It most definitely is not. Oh no, this comes right from the top. To quote Robert Delaney in *The Library Journal* . . .

'Culture for culture's sake has no place in the US informational and educational programs . . . Cultural activities are an indispensable tool for propaganda.' You see, Milly, libraries are not hallowed places of learning, of opening minds to new things, they are not havens for escaping the everyday humdrum of life. No, 'they are propaganda agencies for the dissemination of anti-Communist literature,' to quote a report to the State Department." Susan's chest is heaving with indignation. "Libraries, schools, cinemas, plays . . . the censors are trying to stamp out everything from race, to sex, to liberty, to equality. To *freedom*. On the basis that it is *anti-American*." She spits the words. "Sorry, *sorry*," she says. "I just get a little heated when I allow myself to think about this stuff too much."

"Please. Don't be. I recently encountered a similar attitude against modernizing what they are teaching at the school. I was shocked, if I'm honest."

Susan exhales, places a palm on her still-heaving chest. "Thank goodness. I thought I'd said too much. I do have a tendency. I *thought* you would be sympathetic, but you never can tell. I really must learn to keep my mouth shut."

Milly smiles. "I'm guilty of having a runaway tongue too!"

"I think we are going to get along just fine, you and me." Susan taps her handbag. "So, what did you think of the book?"

"I thought it wonderful," Milly replies. "Painful, upsetting, but powerful."

Susan nods encouragement.

"I couldn't help but dislike the way Curley's wife was portrayed, though. I mean, she doesn't even have her own name. It's as though she has no identity and could be interchanged with any other woman. Just there to flirt and tempt as though that is a woman's only purpose in life and literature."

"Oh yes, but that's the author's intention, wouldn't you say? To challenge us, the reader, to be uncomfortable?" Susan glances furtively about her for anyone listening, but the women seated at the surrounding tables are engrossed in their own conversations.

The discussion of the book goes back and forth. Milly becomes quite heated on the subject of giving women a voice in literature, "Why are there so few women whose work is taken seriously?"

"I think," Susan says, "you might have landed in the wrong country if you want women to be taken seriously. A book that topped *The New York Times* bestseller list last year, *Washington Confidential*, meant to be an exposé of the Washington establishment, apparently a cesspool of drunken debauchery, homosexuality, corruption, exposes it to be a *femmocracy* . . ."

"Femmocracy?"

"A place of emancipated, sex-starved women who are taken advantage of by communists, naturally, and whose unhappiness proves the emancipation of women is baloney. Oh, and it gets much worse than that. It's a terrible book, don't read it."

"I won't," Milly says, making a mental note to do just that. She wants to learn more about modern America, after all.

The coffee is drunk, and they move on to talk of other novels they have enjoyed, of Milly's studies at Oxford, of how the war changed everything. The death of her parents and how she managed to scrape out a living after the war through her writing. How she met George. Susan tells her she lives in Hicksville and has worked at the library here since it first opened a few years back. That books are her passion and that most people would think her sad for being childless and alone, but that she is happy and fed up with those who look down on her for not having married, thinking that she is a creature to be pitied. Milly remembers her own pity, and shame crawls the length of her spine. But still, she can just imagine how other women might avoid Susan as though her lack of husband, her barren insides, might rub off on them, like a disease.

"So," Susan asks, "why the interest in sixteenth-century Europe?"

"Oh," Milly hesitates. She realizes how comfortable she is in Susan's company. How she'd love to confide in her about the manuscript. But if she can't tell George, how can she tell an almost-stranger? *When lying it's always best to stick to an almost truth.* "I'm just a little bored and a distant cousin of mine, back in England," she tells Susan, "is a rare book collector. He mentioned something in a letter about a book he'd acquired, and how he is looking into its background. I thought I would try and help him. He reckons it dates from the early 1500s." She laughs. "It's silly, I know, but I've always enjoyed keeping my mind occupied . . ."

"That's not silly at all." Susan glances up at the clock on the café wall and lets out a little gasp.

"Oh dear, look at that. How time flies when you are enjoying yourself! I must get back—my break is over." She reaches behind her for her coat then stops. "One day, I should like you to meet a very great friend of mine, Myra Bougas. She's the Features editor of a woman's magazine, *My Life.* You heard of it?" Milly has. It is prominently displayed on every rack in every newsstand. Milly has even bought the odd copy herself. It's a typical women's magazine, aimed at middle-class married women, with articles about how to get your kids to work harder at school, fun things to do as a family at weekends, how to keep your husband happy. There is always a feature on a beautiful home with furnishings to die for, a short story—usually a soppy romance—a women's interest article of some sort, and an agony aunt section. "I've a feeling the two of you would get along splendidly." Susan looks anxiously about.

"Where has the waitress gone? I need the check."

"Please, you get back to work and I'll settle up."

"Well, that is kind, Milly. Next time, it'll be my treat."

Milly sits back and watches Susan scuttle toward the door. How nice to think there will be a next time.

"Please, may Elephant, Tiger, Dog, and I have a picnic for lunch today, Mummy?"

"Not an outside picnic, Olive, it's much too cold."

"Not *outside*. Here. On the floor. I can get the picnic blanket. I know where it is."

Milly stares down at her daughter. "You do?"

Olive sighs heavily. "It's at the back of the cupboard beneath the stairs. Behind Daddy's golf clubs. I saw it when I was playing hide-and-seek."

And with that, Olive skips out of the kitchen to retrieve the picnic blanket and her toys. Milly shakes her head. She makes her some egg sandwiches and cuts up small slices of cake, with a little extra for the teddies. Winton Harvey-Jones will be sailing back to England tomorrow, so this afternoon is decision time.

Will she keep the manuscript here, or won't she?

While Olive is preoccupied with her picnic and her toys, Milly brings down the manuscript one last time before Winton arrives. Aside from yesterday when she had coffee with Susan, as soon as the children were dropped at school each day, Milly rushed home to take the manuscript from its hiding place, working on it until it was time to collect the children again. George doesn't seem to have noticed, thankfully, that the housework has largely been forgotten and meals rather hastily put together.

She looks at her notebook and reviews her progress. By careful study of the formation of the symbols and characters, Milly is now confident she has identified three different authors of the manuscript, despite the efforts that have been made for this to look like a seamless piece of work.

She is also certain that the book has been taken apart and put back together, in all probability in an incorrect order, which will certainly not help any efforts to decipher it. She has carefully studied as many pages as she has had time for, to spot recurring symbols and characters. She has made a list of all the letter-like characters and symbols. There are almost eighty in total. Too many for each to represent a letter of the alphabet. What *is* clear is that the way the text is written, the formation of it, such as the common recurrence of certain characters, the use of symbols perhaps as a shorthand for people or place-names, the structure of paragraphs, and the use of numbers is all very much like an ordinary text might be written, which, she thinks, again points toward this being real and encrypted.

Milly pulls the book in close and carefully turns a couple of pages, pausing at an illustration of a ludicrous plant that dominates a page. There is only a short paragraph of writing beside it. The plant has a large woody base, out of which grow three tall, spindly stems, topped by enormous red and blue flowers, of a type that could not, and do not, exist in the real world. It isn't the only invented plant or creature in the book. Perhaps their purpose is to make people think the document is a hoax? Or could they serve some other purpose?

Milly has noted her thoughts as she has gone along to ensure she doesn't forget anything important to discuss with Winton. *Just because this manuscript was found in a monastery in Northern Italy doesn't mean it started life there. Could it have originated in an-*

other part of the world? There was, after all, an explosion of exploration and conquering in the early sixteenth century by European settlers. From her recent reading she recalls their names. Cortés, Córdoba, Marin, Fernández de Valenzuela. Could this manuscript have been brought back from a far-flung part of the world? It might explain why the manuscript is handwritten. The printing press had not yet spread throughout the world. Could this be written in an obscure and long extinct Eastern language? She stares at the rust-brown writing on the page, willing it to release its secrets.

Her eyes stray to the margins where there are clear Latin letters and numerals. Which brings her back to Europe. Fine, so she will assume that it is a text written in Europe. Why might someone have wanted to encrypt it? Apart from Winton's theory about women wanting to keep their writing hidden from the eyes of men, the most obvious reason would be the religious wars. The Protestant Reformation was a dangerous time. England was in turmoil. Rome was sacked. Germany had the Peasants' War. The Ottomans presented an ever-growing challenge to Christendom, even threatening Rome itself. It was a time of unrest and fear. Heretics were burned at the stake. It was also a time of a proliferation of encoded correspondence and increasing sophistication in methods of encoding to keep messages safe, should they end up in the wrong hands.

Milly sighs. Messages, letters, yes. But whole books? And besides, the illustrations seem at odds with such a theory. But this, too, was a time of witch hunts and burning women accused of witchcraft. Her skin prickles. This feels more likely. Could this be a book of herbal treatments, and even contain incantations? That would fit more with the illustrations, and there appear to be pages of medical treatments and a focus on plants and animals, even if there are none she recognizes.

Turning to the four pages she calls the astrology pages, Milly is still troubled by the distinctive symbol of the blazing sun that appears on each. It still feels familiar, but she hasn't yet been able to place it. And now, at the eleventh hour, she is beginning to wonder if she recognizes it because she has been staring at it for so long.

The knock at the door makes her jump.

Winton.

Olive, after greeting Winton as though she has known him all her life, is now happily chatting to her toy animals, placed in a circle on the picnic blanket with the plate of food and beakers of juice in the middle.

Once Winton is seated at the table, the manuscript between them, Milly fills him in with her progress. It is just then, as she is talking him through script that looks like Latin, but isn't, the penny drops.

"Oh!" she exclaims, as she turns rapidly to the first of the astrology pages.

"What is it?"

"This image," she explains, pointing at the sun with the human face at its center, the flickering rays curving outward. "On each of these pages, beneath the drawing of the sun is a symbol that looks like a number four above a zero with a line through it. Inside the zero are tiny letters that look like *CG*, and beside the symbol, a couple of ornate looking lions, who appear to be holding it up. It looked familiar. I've been staring at it all week. I *didn't* dream it," she says looking up at Winton, who smiles encouragingly at her excitement. "I remember now where I've seen it!"

"And that was . . ."

"Before I was recruited to work at Bletchley, you remember I was at Oxford, studying Greek and Latin. Well, there was a book there—in the Bodleian Library. I got to go into the rare books section once to see a Greek to Latin dictionary we learned about in one seminar. It was the most comprehensive ever produced. I think it was commissioned by a monastery in France, if I correctly recall. Anyway, a handful of us had special permission to examine it. It was hundreds of years old and over two thousand pages long, separated into two volumes. We had to wear silk gloves to touch it."

"Mummy," Olive calls from the corner of the room, "my naughty animals have drunk all the juice. Please can I have some more?"

"There was quite a lot of juice in those four beakers, Olive. You will all have to have water now." She refills the beakers with water, resulting in some dramatic huffing from Olive.

Milly returns to the table. "Anyway," she continues, "I think now that's where I saw a symbol, identical to this. Or maybe identical. It was a long time ago, and I only saw it briefly. In the front of each volume, behind the front cover. A printing mark, I think."

They both stare at the symbol.

"But," Winton says slowly, "the image of a sun with a face at its center isn't unusual. Could it be that you remember something similar?"

"It's possible. But I think I remember these stars, the lions. All of it. I could take a photograph of this one and send it to the Bodleian Library for confirmation. Wait! George has a Polaroid camera; maybe you could take it there in person? It might be quicker."

"Polaroid?" Winton looks confused.

"Oh yes, it's a new contraption. His parents bought it for his last birthday. It takes black-and-white photographs, and they develop instantly. It's a bit of a knack, you have to time it, one minute exactly, pull out the print, and then you peel off the film. It's rather clever—I'll get it now."

After a few tries, they manage to take a decent photograph of the image, and Winton promises to deliver it to the Bodleian when he is back in Britain. He'll telephone just as soon as he has news.

"You see?" Winton has a look of triumph on his face. "I *knew* you would see things others missed. You are definitely onto something, Milly." He pauses. "Can I assume you will be carrying on with it then, and I can leave the manuscript with you until the spring when I return?"

Milly hesitates. Her recognition of the symbol feels like a breakthrough, and there is a fizz of excitement at the base of her belly. But that doesn't mean she will have more success.

"I can see you are tempted," Winton says.

"I am, but . . ."

"But?"

"It's such a huge responsibility Winton. And I still can't see how I can succeed where others have failed."

"I'd love you to give it your best shot," Winton says, his eyes filled with a gentle pleading. "I shan't think any worse of you if you don't succeed," he adds. "I've been trying for five years and failed."

She looks down at the manuscript. "All right. I'll give it my best shot."

She raises her gaze to meet Winton's. His face cracks into a wide smile.

"Thank you," he says. "I have a good feeling about this, Milly Bennett, and I want you to know, you have made an old man happy today."

"I think this deserves a drink!" Milly says, jumping to her feet. Winton's excitement is infectious. She runs to the drinks' cabinet in the sitting room, pulls out two tumblers, and the whiskey bottle, pouring a finger measure into each.

Milly and Winton toast to the success of unraveling this manuscript.

They agree to keep in touch by writing and exchange telephone numbers.

Winton Harvey-Jones slides on his coat, and Milly watches as he walks along the pavement to the waiting taxicab. He raises his hat and gives Milly, and Olive, who has joined her mother to see him off, a jaunty wave as he goes.

"Don't tell Daddy or Edward that Winton came to visit again, Olive," Milly says as they go back inside. "We don't want them to feel jealous that they missed out, now, do we?"

Chapter 10

Charlotte

Paris, July 1552

I t was never wise to stray onto the streets of Paris at night.

During the day the city was perilous enough with its narrow, winding streets where the sun never shone, rendered in perpetual shadow by tottering, half-timbered buildings that clamored ever upward and outward such that if a man leaned from the top window of one, his fingertips would almost meet those of a man leaning from the window of the building opposite. Down on the ground in the rank filth of the sewage-strewn streets, thieves and miscreants could operate with bold impunity, knowing there was little chance of their being caught. Swelling the numbers of the discontent, ever more young men poured into the city day after day, expecting, hoping, to find their fortunes, but instead they encountered only unemployment and pickpockets to strip them of their dwindling livre.

But at night, Paris was a cesspit of vagabonds and drunks, whores and murderers. Nobody in their right mind would dare walk anywhere but the wealthiest streets if they wanted to return home with their lives intact and hard-earned coins in their pockets.

Charlotte had not stepped outside of her house on foot and alone during the hours of darkness since the death of poor Claude these fifteen years hence, God rest his soul. Yet here she was, creeping away from the safety of her *hôtel*, along rue St.-Jacques, before the cocks began to crow and the diamond-studded black sky carried the merest hint of softening toward the east.

Fool, she admonished herself as she walked, grateful at least that the night was clear and the low-hanging full moon lit her way with a pale, unearthly glow. Lighting her lantern would only draw unwanted attention to herself. But how had a woman of her age and standing allowed herself to be hoodwinked into this mission by a complete stranger? And yet, here she was, so against her better nature, walking the blessedly quiet streets of Paris in the dead of night. All to meet Lysbette Angiers at the gates of the Convent of the Blessed Heart before the bells sounded for lauds prayers.

Claude would be turning in his grave.

But this, she told herself, was all in the Lord's plan for her. A test of her mettle, and she would not fail.

Strange night noises set her teeth on edge. During the day, the Grande Rue St.-Jacques was a seething mass of merchants, lawyers, booksellers, university professors, tradesmen, and the like, the air filled with a cacophony of hooves and wheels, shouts and chatter. Now, as she crept down the empty thoroughfare, somewhere in the treacly dark, hidden in the shadows of the buildings standing six stories above the street, she could hear rustlings and movement. Was that the sound of breathing? The scurrying of feet? *Foraging animals*, she told herself firmly. *Drunkards slumped in alleyways.*

Or maleficent eyes, watching.

Charlotte walked resolutely in the middle of the road, lifting her skirts and stepping as best she could around mounds of animal dung. Hopefully here she'd be out of arm's reach from being pulled into an alley or accosted from the black recess of a doorway.

Besides, she was less likely to encounter the slops and spills from emptied chamber pots. There was no sign of another human soul, not even the night watchman.

With the university buildings, the city walls, and gates of St.-Jacques behind her, Charlotte headed toward the mighty river Seine, tripping on the uneven ground beneath her shoes. At least the air at this, the hour before dawn, was cool, and Charlotte could breathe without fear of the miasmas that came with the midday stench.

A shape shifted and unfolded itself from a doorway. Charlotte's blood roared in her ears. She sidestepped and doubled her speed, cursing herself again for giving in to the pull of the woman and her mysterious manuscript. But the intrigue of it was too much and Charlotte's will was weak when it came to the power of words and the notion that she might find a way to outwit those who tried to curb them.

Were those footsteps behind her? But when she checked and rechecked over her shoulder, peering through the darkness, she could see no one.

Charlotte hurried across the bridge, keeping always to the center of the street. When the convent buildings finally materialized through the gloom, tucked into the shadows of the great shape of the church of the Notre-Dame de Paris, she slowed her pace. She stopped for a moment to stare up at the heavy stone walls of the Convent of the Blessed Heart, its pitched roofs and tall spire of the church behind reaching into the paling sky, then continued on toward the main gates of the convent. Candlelight flickered faintly from an upstairs window in the convent gatehouse and Charlotte exhaled with relief. She leaned her back against the rough wall to wait for Madame Angiers.

The street was growing lighter by the minute, and it would

not be long before Paris awoke, and the frenzy of a new day began. She remembered the scurrying feet, the figure in the doorway. The eyes, she had been certain, that followed her. Women who misbehaved were considered fearsome creatures who must be brought to heel. She thought about her obstinacy in printing the works of Erasmus. Her plan to take the Paper Guild to court. She had enemies out there who would be only too happy to see her business fail, her reputation tarnished. Better still, locked up and tried for heresy. She thought of that troublesome typesetter, Nicolas. Was it possible he had spoken loose words in the taverns he frequented? Words that had been whispered from ear to ear and finally reached those of de Mouchy, already suspicious of her, and whose spies had followed her here?

She stared up and down the street, eyes straining through the gloom. The only movement revealed itself to be a skinny cat slinking on silent paws beside the wall. Then, with an ear-shattering clang, the lauds bells rang out, so sudden and so loud that her teeth shook in her gums. Charlotte covered her ears and felt the ground tremble as the mighty bells tolled five thunderous times. In the aftermath, ears still ringing, she checked both sides of the street, but there was no sign of shadowy men, nor of Lysbette Angiers.

Time passed. The day brightened and her nerves eased. People began to appear from their houses, yawning, stretching tired and aching limbs as they set off to begin their day's toil. Charlotte peeled herself off the wall and paced a circle, her back complaining at too much standing still. Lysbette Angiers must have been held up. Or perhaps her husband had forbidden her to come? A knot of irritation wound itself around her gut.

The church bells rang out again, six this time, calling the nuns to prime prayers. Back at the printworks, the journeymen and their apprentices would already be hard at it. Frédéric would wonder where she was. With a sigh, Charlotte gave one last look around, then set off for home, hurrying to get back before anyone became alarmed at her absence.

Lysbette Angiers had taken her for a fool.

When Charlotte reached the corner of the street, allowing a wagon to pass before stepping out to cross, a commotion beside the wall of the convent caught Charlotte's eye. A small crowd had gathered beside the arch of a smaller side entrance. Someone was hollering and a woman shrieked. There were cries of, "Call the militia!" and "Fetch the *sergents*!" A man peeled away from the crowd and took off at a run. Another passed her and jogged toward the gatehouse of the convent, knocking loudly on the door. Curiosity pulled her to the back of the circle of people. She stood on tiptoe, peering over shoulders to try and make out what was in the center causing the disturbance. But all she could see were heads, broad shoulders, and the solid backs of the crowd.

"What's happened?" she asked a tall man standing beside her.

"A dead woman," he grunted. "Murdered, by the looks of it."

"How do you know she was murdered?"

The man peered down at her from his great height.

"She's had 'er throat slit," he said. "Road drenched in 'er blood. Don't s'pose she did that to 'erself, did she, eh?"

Charlotte's heart plunged.

Surely not?

Using her elbows, she shoved her way through the crowd until she reached the front.

Somehow, she already knew it to be true. But she had to see it with her own eyes.

There, sprawled in the dirt, her cloak stained red with her own blood, lay Lysbette Angiers.

Charlotte's stomach churned as she remembered the flash of fear she had seen in the woman's eyes as she had spoken to Charlotte in her study only the previous day. Alive, breathing, full of life. A pulse beating at her delicate throat, where now there was but a ghastly, gaping hole. Could this have happened while Charlotte stood but moments away, waiting and fearing nothing but shadows?

"I know this woman," Charlotte gasped, turning from the body and clutching her sides as nausea rose swift and strong. She fought it, bending double, her head swimming. Strong arms caught her, kept her upright. She found herself clasped to a manly chest as she heaved her breaths, in and out.

"A friend?" the man queried.

"Acquaintance," Charlotte corrected. "But . . . She was a good, decent woman." Or so she thought. "One who didn't deserve this . . ."

"Someone has gone to fetch the commissioner. You had better stay to identify the dead woman."

While they waited, Charlotte tried to calm her jangled nerves. Tried to think back to her conversation with Madame Angiers the previous day. Why did she not question her more? Insist she told her whom she had feared?

A woman whose life had been snuffed out too soon was not so unusual in Paris. Whores, paupers, errant wives, witches, crones, seductresses, and the like were among those most at risk from strangulation, burning, beating, stoning. But Lysbette Angiers was a wife. She was educated and respectable, intelligent and of the merchant class, cared for by her husband and her family. This was not the type of woman who was likely to suffer a violent and sudden end at the hands of a man with a dagger or a hunting knife.

Charlotte's thoughts were interrupted by the arrival of the commissioner, a gruff, elderly man with the ruddy cheeks and bloodshot eyes of a drunkard, and his *sergent*, who looked to be barely more than a child. They bent over the body in contemplative silence. A couple of flies already buzzed around the gash in Lysbette's neck. Charlotte waved an arm at them, but they paid no heed and more arrived, settling and feasting on Lysbette's blood, making Charlotte gag.

"Madame . . ." The commissioner straightened and turned to her. "I understand you knew the unfortunate lady?"

Most of the crowd had dispersed now that the commissioner of the law had arrived. Perhaps they feared being accused. The remaining gawkers were shooed away by the *sergent*, leaving only Charlotte and the man who had kept her on her feet and on whose arm she still leaned for support.

"My name is Charlotte Guillard," she said, unable to stop her voice from quivering. "I am the proprietor of the printworks beneath the Soleil d'Or on La Grande Rue St.-Jacques." She took a breath. "This woman . . ." She pointed a shaking finger to the sprawled body on the ground. The buzzing of the flies intensified. Charlotte swallowed hard, turned her head away. ". . . is Lysbette Angiers. All I know of her is that she had recently arrived from Calais with her husband, Matthew, a cloth merchant." She paused, fighting for breath, her brain whirring as she wondered how much more to divulge. Lysbette had been so afraid, and if Charlotte told them of the reason for her visit to the printworks, she might put herself in danger too. And what of the manuscript she had gone to so much trouble to protect? On the other hand, whoever did this heinous thing should be hunted down and punished for his crime. And if they were to find who did it, the commissioner would need to know *something.*

The three men stared morosely at the body. Charlotte stared at the men, unable to bear looking at Lysbette. It was hard to know how much they truly cared about one unremarkable, foreign, dead woman, and whether they would go to the effort of finding her killer.

"Do you know of any reason why she might have been murdered?"

"None. I barely knew her," Charlotte said deciding it might be best to stick to minimal details until she could think straight. Despite the shock, her instinct was to protect her reputation, and that of her printworks. She had quite enough trouble of her own without getting drawn into this stranger's world. "I met her only yesterday. She came into my shop, looking for some reading matter . . . She asked my advice on the French poets, Marot, Rabelais. She told me she hadn't been required for her husband's meeting that day because it was in a tavern—an unsuitable venue for a woman."

Close to the truth, but not the complete truth.

The commissioner tightened his mouth and nodded.

Two nuns appeared beneath the arch of the side entrance to the convent, black habits flapping as they strode to the small group, faces pale with shock.

They crossed themselves at the sight of Lysbette's body, so unceremoniously dumped in the dirt. "We've sent for the priest."

"May her soul be safe in heaven," breathed one.

"Amen . . . Sir, we must take her into the convent. She can't be left like that in the street. We will wash and dress her. Prepare her for burial."

"That might be for the best . . . Her husband will need to see her and identify the body. Best he doesn't see her like this," the commissioner said.

"Perhaps someone in the convent heard something." The commissioner turned to Charlotte. "Where might we find her husband, Madame?"

Charlotte cast her mind back. "She mentioned Les Halles. That's all I know."

"No matter, I'll send men to make inquiries. They can start with the cloth merchants' guild . . . I can't imagine what a woman like this would have been doing out alone at this hour . . ."

Charlotte bit her lip.

"Do you think it a robbery, sir?" she asked.

"I do not," replied the commissioner looking grim. "This is no random attack." He stroked his beard. "It looks to me like an execution."

Chapter 11

Lysbette

Chelsea, England, November 1530

Lysbette tucked herself into the window seat in the library and pulled out the letter from John she had concealed earlier inside the lace of her sleeve. She liked to read his letters here, where she so often used to sit with him, and where she could still feel his presence.

With Mary's help, she and John had been writing to each other regularly since he left the house three years ago. The letters, in the early days, were those of two young friends exchanging news and gently teasing each other. But over time, they became something more. Feelings were expressed, gingerly at first, more openly lately. And when John visited Chelsea, at least every month, they would exchange long, lingering looks. They became adept at snatching precious moments together, just the two of them, as they had done when they were children. Only now they teetered on the edge of adulthood, straining against the propriety, longing to take flight on the rising draft of their feelings.

Lysbette took a breath and opened the letter.

My dearest Lysbette,

It is only a week since I last set eyes on your beautiful face and, oh how I have missed you! Not an hour, not a minute, goes by when

I don't think of you in Chelsea. I should be focused upon my work, but my thoughts always stray to you. I have so much to do in preparation for tomorrow's court hearing that I fear I shall have no time for sleep tonight.

How fares Sir Thomas? Now he is made Lord Chancellor in place of Cardinal Wolsey, his favor already falls with Henry. Is it true, Lysbette? I see so little of him these days. They say Sir Thomas's silence when the King asked for his support for the annulment of his marriage to Queen Katherine makes the King more frustrated with him by the day. If this is true, then I fear for him. As I write this, Wolsey is traveling from York to London to face charges of treason for his inability to solve the King's Great Matter. I worry Sir Thomas, too, shall be in an impossible position. What do you think, dear Lysbette? I know Sir Thomas confides in you. He values your, like his daughter Margaret's, keen intelligence and thoughtful advice.

I shall travel to Chelsea this Sunday morning and hope that Sir Thomas will be present and may spare me some time to talk these matters through. And then, with luck, you and I shall have time in the afternoon to spend together while Lady Alice naps and Sir Thomas is busy with his prayers and good works. There is something very particular I would like to ask you. I cannot wait to hold you in my arms.

Till then,
John

Lysbette pressed the letter to her heart. *There is something very particular I would like to ask you.* Could it be possible that, against all odds, John has thrown off the weight of expectation from his

gether for an hour while Sir Thomas regaled John with the sorry tale of the tightrope he walked between being true to his faith and the King's desperate desire to marry Anne Boleyn. Thomas was under increasing pressure, too, to be ever more hard-line on the plague of heresy that infected the nation. The constant worry was aging him before his years.

Finally, Sir Thomas went to pray alone, and Alice retired to her chamber for a rest. Lysbette and John stole unseen from the library door into the garden and fled to the old yew tree near the boathouse by the river. Forgetting to be demure and shy, as she should be, Lysbette threw herself into John's waiting arms.

"My love," he whispered into her hair.

"How I've longed to see you."

He pulled back a little, cupped her face in his hands. His warm brown eyes searched hers.

They were both silent for a moment.

"Lysbette . . ." he began and swallowed. Her pulse beat hard and hot through her veins. "I had planned, before coming here, to ask Sir Thomas for his permission, before I spoke to you, but—

"Permission?"

He smiled shyly. "Permission to ask you a very particular question." His fingers traced her cheek, sending shivers down her spine. "But, given all he has on his mind this day, I didn't want to bother him with this too."

"Oh . . ."

"It's complicated, you see, because my father—"

The loud crack of a dry twig underfoot made them jump and spring apart.

Alice stood before them, a look of triumph upon her face. Lysbette's cheeks flamed. Dear Lord, she would be in trouble now.

"I have been searching all over the house for you, John," she said, her tone carrying a hint of ice. "Surely you should be returning to London soon. Sir Thomas wishes to see you before you go."

Alice turned to Lysbette. "As for you," she said, "I see the mischief you make with John Haydon. Do not think what you do goes unnoticed."

She turned on her heel and strode back toward the house, her back tight with anger.

"Don't worry, Lysbette," John whispered before he turned to follow her. "You know I can handle Alice. With me, she is like dough in Cook's hands. You'll see."

But despite his comforting words, sick fear stirred in her belly.

Alice would not let Lysbette, found alone in the garden in John's arms, go unpunished.

Chapter 12

Milly

Milly stands on Mrs. Humphries's doorstep, takes a deep breath, and knocks. She grips Olive's hand a little tighter and bites her lip. If only she hadn't been so rash when she had encountered the woman two weeks ago. She'd insulted her, throwing away her offers of friendship. To Milly, in the moment, Mrs. Humphries had been nosy and intrusive, overbearing and unwelcome. Later, she could hear her mother's chiding. *Really, Milly, she was only showing an interest. You must give people the benefit of the doubt.*

So, here she is, tail between her legs, poised to apologize with a bunch of flowers from Gracie's and a well-rehearsed speech. Only if that goes down well will she ask the favor she is hoping to ask.

There is a sound of footsteps down the hall and the door swings open to reveal Mrs. Humphries, hair in curlers and a blond, wriggling, sausage-shaped puppy tucked beneath one arm.

Olive lets out a squeal of delight and the puppy wriggles more violently, short legs scampering against Mrs. Humphries as it lets out howls of delirious pleasure at the sight of two potential playmates on his doorstep.

"Oh my goodness," Mrs. Humphries gasps, struggling to keep hold of her squirming pet, "come in, come in!"

They are ushered through the front door, which Mrs.

Humphries slams shut with her foot then releases the puppy. Olive collapses to the floor and puppy and child fall on each other with paroxysms of delight.

Mrs. Humphries watches them, hands on hips. "I never realized what hard work puppies were," she says. "It's gone midday and I've yet to remove my curlers." She pats her head. "But isn't he adorable?"

Olive and the puppy scamper on hands and knees and paws respectively into the sitting room.

"I've called him Noel, on account of it being almost Christmas. I'd have preferred Holly, or Ivy, but those don't really work for a boy."

Milly agrees and hands Mrs. Humphries the flowers. "For you," she says. "An apology."

Mrs. Humphries looks momentarily confused and ushers Milly into the kitchen. "Apology? For what? Would you like some coffee?"

"Please." She'd rather tea but doesn't dare ask. "I fear I was rude the other day . . . When you were kind, and invited me to one of your lunches, or knitting parties."

"Oh goodness." Mrs. Humphries laughs and fills the kettle. "My skin is thicker than that. I just like to be welcoming to newcomers, young mothers, like you. And I understand you want to be with women your own age. No offense taken; I promise. And you are here now, aren't you?"

"That's very kind. Sometimes my tongue gets the best of me."

"Now don't you worry. In fact, I'm mighty glad you dropped by with Olive. She can play with Noel anytime she likes. It might give me time to get my hair set." Mrs. Humphries fills a vase and arranges the flowers in the center of the kitchen table, standing back to admire her handiwork. "Don't they look pretty?"

"Actually, Mrs. Humphries, I hope you don't mind me asking, and if it is too much, please do say, but I need to go into the city tomorrow to do some Christmas shopping, without the children, and I wondered, might you be willing to have Olive?"

"It would be my pleasure!" The woman's face lights up. "I could collect Edward from school, too, if that would help? In case you aren't home in time? And besides, having the children to play with the puppy for a while would be a relief. Between you and me, I've not spent so much time on the floor since my kids were crawling. Now, let's get you that coffee."

As Milly emerges from Penn Station the following day, snow-heavy clouds hang so low that Manhattan skyscrapers are half shrouded from view. Nonetheless, it is exciting to escape into the city, to lose herself in Gimbels and browse the shelves groaning with all manner of toys in FAO Schwarz.

Once her shopping is done, Milly, weighted down with bulging bags, heads to Bloomingdale's to meet Susan and her friend, the *My Life* editor Myra Bougas, for lunch.

It was Susan's idea, and although Milly would have preferred to spend the day working on the manuscript, she really did need to do some Christmas shopping if George and the children were going to have any presents to open at all on Christmas Day. Besides, she is becoming quite fond of Susan. Milly admires the librarian's pluck for standing up for her own principles and lending out banned books. It is a risk—she could lose her job, or worse, she could be hauled up in front of the Un-American Activities Committee. Besides, Milly is intrigued to meet Myra, whom Susan thought Milly would get along with so well.

Myra Bougas turns out to be nothing like Susan. Myra is as polished, smooth, and glossy as a marble, sitting elegantly with a cigarette nestled between red-tipped fingers. Apart from the very daring of those impossibly long fingernails, does she never do any housework? To be fair, Myra does not give the impression she would know what housework is. Which is ironic, given her role as the Features editor of the most widely read women's magazine in recent years. Milly cannot imagine what this fearsome, powerful woman has in common with the vast majority of her readership.

Over oysters Rockefeller, Myra talks about her work at the magazine, and asks Milly polite questions about her background. Susan encourages Milly to describe the books she had written, which, she explains, were not exactly bestsellers. Myra sits back in her chair and regards Milly with sharp, narrowed eyes.

"So," she says in a tone that makes Milly sit a little taller. "You are a scholar of ancient Greece. The birthplace of democracy, huh?"

"Well, Athens, if you want to be precise."

Myra smiles. "Freedom, equality, and government by the many, not the few, or something like that?"

"Something like that. Although, of course, the many didn't include women or slaves."

"Ah, well. We have come a long way since then."

"In some ways . . . But it's a mistake to think we follow a steady line toward greater enlightenment and civilization when in fact, we are just as likely to go backward as forward." Milly is thinking, indeed, of the awful book Susan told her not to read, *Washington Confidential*, which certainly does not reflect well on its two authors, who appear to her to be far from civilized in their reflections on women, anyone of color, and homosexuals.

Myra nods, tilting her head and gently tapping ash from the

end of her cigarette. "And," she says, "which way do you think we are headed as we approach 1953?"

"I do worry about that," Milly replies. "My hopes and my fears seem to extend in different directions."

Myra laughs. "I like this girl," she says, turning to Susan.

"As I knew you would." Susan gives Milly a wink.

"I worry," Milly says, warming to her theme, "about the messages my children are being taught at school. I worry about the existence of H-bombs, and what will happen when the Soviets get their hands on them, as they inevitably will. I worry about the world my children are growing up in. I worry about those of influence brainwashing people with reprehensible untruths. A truly free, democratic nation at ease with itself should allow unrestricted access to knowledge."

"Free speech is being eroded by the day," Myra drawls. "I wonder what your ancient Greek creators of democracy would make of that."

"Actually, *free speech* can be interpreted however someone wants. The Greeks had two different types of free speech. *Isegoria*, or, the equality of public speech, which was the right of anyone to a public platform, whereas *parrhesia* was the freedom to say anything you want in a social, rather than a political capacity. So, the freedom to say what you want in poetry, or on the stage or in comedy, rather than in a political forum. Splitting the two can be useful. I'm simplifying, of course, and nothing, no system of government or extent of freedom of expression, will ever be perfect, and someone will always be left worse off or offended or not listened to, but if there is wide and honest discourse then there is more of a chance that the decent, moderate views of the majority will be able to throw out the extreme or the bad." She stops to take a breath. "At least. That's the theory."

"You are preaching to the converted here," Myra says, "but what about the rhetoric our politicians use that is so utterly false and yet people swallow and believe it?" Myra takes a long drag on her cigarette. She closes her eyes for a moment.

Milly shrugs. "If voices of dissent are silenced, if people can't, or don't want to hear different points of view, then it is not a healthy society. Which is why culture is so important. The Greeks used plays and comedy, poetry and song to explore all manner of subjects, from government to obscenity to everything between."

They sit in contemplative silence for a few minutes.

"Now, Milly," Myra says, "I'm sure you didn't come here to talk about politics. Susan thinks you have an interesting mind. That you might be . . ." She pauses as though searching for the right word. "Unoccupied?"

Milly glances at Susan who smiles and nods encouragement. "Well, suppose I was a little bored, but now I'm helping a distant relative of mine in England with some research about old books. He's a collector. Keeps my mind busy, you see. I'm not sure what men think happen to women's brains when they have children, but mine just didn't switch off when the babies arrived, and I find everything so interminably dull. I mean, don't get me wrong"—she laughs—"I love my children, but all the washing, dressing, cooking, housework, even the level of conversation. It's mind-numbing."

She's doing it again, she's talking too much.

"Would you," Myra asks, leaning toward Milly, "be interested in writing for *My Life*? It would be something to keep your mind occupied, and you could do it at home, so you wouldn't be barred from contributing as a married woman."

"Goodness . . . Oh, I don't know if I could." Milly looks from Myra to Susan in surprise. It's been such a long time since she wrote anything other than a shopping list, she isn't sure she remembers how. And what would George think? Perhaps he might mind? She really has no idea.

"I think it's a marvelous idea," Susan says, looking genuinely thrilled.

"But, Myra, I have no interest in fashion or hairstyles or the latest home appliance. I don't like romances and I'm probably a terrible mother. I'm bad at sticking to mealtimes and bedtimes and I'm always doing silly things on impulse, so I couldn't give good advice. I rather think other mothers look down on me . . . This is probably a long-winded way of telling you, I don't think I'm the ideal contributor to your magazine."

Susan deflates before Milly's eyes. Poor Susan, who set this up. Oh dear, now she has let her down, too, the only person she has felt really drawn to since she arrived here.

"Well now," Myra says, stubbing out her cigarette. She fixes Milly with steely eyes. "I think you are *exactly* what I'm looking for. There's no rush. Finish your relative's project and have a think. Send me some ideas. Wild as you like."

Snow begins to fall as Milly hurries across the darkening street to collect the children from Mrs. Humphries.

"Thank you so very much for having them, Mrs. Humphries," Milly says as the children gather coats, boots, and school satchels.

"It was my absolute pleasure. Any time. I mean that, really." She points to the dog basket in the corner of the kitchen. The puppy is fast asleep. "They wore him out! Like I said, you are doing me a favor too."

"Can we get a puppy?" Edward asks as they make their way

back to number 26, stopping at the mailbox to bring in the mail. "Noel is *so* sweet."

"They don't stay puppies forever, Edward. Soon Noel will be a big, grown-up dog. He'll need lots of walking and taking care of."

"I don't mind doing the taking care of."

"You say that now, Edward, but it will be me who ends up doing all that."

Later, when the children are tucked in bed and Milly is waiting for George to come home, she flicks through the pile of mail—Christmas cards, the electric bill, something from the garage. A thick cream envelope is at the bottom of the stack. It's addressed to her in Winton's handwriting. She tears it open and pulls out a letter and a short note.

Scrawling this in haste, Winton wrote, *to catch the morning post. I thought you would want to see this soonest. You were quite right, Milly! Well done. Write and let me know how you are getting on. Best Regards, Winton.*

MILLY UNFOLDS THE enclosed letter. *The Bodleian* is embossed at the top.

Dear Mr. Harvey-Jones,

12 December 1952

I write with reference to the enclosed photograph of the sun symbol that I believe you delivered by hand for my attention. I was most interested in your inquiry.

In answer to the query, your colleague's memory is correct. The sun symbol as depicted in the photograph does exactly match that on the inside cover of the Greek/Latin dictionary that you men-

tioned your colleague had recalled. It therefore seems likely that the document you have in your possession was printed by Soleil d'Or, the same printer that produced a handful of texts we hold here at the Bodleian. Although you mention "handwritten" in your note, I am wondering if this was a mistake? Soleil d'Or was a large and well-respected printing house operating in Paris in the sixteenth century. The proprietor at the time of your print mark was Charlotte Guillard. She was a female printer of notoriety in sixteenth-century Paris. She ran the printworks jointly with her first husband, Berthold Rembolt, then after his death with her second husband, Claude Chevallon. After her second husband died, she ran the printworks single-handedly until her own death. By all accounts, Charlotte Guillard was an excellent and shrewd businesswoman of her day.

From the illustration you have provided us with, we are confident that this mark dates from the time Charlotte ran the printworks alone. Indeed, the picture looks so similar to the mark we have seen in the folio of Jean de Gagny, Clarissima et facillima in quatuor Scholia, printed in Paris in 1552 that I suggest your document dates to around this time.

Please do not hesitate to contact us if you have any further questions, or if you require more assistance with your work.

I remain,
Yours sincerely,
Mr. C. G. Clarke
Chief Archivist
Bodleian Library, Oxford

Milly lets the letter fall. Her pulse ticks faster. She's too excited to sit still. She paces the kitchen floor, her mind whirring.

So now she has a possible date for her manuscript:1552. She has a place: Paris. And incredibly, she has a name: Charlotte Guillard. A person, a woman. Tantalizingly real.

Milly longs to talk to Winton, but overseas calls are eye-wateringly expensive. And how would she explain it to George when the phone bill arrives? She will write a letter instead.

Who was Charlotte Guillard, she wonders, and why, if she was a printer by profession, would she need to write an encoded man-uscript by hand? She will write to the Bodleian, too, to ask them to let her have all the information they have about this woman, or to direct her as to where she can find it.

This has to be a breakthrough. Some of the other lingering questions can probably now be answered. The biggest one of those being which language underlies this code. It could have been any-thing, but now, having narrowed down the place to Paris, and if the document had been put together by Charlotte Guillard, then the most likely languages would be French or Latin. Her hunch is Latin, the language of the Bible, of legal and religious documents, and of the courts of Europe.

And Latin, being a "dead" language, hasn't changed from that day to this, unlike a living, evolving language. That makes things *much* easier.

So, Charlotte Guillard, if this really was your work, what was it you wanted to say, and who were you trying to hide it from?

Chapter 13

Milly

Levittown, Long Island, New York, December 1952

Saturday dawns fine. A brisk wind sends clouds skittering fast across a pale blue sky. It's the type of breeze that lifts unfastened hats from heads and whips handkerchiefs from loose fingers. The Bennett family pile into the Buick and head out on the highway toward Oyster Bay. The radio is tuned to WQXR and Frank Sinatra accompanies them as they sail past stores and restaurants, cinemas and bars, parking lots and gas stations, strung out along the main road before they at last hit open country.

George believes children should be exercised daily, like dogs. And nothing can beat a blustery march along the coast in winter to wear out the young ones and ensure they sleep soundly. Although Milly suspects it is George, rather than the children, who is in need of the head-clearing douse of nature after his long week in the office.

As the countryside slides past, Frank sings about how the blues began. Her mother would have loved this song. There is a familiar tug of sadness as she thinks of how beautiful Mother was, how she used to sing along to Frank on the gramophone as she mopped and dusted. Never, not once, had she tried to make Milly behave like other little girls. Instead of forcing her to learn interminably boring skills like needlework, knitting, and cooking, she nurtured her love of the Greeks and Romans by buying her books on the ancient world. Later, when Milly announced she wanted to go to university, and had won her place at Somerville, Oxford, her mother had cried, then told everyone she knew that her Milly was a genius.

But of course, life has a way of reminding one that happiness is only ever transitory, and that, as the ancient Greeks would tell us, time is not only chronological, but *kairos*. That, for every opportunity, the right time and context must exist.

And the best of plans must change through war, or more specifically, a telephone call.

The first call had come during her early weeks at Somerville College, from Mother, with the terrible news that Milly's father had so suddenly and unexpectedly been taken from them by a heart attack. Then came the second telephone call, from Winton Harvey-Jones who wanted to recruit her for the war effort, and Milly willingly went to do her bit. Then, inevitably, the third telephone call came, informing her of her mother's cancer diagnosis.

Now, as they travel along the freeway, Frank is crooning about his *Bim Bam Baby coming home tonight* and George is jiggling and jiving along to the music, which makes the children laugh and they join in from the back seat. But Milly is remembering the time when Mother's life began to peter out. Her eyes grow hot and her vision blurs as she recalls the day she sat on the kitchen floor, her head in her hands, broken and sobbing.

"Oh my darling," George had said and swept her up into his arms.

"I can't do it," she'd cried into his shoulder. "I can't help her, and I can't bear to watch her suffer. I'm a coward."

"You are *not* a coward. You're one of the strongest people I know. Let me take over. Your mom and I get along just swell. She doesn't want you to see her like this. She knows how much pain it causes you. You focus on the children. We'll help your mother together."

And he did. He took control. Dearest, gentle George had sat beside her as death crawled in, inch by torturous inch. He'd said Milly shouldn't remember her mother like that. That she should hold on to the *good* memories.

He'd done that for Milly, and for her mother. For love. So, after the funeral, after they'd tidied up Mother's affairs, when he'd suggested they move to New York, she couldn't refuse him. Through one of his father's friends, George told her, there was a chance of a marketing position at a bank, and, with the small amount she had inherited from Mother, they could afford to put a down payment on a house to buy. It was a chance of a career, a proper one, and a good life for her and the children. He was desperate to provide for them. To prove he was the man the world expected him to be.

Milly turns her face from George now so he can't see her wipe the tears from her eyes. She owes him so much, and she isn't going to ruin his happiness by letting on about her own struggle with living here. It is her failing, not his. He's doing everything he can to make her happy, working so hard, making such an effort, and perhaps she needs to show him more often just how much she appreciates him. On impulse she reaches out and grabs his hand, giving it a squeeze. He turns to look at her, his eyes warm, liquid hazelnut, and laughs.

"You *are* happy, aren't you, Milly-Moo?" he asks, as he had done at least every few days since they moved here.

"Of course I am," she says without hesitation and leans across to kiss his cheek.

They park in the pretty town center of Oyster Bay, bare trees lining the streets, and buy the children a soda and a kite before making for the coast path. Out in the sound, waves cap white beneath circling, crying gulls. On the beach, George grasps Milly's hand while the children run on ahead, arms out, leaning into the wind.

"I love it here in winter," George shouts above the gusts of wind. His face is pink, happy. There is no sign of the weariness and hunched shoulders he bears after a long day at the bank.

"Who wants to go first!" he yells, kite in hand, and the children tear across the beach toward him, laughing and shouting.

Watching them, Milly's heart swells with love but she's also quite alone, standing here on the sand, her hands dug deep in her pockets, her eyes wet from the cold. As though she is watching their joy but isn't part of it; she's outside the window, looking in. Apart from the brief time at university and Bletchley, when she was as inside the room as she has ever been, she's always felt different, not part of the gang. And something in the pit of her belly opens. Something uncomfortable, like pain or regret. Melancholia or loneliness. She can't work out which. And it is in that moment that an inkling of an idea for an article in *My Life* comes to her. She thinks of her lunch with Myra and Susan, of their discussions about the state of modern American life, and that of Athens, and she wonders.

As she watches her husband and children laugh and gambol across the expanse of flat, dark sand, the kite dipping and diving high above them, she allows the idea to percolate and solidify in her mind.

Sunday evenings, until very recently, were usually accompanied by a tightening inside, as though Milly's intestines were slowly being twisted and squeezed until the pain came. It made her jittery and short-tempered. George called it her *Sundaynightitis*. She'd been just the same when she was at school and the week ahead loomed horribly, filled as it would inevitably be with gibes and laughter from the boys about her bottle-thick calves, thicker glasses (on account of her squint), or hair so like a horse's mane that they would neigh in her presence. And the girls weren't any better, closing ranks to keep her out of their cozy circles, making sure her status at the bottom of the social scale wouldn't hurt the rest of them with some sort of infectious unpopularity. Over the years she had lost the glasses and grown into her calves, but the end of the weekend meant George would be gone for most of the week and the children would be at school. The idea of coffee mornings with the neighbors or trying to fit in with the PTA mothers filled Milly with a similar sense of dread.

But since Winton's visit, now that she has his precious manuscript to work on, she finds she looks forward to weekdays in a way she hasn't ever since they moved to New York. Now she has a reason to avoid the gossip and the small talk, the eyes that rake her bad hairdo and substandard clothes.

"I'm going to meet with Susan from the library again this week," she tells George as they eat chili con carne for dinner. "She and I at least have a love of books in common."

"That's good, Milly. See, I told you it would take time, but that you would find friends and good company here soon enough."

He chews, swallows, frowns.

"Is this tinned?" he asks, waving a fork at his bowl.

"Is it no good?" She'd buried the tins in the rubbish and hoped he wouldn't notice.

He looks up at her. "It's er . . ."

She puts up a hand. "Don't say it. It's mush. Sorry."

He stares down at the food. "It's lucky I didn't marry you for your cooking," he admits finally, and he gamefully shovels the tasteless muck down while she stirs hers around in the bowl.

Poor George. She really has served up some shockers in her time. Grilled apple cake, burnt on top, raw at the bottom. Chicken that was still pink in the middle. Beef topped with Heinz tomato soup. Lumpy gravy, soggy carrots. It's a miracle they have survived.

"What did you marry me for?"

He smiles at her. "Your extraordinary mind, of course. Your pluckiness. And you are beautiful." She snorts at that. "Well, you are to me. And you are a wonderful mother, if unconventional."

Milly smiles and thinks about the idea she has in mind for *My Life*. She is keeping the work on the manuscript from George, but there is no reason to keep this from him too. She takes a deep breath. "Actually, George, Susan's friend, Myra Bougas, is an editor at a women's magazine and she has asked me if I might be interested in writing some articles for it. Just a bit of fun."

His face falls. "But . . . You don't need to work now, Milly. I have a decent job, and an excellent chance of promotion. What is it you need? More clothes? A trip to the beauty parlor? You only have to ask, Milly-Moo. I know you spend most of the housekeeping money on the children, but you should treat yourself too. I can afford it." He pushes his empty bowl away and slaps the table. "Sweetheart, I'm sorry, I didn't think to say that before. And you are too good to ask—"

"The articles— It's not about money, George. Although to tell the truth, if I earned a little of my own money it might be nice not to *have* to ask—"

"I don't mind you asking. Not one little bit."

"I know you don't. That's not the point."

His face clouds in confusion. "Then I don't get the point."

Milly sighs, stands, gathers the dishes, and starts to wash up. She hands George a freshly rinsed plate, which he dries with a tea towel. "The point *is* I thought I would quite like something to keep my mind busy while the children are at school. You know, like I used to."

"But you were so upset when those books stopped selling. And it was hard to juggle everything, with the children being so little, and your mother unwell . . ."

"I know, but this is different. The children are older, and I don't have my mother to worry about. Besides, this would be writing something for *me*."

Milly pulls out the plug and watches the dirty water drain away. She wrings the dishcloth. George dries the last plate and puts it away before tossing the wet tea towel on the laundry pile.

His face is still twisted in discomfort.

"I really don't think that's how it works, sweetheart. These editors, they all have their own agenda. They'll reel you in with all sorts of promises and before long you'll be tied into some god-awful contract with tight deadlines and content you have no interest in. I don't think it's a good idea, Milly. You have your hands full anyway with the children and the house. Isn't that enough? I know you are lonely, and this new friend . . . Well, I can see you want to please her and that's perfectly understandable . . . Is she married? Does she have children?"

"No, but—"

George slides his arms around her waist. "Well, there you are then. She wouldn't understand your situation. Wouldn't it be better to make friends with the other mothers? You'd have more in common. Or maybe you could do something that will get you out of the house. I know housework isn't your forte . . . Do you mind me saying that?" He smiles and strokes her hair.

"I don't mind. It's true, and that's why I thought . . .

"My mother used to do charity work. She had a wonderful group of lady friends doing . . . Whatever good works they used to do." He gives her a little squeeze. "By all means have coffee with this Susan and talk books, but don't go taking on work when you don't need to."

She looks up into his kind eyes.

"I worry about you, that's all."

"I know you do, George. There really is no need."

"Promise me you won't do it?"

"All right, I promise!"

"Good girl. Now, how about a little nighttime brandy while we watch the evening news, and then an early night?"

"That would be lovely."

And she follows him into the sitting room where *America in View* gravely informs them that 1952 has seen the worst polio outbreak since 1916. With over fifty thousand cases and over three thousand deaths, can anyone be safe? Milly's insides wind tight all over again until George switches channels to CBS and *The Fred Waring Show*, which he says will be much cheerier.

But still, the knot inside Milly refuses to unwind, however sweet George is trying to be.

Chapter 14

Charlotte

Paris, July 1552

B ack at the printworks, Charlotte took a large tankard of wine and a hearty breakfast of bread and sliced meat to settle her stomach. Normally, this worked like a charm, but not today. The sight of Lysbette's gaping throat, her blood, so much of it, soaking into the dusty road, kept flashing before Charlotte's eyes. Work. That was what she needed to take her mind off it. None of this was her concern. She didn't even know this woman. But still, the visions kept returning, alongside the worry that perhaps someone had, after all, been following her that morning. Could that have been the someone who had slit Lysbette's throat? All day she shook inside, overcome by sudden waves of nausea and crushing panic, making her head swirl and her body slick with sweat.

She struggled to stay focused during the meeting with her lawyer, Monsieur Riant, and fellow printer and friend Yolande Bonhomme. Monsieur Riant did not appear to notice Charlotte's lack of attention, speaking at length on the law. Paris was awash with courts—ecclesiastical, feudal, royal, as well as different types of justice—high, medium, low. No wonder the lawyers were getting so fat. This case, he said, must be brought before the University of Paris, for they regulated the book trade in Paris. He sat back in his chair, scrawny legs outstretched from beneath his full midriff, absentmindedly stroking his luxurious beard with long, ringed fingers. He ran through the process of the proceedings, how Charlotte and Yolande would not be allowed into the courtroom, given how they were women, but he would report to them at the end of the proceedings. Somehow, the paper problem mattered rather less today than it had yesterday.

Think of the printworks, she told herself. *Of course paper matters.*

"What do you think of our chances, Monsieur?" Charlotte asked.

Riant regarded her with grave eyes. "Poor," he said after a pause. "And Monsieur Baubigny, in his role as head of the Master Papermakers is, how can I put this . . . robust in defending the practices of his members."

"Oh?" inquired Yolande. "How so?"

"There is anecdotal evidence that his members are *encouraged* to maximize their profits by using only the cheapest fiber in their vats. The vatman must deposit an ungenerous scoop of the fiber slurry into the mold, which the *couchers* are told to ensure forms the thinnest possible wet sheet of paper. This, and the disregard of adding sufficient pigment, lime, and glue into the vats, leads to inconsistency of texture and thickness. It also means the paper is likely to disintegrate much faster than if greater amounts of these constituents are used. But in short, *mesdames*, no master, journeyman, or apprentice would be willing to give evidence of these practices in a court of law and risk losing their livelihood, or worse. I hear that Baubigny isn't afraid to use violence when he thinks he needs to keep certain people in line."

Yolande squared her shoulders. "We shan't be so easily dissuaded, shall we, Charlotte?"

"Indeed not. The problem of sourcing substandard paper continues. I had a papermaker here last week, a Monsieur Faivre. I could see right through his samples when I held them to the light.

He wanted to look around the printworks, which I gladly showed him, if only to exemplify good paper quality versus bad, and the enormous quantities we require here. I regretted my decision as he seemed keen to poke his nose into corners he had no right to look in."

After the lawyer had taken his leave, Yolande turned to Charlotte.

"My dearest friend. Are you unwell? I have never heard you utter fewer words." She fixed Charlotte with a probing look. "Are you thinking of withdrawing from the case?"

Yolande was the daughter of a printer, widow of another, and had been successfully running the House of Kerver printworks, alone, for the past thirty years. Of similar age and life experience to Charlotte, they had fallen easily into friendship and collaboration. For particularly large or challenging projects, they always assisted each other. Lone women who understood the world of commerce were a rarity and treated with suspicion by their male counterparts. The legal case against the papermakers was going to be their most challenging collaboration yet. If it failed, it could cost them a great deal in livres and, crucially, the longevity of the books that they printed.

Charlotte sighed. "No, but it has been quite the morning. Come, take a turn with me in the garden. We can talk freely outside." One never knew when a servant may have their ear pressed to the door. Information always had a value, particularly a trade secret that might fetch a tidy sum from a competitor or a disgruntled paper manufacturer.

They sat on a bench beneath the shade of an arbor covered thickly with vines. The temperature was blessedly a little cooler today, and the sounds of nature—birdsong, the rustle of leaves, creatures shuffling in the undergrowth—calmed Charlotte's shattered nerves. As she found herself pouring out the story of Lysbette's strange visit yesterday and the shock of this morning's discovery, she wondered if the commissioner or one of his *sergents* might at this very moment be banging on her front door. How then the questions would flow from her servants and employees. And more worryingly, could Lysbette Angiers have brought danger to Charlotte's own door? She considered again her sense of being followed as she had made her way to meet the dead woman. It would certainly be best, personally and for the reputation of the printworks, to avoid any scandal of a connection with her. Perhaps if she went to the commissioner at the Hôtel de Ville that afternoon, she might be able to head off any visit he might decide to make to the Soleil d'Or.

And then there was the manuscript itself. What would become of it? Charlotte thought of her promise to Lysbette Angiers who, for reasons that were beyond her earthly understanding, fate had brought to her.

"I think," she said out loud to Yolande, "that in spite of all the risk, I should find out what is in that manuscript. I don't know why I feel so compelled, but I do."

"Instinct," Yolande said at once. "You must always trust it . . . I suppose you are keen to protect the written word, just like Lysbette was."

The sentiment was left, hanging in the air like dew. *The written word*.

What power lay there, in words on a page.

And with that thought, Charlotte knew she would not rest easy until she had seen what was in the manuscript that Lysbette so desperately wanted to preserve in print. And probably had lost her life for. She felt a strong sense this was the right thing to do. Was this God directing her? She had a hard time, sometimes, discerning whether it was God, or her own self, behind her decision-making.

Yolande placed a strong hand on Charlotte's forearm. Her friend's eyes were solemn. "Be careful, my friend. I couldn't bear for anything bad to happen to you."

The sun was still high when Charlotte announced herself at the convent gatehouse later that same afternoon, its rays glinting off the steep rooftops and the huge glass windows of Notre-Dame.

The gatekeeper led Charlotte to the main building, and she was shown into a parlor to await Dame Agnes. Moments later, a diminutive woman in the black habit of the Benedictines entered the room, her expression grim. But as she greeted Charlotte, she smiled warmly, offering her a seat and a cup of wine, which she accepted.

"My name is Charlotte Guillard," she began, "of the House of Soleil d'Or."

"It was you," Dame Agnes asked, "who found Lysbette in the street?"

"Yes. I'm afraid so . . . She told me you had been close friends some years ago?" The nun nodded. Her face was contorted in pain. Even if they hadn't seen each other for years, that friendship clearly meant a great deal to Agnes.

"I cleansed her body, tended to her wounds. I have prepared her for burial and for meeting her maker. It was something I never expected to have to do. Lysbette Angiers was . . ." She appeared to be searching for the right words. ". . . so full of life and vigor, as well as a dear friend. She will have her place in heaven, of that I am in no doubt. We will pray for her—you are welcome to join us, Madame Guillard, should you wish to do so."

Charlotte, surprised, found that she did.

"I did not know Lysbette—I had met her only once—but in that short meeting, she made quite the impression on me. When she visited me," Charlotte said carefully, "she mentioned a manuscript. She said there were those who wanted it destroyed. She seemed to fear for her life, and she told me she had left the manuscript with you for safekeeping."

"Lysbette had a habit of making an impression on people," Agnes smiled. "Yes, she left the manuscript with me yesterday—before she went to see you. She was agitated, and in a hurry. She said she didn't have long. I think she was worried someone might be following her, and she had no idea if you would agree to print her work. She told me she would collect it this morning, hopefully with you, if her powers of persuasion worked."

"Do you know what is in it?"

Agnes shook her head. "No. She asked me not to look inside, for my own sake. She also said that if you wouldn't help her, and if anything were to happen to her, a man named John Haydon would come to collect it."

Charlotte frowned. "This is all very mysterious . . . Please, if I am to be enticed to take this on, and not walk straight back out of that door to my comfortable life, I need to know everything there is to know about Lysbette Angiers."

Agnes gave her a long look, then sank back into her chair.

"I will tell you what I know about Lysbette," Agnes said. "But remember, I knew her for only a portion of her life. I pray you do not find yourself in the midst of something you have no wish to be mixed up in."

The vast bells of Notre-Dame rang out for vespers as Charlotte left the convent, the manuscript tucked safely at the bottom of her leather pouch among the lawyer's papers. She felt her pulse quicken as she tried to imagine what it may contain, but before she could give in to the urge to read it, she had to pay a visit to the commissioner at the Hôtel de Ville. She tried to hurry across Le Pont Notre-Dame, but her way was blocked by wagons, horses, donkeys, carts, and a heaving mass of humanity. Beneath the sturdy stone arches of the bridge swirled the dark waters of the Seine and barges and sailboats carrying cargo to and from the port at the Place de Grève, close to the teeming market of Les Halles.

Finally, her feet on solid ground, Charlotte turned right toward the bustling port, La Place de Grande Eve, and the impressive new stone building that housed the Hôtel de Ville.

The commissioner looked even more disheveled and disgruntled than he had when Charlotte encountered him earlier that morning.

"You had better come in, Madame Guillard," he said observing her with his bloodshot eyes. She caught a whiff of his rank breath, soured, undoubtedly, by drink. "Your timing could not have been better," he added, his words at odds with his manner. "I have Monsieur Hatt here." On seeing Charlotte's blank look, he added, "He is Madame Angiers's husband."

"Oh!" Charlotte stopped in her tracks. "But why . . ."

"That is a question in my mind too," said the commissioner. "She introduced herself to you with her maiden name. It is a mystery, this business of the names and her visit to your establishment. I was just discussing this very matter with her husband. I am sure he would like to meet the woman who discovered her body. Come this way."

Charlotte followed him into the room, her stomach heaving like the grim, swirling waters of the Seine. Inside, a fine-looking man sat on a chair beside an unlit fireplace. She imagined him with Lysbette and thought what a handsome couple the pair must have made. Two chairs were placed either side of the fire on a well-worn rug and the commissioner fetched a third from behind his desk for Charlotte to be seated before the two men.

"This, Monsieur Hatt," he addressed the man, "is Madame Guillard, the woman who identified your poor wife in the street."

The man stood in a rush, bowed, and greeted Charlotte with a "Good morrow to you, mistress." Apart from the regular features of his face, everything about the man seemed somewhat askew, from his hair to his expression to his clothes. She supposed he had suffered a most terrible shock. He began thanking her, in broken French, for looking after his wife's body, and what a shock it must have been for her to have come upon her, as it was for him to hear of it. Indeed, he seemed unable to fully take it in, to know that his wife was gone. It was, he lamented, impossible to believe. And to think of the violence of her death. He gave a small shudder as he sank back into his chair.

"I am so sorry for your dreadful loss," she said to him, and he nodded, his face downcast, his eyes red-rimmed. His hands shook a little and his brow beaded with sweat. Her heart melted for the man.

"Are you any closer to finding who committed this heinous crime?" Charlotte asked the commissioner.

He grunted. "Not yet. But Monsieur Hatt was enlightening me on his wife's nature. It seems she was rather difficult to control, taken to wandering about at all hours of the day or night. I believe her humors were unbalanced. Indeed, Monsieur Hatt feared the onset of a hysteria of the mind, perhaps brought on by the fact she was not blessed with children. That can do terrible things to the female mind." He paused as though deep in thought. Charlotte bristled. *She*, too, had not been blessed with children and her mind was perfectly sound. What did men know of these things?

"And, given what he has said," the commissioner continued, "I rather fear the poor madame brought this grisly end upon herself. No sensible woman would wander the streets of Paris, alone, at night."

Charlotte stared at him in astonishment. How could anyone suggest a person brought murder upon themselves? She wondered if the commissioner would have the same attitude if it had been Monsieur Hatt who had been wandering the streets and ended up dead.

"That surprises you, I see, Madame Guillard," the husband said, turning to Charlotte. He shifted in his seat, rubbed a hand across his chin. "I hope you don't mind me asking . . . But my wife, it seems, was full of secrets, and you are another of them. I'm just trying to understand . . . Please, tell me, were you on your way to meet her when you encountered her body?"

Charlotte opened her mouth to speak, then closed it. Her mind was racing. She was unprepared to be questioned by the bereaved husband.

"I am sorry, Monsieur," she began, "but I'm afraid you are mistaken. I did not know your wife at all. I only struck up conversation with her while she browsed my shop for poetry. She did mention having a friend at the convent near the Notre-Dame church, and that she planned to visit her there. That is all I know."

"Odd that you were so close to her, then, when she met her untimely end." His face was full of suspicion as he regarded her.

Charlotte almost choked on her surprise. "I hope you are not accusing *me*—"

"Monsieur," the commissioner interjected, waving his hands in a manner Charlotte supposed was meant to be placatory. "Madame Guillard is a woman of upstanding reputation in this city. She is a master printer and bookseller, and her word is to be trusted. As you can see, she is also of advanced years and I'm sure incapable of . . ." He let the sentence drift and cleared his throat. "I understand you are upset, but we will do our best to find her killer, I assure you. Now, what you have told me does shed some new light on the matter."

"And what is that?" Charlotte queried, eying Monsieur Hatt who had now sunk back to rest his head against the chair back, his face pale, shoulders slumped with apparent exhaustion.

He gave a nod to the commissioner, as though granting his permission to speak. "It seems," the commissioner began with a sigh, "that the madame may have had a . . . *gentleman* friend. Perhaps she was on her way to an illicit meeting when she met her untimely end. Monsieur Hatt found a letter—"

"Letters," Monsieur Hatt corrected.

"Letters among her things when he was going through them after her death. He has shared them with me." He sighed. "Having read them," he said, "it seems fairly conclusive to me."

Charlotte's mouth fell open for a second time. She had barely known the woman, but she thought that to be highly unlikely. Lysbette Angiers had once been a nun. She was not the type of woman who would seek a lover. And besides, such a tryst by a married woman would be foolhardy—even downright dangerous. For everyone knew that in France husbands were entitled to kill their wives for cuckolding.

"But can you be absolutely sure?" Charlotte pressed. "From the letters?"

Monsieur Hatt looked at her with abject misery in his eyes.

"They leave little doubt in my mind," he said. He let out a long sigh. "My wife was at one time a nun. Such an unnatural state makes women . . . How can I put this . . . voraciously wanton. Unbalanced, if you understand my meaning. Perhaps this man was trying to extricate himself. Maybe there was an altercation. The scoundrel became angry and . . ." His voice faded, letting the implication of his words sink in.

The commissioner nodded and picked up his quill. "The man's name, if you please?"

"John Haydon," said the husband. "His name is John Haydon."

Chapter 15

Lysbette

Chelsea, England, November 1530

Two weeks had passed since Alice had caught Lysbette alone in the garden with John. Two weeks when, each day, Lysbette rose, guts clenching, wondering if today would be the day when Alice's wrath would be unleashed.

But so far, there had been no consequences at all. Alice greeted Lysbette politely at breakfast, ignored her mostly during the day, which was not unusual, and made small talk over dinner as though nothing had happened at all.

Perhaps, Lysbette thought, as Mary helped her dress for Sunday chapel in the chilly early morning, she had been forgiven. Perhaps Alice was not so mean-spirited, or John, as he had promised, had worked his magic.

She had received three letters from John in the interim, had written back three times. He promised to speak with Sir Thomas, respecting the particular question he wanted to ask her. Promised to visit soon. But there was no sign of him in the chapel that morning nor at lunch. Afterward, Sir Thomas suggested Lysbette accompany him to his study, which she often did on a Sunday afternoon, where they might spend a pleasant hour or so discussing some matter of philosophy or theology. Or, less pleasantly, some matter of state that happened to be on Sir Thomas's mind. But today, he nodded to Lady Alice to accompany them, too, and that was not usual at all.

Lysbette's limbs turned to rubber as she followed Sir Thomas and Lady Alice to his study. The fire had been lit and Sir Thomas crouched to stoke it. Alice edged her chair closer to the heat. There was a sly look in the woman's eye. A flush to her puffy cheeks. Lysbette looked from wife to husband, who stared at the floor somewhere around Lysbette's feet.

Finally, Sir Thomas raised his solemn eyes to hers.

"Lysbette, my dear," he began. "You are sixteen years old. We know you and John have formed an . . . attachment, and that you are well into marriageable age. But, after giving the matter much thought, Alice and I think it is not the best option for you. Your talents with the pen would be wasted. We believe the place you will be happiest and most fulfilled is within the warm arms of the church. As you know, it is a route I almost took for myself and sometimes I wonder if my life would not have been more content had I taken orders after all." He sighed. "I heard only yesterday that the place I sought for you as a novice at Barking Abbey has been secured with the promise of a substantial dowry. I shall take you there myself, next week."

Lysbette sat frozen, her mind snagging on the words, unable to quite absorb what they meant. She could feel Alice's eyes willing her to turn and see the look of triumph on her face. She would not.

"But . . ." Lysbette swallowed a lump in her throat. If she didn't say something now, it would be too late. She clenched her hands tight in her lap and gathered her nerves. "What if I do want to marry? We never discussed it . . ."

There was a moment of silence.

"I want to marry John," she blurted.

Alice snorted. Lysbette kept her eyes firmly fixed on Sir

Thomas, silently praying for him to consider her plea. "We are . . . fond of each other. More than that. He loves me and I know he wishes to marry me."

"You *know* he wishes to marry you?" Alice spluttered, her face growing purple. "Has he proposed?"

Lysbette ignored her. "I could help him with his work. And I know he would be happy for me to continue with my studies— just like William Roper allows your daughter Margaret—and now that John is at the bar, soon he shall earn sufficient income to support us both and—"

Sir Thomas glanced at his wife as he raised one hand to stop Lysbette's flow of words. "I spoke with John yesterday, once I received the news from Barking. He told me he would like to marry you, but I made clear to him marriage to you is out of the question. His father wouldn't allow it and besides, as John well knows and you are conveniently forgetting, he is already promised to another. She will bring him a substantial estate, which I am afraid, you cannot. That is why I forbid him to come today. Besides, a childish attachment is not *love*, Lysbette–"

"Please! I know I can't bring him wealth or a good name, but I can make him *happy*, and it *is* love. He feels the same, I know—"

"*Enough!*" Alice barked. She pointed a finger at Lysbette. "Any *attachment* is your doing. Don't think I haven't seen the way you turn your doe eyes on him. The poor, defenseless boy . . . Can you not see the master is under great strain with the King's business? The last thing he needs is you making trouble! After all he has done for you. Such ingratitude . . .

"I'm not ungrateful!"

"Leave us." Alice pointed at the door. "And don't return until you can remember your manners!"

Lysbette stumbled from the room, hot tears welling as she

went.

How could she bear a life without John?

Back in her room she threw herself onto her bed, allowing the racking sobs to come. Lysbette Angiers was, and always had been, an outsider in this house, never truly belonging.

It was always there, that wedge of foreign blood, that taint of inferiority.

When it came down to it, she was an orphan girl with no money and no say in her future. John was promised to another, and she was to become a Bride of Christ.

Somehow, she, and he, would have to come to terms with that.

Lysbette took her seat in the prow of the barge as it bobbed and swayed. Close to the water, the raw chill seeped fast through the layers of her clothes. Sir Thomas took his place beside her, and the boatman steered them out into the center of the river. A fine, ethereal mist rose from the water, shrouding the banks.

She leaned forward and met Sir Thomas's eyes with her own. "You have been good to me. I know how lucky I am that you took me in . . ." It was the truth. She wondered, as she had so many times these last days, had it not been for Alice, would he have made a different decision about her and John? But she reminded herself it had been John's father, too, who was against the match.

She watched Sir Thomas swallow the emotion that rose inside, then nod firmly. "I did what I promised your mother all those years ago. I am glad to be releasing you into the safe arms of the mother church. We will miss you at Beaufort House, but I let you go with a glad, if heavy, heart."

"I shall worry for you, sir."

Sir Thomas patted her hand.

"It is Christendom itself you should worry for. I fear a disease, brought to these shores by the Lutheran heretics, has infected the body of the Christian world and shall be the death of it."

Lysbette had seen the piles of forbidden texts Sir Thomas had been given special permission by the King to read, such that he may hunt down the heretics spreading them. *Think on it, Lysbette. The clerics alone understand the sacred scriptures. If any person can translate the Word of God into English, however corrupt and distorted it may be, imagine the consequences when the masses in their thousands read such violations? The devil's work will be done; faith itself will be at risk.*

"However many copies of the pestilent works we confine to the flames," he said, "more pour in from the continent and are openly sold on London's streets. God's punishment is plain to see, Lysbette. Drought and another failed harvest with thousands set to starve. I can only feed so many of them at my own door . . . Then there are such outbreaks of plague and the sweating sickness that the courts at Westminster are suspended, and the King has fled London." He stared morosely into the dark water that swirled around the barge.

"And in Europe the attacks on Christendom come on all sides. To the east, the Turkish infidels press farther west than ever before, threatening Rome. From the north, the Lutherans in Germany, Switzerland, and the Low Countries spread their tentacles ever farther south." He looked gray with worry and Lysbette felt a rush of love for this man who tried so hard to defend the faith from this unprecedented onslaught.

It was a task, Lysbette knew, that weighed so heavily upon him that he was bowed by it, like a donkey buckling beneath a great load. And as for her, the loss of John had made her feel as though her heart had been ripped from her body. She knew she would never feel anything, not love, or joy, or sorrow, not deeply like she had before, ever again.

Their fate was sealed, and she must accept her future without him.

They lapsed into silence, and she finally released Sir Thomas's hand, slipping her own into her muff for warmth as they drifted past the looming white walls of the Tower of London and the Traitors' Gate. Three putrefying severed heads stood on gruesome display upon tall spikes. Lysbette shuddered as the barge floated on beneath Tower Bridge, blessedly obscuring the heads from view.

The great church and soaring steeple of Barking Abbey reared high above a cluster of red-tiled roofs and high walls marking the abbey grounds. Departing the boat, they rode on horseback through the hodgepodge of dwellings outside the walls, the scale of it catching Lysbette's breath; her stomach lurched with nerves. An abbey had stood here, Sir Thomas said, for almost nine hundred years.

And now, here she was.

The abbess's house was bigger and grander than she could have imagined, and they were shown into a comfortable reception room. Wine, bread, cheeses, and meat were brought and Lady Dorothy Barley, the abbess herself, swept into the room, black habit billowing, smiling broadly.

"Sir Thomas—I'm honored to see you again. The journey wasn't too long and arduous, I hope?"

Dorothy Barley was one of the most important and revered women in the whole of England. She was a baroness, Lord of Parliament (not that she could take her seat on account of her sex), and King Henry himself was a patron of the abbey.

"My lady . . ." Sir Thomas gave a low bow. "I present to you my ward, Lysbette Angiers."

The abbess took her hands and studied Lysbette's face with quick, hazel eyes. "Welcome, Lysbette. I know from Sir Thomas how you love to study and are passionate about classical learning. Perhaps, in time, you will become obedientiary of our library."

"Thank you, my lady."

"Come, let me show you around before I hand you over to Dame Amelia, our mistress of the novices."

"Take care, dearest Lysbette," Sir Thomas said. "A life close to God is the greatest honor. I rather envy your choice." Not that she recalled having been given one.

She bid him goodbye then followed the abbess around a maze of dormitories, kitchen and warming room, infirmary, chapter house, chapel, washhouse, library, schoolroom, and umpteen other assorted buildings. As they walked, Abbess Dorothy spoke.

"We have over seven thousand acres spread over several counties and thirteen manors. We provide care for the sick and the poor. Alms are given through pittances to keep them fed and clothed, and sometimes we provide money to help put a roof over their heads. We also, of course, look after the temporal and spiritual welfare of everyone, from royalty to the homeless. Living here are members of the royal family, the aristocracy and the gentry, as well as those less well connected. I have several dozen children under my care, too—children of patrons and royalty. We have hundreds of tenant farmers to manage, crops to harvest, grain to mill, animals to tend. We have legal cases to fight and the books to balance."

Looking around, Lysbette realized her naivety at thinking a nun's life was all prayers and contemplation.

The abbess nodded. "Barking Abbey is an enormous enterprise, and all of it is overseen and managed by us nuns. Such responsibility, influence, and power that we have is unique in the world of women."

Days at the abbey melted into weeks, which melted into months.

Time passed in a blur of learning. Lysbette spent time working with the different obedientiaries—the sacristan, cellaress, kitcheness, fratress, librarian, infirmaress, treasuress, chambress, and the laundress, as well as the prioress who was second-in-command to her lady, the abbess. It would take Lysbette seven years to learn enough to be professed. The nuns prayed several times a day for the souls of the founders and the benefactors, as well as celebrating Mass three times a day. The rhythm of rising at two a.m. for matins prayers, then again at five, took some getting used to, but, once she did, it began to feel as though it were something she had always done.

The priests and chaplains who led Mass and attended to the nuns' spiritual needs, being male, lived separately within the abbey grounds. For a female-only community, the place crawled with men. But, unlike the patriarchal world outside the abbey walls and in the hierarchies of the church itself, here Lysbette found the illusion of a matriarchy. Here, everyone, from the steward and bailiffs to the gardeners and laborers, reported directly to the abbess. The great lady herself traveled often, an impressive sight on her horse, commanding respect from all she encountered.

Indeed, in this rarefied environment, Lysbette saw how differently the nuns were treated by men. Outside of these walls and the rather unusual More household, womenfolk were generally treated with disdain. Only a husband, a father, a man made decisions and gave instructions. Women, inferior with their weak minds and moods prone to hysteria, must be silent and bow, always, to a man's authority. But a woman in a habit was treated altogether differently. She was deferred to, revered even. Her purity and proximity to God gave her a status that lifted her above the standard, flawed woman. A nun was not to be feared like other women. A nun was not a temptress. Men need not be concerned she might use her beauty or wily ways to seduce them. A nun, as a bride of Christ, was clean of the devil's influence and trickery.

Between the learning, praying, handing out of alms, and attention to godly duties there was, as Abbess Dorothy had promised, time for relaxation and reading. Many of the nuns were talented seamstresses, embroiderists, and painters. Many copied and translated manuscripts, illuminating them with exquisite illustrations. Almost all were highly educated and discussions between them were lively and varied.

As the weather grew warmer the following summer, Lysbette and her friend Agnes, who had joined Barking two years earlier, took to strolling in the gardens and sitting beneath the spreading limbs of a great, old oak tree that overlooked the meadow where fat, brown cows grazed, swishing lazy tails at flies.

"Do you ever regret coming here?" Lysbette asked Agnes one day as they lay side by side on the warm grass.

"No, why would I?" Agnes looked aghast. "What would be the alternative? Marriage to a weak and ugly man, or a cruel one. Producing child after child and then probably death by one. Here, I have purpose. To grow closer to God. To improve myself for his benefit. To pray for the souls of others. I am able to sing, and singing makes me happier than anything on this earth. Why, do you?"

Lysbette hesitated. She still thought of John, even though she knew she should not, and she wondered what her life might have been had she become his wife. Since leaving Chelsea she had had no more contact with him. Writing to a man who was neither father nor brother was impossible. Sir Thomas had mentioned in a letter that John was married now to Isabelle, to whom he had been promised since the age of fourteen. They lived in his new wife's grand house, Tappers Court, Holborn, and were expecting a child. The sharp pain of his loss had been numbed to a dull ache through the passage of time.

"I hoped to have been married," she said, staring out over the meadow toward the woods in the far distance. "But, John, the man I loved, and who loved me, was a nobleman, and I a poor orphan. We couldn't have made a match. I try not to let myself wonder how my life might have been. If I do, I only become bitter. We must look forward, don't you think, Agnes? I am reconciled and find I can be happy." She turned and smiled at her friend.

Agnes laughed. "I hear you spend every spare hour in the library." She lay back and stared at the sky, chewing the end of a long grass stalk. "What is it you do there?"

"Translation. I was always good with Greek to Latin. I found some books of the Greek Church fathers. Beautiful printed and illustrated books, with the printer's symbol, a golden sun, on them. I have been translating them to Latin. But recently, I've found other texts, more modern ones, which are fascinating."

Agnes turned to look at her. Freckles were appearing on her pale skin, brought out by the sun. "Tell me." She propped her head up on her elbow. Lysbette considered her for a few moments, wondering how much could be safely said. Agnes, she concluded, seeing nothing but honest curiosity in her eyes, was the closest friend Lysbette had ever had. Of course she could trust her.

"I found a text, *Declamation on the Nobility and Preeminence of the Female Sex*, written by a man, Henricus Cornelius Agrippa. He believes he has been ordained by God to argue for women's superiority over men. He says it is men, not women, who introduced murder, bigamy, drunkenness, tyranny, idolatry, adultery, incest. I've never read something like this before. And he mentions others writing on a similar topic too."

"What he says is true . . ." Agnes sighed. "But one enlightened man among the rest won't make any difference."

"True, but if others take up his cause . . ."

"What men are ever going to admit to women's superiority? It suits them to have us believe in our own inferiority too."

"'Tis true. Since Aristotle, and probably before, women have been taught to believe we are inferior. But if we could at least be treated with respect and honor. Be listened to, as men are listened to. That we may not be ruled over by our fathers, brothers, husbands. Marriage should be of equals. Man should recognize *he* is responsible for his own base desires and not blame us, or the devil inside us, for them."

Agnes gave Lysbette a long look.

"It is a tantalizing notion, Lysbette, but it will never happen. If owning the Bible written in English is enough to burn a person alive, imagine the chaos if *women* read and begin to have their own opinions too? I'm afraid your Agrippa is but one man. No doubt he will be called a madman at that."

"We are far more capable than men would let us think. Besides, I have been reading about matriarchal societies that exist in the far reaches of the world. Perhaps things beyond our abbey walls might be better if we had equality with men. Even my guardian, Sir Thomas, thinks women are just as clever as men. Sometimes more so."

"Well," Agnes said after a pause. "Then he is an unusual man."

"He is indeed. Although he is also a great traditionalist, and I suspect the idea of women having full equality with men might not sit well with him." Lysbette sighed.

"And, of course," Agnes added, "let's not forget that Eve tempted Adam. That women tempt men into sin. That the devil chooses a woman's body to inhabit to carry out his evil deeds." Her face twisted a little, reddening as though in anger or anguish. More words came in a rush. "Let's not forget it is the devil that chooses women to carry out witchcraft. Have you read that awful book *Malleus Maleficarum*?" Lysbette shook her head. "It's an abomination. It gives men an excuse to hunt women, torture and burn them alive. It spreads hatred of women, *fear* of women." Agnes stopped, took a breath.

Lysbette reached out a hand and touched Agnes's. She hadn't meant to upset her friend.

Agnes sat bolt upright and wrapped her arms around her knees.

"Agnes?"

"Something happened to me," she said quietly into her knees. "Before I came here. I was thirteen. My uncle. He . . ."

"Oh god in heaven."

"Of course, he blamed me. I had taunted and enticed him with my beauty. I was the evil witch, he the victim. I can tell you, it certainly did not feel like that. I did nothing to entice him. I knew nothing of . . . what a man could do to a woman. The violence and pain return to me, night after night in my dreams . . ." Agnes let out a sob. Lysbette wrapped her in her arms and Agnes's tears flowed freely.

"I am sorry."

Agnes dried her eyes. "They sent me here. I think as punishment. But I am glad. Here I am safe. My uncle cannot get to me, nor any other man."

"Yes, yes. I am glad of it, Agnes. But . . ."

"But?"

"But . . . What about other women? Women who are not protected by this . . ." Lysbette flapped her habit. "The accusations, the cruel treatment won't stop unless we *do* something."

Agnes snorted. "And what can we do? Men have no interest in elevating women. Why would they? And besides, men have been telling women of their inferiority for so long, we have come to believe it."

"But look at us here, in this abbey. Aren't we doing the jobs of men? Managing staff, running the estates, balancing the books? We are living proof it can be done. And other women need to know this." She sat up straighter. "You asked what can we do? Well, I can write, Agnes. I can write *well*. I could write in English, publish a pamphlet, perhaps called . . . *One Hundred Reasons for the Elevation of Women* . . ." Agnes wrinkled her nose. ". . . Or something better."

"I don't think the lady abbess would be pleased."

"But she wouldn't have to know, would she? Not if I remained anonymous. I could write under a pseudonym."

Agnes took Lysbette's hand in her own. Her eyes were serious. "You won't really do this, will you, Lysbette? We may jest, but it would be far too provocative. Dangerous, even. Promise me?" She gave Lysbette's hand a shake.

"I doubt I am bold enough," Lysbette replied, and she smiled at her friend.

But something like a spark was lit inside her, and sparks ignite into flames that good sense alone cannot dampen.

Chapter 16

Milly

Levittown, Long Island, New York, January 1953

Christmas comes and goes in a whirl of neighborly drinks parties (Milly's idea of what hell must be made of); a beautiful candlelit church service; excited, bouncing children and presents in pretty boxes. Early the following day the Bennetts climb into the Buick and drive over seven hundred miles, stopping overnight at a motel near Harrisburg, Pennsylvania, to break the journey, then onward to George's parents' racehorse farm in the heart of the rich bluegrass fields, thirty miles outside Lexington, Kentucky. Milly marvels, as she did the first time they made this drive, at the mind-blowing size and resources of this beautiful country, and this, even though it has taken them nigh on fourteen hours to get here, only a tiny slice of it.

They spend the next week of George's holiday from work admiring the horses on the farm, the children even getting to sit on their cousin's ponies. Olive isn't sure that sitting on horses' backs is fair to the horses and tells her grandparents quite firmly that she thinks they should all be set free to gallop wild on the plains, rather than on the racetrack with a jockey on top.

"What a strange creature you are," Patricia tells Olive. She laughs and musses her granddaughter's hair. "Turning out like your mother, aren't you?"

Patricia's daughter, George's sister, Ida, lives on the farm with her husband, Pete, and runs the household like a well-oiled machine. No doubt she will, in time, inherit it, George having no interest in either horses or living in Kentucky, failings that, Milly is sure, are laid firmly at her feet, rather than at their son's. Ida is all Milly is not. Her three children, a few years older than Edward and Olive, are pink cheeked and robust, earnest and courteous. Ida is simultaneously a talented horsewoman and homemaker, able to turn out a perfectly light and fluffy cake for tea at five, a three-course meal for ten by seven, and still not have a hair out of place. Milly has never felt more of a spare part. She watches Ida all week, imagining that she is the ideal reader of *My Life*. Thirtysomething, mother, wife, entertainer, intelligent and accomplished, yet modest. The central spoke of the family wheel, the piece that holds them all together. Perfect and accomplished in all the ways that matter. Sometimes, though, Milly catches an expression on Ida's face, one she thinks may reflect a different reality. Is Ida happy?

On the morning of New Year's Eve, the men in the household take themselves off for a long, soul-enhancing ride in the beautiful countryside that surrounds the farm, leaving the women at home to watch the children and prepare the house and the food for the planned evening festivities. Patricia trusts Milly only with the task of setting the table, then dispatches her to keep an eye on the children who are now outside, happily poking about in the stream that winds its way around the bottom of the garden, hoping to spear a passing fish.

It's not unpleasant sitting on an upturned log, the children's chatter washing over her, and it's a relief to be out of the kitchen with Patricia's incessant chatter and Ida's easy domestic confidence. Less than half an hour later, there are footsteps on the graveled path and Milly turns to see Ida striding toward her wrapped in a camel coat and matching scarf. Milly shuffles along to make room for Ida on the log.

The children are now poking about in the stream with long sticks, apparently having changed games and are in the midst of some sort of Robinson Crusoe adventure. Ida offers Milly a cigarette and lights her own, inhaling deeply, sighing audibly.

"Everything okay?" Milly asks. "Do you want me to come back and help?"

Ida shakes her head. "Everything's under control."

"I'm sorry, I'm pretty useless in the kitchen department."

Ida smiles. "Are you really as bad as you seem?"

"I am. I spent more time with my head in books than doing anything domestically useful when I was young."

"Lucky you. Doesn't George mind?"

"You know George. He's so easygoing. I am fortunate to have found him." Milly turns to look at Ida. "You said, *lucky you*. Are you not happy, Ida? You seem so accomplished. So naturally at ease doing all the cooking and housekeeping."

Ida takes another drag on her cigarette, her gaze fixed on the children. "You are very direct, Milly." She pauses. "I like that. A direct question deserves a direct answer. Am I happy? Sometimes, I guess. But some days, I feel like I'm suffocating—spending every single day going through the motions in a state of bored numbness. I think to myself, is this all life is? To be in the service of others? To spend my days doing never-ending, dull tasks, and to be grateful for it." Ida pauses. She raises her cigarette to her lips again, only this time, her hand trembles. "I sometimes wonder," she adds, "why we women have been given brains. It's our bodies men want. I think that if men could produce children without a woman's body, we wouldn't be required at all."

Milly watches her in stunned silence. She suspects Ida rarely speaks like this to anyone.

"It was always clear," Ida continues, "that George wasn't interested in taking on the farm when it becomes too much for my parents. I'd love nothing better than to spend my days out in the yard, with the horses. I have a good eye for a horse. I know the bloodlines. I know I could breed and train horses as good as any man. Better than Pete, anyway. But my parents, my husband, they'd never contemplate it. It's not even in the cards. My place is in the house, raising the kids. My mother is always telling me how lucky I am. I smile and agree but inside I'm screaming with frustration."

"But . . . Why don't you tell them that's what you want? Pete seems a reasonable man. Your parents would come round, wouldn't they?"

Ida shakes her head and half laughs, half sobs. "You don't understand. My father is going to leave the farm to Pete. He entrusts him with everything: financial, strategy, land. The lot. Pete often asks *me* for advice when he's out of his depth. Then I hear him talking to the trainers, the customers, the other breeders as if these are his ideas. But if they heard it from me, they'd never listen. Nobody would take me seriously, from bank managers to auctioneers to jockeys to trainers, to my own mother and father. Pete *is* a reasonable man, you're right. But it isn't just about him, is it? It's about the entire world around us, do you see?"

Milly nods. She does see. She thinks back to her conversation with George about writing the magazine articles. George is a reasonable man also, who loves her very much, but still, he didn't want her to take that on. And she agreed to comply with his wishes. She wonders how many other women there must be, out there, all across America, feeling just like Ida, or worse.

She reaches out and gives Ida's hand a squeeze.

"I'm sorry," she says, because she is, and because really, there is nothing else to say.

Two days into the new school term, Doris Sykes invites Milly, Edward, and Olive over after school. Betty and Olive are still best buddies, which is a friendship record for Olive. Doris's second son, Larry, who, at seven, is a year older than Edward, reluctantly offers to show him his train set, while the eldest, eleven-year-old Ronald, reclines on the sitting room sofa reading *Amazon Adventure*.

The women exchange stories of their respective holiday seasons, and then Doris talks at length about her husband, Frank, who works in the governor's office of the New York State Executive Government. They'd met when Doris was a freshman in college and Frank an ambitious hopeful for political office. He'd persuaded her to leave before she'd graduated as he couldn't live without her and needed to move to New York for the sake of his career.

"Oh," Milly exclaims, horrified. "Couldn't he have waited for you?"

Doris smiles serenely. "He said not. And he didn't dare leave me behind in case I was tempted by one of the college boys . . . I had thought of going into law, but well, love, marriage . . ." She shrugs her shoulders with apparent hopelessness. "You know how it is, don't you? Frank is so fiercely ambitious. It's what he lives for, and I'll do everything I can to help him achieve his dreams."

Don't you have dreams of your own, Doris? Milly wonders as she watches Doris talk animatedly about Frank. She strikes Milly as someone with great passion and energy, but someone who only sees herself in the context of her husband.

When it is time to leave, Doris stands by the front door to see them out.

"Listen," she says, placing a leaflet in Milly's hand. "There's a meeting of the All-Women for Families Group tomorrow evening at the town hall. Why don't you come along?"

"All-Women for Families Group?" echoes Milly.

"The leaflet explains what we're about," Doris says airily, handing it to Milly. "It's just a small group of women who want to do some good in the local community." She smiles. "It might be a nice way to get more involved around here."

Milly puts the folded leaflet into her handbag, then forgets about it in the flurry of goodbyes. It is only much later after the children are asleep and she and George settle on the sofa for a nightcap that she remembers it.

**Do you put your family first, above
everything else in this world?**
If you want to make sure your kids grow up in a safe,
nurturing environment where good Christian and American
values are upheld, then we are the group for you!
The All-Women for Families Group
has been set up to support our schools and wider community
to deliver a first-class American education. Join us, learn,
have fun, make new friends as we fundraise, educate,
and deliver to our local communities. All American
women, whatever your age, you are welcome!

"You should go," George says, leaning over her shoulder, reading. "It's a swell idea for you to get involved in charitable things. You might widen your social circle, outside of that librarian."

"There's nothing wrong with Susan," Milly snaps.

"I never said there was. I can babysit the children. It will be nice for you to go out for the evening."

Milly sighs. "I'm not sure I'm the charitable type."

George nudges her. "Well, you won't know if you don't go along and find out, will you?"

Doris Sykes, president of the All-Women for Families Group, stands before the raised platform in the town hall, resplendent in a shell pink dress with trumpet skirt and nipped-in waist. Her hair, the color of a fiery evening sky, is curled delicately around her ears, topped with a neat pillbox hat. Even though it's eight o'clock on a weekday evening, there must be at least fifty women present. Milly recognizes some of the other mothers from the PTA and the school gates. There are older women too. Milly spies Mrs. Cross and Mrs. Humphries sitting together in the front row.

She slides into an empty seat at the back.

"Ladies, ladies . . ." Doris looks around the hall. "Welcome! I see some new faces out there . . ." She catches Milly's eyes and gives her a small smile. "So I will give a short recap of who we are, and why we are here today." She clears her throat and begins a slow walk back and forth across the stage. "As far as any of the menfolk in our lives are concerned, we are the All-Women for Families Group of Levittown who raise funds for playgrounds, plant trees, gather money for a scholarship fund, and do good deeds. That is a cover story. What we *really* are is the local branch of the Minute Women." She pauses.

Milly leans forward in her seat. She was expecting they'd be standing around with biscuits and hot drinks discussing bake and yard sales. This, clearly, is not that.

"Most men, my husband whom I love very dearly, included, do not think women should dabble in politics, perhaps apart from assisting them in their work when they have too much to do." There is a low rumble of laughter. "So, when you leave here, you mustn't breathe a word about our true purpose . . ." *What is your true purpose?* ". . . We are not, please understand, feminists or anti-men. On the contrary, what we want most in the world is to support our men in all that they do. Many of your menfolk will be, at this very moment, fighting communists in the hot, steamy jungles of the East. Our job, here, is to make sure they come home to the America that fills their dreams at night. The real, traditional America. A happy home, healthy children, and loving wife."

There are murmurs of agreement among the audience.

"We women are the bastions of the home front. And the frightening reality is, the communists, the socialists . . . They fight a dirty game. The Red Threat is right here, infiltrating not only our national institutions, our literature, our theaters and cinemas, but the very heart of our nation. Our homes, our families, our children." She stops to take a breath, and the hall is deathly silent.

Milly swallows her shock. *A clandestine group of communist-fighting housewives?*

"Here is a fact," Doris is saying. "The number of people living under communism has increased by four hundred percent since 1945. Why does this matter? To quote Senator Nixon, if Europe were to be allowed to go communist, within five or ten years, we will be faced with a war we are likely to lose. Ladies, this war is not confined to Korea. We are facing not only the potential destruction of *this* nation, but that of civilization itself." There is a collective, uncomfortable shuffle. "And if *that* isn't enough, I know you are good Christians. We must do all we can to protect our faith. As J. Edgar Hoover has so wisely said, the *real* danger in communism lies in the fact it is atheist. It wants to replace the Supreme Being."

The Minute Women. Doris mentioned they were a national organization. Milly has never heard of them. Perhaps George has? Then she remembers she isn't supposed to mention this to her husband. She seems to be making a habit of collecting secrets from George.

"The Minute Women of America," Doris continues, as though listening to Milly's thoughts, "is organized nationwide through local chapters because we women care just as much as men about liberty and democracy. Should it fail, your little one will be placed in a state-run nursery, followed by a special indoctrination school. That would mean you mothers"—she now looks across the hall—"will have no childcare responsibilities and will be sent to work in government-run factories and mines." Doris plants her feet, raises her chin. "Are you going to sit back and let our society be destroyed, our children brainwashed? Or are you going to join me in fighting for the survival of the free world?"

There is a rising clamor of agreement from the audience, clearly stirred by Doris's terrifying dystopia.

"It's an uncomfortable truth," Doris states, "that any neighbor, friend, local shopkeeper, librarian, or, perhaps worst of all, schoolteacher, might be harboring *leanings* toward an ideology that is anathema to our own." The hall falls silent again, the only sound Doris's heels clicking on the wooden boards as she begins her pacing again. "One we would rather not have. For if it is the case that that friend, or acquaintance, is in fact, an enemy in our midst, what are we going to do about them? Keep quiet? Or do the *right* thing and report our concerns to the authorities?"

Milly is beginning to feel hot. There is a squirming in her belly.

All this talk of reporting your neighbor, your friend or acquaintance. Isn't this what the communists *themselves* do?

"Anyone who claims to support liberal values must be held in suspicion. Anyone who supports women's rights. Foreigners. Homosexuals. They are, by their very nature, fellow travelers with communism." Doris sniffs. "Be suspicious of those who support workers' rights, Social Security, or other policies that may *seem* innocuous . . . Remember, Julius and Ethel Rosenberg, who were hiding in plain sight in the midst of a pleasant community, were convicted of spying for the Soviets only last year. They can be anywhere, even right here, in our town."

This is madness, Milly thinks. How can Doris, in her right mind, be throwing feminists, foreigners, those in support of Social Security, or any other group that springs to mind, in with the communists? How much of this *is* Doris? Or underneath it all, is this Frank? Frank and all the other politicians influenced by McCarthy and his ilk, spreading hate and hysteria out into the attentive ears of women like Doris who fear new ideas and a changing world and hope to resist it by clinging to some fictional, traditional America as though it were Utopia itself.

"Starting with the schools," Doris continues, "many of us are unhappy with the way the superintendent of the Board of Education has been acting, and some of the teachers too."

"And the public libraries," someone else shouts. "I heard that if you ask the librarian right here in Levittown for a banned book, she will get it for you. And there are rumors she is a *fellow traveler*."

Milly's heart stops, then jumps violently in her chest. *Susan!* Oh dear god, she must warn her. Sweat trickles down Milly's back.

The talk goes on around her, names of teachers shouted out, things people have said, newsletters they plan to write, reports to be gathered in.

Once the meeting is over, Doris speaks to the women as they file out of the hall. "Can I count on you for support?" she asks each of them as they pass by. Milly shrinks down low, skirting the women gathered around Doris. She manages to sneak away without being seen and begins walking home.

Should she mention this to George? She was told not to, and she certainly doesn't plan to go back. But the most pressing thing on her mind is Susan. At the first opportunity, she will call in at the library and have a quiet word with her. She must stop lending unsuitable books.

Susan's secret seems to be not so secret, after all.

Chapter 17

Milly

Levittown, Long Island, New York, January 1953

It is gone midnight the next night, and the rest of the household are asleep. Milly lies on her back staring up at the ceiling. Beside her, George is turned on his side, his breathing heavy and even. Outside, a storm is brewing. The rattling, flapping, creaking she can hear from outside combined with the whip of the wind through the trees leave her on edge. Her heart thumps too loud in her ears.

Her mind keeps returning to Doris and the Minute Women, to poor Susan who had stared at her with alarm in her eyes as Milly whispered her warning. *I cannot lose this job*, Susan had said, almost in tears. *It was hard enough to get this one. And if there is any whisper of being a fellow traveler. Well, it would be the scrap heap for me, true or no.* Milly had left her then, to gather her illicit books and her wits. She thinks of Ida, frustrated and restricted back in Kentucky.

The discomfort is turning to anger. What had they all fought for in six years of war if it wasn't for freedom and democracy? She'd lived through it. George had risked his life daily for it, only now to be facing the threat of communism with restrictions and fear and suspicion. Allowing those with agendas she can't begin to fathom, but suspects it is all to do with power and self-interest, to conflate freedom with communism. What was the point in the thousands of women like her stepping up to do their bit for the war effort, to take on the jobs of men while they were away fighting, to prove their capability as equals, only to slide backward now?

And it is in that moment that she resolves, finally, she *will* write for *My Life*. Her own small, symbolic act of rebellion on behalf of all of them: Susan, Ida, herself. Through her stories, she might just connect with other isolated women. Those who feel alone and powerless, and that makes it feel worthwhile. An inkling of an idea begins to form—a series of stories that will get the readers thinking, not the usual romances or happy-ever-afters, but in the vein of those the ancients told, which she spent many years studying. This storytelling might be two thousand years old, but it's as relevant now as it ever was.

George needn't know. She will write under a pseudonym.

Milly feels prickles of sweat forming as she acknowledges her deception. She is gathering secrets around her like illicit love affairs. But she shoves away the thought and slips out of bed, reaching for the dressing gown she had tossed on the floor hours earlier, on impulse silently sliding the box containing the manuscript from the cupboard. Downstairs in the kitchen, she looks out at the stark outline of the bare tops of the oak trees, tossed violently against a curiously pale sky. Above the trees, the backlit shapes of dark clouds race. Milly shudders and turns away, flicking on the light and busying herself with heating some milk.

Milly pours the hot milk into her cup of cocoa. She spoons in some sugar and stirs. She thinks of Charlotte Guillard and the anonymous women who were so compelled to hide what they wanted to say beneath a web of encryption. Doris's speech, the threat to Susan, all the talk of book bans and stifling what their children can be taught at school has made her feel a connection with these women across the centuries. Perhaps times haven't changed as much as people believe they have. It makes her desire to know what is in this manuscript stronger than ever.

She opens it and gets to work.

The basics of coding have not changed so much between the sixteenth and the twentieth centuries, with two main methods of encryption. The most straightforward and easiest to break is the simple substitution method, like where a Caesar cipher might be used, so the plaintext is replaced with another in a fixed position (monoalphabetic), that is, shifted along by the same number of places. This is easy to detect by running a frequency test, as the distribution of the plaintext letters and ciphertext will be identical.

A substitution method can be made harder to break by changing the substitutions at different intervals throughout (polyalphabetic), or by using symbols in place of letters.

The other method, transposition, is where the plaintext isn't altered but is rearranged in a different and complex manner. For example, a repeated word or phrase could be used for the key.

The most complex encryptions might have been a combination of the two. In this manuscript, given the lack of any frequency of appearance of the letter-like characters, Milly has already concluded this is more sophisticated than a simple monoalphabetic substitution code. It is also very likely that the authors of the work have used certain symbols to represent syllables, phrases, whole words, names, dates, and places.

She's compiled a list she thinks represents some of those as they occur at inconsistent intervals throughout the document. There is a triangle, a sun, a moon, a star, an arrow, a key, and more. Aside from the letter-like characters themselves, some of which look tantalizingly close to the Latin alphabet, and the symbols, there are beautiful illustrations, which Milly has examined in great detail. The women are central almost everywhere, except in a couple of scenes where battles are depicted. It makes Milly think of Sparta in ancient Greece, where women were permitted to own their own property and ran everything to do with the household, while men's roles were confined to training for fighting wars for Sparta. Although it didn't, in the end, turn out well for the Spartans.

Ancient Greece.

Always, somehow, her thoughts bring her back to it. *Why?* She thinks about Charlotte Guillard and the two volumes of the huge Greek to Latin dictionary that also bear the sign of Soleil d'Or, and a thought pops unbidden into her mind.

What if the base language is not Latin. What if it were ancient Greek?

On impulse, Milly goes to the drawer in the kitchen where all the odds and ends are kept. She rifles through sticky tape, scraps of paper and pens, coloring pencils and a half-used tube of glue, until she finds a magnifying glass. She turns to the first of the astrology pages that bears the printing mark of Charlotte Guillard, and she slowly traces the magnifying glass across it. There is the magnified *CG. Charlotte Guillard.* Milly examines the spray of stars, the wiggling lines of the sun's rays. There are a few marks along the line of one of the sun's rays. Without the magnifier, they are tiny, so easy to miss. One might think them dots or splotches of ink, and besides, they are almost obscured by a profusion of stars that fill the gaps between the rays. Studying them closer, she makes out what she recognizes to be Greek numerals. It reads αφνβ.

1552.

Her heart begins to thump faster. Could this mean the book

was written in 1552? She sits back in her chair and stares at it, hardly daring to breathe. Surely it can't be this simple. But maybe it is. And maybe, just maybe, she has unlocked a key to what else lies hidden on these pages. If she really has found the base language, that would be one enormous step forward.

Charlotte, whatever it is you had to conceal, I know you want me to see. And I will find it.

The following morning, Milly finds Winton's telephone number written on the card he had given her. She takes a deep breath, picks up the receiver, and asks the operator to make an international call to England. Winton will want to know of her discovery last night, and she will think of some plausible explanation for the call before the phone bill arrives in the mail.

The distant ringing at the other end of the line through the crackling goes on and on until Milly is certain nobody is home, then, a series of clicks and a distant female voice. After accepting the international call from the operator, Milly is through.

"This is Mrs. Harvey-Jones. To whom am I speaking?" The faint voice sounds very far away.

"My name is Milly Bennett, I am calling from New York. You don't know me but—"

"Who?"

"Milly Bennett. I am helping your husband with a manuscript he left with me when he was here in November. I think I've made some headway and wondered if I may speak with him."

"Oh dear me . . ." The line goes quiet for a moment, then Mrs. Harvey-Jones speaks again. "He did mention you." she says, her voice sounding so very small and distant, the crackling on the line so loud. Milly presses the receiver closer to her ear. "I'm afraid I've been remiss in letting everyone know. There are so many, and I don't know half of them . . . I am so sorry, Mrs. Bennett, but my darling Winton passed away the week before Christmas."

"No!" Milly's legs give way, and she sits with a thump on the staircase. "I am so very sorry, Mrs. Harvey-Jones."

The crackles on the line increase, and Milly can only make out part of what she is saying. "Thank you, dear . . . dodgy ticker . . . long time. Doctor warned him . . . port and stilton . . . never listened. The old fool . . . terribly sudden."

"What an awful shock."

"Blessing . . . He'd have known nothing about it . . . Comfort from that . . .

"You must miss him terribly. I hope you are managing?"

"There is an awful lot to do. He was a hoarder . . . every scrap of paper . . . book that ever . . . seventy years of life."

"I can imagine . . . But, Mrs. Harvey-Jones, I have this manuscript here. The one he told you about. I must return it. I shall send it special delivery just as soon as I can get to the post office—"

"Oh no, you mustn't do that. Please, keep it . . . doing me a favor. He's not been gone long and already these darned people from the university, some library or other, they've been calling, asking if they can have it . . . Scavengers, the lot of them. No, he would have wanted you to keep it, *I* want you to keep it . . ."

"I couldn't possibly! It must be very valuable. You should let the university or library have it. It would be safe, and it should fetch a good sum . . ."

"I have plenty enough money. Winton would not have wanted that at all . . . Very obstinate . . . I don't know anything about it, and they should leave me alone."

"But—"

". . . Won't hear of it . . . Go well, Mrs. Bennett, and keep your family close. They are the most precious things of all."

The line clicks, and the operator informs Milly that Mrs. Harvey-Jones has ended the call.

"Goodbye," Milly says to the empty air and replaces the receiver. She sits, numb, on the steps for several minutes. She finds she is shaking. *Shock*, she thinks and goes to pour herself a tot of whiskey.

She tips it back and there is fire in her throat, scalding down into her belly, which calms the shaking. How can Winton be dead? Not another person who seems so suddenly important to her, gone. Poor, dear man. He had just come back into her life, given her purpose again. She remembers his tight face and tired eyes as they worked through the dead of night at Bletchley. His slumped shoulders when they had an impenetrable message they couldn't untangle. His quiet elation when they broke through. A heaviness comes over her, as though the effort of moving her limbs is simply too much. How we take life for granted. How swiftly it can be snuffed out.

How sad that Winton will never know if his dream of untangling this manuscript's mysteries will ever come to be.

I'll keep going Winton, she promises. *I'll do my best not to let you down.*

Then she pours herself another whiskey and toasts his memory.

Over the next few days, Milly's mind keeps flipping to Winton and her disbelief that he has gone. She wishes she could have gone to his funeral to say her proper goodbyes. The only thing she can do, because it is what he would have wanted, is work whenever she can on the manuscript.

Remembering her conversation with Winton about how they both believed the manuscript had been bound incorrectly, Milly decides to double her efforts in her search for a catchword. Such an identifier could be a character, word, or image at the bottom of one page, then mirrored or continued at the top of the next, so the reader can keep track of the pages. Over several days, by carefully studying the top and bottom of each page, she realizes there could be a continuity of symbols that are repeated from the bottom of one page to the top of another, but she had missed them previously because the pages are not arranged in the order of the identifier. Instead, the pages are currently grouped in accordance with the illustrations, and she concludes this is wrong.

Carefully, she unbinds the book, reordering the pages as she thinks makes sense with the identifiers. Placed in what she hopes is now the correct order, the four astrology pages are no longer together but occur at intervals in the book, dividing it into four roughly equal sections.

Staring at the rearranged pages, she has the sensation this is significant, and she longs to discuss it with Winton. The pain and shock of his sudden death strikes her once more, like a physical punch to the stomach. Her aloneness in this task he has left her with eats away, leaving an aching, empty space inside.

The following day, in need of a break, Milly confides in Susan as they take a loop around the village green during Susan's lunch hour. She tells her that her *relative*, as she had previously told Susan he was, the one she was doing the book project for, passed away suddenly and unexpectedly. That she is more devastated by his death than she really has a right to be, given that she had barely seen him for years.

"Be kind to yourself," Susan says, giving Milly's hand a squeeze. "You've had a horrible shock."

"And you, Susan?" Milly asks, remembering the Minute Woman and the nasty, terrifying things said about Susan at the meeting.

Susan bites her lip.

It's only then that Milly notices her friend's eyes are purple rimmed, flat and dull as though she's not been sleeping. "What is it? What's happened?"

"Nothing. Not yet. But . . . Oh, Milly, there is something I should have told you. Something you might hate me for, but it's only right you should know. You are a good friend and I've not been straight."

"You're a communist?" Milly takes Susan's arm and guides her to a nearby bench where they sit on damp, cold wood and stare out over the expanse of frozen pond. "I don't care."

"Oh no, I'm not, actually, a communist, but I *am* living with another woman—and we are more than friends . . ." She stops talking and bites her lip again. "It's Myra . . . I should have told you," she says, quieter, "but there never seemed a need, or the right way to put it. And I didn't want to ruin our friendship."

A flock of Canada geese fly so low overhead, they can hear the beat and thrum of their wings. They watch as they land beside the ice in a volley of haunting cries.

Milly turns to Susan. "It is not my business who you choose to be with, and, if I'm honest, it makes me happy. I like you both, very much. And I'm relieved to know that each evening after the library you aren't going back to a lonely flat with just the television set for company. It's much nicer to think of you with Myra, cooking her supper and she massaging your feet while you watch the evening news." Susan splutters and turns scarlet. *Too much again, Milly.* "Well, it's true, I'm pleased for you."

"Well, not everyone shares your view on that, Milly. Most people see it as a sin. And especially now, if you are a *fellow traveler*, then you are a misfit, along with all sorts of other misfits, and therefore in league with the communists, whatever your political persuasion. Anyone can be a threat to the nation."

"You sound like the Minute Women." Milly feels a tight knot of anger take root. It makes her feel hot, despite the subfreezing temperatures in the park.

Susan sighs. "Mr. O'Malley called me in to his office yesterday. Said he had received an anonymous letter about me, making salacious and upsetting allegations. I denied everything of course. And he seemed satisfied, said if a person wasn't willing to sign their name at the bottom of a letter, he was going to assume they had some axe to grind and couldn't be taken seriously. I think he probably searched my office, but thanks to you, all the offending books are now in my flat." She pauses. "But I don't suppose whoever wrote that letter is going to let things rest. And just being the subject of a complaint alone could be enough to lose me my job. I wouldn't be the first librarian to go, nor the last."

"But . . . If you aren't a communist spy, they can't sack you, surely?"

"Milly . . ." Susan turns to her, her face drawn and pale, eyes laced with fear. "This whole nation is infected with a crazed, religious zeal that started with Mr. J. Edgar Hoover and fans out not only through the FBI, but through all the wildly popular essays he writes for *Christianity Today*. These people, they have an agenda, see? America is God's chosen nation. Chosen for white men. Ambitious women, Black Americans, homosexuals, the foreign born—we cannot be *real* citizens. He can't say that, of course not. But what he *can* do is lump us all in with communists. Give ordinary people a reason to fear us because we are a threat. So, if we lose our jobs, our voice, our dignity and status, well. Then they will have won, won't they?"

"This is terrible, Susan."

"It is."

"Is there is anything I can do . . . for you, I mean?"

"What can any of us do?" Susan says, a note of resignation in her voice. "We are all just lackeys, Milly. We none of us are in control of our own destinies."

That evening, when the children are in bed, Milly sits down at the kitchen table. Now she has resolved to write a piece for Myra and *My Life*, and with George at a bank function this evening, it's time she put pen to paper. Indignation burns inside for Susan, and her words have been echoing around her head. *We are all just lackeys, Milly. We none of us are in control of our own destinies.* She thinks of all the banned books and Susan's valiant, one-woman effort to circumvent the rules. She thinks of all the war years, of those who fought and lost their lives, in the name of freedom. She thinks right back to where it all began, to the literature of the ancient Greeks, in whose tradition and footsteps two thousand years later, writers unwittingly still follow. She thinks of the epic heroes' journeys of Homer, the lyrical poems of Sappho, the first writer of prose, Herodotus. She thinks of the dramas, the comedies, the tragedies, the philosophies, and the histories. Since those earliest days men, and women, have sought to explore the world, the way they live, their philosophy and their soul, through story.

How can we live without freedom to read? How poor, how narrow this life if only one point of view is allowed to exist?

And she begins to write.

Agnoeo was an old man, set in his ways. His amenable and quiet wife of many years had passed away some time ago. The couple had three sons and three daughters. They had all taken wives and husbands, and lived close by, the wives and daughters making sure to look after Agnoeo as they went about their days. But at night when the women were in their homes taking care of their husbands, he was all alone and grew more and more morose as time went by.

One day, Agnoeo was taking a stroll beside the river when he heard a young woman singing a beautiful song. He stopped and listened, mesmerized by the sound. When he caught sight of the woman herself, he fell instantly in love. She was as beautiful as her voice, tall and slim with sleek dark hair and bright green eyes. Her name, he discovered, was Philomena. But when he tried to engage her in conversation, he could find nothing interesting to say to her. She told him she was bored of this small village, that she wanted to travel to the ends of the earth, to learn its secrets and to pass them on in her songs, so that other people might learn those secrets too. Agnoeo had lived a dull life, he realized, never leaving his village, doing the same thing each day. He had had no need to leave or think about doing things differently. Why should he? He had all he needed right here. But not anymore. That night, sitting alone in his house, Agnoeo told himself he was not so old to take such a lovely young woman to be his wife. She would brighten up the place with her beautiful song and her youthful vivaciousness.

So Agnoeo prayed to Athena, the goddess of wisdom, to make him wise and witty so that Philomena would fall in love with him and agree to become his wife. He made her offerings of the finest olives, flowers, milk, and incense. That night, when he heard the hoot of an owl from a nearby tree, he knew Athena would answer his prayers.

The next day when he encountered Philomena, he found he stood just a little taller than before, more energy flooded his body than it had for a very long time, and when he spoke to her, he found himself speaking with such wit and eloquence that it wasn't long before Philomena was utterly smitten and agreed with a full heart to become his wife.

As the days went by, Agnoeo grew used to his new skill with words. Soon the whole village was in his thrall. How did we not know that Agnoeo was such a clever man? they said in wonder to each other. How have we only just discovered what good company he is, how wise, how funny? Soon, Agnoeo's house saw a steady stream of visitors. Each evening, they would flock there, and his house was filled with laughter and conversation, music and the beautiful voice of his new wife, Philomena.

But in the days following his wedding, Agnoeo grew tired. When he tried to amuse and enthrall, his words fell flat, and he drew only withering looks. His house slowly emptied, and his mood darkened. The gods were smiling on him no longer. Only Philomena remained. Soon he grew weary of her bright woman's chatter. He didn't need to hear about the books she read, the poetry or the plays. Stop your wittering, he told her, shutting his ears to her words, so he couldn't know what wisdom she had to offer, what stories she could cheer him with, what songs could ease his sorrow. He was not interested in what she had to say at all.

It wasn't long before Agnoeo could bear Philomena's presence no longer. Why had Athena punished him so? He made another desperate prayer to her to forever shut this woman up so he could have some peace and quiet. But Agnoeo had angered Athena, and she decided to punish him for his stubborn ignorance. In a fit of rage, she turned Philomena into a nightingale, banished forever from her home.

Philomena traveled far and wide on her new wings, looking down upon the earth and seeing all there was to see. But each and every night as the moon rose, she would return to sing of all that she had seen and learned right outside Agnoeo's window, keeping him from sleep until dawn broke. Agnoeo lived the rest of his days in lonely misery. He would never learn about the wonderful things Philomena sang of, because he could not understand the songs of birds.

Milly sits back and smiles to herself. She envisages a series of these Tales, or perhaps, Myths and Fables. She's made this one up, of course, but there are others she could write. She thinks of a twist on Theogony. After Chaos came the earth, then the Titans, followed by the gods. There is a metaphor in there, surely, for democracy and autocracy. Instead of the Titan, Cronus, swallowing his children for fear they would one day defeat him, Autocracy can swallow all the books.

Okay, it needs work, but that will be for another day. She yawns, tired suddenly, and puts away her work. George will be home soon, and she must make the evening meal. In the morning, she will post this to Myra.

Three days later, Myra calls.

"Milly, darling, we have nothing like it at *My Life*. I ran it past the board at our meeting this morning and they have said yes, one a week for six weeks. Keep them short and snappy. Busy housewives don't have much time for reading. I'm assuming you have more like this?"

"Of course! That's wonderful, thank you."

"We'll pay you the going rate."

Milly grows warm at the thought of having her own money. Money George doesn't need to know about.

She twists the phone cord around in her fingers.

"I don't have my own bank account, Myra," she says finally. "And George doesn't really approve of me doing this."

"Ah," Myra says, quiet for a moment, thinking. "We can make out the checks to cash. Then, you could pick up the checks once a month and simply cash them at any bank. You won't need an account for that. And how about a pseudonym?"

"Oh, yes. I would be grateful."

"Can you think of one? Just a Christian name will do." Milly's mind is momentarily blank, then she thinks of the manuscript, and its author, Charlotte Guillard. There is irony in the meaning of her name and the words hidden behind the code.

"How about Charlotte?"

"Okay . . ."

"It means, *free*."

Myra's throaty chuckle floats down the line.

"How very apt. I look forward to working with you, Charlotte."

Chapter 18

Charlotte

Paris, July 1552

It wasn't until the day's work was done, supper had been cleared away, and the sparrows quit their twittering and took to the trees in the garden to roost that Charlotte found a moment of quietude to take out the box containing the manuscript the nun had given her earlier that day. By candlelight in her study, she carefully removed the bundle of pages laced together with leather ties.

Charlotte found her hands were trembling so much the pages shook. Her head swam and the room swayed as though it, and she, were drifting somewhere above the city, floating in the warm night air. *Dear sweet Jesu, what is happening?*

I'm merely tired, she told herself firmly; the day had been long and really she should be in bed. She stood and went to help herself to wine from the carafe that stood, regularly refilled by her maid, Sophie, upon the bookshelf. *Wine replaces sleep* had been Berthold's mantra, and of late, she found herself taking his advice and drinking more of it. She hoped that Berthold, in his wisdom, was right.

Back at her desk, Charlotte took a deep breath, opened the manuscript, and began to read. Lysbette had written the work in Latin and illustrated it in her own hand. The illustrations were crude drawings and lacked vitality and form. She was no artist, Charlotte concluded, and hoped the words were better in skill and content. The title was curious and simple.

Just one word: *Alius*. Another.

Charlotte took a mouthful of wine, heavy and sour on her tongue. There was no explanation, no further words. Another what? She turned to the next page. Here, more text, written as a letter. Lysbette had addressed it, *To All the Women of Europe, and Elsewhere. Est Alius Modus.* There Is Another Way.

Curiouser and curiouser. And in honesty, somewhat *pompous*? Charlotte took another mouthful of wine, this second less of an assault on the tongue. By the time she was halfway down the glass, it began to taste almost pleasant. She read on.

What right have I, to address all women as my friend? Why should you listen, why read my words? Charlotte shifted in her seat. It was as though Lysbette had read her mind from beyond the living realm and was talking directly to her. A shiver ran down her back. She continued to read, but the voice she heard inside her head as she read the words was Lysbette's.

Women, friends, I hope you will read and ponder. I hope you will talk with one another. I hope, in time, and I have no idea how much time, you might all rise together, as one great body, so that men may see we women deserve an equal place in this world. That we have the brains and the strength, the courage and uniquely female talents, to make all our lives better. It won't be easy. Men will resist. They will tell us over and over we are inferior, that we are weak and stupid. They will tell us we are dangerous seducers, that we are witches and harbor the devil beneath our skin. They will tell us it is we who drive them to their terrible behavior, that we have no place in this realm of men. None of this is true. We must no longer shoulder the blame for their weakness, or their desires. We must no longer allow them to hold us down.

There is another way.

I have lived a strange life, but one that has given me, I humbly submit, an unusual wisdom. During my life I have been, variously, treasured daughter, penniless orphan, ward of one of the most venerated men of England, educated nun, wife. I have seen and experienced the world from each of those vantages and I have read widely, from the teachings of the ancients to the most modern thinkers of today. I have read of past civilizations and civilizations only recently discovered in the outer reaches of the world. We, in Europe, live in troubled times. If we are to save ourselves from disaster, we must consider different ways to live.

Many years ago . . .

A dreadful knocking and banging jolted Charlotte from sleep. Her head was upon the desk, her mouth open and dry like she had been parched in a desert for weeks. She sat up, her joints creaking and her neck sore from the awkward angle at which she must have fallen asleep on her desk. She rubbed her eyes and her neck, her head pounding in time with the distant knocking at the front door. The candles were burnt out, and pale moonlight seeped in at the window.

Downstairs, the banging stopped. Whoever was at the door must have been admitted to the house.

Before her lay Lysbette's open manuscript. She must have fallen asleep as she read. Memory of the content flooded back, and she closed it, meaning to push it to the back of a drawer in the desk before anyone saw but she was too late for at that moment, Sophie appeared in the doorway.

"*Madame!*" she cried, running toward her mistress. She placed her hand on her heaving chest. "Thanks be to heaven. Your bed was empty! I was so worried."

Charlotte snorted, gathering herself. "What catastrophe did you imagine had befallen me, Sophie? Did you think I'd broken my neck on the stairs? Or been snatched in the night by a thief?"

Sophie raised her chin. "No, Madame. I merely wondered if you had taken to walking about the city again, just as you did two nights ago." Her voice was crisp and firm. Sophie was smart and had razor-sharp senses. She knew Charlotte too well. She'd been her loyal maid for more than thirty years after all.

Charlotte sighed. "All right. I wasn't out in the city; I was here all along. I must have fallen asleep over my reading."

She looked down at the manuscript open on the desk, then back at her maid. Sophie was staring right at its open pages.

Charlotte had taught her maid to read and write Latin some years ago. But could she read it upside down?

Sophie pursed her lips. "I pray you won't go getting yourself caught up in anything you shouldn't, Madame." Sophie had a habit of making the sort of bold statements maids should not be making to their mistresses. Charlotte should chide her to mind her place, but she let it pass, as she always did. Since she had lost her husbands Sophie had come to be much more to Charlotte than merely a maid. She was a friend, a confidante. Her loyalty was without question.

She was considering whether to tell Sophie everything about Lysbette and the manuscript when Sophie said, "Indeed, there are two gentlemen downstairs who wish to see you."

Charlotte frowned. "Who are they?"

"The commissioner and a Monsieur de Mouchy, Madame, from the university. Should I bring them up?"

Charlotte's breath caught in her throat. Instantly, she was wide awake. She gathered the pages of Lysbette's work. "Take these to my chamber, please, Sophie. Hide them, for now, beneath the mattress. I will find somewhere better later. Two nights ago, a woman was murdered on account of this manuscript." Sophie met her eyes with a steady gaze. "If you would rather not play a part in this, I will understand, and we'll say no more of it." She looked about her. "But I'll need to hide it well somewhere."

Sophie held out her hands. "I'll take it, Madame."

"Nobody can know of its existence, understand?"

Sophie nodded and took the pages, concern deepening the lines on her face.

"Of course, Madame. I will do that first, then bring the men up."

"No. I don't want them here. I'll come down." This room was her sanctuary. She couldn't bear the thought of Antoine de Mouchy sullying it with his noxious presence.

The men were waiting, stern faced, arms crossed behind their backs, in what was once the library, but since adopting the upstairs study for her own space, Charlotte now used this as a formal room in which to receive visitors. Here, the drapes were heavy, the furniture dark and solid. There was a lingering scent of dust. The place had an air of dreary neglect rather than warm welcome. It was the perfect place to put unwanted guests who might otherwise be tempted to outstay their welcome. The shelves bore a collection of Charlotte's own, carefully curated religious and legal works. Serious, dull volumes, too, collected by her dead husbands. Those of a more scientific nature, of astrology and medicine, of modern thought and poetry were kept upstairs, in Charlotte's private quarters.

"Good evening to you, sirs," she said entering.

The commissioner nodded. "Apologies for the late intrusion, Madame."

"And the nature of your business?"

The two men exchanged a glance.

"You have met my friend, Monsieur de Mouchy?" the commissioner asked.

Charlotte looked at the man properly. She had heard of him, of course, but never yet made his acquaintance, something she was not sorry for. Antoine de Mouchy, canon and rector of the University of Paris, professor of the Sorbonne, *Inquisitor Fidei*. Heretic hunter, and one of the most feared men in Paris. Standing right here, inside her house. Her empty stomach curdled.

But instead of the man of presence she had expected, de Mouchy was barely taller than Charlotte herself. She had the sudden urge to laugh, but she bit her lip. *Do not be fooled, Charlotte*, she imagined Berthold saying. *Pathetic men feel they have something to prove and are often the most dangerous of all.*

"I am pleased to meet you," Charlotte said, nodding her greeting. "Your reputation proceeds you."

"I am glad to hear that," said the man, lifting his weak chin. She met his eyes. Hard little eyes. Like bullets.

"Please, sit."

Once they were settled, de Mouchy nodded at the commissioner to begin.

"Monsieur Hatt has left Paris rather suddenly."

"Oh?"

"His wife has yet to be buried, and we can find no trace of him. It would appear he has left without word. It is most irksome."

"But what about her funeral?"

The commissioner sighed. "It must be the pauper's grave, unless someone else were to . . ." He left the sentence hanging, unfinished.

Charlotte said nothing. Her instinct was to offer to pay for the poor, murdered woman to have a proper Christian burial, especially since she had once been a bride of Christ. And yet . . . Intuition warned her this might not be a good idea.

"Why would he leave in that way?"

"Perhaps," de Mouchy spoke now, in silky tones that sent a shudder down Charlotte's spine, "he knew of his wife's dalliance with the devil and wished to distance himself."

"Sir?" Charlotte thought of the words in Lysbette's letter addressed to the women of Europe about the tyranny of men, and heat flashed through her veins. "May I ask, what has this to do with me? I had the misfortune of coming upon her body in the street, a shock I am still recovering from. I met her once, when she visited my shop, as I told the commissioner. Other than that, this woman was a stranger to me. So please, gentlemen, enlighten me as to your presence in my house at this hour?"

De Mouchy got up and began to pace across the room, hands clasped behind his back. "Madame Guillard, it seems to me you are involved whether you wish to be or not." He took a breath, looked down at the floor as he spoke. "Word reached me . . ." *Whose word?* ". . . that Madame Hatt did not merely visit your shop for a few minutes, as you would have us believe. No, indeed, she stayed at your establishment for more than two hours and was observed not to remain in the shop. She emerged, in fact, from the house. It therefore seems to me that her business here was not merely to discuss poetry."

Charlotte swallowed as fear crawled like ants across her skin. She forced herself to speak steady and strong.

"Sir, your witnesses are unreliable. I do not know what you imply, nor do I recall being asked for how long this woman stayed on my premises, but yes, she was tired and a little overcome. Perhaps by the heat or her travels or both and hence she took a rest and some refreshment within. If you can find someone to attest to the content of our discussions, good luck to you. I have nothing to hide."

De Mouchy smirked. "I believe, Madame, that contrary to all that you say, Madame Hatt came here with writings of a heretical nature she wanted you to print. Her husband left her things behind him. In among them, we found letters and a page of vile and poisonous content that must have become separated from the rest." He paused.

"What sort of content?"

He ignored her question and continued. "What interests *me* at this moment is that this woman chose to visit *you*, above any other printing house in Paris. It is my belief that it is because your print mark is clearly displayed upon condemned books by that heretic, Erasmus, that she thought she would find a like-minded devil worshipper in *you*."

"Monsieur de Mouchy, I assure you, my soul, and my reputation, are pure."

He swung around now to face her, so close she could see the tiny red veins in the whites of his eyes. "Be very careful, Madame Guillard, for I am watching you."

Charlotte swayed backward as his breath, warm, wet, sour, touched her cheeks. She had the urge to rush from the room and wash the foul-smelling filth of it away.

"Search the place, Monsieur de Mouchy," she said, waving her arm in the direction of the workshops. "You will find nothing on my printing presses that the King himself would not wish to read." She stood firm and the room fell silent as they held each other's gaze.

De Mouchy broke first, letting out a noise somewhere between a laugh and a cough.

"Well," he said, cracking his knuckles, loud as gunshot. "Today that will not be necessary. But should any knowledge reach me that your involvement with this *witch* is more than a casual acquaintance, then I shall return. Indeed, perhaps I shall commission you to print a few works of my own. For now, good day to you, Madame."

"*W-witch?*" Charlotte spluttered. "How come this poor, dead creature is now being labeled a witch?"

De Mouchy was already heading for the door. The commissioner at least had the good grace to look embarrassed.

"I'm sorry, Madame," he said. "It was I who found the stray page together with the letters. I will spare you the details, but . . ." He shook his head. "There were some treacherous and heretical writings. The woman was clearly possessed of a tortured and twisted mind. It seems most likely the devil had found his way inside her and, well, I understand why the husband—poor man—took his leave." He glanced after de Mouchy. "Do not concern yourself with him. He is under much pressure from the Parlement to capture heretics and clean the vile undercurrent from the streets of Paris. I doubt he will bother you again, Madame Guillard."

And then he, too, was gone.

Charlotte sank into the nearest chair, placing a hand over her heart, beating as it was like the hooves of a panicked horse. She thought of Lysbette's manuscript tucked beneath her mattress and prayed to the holy Mother of God that the commissioner was right. She thought about what Berthold and Claude would make of all this. She imagined the advice they might give to her.

Get rid of the manuscript, Charlotte. The reputation of Soleil d'Or comes before everything.

She sat for a long time, thinking. When she was recovered enough, she stood, a little unsteady at first, then firm. Charlotte made her way back up to her chamber and pulled the manuscript from the mattress. She held it in her hands and thought of the hours Lysbette must have put into writing it. She sat heavily on the bed and reminded herself of the part of the letter she had read before she fell asleep. Then she read the rest of it.

Many years ago, when I was a young girl, I read a fictional account of an island that went by the name Utopia. The account had been written by the great Sir Thomas More, who was most dear to me. I am haunted, still, all these years later by the terrible end he met. An irony, given the subject matter of his fictional world. That book had a profound effect upon my young mind. In the intervening years, I have seen my world change beyond anything I could have imagined. I have known loss and terror and seen unspeakable violence, all conducted by those certain they are on the side of right and following God's will. An easy story to make to oneself, to justify wrongs done to others.

But I believe it is within the realm of the mortal world, within each of us, that the power for a better life lies.

The idea of Utopia was unique and, to my mind, good but flawed. For the island to be a peaceful and happy place for its citizens, it relied on a fair king, a good ruler. But in all history there have been as many unfair and cruel rulers as there have been fair ones. And within states, rulers come in more forms than princes and kings. Mere common people are at their mercy, fair or otherwise. Lords and masters, clerics, landlords, employers. And for us women: husbands, fathers, sons, uncles, and, I venture, all men . . .

I'd been content living in the company of women at the great Abbey of Barking. Together we created a community of women who ran a huge venture happily and competently. Until the day my world was destroyed, and, forced by circumstances, a new life of travel ensued. And hence the journey to a place I shall introduce you to in the pages of this book. A place so extraordinary, you will barely believe it could exist. But exist it does, far from England, far from Europe, in the lands of the East. Its name is in a strange tongue, so for the purposes of this account, it shall be called Alius.

Charlotte closed the pages. She thought of how she could throw them one by one onto a fire. She could shove them into her pouch with heavy stones and throw it into the muddy waters of the Seine. She continued to stare at the pages, thinking of how she had devoted her life to the preservation of written words. To the spreading of them. She thinks of Lysbette's desperation to preserve and publish this work. The fact that she must have died for it.

I may get rid of it, husbands, she thinks, *but not until I have read and pondered its contents. Only then shall I decide.*

Chapter 19

Lysbette

Barking Abbey, England, 1535

A letter for you, Dame." The servant girl stepped forward and held out the sealed message with a little curtsy and a dip of the head.

Lysbette looked up from her book. It was a glorious May morning, and the sun streamed in through the library window like liquid honey. The curling letters and sloping hand she recognized to be Mercy's. She unsealed the letter.

My dearest Lysbette,

I am sorry to write to you with terrible news. We are all here in a state of anguish, but I felt certain you would wish to know. Sir Thomas, who last year was arrested by King Henry's men and taken to the Tower in light of his continued refusal to swear his allegiance to Anne Boleyn and her future children as rightful heirs, has been charged with treason and will soon face trial. . I need not tell you what this means for our dear father, and the wider family, should he continue to hold firm against the King in this regard.

Only Margaret and Alice are permitted to visit him. But I wonder if you would be so good as to write him a letter? I know how he always valued your judgment along with Margaret's.

Perhaps between you, you can persuade him to give way. God will forgive him as he knows my father's heart to be true. But I fear Sir Thomas will not move from his chosen path.

We are in turmoil, as I'm sure you can imagine. I know this news will bring you torment too. But please, with your clever words, you may change his mind yet.

Yours with fondest love,
Mercy

Lysbette sat for a long time, watching the honeyed light play across the open pages of her book. But the ink blurred beneath her eyes and instead of words, she saw the mighty white walls of the Tower of London, as it had looked when they journeyed here five years before, dwarfing the buildings that lay in its shadows. She recalled Sir Thomas, warm and comforting beside her, and the rank, damp stench of the river as the barge slipped silently by. She shuddered to think of him locked in a cell, deep within the Tower's malevolent walls. She remembered the glimpse of the severed, putrefying heads of traitors atop their posts and her stomach heaved at the thought of Sir Thomas's head rotting there, too, should he remain obstinate in his refusal of King Henry's wishes. How could such a thing come to pass? It was unthinkable.

But what could she possibly write that would change his mind? She knew how deeply he would have thought about this. How no words she could conjure would touch him, not when God's almighty grace would not allow him to acquiesce to King Henry's demands. There could be nobody more careful to consider fully all that was asked of him. He would have sought, not only the advice of fellow intellectuals, but also that of God himself, of Mary and Jesus, and all the saints. And this was his brave conclusion. He would be resigned to his fate, and there was nothing that she or Margaret would be able to say that would change his mind.

But she could try.

Words, she knew, thinking of *Utopia*, of Erasmus, of Plato and Aristotle, those of kings, popes, and the Bible itself, held the power to change everything.

If only she could find the right ones.

Lysbette stood abruptly, put away her book and her writing things, and made for the chapel. She must pray for enlightenment.

God, it seemed, was deaf to her entreaties, just as he had been to Margaret's and, no doubt, to Alice's too. Week by torturous week passed with Sir Thomas becoming older and weaker, and those who loved him more desperate than ever, but more resigned too. Lysbette's pleading letters did not, in the end, change his mind. On July 1, 1535, at Sir Thomas's trial for treason, he remained silent in the face of a certain result. Six days later, having been granted the rights of the aristocrat to a better, swifter, less painful death, he was beheaded, to the outrage of the faithful all across Europe. Swiftly, he was named a martyr.

But Lysbette was left with a gaping wound she was certain would never heal. She had failed. Her words had made no difference.

While to the outside world Sir Thomas More had stood solid and faithful, even in the face of his own death, for her, he was all she had left in the way of a family. He was father, teacher, supporter, protector. Suddenly, with a pang, she longed for John Haydon. It was some time since she had thought of him, but in that moment, she imagined, only he might understand her loss. But she was alone. True, she had her sisters in the abbey, but for how long? The King was on a mission to close the smaller monasteries around the country. It was only a matter of time before he came to steal wealth from the larger ones too. His commissioners had already visited the abbess, walking around Barking for days with their notebooks, marking down relics, the contents of the library, noting the treasures and the value of their art. She had seen the greed in their eyes, the worry in the knitted brows of the abbess. Henry's insatiable appetite for money to fund his wars was as unquenchable as his thirst for a son. Soon, the nuns whispered to each other between the cloisters, the King and his greedy men would come to take their beautiful abbey from them.

In the days that passed after Sir Thomas's execution, Lysbette withdrew into herself. She spent hour upon hour in the chapel, kneeling and praying until her knees grew sore and her mind exhausted. She wasn't his daughter, but she felt his death as keenly as if she were. His loss was like the gaping mouth of a great monster who had swallowed her, pulling her down into its dreadful bowels where she would rot from the outside in. Down here, in the hellish pit of grief's belly, God's love abandoned her. She screamed into the void, and he remained silent. Down here, she would suffer pain and anguish for all eternity unless she could find a way out.

And so she did the only thing she could think of that might rescue her soul.

She wrote.

And in the writing, somehow, slowly, painfully, she crawled her way out of the grief-beast's belly, one word at a time, until all that was left was a knot of sadness at the center of all she did.

All around her, the world seemed ever more precarious and the writing saved her. It started with a letter addressed to all women. But what she had first envisioned to be an anonymous pamphlet urging women to come together morphed into something much more. Sir Thomas's execution, *all* the executions, the book burning, the hysteria. It felt so urgent that people find a new tolerance for one another. It was inspired, of course by Sir Thomas's *Utopia*, but with a twist. While his idea was perhaps told in jest, hers was deadly serious. If the world was to survive these convulsions of hatred of man for each other, they must find a different way to be.

After months of pondering, she could see, in full and glorious color, the world she was creating in her imagination. She would illustrate her work, too, she decided. She was no artist, but she began to carefully sketch plants, insects, animals, and birds that would inhabit her world. All God's creatures, and a few more. While creating, she could shut out the concerns of the outside world. She worked by candlelight late into the night. She rose before the bells calling the nuns to prayer rang out in the early morning.

Writing became her solace and her friend.

It became her everything.

The nation I once had the privilege to call home is named *Alius*. It is a temperate region, with warm summers and mild winters, never experiencing extremes of hot or cold, wet or drought. It is not a large country, but it is diverse in topography. It boasts a mountain range, large and fertile plains where crops are grown, ample lakes and rivers stocked with fish, extensive forests and natural resources, as well as a good coastline with enough depth for ports and easy access for foreign trade, which is plentiful, and brings wealth and benefit to the region. Until the year 1529, Alius remained undiscovered by European adventurers.

Alius is a country the like of which is beyond the comprehensions of all the peoples of Europe. In this account I shall lay all of it bare to you, dear reader, in such detail you will come to believe you have visited it yourself. And for the time you live between the pages of this book, you shall be glad of it. Glad to escape your own troubled land, where kings and powerful men in the false name of our Lord go about with such ruthless, murderous intent, so blind with hunger for power and gold, that through their deceitful messages they are willing to take our world and all with it into the fiery pits of hell. Alius will show you a different way. One where men and women can live in peace and honesty. One where tolerance and respect replace greed and tyranny. One where the downtrodden, the weak, and female rise up and prove they are equally worthy. What you read here may shock you, but I pray, open your mind to the possibilities within. Perhaps a different way may be the better one if we are to have any hope of saving ourselves.

Chapter 20

Milly

Levittown, Long Island, New York, January 1953

S ure you won't come with us?" George hovers in the entrance hall, the children, bundled into their winter coats and boots, hopping with excitement at his feet. "Our snowman will have a much better chance of winning with your artistic flair."

An icy blast of air flows in through the open door, and Milly glances at the disappointment in George's face. Saturdays are for them to spend time together. He is largely absent during the week, often working late or attending client events. Lately it feels as though they might live entirely separate lives were it not for the children anchoring them together. She feels a stab of regret. The manuscript *could* wait. She should go with them, join in this impromptu snowman-building competition in the park after the heaviest snowfall of the winter. But the pull of the manuscript holds her back, especially now that Winton has died. She owes it to his memory to solve the manuscript's puzzle.

Since the revelation that the underlying language is likely Greek, not Latin, Milly feels one step closer to making a breakthrough, and time alone at the weekend to work on it is rare. And besides, it will be nice for the children, Edward in particular, to have George all to themselves.

"I'm really not feeling well, George," she says, leaning in for a hug. "Terrible headache. I need to lie down for a bit."

George strokes her hair. "You rest up." He gives her cheeks a gentle pinch. "Lately, you seem as though you have a lot on your mind. You would tell me if anything was wrong, wouldn't you, Milly-Moo?"

"Of course, I would. It's nothing, George. It's just the weather, or something." She waves them off and shuts the front door, listening to their excited chatter fade until the house descends into silence. Telling herself she isn't a bad mother, Milly climbs the stairs and fetches the manuscript from the shoebox at the back of her cupboard.

Settling herself on the bed, propped up with pillows, she turns to the first of the four astrology pages. It is here that the blazing sun with Charlotte Guillard's printing mark at its center shines the biggest and the brightest. And somehow, this feels significant.

Milly considers what she knows so far. First, that she has the manuscript in the correct order, and second, that the language underlying the code is Greek, not Latin. Third, that Charlotte Guillard, a well-respected, apparently religiously conservative printer, had a hand in producing this manuscript.

She also knows that the coder did not use a simple substitution technique, but something more complex, making the code harder to break. Instead, they used a polyphonic technique, so that each character represents more than one plaintext letter. She knows this because the frequency of the characters used throughout the manuscript is spread fairly evenly. If one character represented one plaintext letter, then the characters representing the letters that occur more often in plaintext writing, such as *e* or *a* would appear more often too. What she doesn't know, of course, is how many letters each character might represent, or the key to work out which.

Milly studies the first astrology page with the flaming sun in the middle, its rays fanning out among the scattering of stars. There are four sections divided by lines, like spokes, which fan out to three rings. The inner contains "words" made up of groups of five letter-like characters running inside them. In the middle ring are rough, outline drawings of ordinary women undertaking day-to-day tasks in their work: shepherding, working in the fields, visiting a fish market, traveling by horse. In the top ring, above each of the women, are the twelve signs of the zodiac. In the center are four sections spanning out from the sun's shining face, each filled with rays and stars and each containing the images of beautifully decorated regal men wearing crowns and robes and carrying scepters and trinkets that indicate ruling or royalty. In comparison to the women who are small and apparently insignificant, roughly sketched in outline, the men are exquisitely colored and dominate the page. This arrangement seems at odds with the rest of the manuscript where men, if there are any at all, are in the periphery, while the woman dominate. Here, the eye is naturally drawn to the men. Their images so vibrant, they practically jump from the page.

Ignoring the illustrations for a moment, there is something about the design of this wheel that still reminds Milly of the decoding ring of a Caesar cipher. She looks at the twelve signs of the zodiac, divided equally into the central four sections.

Milly thinks for a few moments, trying to put herself into the head of Charlotte Guillard. She has an image of her: a strong jaw, bright eyes, neat gray hair beneath her hood. She is sure these astrology pages hold the clues. Just like in ancient Greece, imagery in the sixteenth century was full of symbolism with well-understood meanings. From colors to animals to icons, they all meant something. Purple for royalty. Red for power. Dogs for loyalty. Serpents for sin, and so on. But in this manuscript, the meanings are obscured by layers of decoys and red herrings, to put the viewer off the real trail.

Thanks to the letter from the Bodleian Library that Winton shared with her, answering her inquiry about Charlotte Guillard and Le Soleil d'Or, she knows that Charlotte Guillard was the twice-widowed printer of one of the most preeminent printing businesses in Paris. She was a Catholic, and most of the work she produced was religious. But she also printed works of the Christian humanists of the day, including, interestingly, the man labeled as heretical by both Catholics and Protestants, Desiderius Erasmus. Reading about him, Milly concludes he was ahead of his time in his writings and ideas, proclaiming to love liberty and asserting that heretics, witches, and books should not be burned.

Milly pulls her attention back to the manuscript. So what was the seemingly sensible, conformist, and conservative Charlotte doing printing the works of Erasmus? Is this a tiny clue that she was too afraid to tell the world what she really thought?

She studies the preening men through her magnifier.

In one hand, each of the four men are waving their symbol of power—scepter, crown, gold cup, and orb. The other hand is clasping the outer edge of the inner circle, as though to balance or steady themselves. She looks at the symbol above each man's hand. There are four of them. Could this be a clue? Or is it a decoy? She thinks about how her eye has been drawn to them. She decides to ignore them and moves her magnifier instead to look at the "words" in the inner circle. She notices that a drawing of a woman carrying out her daily task is situated above certain characters in some of the blocks of text, and above, is a sign of the zodiac. That pattern is repeated on each of the four astrology pages that appear at intervals in the book. She turns to the other three similar astrology pages. On each one, although at first sight

FPO

Art TK

the pattern looks the same, the characters creating the words in the inner circle are *different* in each one of the astrology pages. Assuming the astrology pages contain the key, then could it be that at each astrology page, the key changes? Thus the plaintext letter or letters represented by one character would change four times through the book, following each new astrology page. If that is right, that would explain the roughly even distribution of characters throughout the book.

Milly leans back against the pillows and closes her eyes, thinking. There are twelve signs of the zodiac. There are twenty-six letters in the modern Latin alphabet, twenty-three in the classical Latin, and twenty-four in ancient Greek. Twice twelve is twenty-four. She feels prickles at the back of her neck. She focuses for now on only the first of the astrology pages.

Slowly, carefully, Milly makes a note of each of the characters that arise in the inner ring below each zodiac sign. If she ignores the accents, there are twelve. If she *includes* the same characters but *with* the accents, there are twenty-four. Could they, therefore, represent the letters of the ancient Greek alphabet?

The remaining forty-six characters she has identified in the manuscript that *don't* appear on the astrology pages she thinks must represent place-names, character names, commonly arising words, phrases, syllables, or dates. She sets those aside and returns to the twelve characters on the astrology pages, and their accented pairs. It really feels like she is getting somewhere. If only she could tell Winton. She takes a deep breath. *Slow down, Milly. You aren't there yet.* The key must somehow relate to the zodiac.

Above the outer ring and below the zodiac signs are the small, insipid drawings of the women who appear to be going about their daily tasks. The first woman is standing with a shepherd's hook with a lamb beside her. The hook points down toward the edge of the inner ring and the first character that sits beneath. She studies the woman very closely with her magnifying glass, then the lamb. She almost missed it, but then she sees the letters *CG* are printed in tiny writing on the side of the lamb, just above its front leg. They are so tiny, it looks like a mistake by the illustrator. The first sign of the zodiac in ancient Greece was Aries, symbolized by a lamb. She looks at the first character in the group of characters that sit beneath the woman's feet. *Π*. Could *Π* therefore be an *A* for Aries? Or just because *A* is the first, the beginning of the alphabet and the first sign of the zodiac?

If Milly is right about the plaintext letters being in ancient Greek, then each character, because there are only twelve, should represent two letters, thus *Π* could also represent the thirteenth letter, which would be *N* in the Greek alphabet (*ν*). Looking back at the groups of characters, Milly sees the same character, *Π*, but with a tiny circular accent above it. Could the accent denote it represents the thirteenth plaintext letter, the *N*(*ν*) in the Greek alphabet? The next group of characters sit beneath the second zodiac sign, Taurus, the bull. Looking back at the blocks of text she tries the second character beside *Π* to see if it represents the second letter in the ancient Greek alphabet (*B*), and searches for its accented equivalent, which should be the fourteenth letter of the Greek alphabet, and so on.

But this doesn't work as she only ends up with meaningless text.

She throws her pen down in frustration. Screws her eyes shut. *Think.*

The women.

She opens her eyes. Stares at them, and the signs of the zodiac above. Of course! The clue is the women. They aren't going about their daily tasks, they are embodying the sign of the zodiac above them. The shepherd has a lamb (Aries), the woman leading a bull by the ring in its nose (Taurus), the two girls skipping are twins (Gemini), the woman at the fish market (Cancer).

Her heart quickens. Each is positioned exactly above a character in a block of text. So, could the following text spell the name of each zodiac sign? There are too many characters in each section for the names of each sign, and too many blocks of text, but perhaps that is a decoy.

Using the Greek alphabet, Milly carefully transcribes the first block beneath Aries, and the characters beneath, stopping at the fifth character. Then she moves to the block beneath Taurus and the woman with the bull.

It works.

She's done it. The nonaccented characters form the first half of the alphabet, the accented characters forming the second half. Swiftly, she transcribes all the characters against the ancient Greek alphabet and does the same with the other three astrology pages, where the characters represent different letters.

Then, barely able to breathe, she turns to the first page of text in the manuscript and begins transcribing the text. She has the ancient Greek dictionary Susan managed to source for her beside her, but she finds she only occasionally needs it. Her own knowledge of the language is quickly returning. It is as though Charlotte is speaking to her from the depths of the book itself.

She cannot work out every word, because there are characters she still doesn't understand, but by using guesswork to fill in some blanks, clear as day, and remembering to work from left to right, then right to left, in the way ancient Greek was written, she manages to decode the following:

FPO

Art TK

Dear Reader,

If you are reading this, then . . . I speak to a friend of the written word. The . . . pages are not my words, but those of a most . . . woman, once a nun, by the name of Lysbette Angiers who met with a violent and untimely end.

I have no . . . . . . that men of high birth, princes, bishops, sovereigns, scholars, lawyers, and all others who wield power . . . will pay heed to . . . , for men pay little attention to the whims of mere women.

But know this, . . . no banning of books . . . will abate a people's thirst for knowledge and a better life. No burning of literature, heretics, or witches will strangle the . . . new ideas. For unstoppable winds have already scattered ideas like seed into the far corners of the old world where they, at this very moment, are taking root and spreading like weeds amongst the . . .

The below account is all truth. The only fiction, I venture, is that which men of influence would have you believe for . . . If you seek truth, look behind their words at their deeds and motivations.

I pray, reader, you will spread what is written herein as far and wide as you see fit. It has been my life's work to do just this.

Charlotte Guillard, this year 1552

Milly lets the manuscript drop from her hands to the bed. She begins to shake. Sudden and unexpected, tears spring from her eyes, and she begins to sob. She isn't sure if this is with elation that she's finally cracked the key to the manuscript, or sorrow that she has nobody, especially Winton, to share this moment with. She is the only person in four hundred years who has been able to read the words of this book, or at least some of them. **She** wipes her eyes, blows her nose. With trembling hands, she **puts** the manuscript and her notebook back in the shoebox.

There is so much work to do, but she has cracked open the **door** and found her way inside. She begins to pace the bedroom, **back** and forth, back and forth. The enormity of it all is almost **too** much to bear. It's too big, too much responsibility.

Milly thinks of Charlotte's words. The woman, through **her** writing on that page, has been able to speak to her from hund**reds** of years in the past. There is magic in that. *I pray, reader, you will spread what is written herein as far and wide as you see fit. It has been my life's work to do just this.* What happened to the woman Lysbette? What was the violent and untimely end she met, and **why?**

She stands at the window, looking out. The street, hous**es,** and gardens are unrecognizable under a foot and a half of snow. Neighbors have been busy, shoveling it from pavements into **huge** banks, the winter sun turning the scene into a dazzling, danci**ng,** glittering white. Milly thinks of George and the children in **the** park, of Winton's widow urging her, *keep your family close, they really are the most precious things of all*, and she has a sudden **urge** to be with them. If she is quick, she might be in time to see **the** finishing touches to the snowman.

Milly turns away, runs downstairs.

She fumbles into her shoes, her coat, her hat. But just as **she** is ready, they are home, pink cheeked and frozen fingered, **filling** the air with energy, chatter, and laughter. She hugs them all.

"Feeling better?" George asks, eyes hopeful.

"Much better."

She smiles at her husband and wishes she could tell him w**hy.**

Chapter 21

Milly

Milly's days pass in a blur of working on the manuscript, writing stories for *My Life*, taking care of the children, and trying not to let the household tasks slip too much so that George will wonder what on earth she does all day. She whips around the house with the vacuum cleaner, the duster, and the mop, thankful the house is small. Each time she thinks about the first stories being published, she experiences a swoosh of nervous energy. What if they haven't gone down well and readers write in and complain?

More problematic is the shopping and the cooking, which gave her headaches even before she found her days filled with decrypting the manuscript. She buys a recipe book from Barnes & Noble, entitled *Fast Family Food for the Busy Housewife*, and hopes it will give her ideas to save herself even more time.

She manages to avoid Doris at the school gates most days, which is a blessing, and even asks Mrs. Humphries to have the children after school a couple of times a week. They love playing with Noel, and Mrs. Humphries is delighted to have them, brightening each time Milly asks her to babysit. She will find a way to thank her properly, sometime.

From the first days of Milly discovering the key, she has managed to piece together the meaning of some of the other frequently occurring characters. She has managed to transcribe around a third of the book into her notebook. What she is unraveling is so gripping that it doesn't feel like work at all. The author of the work, Lysbette Angiers, who died so brutally, according to Charlotte's opening note, invented a fantasy society, so detailed and beautifully described it was as easy to imagine as a modern-day film or novel. A *Utopia*, with a twist. The concepts are sophisticated and well developed, the ideas drawn not only from antiquity, as Lysbette had been born into an era that looked to that distant past for inspiration, but also, Milly thinks, from her experience living in a community of women in an abbey, as well as from her own imagination. The result, even now, is fresh, exciting, and unique. Milly thinks of her own position as a wife, of how she must keep the stories she writes each week for the magazine from her husband. How she can't even open her own bank account without his permission. And George is a good man. The best.

After the cleaning is finished, Milly has several hours until the children need to be collected so she takes the train into New York to visit the offices of *My Life* and collect her first check from Myra. As the townscapes slide by, she ponders what she will do once she has finished translating the manuscript. Who should she approach about it, and how? She feels protective of Charlotte Guillard and Lysbette Angiers. Once she tells someone about it, she will lose control. She imagines a museum publishing what she has found. It will be poured over by academics in some high-brow publication, possibly making a small paragraph in the back pages of the national press, possibly not. Then it will be locked away somewhere for safekeeping, or perhaps put on display beside other old books so that only those with a special interest will see. She thinks again of Charlotte's words at the end of her introduction, where it seemed Charlotte was speaking across the centuries, just to Milly. *I pray, reader, you will spread what is written herein as far and wide as you see fit. It has been my life's work to do just this.*

Seated in a swish meeting room on the sixth floor of *My Life*'s Madison Avenue offices, Myra brings Milly a check for $16 and a selection of letters readers have sent in. She puts the pile in front of Milly, raises her eyebrows to indicate Milly should read them, and lights a cigarette. Milly picks up the top one.

Dear Editor,

I'm really enjoying the new weekly column by Charlotte. These stories are so different and interesting. They really make you think! Keep them coming. I'm off to the library now to see if they have any books about Greek myths!

Yours gratefully,
Edith Hope, California

She picks up the next.

Dear Editor,

The feature you ran last week about childhood illnesses and what to look for was a godsend. . . .

She skips to the final paragraph.

I've been fascinated by the wonderful new stories by Charlotte. The first, about the husband whose wife was turned into the songbird, got me thinking. Have things really moved on for us women since ancient times? I'm not so sure. I've started to look at the world around in a slightly different way. Notice how in everything from everyday language (e.g., "like a girl," meant as an insult) to different expectations of behavior to life aspirations are in place to hold us women back. It is making me pull myself up short, as I catch myself having self-limiting thoughts for me and my daughter.

Thank you, Charlotte, for this insight.

Yours sincerely,
Mrs. D.E. Grant, Missouri

Dear My Life,

I'm a schoolteacher and an avid reader of all sorts of books. I've been so taken with the stories written by Charlotte that I have been cutting them out and taking them into my seventh-grade English class to discuss. They are wonderful. I would love to know if Charlotte has written any novels? If not, please tell her she should!

With admiration,
Henrietta Smyth, Boston

Milly reads them all while Myra sits quietly, smoking her cigarette. The letters talk about how her stories have made readers think, or how a particular story highlights an issue that struck a chord with a reader. A warm glow spreads inside at the words of praise, at how Milly has managed to reach out into the far corners of the United States of America and into the houses of all these women and touched them with her words.

And then it strikes her.

The manuscript.

The parallels, now she comes to think of it, are glaringly obvious. Chillingly so. Four hundred years ago, women were forced to encrypt a manuscript because it contained ideas that went against the prevailing ideals in a world on the precipice of change. Different times and a different cause, of course, but now, in a new era of repression, the pace of change was once again being resisted, only this time under the guise of the threat of communism. Why else were liberal ideals, civil rights, social security, feminism, homosexuals, being conflated with communists?

Milly could see with spine-tingling clarity that the message of this manuscript is as urgent now as it was then. *Spread what is written herein as far and wide as you see fit . . .*

Through *My Life*, the widest-read women's magazine in the country, Milly has the ability to reach more women than in any other way she can think of. She will adapt the message, of course, for a modern audience, if, that is, she can convince Myra to take it on. Her mind hops about as Myra waits for her to speak. She has told no one about the manuscript and is reluctant to for the same reason she can't tell George. How to explain why she has it? No, it would be better *not* to tell Myra about the manuscript yet. Too risky, and besides, what is important is the *message* she wants to spread. If she were to do that first, telling the story Lysbette so beautifully imagined in a serialization in the magazine, then, when it's finished, she will find a rational way to confess to Myra about the manuscript. Perhaps they could do a grand reveal of it in *My Life*. She feels in her gut Lysbette Angiers, writer of words, and Charlotte Guillard, printer of words, would approve of this plan. Winton, too, who, after all, was the one who had a hunch this was a book encrypted by women.

Milly clears her throat. "Myra," she says. "I've an idea for something new. A serialization of a new story."

Myra narrows her eyes. "But the Greek stories are popular with our readers, Milly. The circulation figures have been noticeably rising, and the letters praising you are pouring in. Why change what's working?"

Tension balls in Milly's throat. She has to convince Myra this is a good idea. "It will be similar in theme," she begins. "Indeed, it will be even more thought-provoking, as well as an engaging story. Stories have such power, don't they, Myra? Power to change lives. To change the world, even. Reading these letters"—she points at the pile—"I feel there is a desperate need for something . . . Something that could help lonely or frustrated women across America. Something that will get readers talking. That will be easier to do in one long story, where readers will be desperate to know what happens next. And they can only do that if they buy the next issue."

Myra nods slowly, taps the table with her nails as she thinks. "I don't see why you shouldn't run with something longer," she says at last. "And a serialization might be very popular . . . What did you have in mind?"

So Milly roughly outlines what she has read of the manuscript so far, but making it sound like this is her idea, not Lysbette's.

"Anything that keeps the readers buying is going to be popular with the board," Myra says. "And Charles Dickens certainly managed to make his serialized novels a popular thing. I'll need to run it by the board, but I'd like to give it a shot. When can you start?"

The PTA board members of Abbey Lane Elementary School have

hired a room at Bethpage Black Golf Course for the PTA's annual fundraising dinner. Tickets were an astronomical price, according to George, but they should do their bit, and it is all in a good cause, the profits going toward playground and sports equipment, art supplies and theater props. Mrs. Humphries has kindly agreed to babysit, and Milly, in her best dress and hat, walks arm in arm with George into the clubhouse.

Everyone is standing in the bar, talking about President Eisenhower and how he has refused clemency for the Rosenbergs.

"It's a good thing," opines one man. "Sends out a strong message that there will be zero tolerance of these commie bastards. They've been allowed to operate under the radar for too long."

Milly can't help herself. "From what I understand, though, the evidence against Ethel was weak. They have two children aged ten and six. What about them? They will be left orphans. Those poor children."

The man guffaws. Then he bends down toward Milly, keeping his voice slow and steady as though he is talking to a young child. "They should have thought of *that* before spying for the Soviets then, shouldn't they?"

"But what if it was *him* not *her*," Milly persists.

"Who cares?" The man shrugs. "She was his wife. She should have known what he was doing. Wives always *know*. And she said nothing. Which means she agrees with him, so it's right she should die too . . ."

A ball of hot indignation rises inside Milly, and she opens her mouth to reply but George silences her with a glare.

"Do you play golf?" George asks the man instead. "I hear this course is tough. I'd love to give it a whirl sometime . . ."

Milly tunes out of the golf talk and tips back the glass of champagne that has been pressed into her hand. The man's wife is telling another woman how wonderful the Peter Pan animation is, and how her kids loved it. Across the room she sees Doris, Sissy, and some of the other mothers in their usual huddle. She catches Doris's eye. There is no getting out of it. She will have to go over and speak to her. *Still, anything would be better than present company*, she thinks, slinking away.

"Milly!" Sissy exclaims. "Where *have* you been hiding yourself?"

Doris turns and gives Milly a tight smile. Is she out of favor because she's not returned to the Minute Women's meeting or the PTA?

"Anne Humphries tells me you're awfully busy these days," Doris says before Milly can reply. It's lucky she isn't having an affair. The entire neighborhood would know before George.

"That's right," Milly says, trying to keep her voice bright. "I'm helping a relative of mine with some research—he collects old books—it's been more involved than I first imagined. But I'm making progress."

"How nice. And when you've finished, you'll have more free time?"

"Perhaps. It depends whether he decides to involve me in anything else." She smiles and takes a gulp of her champagne, swallowing down the guilt of pretending Winton is still alive along with the bubbles. Then she thinks perhaps Doris was making some pointed statement about her not having Betty back to play. "I'm sorry we've not invited Betty to come and play with Olive. I've been meaning to . . ."

"Goodness, don't you worry," Doris says. "You sound so awfully busy."

"Yes, well—"

"We've missed you at the PTA," Sissy says, her voice as smooth and sweet as maple syrup on morning pancakes. Someone stifles a snigger. "Hopefully you'll find the time to come back soon."

"Oh yes, I'm sure I will."

There's an awkward silence.

"I do love your dress," Doris turns to Sissy. "It's not Jacques Fath, is it?"

Sissy gives a whirl. "Oh, I wish! No, but I'm glad you think so. I had a dressmaker make this for me. I sent off for the pattern from one I saw in *My Life . . .*" Milly's ears prick up at the mention of *My Life.* ". . . And had a girl make it for a *fraction* of the price."

"I'll have to get the name of the girl from you," Doris says. "Frank has some important functions coming up, and I could do with some new dresses."

Milly's mind spins off to consider the contrasting conversations of these women to the men at the bar. How *these* women are just what men in power would like *all* American women to be. Concerned only with pretty dresses and pandering to their husbands. Thinking for themselves, having their own opinions, could be a dangerous thing. Fear of women's progression in society was among the abysmal warnings of men like the authors of *Washington Confidential* who painted a horrifying picture of the G-girls, the Government Girls. Sexual predators, hungry for power, and willing to do anything to get it, sleeping their way to the top, not caring if their lovers were communist or any other degenerate. It was written as a warning to men: Keep your women at home, or this is what they will turn into.

When it comes down to it, she thinks, considering the troubled times in which they live, the message in the manuscript, and the times in which *it* was written, when those with something to lose were pitched against those with nothing to lose, men will do anything at all to hold on to their power, to control the masses, to silent dissent.

"And yours, Milly?" Sissy turns to her, jolting her from her reverie.

"Oh! This old thing?" Milly holds up the skirt of her dress, then dops it again when she notices her bitten and unpainted nails. "I brought this with me from England. It's nothing special."

"You should treat yourself to something new," Doris says. "We all need some pampering from time to time, don't we, girls? Treat yourself to a new hairdo, or a manicure. George might appreciate it."

"You are probably right," Milly says, deciding to ignore the barb. "Sissy . . . Do you recommend *My Life*? I was always a *Good Housekeeping* fan back in England . . ."

"Definitely *My Life*," the others chorus.

"*Good Housekeeping* is rather staid," Doris explains. "I have a subscription to *My Life* and look forward to receiving my copy every week." The others nod their agreement. "There's something for everyone in that magazine. In fact, there are some fascinating stories by a woman called Charlotte, which, I must say, get me thinking. I believe you would like it, Milly."

The conversation moves on, but Milly's mind is hooked on Doris's words.

And inside, there is a fizz and crackle that has nothing at all to do with the champagne.

A few weeks later, with shaking hands, Milly picks the new edition of *My Life* off the newsstand and hands the clerk a quarter. She can't wait until she gets home, so she retreats around the corner of the street, props herself against the side wall of the newsstand, and flicks through the magazine until she finds her new story covering a two-page spread. Her breath catches. There's an illustration beside the story's title of a beautiful, green island, topped with a mountain and flanked by yellow sand, surrounded by blue seas dotted with white-sailed yachts.

ALIUS—THE 49TH STATE

Good morning America! Today is a historic day.

My Life can exclusively reveal that the United States of America, today, becomes not 48 states, but 49!

Not since 1912 when Arizona became the 48th addition to our great United States, have we welcomed a new nation into our country. But today is the day when Alius does just that.

Why have you heard nothing until now?

Because this whole deal has had to be conducted in a complete news blackout.

Alius has been secretly negotiating terms of membership with the federal government for several years, and now, finally, with all terms settled, the news is out! Alius is a very special place, so the terms of admission have had to be truly unique.

What is special about Alius? Well, for starters it is a beautiful island in the Pacific. Never heard of it? That is because its location is very remote and it has, purposefully, not wished to be discovered by the outside world, until now. It is a large island, rich in resources and, being isolated for hundreds of years, it has developed in unique and surprising ways. Ways it will be permitted to retain now it is ceded into the United States. The problem for Alius in this, our modern world, is that it is vulnerable to other, less friendly, foreign nations who would like to claim it for themselves and destroy its extraordinary culture. Alius is a wealthy nation, and in return for the protection of the United States armed forces, Alius will, of course, be paying taxes.

The government of Alius has been very particular about how the truth of this extraordinary island will be revealed to the American people. And for reasons that will become clear, dear reader, as you discover all the secrets of Alius in the coming series, we are thrilled to reveal that *My Life* has been given exclusive access to the island to learn all there is to know of it. Our journalist, Charlotte, was permitted to live there for three months, to watch the government in action, to travel to all corners of it freely and to speak to whoever she chose. She visited schools, houses, farms and industry, and what she found is profound. You can read it all here, week by week. And we think you will be amazed, inspired, and it might just change your life.

Milly shuts the magazine and smiles to herself. She'll read the rest when she gets home. But for now, she is happy. It looks good, the way *My Life* has presented it. It's bold, fun, and engaging— just as she had hoped. What a relief.

Before they had gone to print with this first part of the series, Milly had had cold feet and telephoned Myra.

"In the current climate," she'd said, twisting the telephone cord between her fingers, "do you really think this is okay to print?"

She'd sunk down to sit on the stairs waiting for Myra's response, the silence heavy down the line.

"Never a better time," Myra said, her voice strong with confidence. "Listen, honey, I understand your qualms and were we a more serious journal, then of course there might be question marks. But the fact is, we are a lighthearted women's magazine. This is a female fantasy. Nothing serious at all. And as such, no man is going to give a damn. Certainly not the board members of *My Life* who are far more interested in being on the golf course. As long as our circulation figures are healthy and the ad money comes rolling in, they will be happy."

"You really think so?"

"Of course I do. I'd never commission it otherwise."

And so, here it was. Real and in print.

Milly had taken what Lysbette wrote and updated and adapted it for a modern audience. But she was faithful to Lysbette's ideas—to the central concept in her work that Alius is a place where everyone, whatever sex, race, or religion you may be, is treated equally. A place where women should be in control of their lives, that no one person should ever assume too much power, and that life in a more equal society can be better for everyone.

Milly turns in the direction of home. She must work on the manuscript this morning, to decode more of Lysbette's story so she can finish writing her next installment for *My Life*. But she is too excited, too energized to go back to her quiet, empty house. Instead, she makes for the library. She checks her watch. She should be just in time for Susan's break.

In the library, Milly finds Susan's young assistant, Meg, behind the counter, and Susan is nowhere to be seen.

"She's with Mr. Sullivan," Meg explains when Milly asks for

her. Meg looks around then leans forward and says in a low voice. "Truth is, I'm a bit worried for Susan. Mr. Sullivan seemed mighty angry when he arrived this morning. He took her into his office, and they've been gone almost an hour." Meg looks at the pile of books on the counter, takes one, opens it and stamps *Returned* over the last borrow date. "Lucky it's not been busy this morning."

"I'll wait," Milly says. Distractedly, she browses the fiction section. What can Mr. Sullivan want with Susan? *Please let her be all right.*

After ten agonizing minutes, Susan and Mr. Sullivan appear. Susan is pale, her cheeks pinched, lips tight. Mr. Sullivan throws on his coat and marches out of the library looking grim.

Milly darts to Susan's side.

"Susan . . . Are you okay?"

Susan's face relaxes when she sees Milly. "I sure am glad to see a friendly face."

"Is it time for your break? Can you escape for a coffee?"

"I need something stronger," Susan says, "but a coffee will have to do for now."

In the café, Susan tells Milly someone has reported her to HUAC.

"HUAC?"

"The House Un-American Activities Committee," Susan explains. "They investigate any private citizen suspected of communist activities. Mr. Sullivan received a letter from them this morning, detailing the allegation: that I have been lending out banned books. I'm going to be called to appear in front of the committee."

"Oh, Susan! When?"

She shakes her head. "I don't have a date yet. I should hear in the next week or so."

"What did Mr. Sullivan say. Is he going to support you?"

"He was furious, as you might have noticed. He asked me straight out, are the allegations true? And is the rumor that I'm a fellow traveler, true?"

"Oh my, what did you say?"

Susan shrugs. "I denied everything. If they have evidence to prove my guilt, let them produce it. I sure am not going to make anything easy, but I do *not* want to lose the job I love." She curls her fingers around her cup of coffee. "It's all so unfair," she adds, in a small voice.

"I am so sorry. Can I help? Maybe I can give you a good character reference?"

Susan smiles. "You are too kind, Milly. I don't think it works like that. There is nothing balanced or fair about the process, from what I gather. If you produce names of people you think might have left leanings, you might be treated leniently."

"*What?*"

"Yes. But I would never do that."

They sit in silence for a few minutes.

"Well," Susan says finally. "Nothing awful has happened, yet."

"I really am sorry."

"I know." She gives Milly a weak smile. She drains her cup of coffee. "Now, I must get back."

Milly watches her friend leave the café and wishes there was something she could do to help.

She sips her unfinished tea, letting the chatter from surrounding tables wash over her, catching snippets here and there, *Bob got a raise . . . Mother is driving me crazy . . . Sale at Macy's . . . Have you seen Caroline's new haircut? Do you think it could be for real? It certainly reads that way . . .*

Milly glances over, her skin prickling when she sees the two women are discussing a copy of *My Life* open between them. She strains to hear their conversation over the background hum of conversation.

"It can't be," one of the women says.

"But it *sounds* plausible. Have you ever heard of Alius? Is it really going to become the forty-ninth state?"

"Don't be a goof, Annie. Of course it isn't true. We'd have read about it in the papers."

"But it says all negotiations have been held in absolute secrecy," Annie insists. "And we know the government does many things in secret, so maybe it *isn't* so silly."

The other woman shakes her head. "I tell you; it is just a story."

Milly holds a handkerchief over her mouth to hide her shock.

"Well," says Annie, "even if it *is* only a story, it sure is a good one. I'm hooked! And I'm looking forward to the next part."

She goes on, "And just a story or not, it does make you wonder, doesn't it, if there *could* be any truth behind it? Alius sounds quite fascinating. If it *does* turn out to be true, I'm going to visit!"

The women's words ring in Milly's ears long after she has left the café. They are discussing *her* story. In how many other cafés or living rooms across America could other women be doing the same?

Chapter 22

Charlotte

Paris, October 1552

Charlotte waited impatiently for the last of the customers to leave her shop so she could lock the door for the night. Two men and a woman browsed the shelves. Finally, the woman chose a *Book of Hours*, paid, and left, but the men lingered; up and down they went, eyes moving over every volume on her shelves.

"Can I help you?" she asked each of them.

The older man shook his head and took his leave. The other mumbled, kept his head down, and flicked through a book of poetry. At last, he replaced it on the shelf, tipped his hat, and, with a *Good night, Madame*, left the shop, limping slightly as he went.

Charlotte locked the door with relief, then, from the packing box behind the counter, she lifted the two finished volumes of the Greek/Latin dictionary, so large and heavy they wobbled in her hands. She held them up to the light of her lantern and screwed up her eyes to inspect the delicate design on the honey-toned, calfskin covers, nodding in satisfaction. They looked good. She placed one volume on the counter and opened the other, her heart swelling at the elaborate design of her printing mark just inside the front cover. In the center, the golden sun nestled between the branches of a great vine from which full and succulent bunches of grapes hung, two lions reaching up either side of the sturdy trunk clasping her printing mark in their paws. The design spoke of excellence, prosperity, professional reliability, and above all, the endurance and transcending importance of the written word, and her profession in ensuring the spread of it.

The dictionary had been produced for Jacques Toussaint, who had died suddenly one month before Charlotte had been able to print it. She'd had a number of competing projects that summer, and, what with the dreadful shortage of good quality paper, the sudden and unexpected death of a nephew, the worry of the Paper Guild trial, not to mention the matter of Lysbette Angiers, this project had been delayed. It was against every one of her own rules to miss a professional deadline, but something had to give.

For the first and only time Charlotte had included some words of her own in a preface to the dictionary. It summed up her sorrow that her choice of which projects to prioritize had resulted in Toussaint not living to see its everlasting beauty.

I bestow on you, she wrote to future readers, *this significant work, not only of the author, who is highly deserving of your gratitude, but also for my sake, who continuously for the last fifty years have been carrying on the duties of a printer which are a very heavy weight, both of cost and concerns. Fare thee well, Paris October 6, 1552.*

She ran her fingers across these, her only ever printed words, and wondered who might come to read them in the future. Then she closed the book, gave it an affectionate pat, and placed it carefully in the padded packing box ready for the delivery boy to take forth into the world. She turned back to the window, staring out at passersby in the street holding onto their hats for fear of losing them to a strong gust of wind. Clumps of leaves and debris collected in eddies along the cobbles. Winter was around the corner and Charlotte shuddered at the thought. Much as she disliked the hot, sticky days of summer, the biting cold, incessant rain, and long, dark, nights of winter that brought with it sickness and death were worse. Was this the last winter she would see? She could almost feel death hovering, awaiting his chance to pull her into his embrace. She straightened her shoulders against him.

Not yet, you brute. I've too much still to do.

Not least was the trial against the Paper Guild. Now that they had a court date, Monsieur Riant had approached other printers to gather additional evidence as to the inferior paper quality across the whole of Paris, and notice of the prosecution had been served upon Monsieur Baubigny. Frédéric brought Charlotte tales of the man's rage. Of what he would do if he got his hands around her interfering, audacious hag's neck.

Outside, although the afternoon was edging toward evening, the street remained busy with the billowing robes and hoods of the university professors hurrying to or from the Sorbonne. In the early days of the business, when she and Berthold had worked so hard to make a good reputation of their fledgling printworks, the university had fast become their lifeblood. She wondered what Berthold would make of its recent condemnation of over five hundred works as heretical, and therefore destined for the flames.

Since Henry II's Edict of Châteaubriant had been issued last year, all books printed, sold, or imported had to be approved by the Faculty of Theology at the University of Paris. Charlotte had had to remove several titles from her shop. She also had to display in the window the faculty's list of banned books alongside a list of books she had for sale. Inspectors could visit any time to check her compliance. Should she be caught trading in banned books, she, too, could be accused of heresy and face death by burning. Now she was forced to take on only commissions of a conservative nature. She was sad to think of Erasmus's words, the man who predicted terrible religious wars if the church and the rulers of nations did not embrace tolerance, now lay hidden in the darkness, gathering dust, all but forgotten.

I have not forgotten you, she assured the dead Erasmus. *Or you, Lysbette Angiers. And for you, I have a plan.*

It was time. Her heart ticked a little faster. Charlotte locked the shop, smoothed her skirts, and retrieved the leather satchel from behind the counter. Inside it lay the precious manuscript Charlotte had kept hidden since Agnes entrusted it to her that hot July day three months before.

The printworkers were spilling out into Rue St.-Jacques in chattering, laughing groups, happy, Charlotte supposed, to be released from their duties early. She imagined many of them would take advantage of the hour before they were expected home and visit the alehouse. She closed the large double doors, shutting out the clamor from the street. In the sudden dimness of the workshop, silence settled, soft as falling snow. Five pairs of eyes watched as she made her way toward the small group of the men that remained. The acerbic mix of ink, wet paper, and metal hit the back of her throat. Frédéric busied himself lighting the lamps by which they would work into the dark of night.

Charlotte cleared her throat to begin her explanation of the strange mission they had been recruited for and looked at the faces of the team Frédéric had put together. She started at the sight of Nicolas, the difficult journeyman, cross-armed before her, his apprentice, Jean, by his side. *Surely not!*

"Just a moment," she said, raising her finger and crossing the workroom to hiss in Frédéric's ear.

"Why Nicolas? We need our most trustworthy people, and he is as slippery as a box of eels. As for his apprentice, I'd no sooner trust him than a fox in the chicken coop. Why did you not ask Pierre, like we discussed?"

Frédéric sighed. "Pierre's wife is about to give birth to their fifth infant. He cannot be absent these nights from home. Nicolas is our only yet-to-be married journeyman who wouldn't have to explain why he is absent half the night. I know you think ill of him, but he is trustworthy, I assure you."

"But—"

Frédéric's dark, sincere eyes met hers. "Madame, truly. Nicolas is ambitious and headstrong. But his heart is good. He would never do anything that would harm you or this"—he waved his free hand at their surroundings—"his livelihood."

Charlotte wanted to believe him. Really, she did, but every instinct was on high alert.

"And Jean?"

"He is well controlled by Nicolas. He would never dare to cross his master."

Charlotte was silent. The risk was enormous, but if she was going to do this, she had little choice. She regarded Frédéric, biting her lip while she thought. She had known this man for over twenty years. He lived beneath her roof. She knew everything about him, his thoughts and beliefs, which were so aligned to her own they could anticipate the other's before they spoke. She would trust him with her life. Frédéric himself was taking an enormous risk by accepting this project and her heart swelled with gratitude. If he trusted these men, then she must too.

It was this team, or the manuscript stay hidden for all eternity.

She turned and walked back to the waiting men.

"Monsieurs," she said finally, "I am about to ask you to undertake what I think is an important but dangerous commission that, for the safety of us all, must remain only between us. You will, of course, be well rewarded in extra pay for your labor, but you must never, ever speak of it to anyone. If you do not wish to go further, I shall not judge you harshly, but you must leave now before I reveal more."

She looked at each of the group in turn, but not one of them spoke.

"Fine, then I shall begin."

For three nights, all went according to plan as the select group set about printing the thirty secret copies of Lysbette's book, a small run, by normal accounts, but large enough that care would be needed to conceal the copies until they could be sent in secret to their final destinations. She made the decision to print in ancient Greek, largely because fewer people would be able to read the contents than if she decided to print them in Latin, including the workers in her printing press, bar Frédéric, and this seemed a sensible precaution, in the circumstances. Hers was one of the few presses able to print in Greek, as she had invested in a stock of the movable metal letters in that language, alongside the Latin and French she could offer her customers.

The task of printing was labor-intensive and required skill and precision. First, the frame must be set with the rows of metal letters set into the words, page by page, copied from Lysbette's manuscript. The ink was applied evenly, then dampened paper was pinned into place and pressed by the machine mechanism. Once all the copies of one page were completed, they could move on to the next. The pages of the manuscript were thick with illustrations, which slowed the process further, for illustrations needed to be added using inked woodblock engravings. It would be too time-consuming and expensive to make all those Lysbette had included, so Charlotte had to make the decision to only include a few where she deemed absolutely necessary, and she tasked one of her illustrators with making the woodblock engravings.

After working long into the night, Charlotte would release her workers, who were being well rewarded for this extra work, to get some rest until their morning shift began. The men were efficient at changing the type, putting the workroom back into the state it had been when the other workers left each evening, ready for their arrival the following morning so that no suspicion was raised.

But on the fourth night, just before midnight, there came a crashing and banging on the street door that stopped their hands, their breath, their hearts. They exchanged wild-eyed looks. The banging continued unabated, accompanied by shouts.

Charlotte grabbed the loose pages of Lysbette's manuscript from where they lay, making for the back door. As she passed Frédéric, she paused.

"Let them in. We've planned for this."

He nodded grim-faced.

She slipped silently into the yard at the back of the house while the others hid the newly printed folios between the religious texts printed earlier that day. They must hope that whoever was at the door did not examine the metal type laid in the printing frames too closely. Though even if they did, they would likely not understand them, set as they were in ancient Greek.

Charlotte ran to the dark house, her breath dragging through her constricted throat, limbs trembling. *Dear God, keep my men safe.* She stole along the maid's corridor, feeling her way in the dark, stumbling up the back stairs, not daring to light a candle. She clawed her way along the top corridor, finding her way to Sophie's room. A faint gleam of candlelight seeped beneath the door. Thank heavens the maid was not yet in bed. Charlotte knocked lightly, not waiting for an answer before entering.

Sophie, in her shift and nightcap, stood frozen in shock at her mistress's sudden entrance.

"Madame? Are you taken ill?"

"Not ill, Sophie, but afeared . . ." She handed the precious manuscript to her maid. "You must hide this once more for me. I fear someone has talked and at this very moment there are men searching the workshops for it. The inquisitors will destroy it if they find it, and I will be for the pyre, the men for the rope." Sophie's eyes widened, but she nodded, a grim expression on her face.

"I have a place," she said without hesitation, taking the manuscript. "I'll blow out my candle and should I be questioned, I'll have been asleep all along."

Charlotte reached for her hand and squeezed it. "Thank you."

Back in her own room, she stripped off her skirt and bodice down to her own shift as though she, too, had been sleeping all along. Heart thudding, she climbed into her bed and waited in an agony of not knowing, the darkness dense and mocking. What terrible risks she had taken, and at what cost? Worse, who had spoken? Who was the traitor in their midst?

Was it Nicolas? Or Jean? *What had she done?*

It didn't take long. Just minutes later, there was a sharp knock on her door.

"Madame," came the voice of Luc, the manservant. "You are needed, urgently, in the printworks. There are some men . . ."

A shawl wrapped around her shoulders, Charlotte allowed herself to be guided by the light of Luc's lantern. Inside the workroom was a scene of mayhem. Folios scattered in disarray. Benches upturned, the drawers of the huge cabinet on the back wall hung out, the contents spilled onto the floor like guts from a carcass. Charlotte cried out in horror.

"What has happened here? What have you done?" The four

men stopped their ransacking and turned to face her. Her blood burned hot with fury that they should march in here and lay waste to the business she had spent a lifetime building. "Who in hell's name are *you*?"

A hard-faced man stepped forward. "Madame Guillard?" She looked from him to the other man who limped backward, his face swallowed in shadow. There was something familiar about him.

"Yes?"

"I am Monsieur Heureux, and this is Monsieur Faivre." He waved a hand at the man in the shadows. *Faivre.* The name was familiar too. "We are sent by the Inquisitor Fidei"—he pointed to the two other men—"assisted by these *officiers de police*. You are accused of printing heretical material in secret, at night . . ."

"Someone lies! Who was it?" Charlotte turned her eyes on Nicolas who was staring at the floor.

"*Madame*, I'm arresting you and Frédéric Morel for further questioning." His eyes dropped to her shift. "I suggest you dress warmly, Madame." He smirked. "One long night, or likely many more, locked up in the *Palais de la Cité* will be very cold, and for one so used to such a comfortable life, I'd say, dreadfully bleak."

Chapter 23

Lysbette

Barking Abbey, England, November 1539

Lysbette was woken by rain blowing in vicious gusts against her small window. She could hear it pounding on the red-tiled roof above her head. She rose, dressed, lit a candle. Outside the glow of her sleeping cell, night was heaviest black, and the wind howled as though the very devil was hurling himself at the building. She turned her back on nature's demons and busied herself with a comforting ritual: the making of ink.

Each morning, she crushed and soaked oak galls in red wine, adding copper sulfate, leaving it to soak all day. Now, she stirred the mixture and strained it into the waiting inkpot. Carefully she measured and added a couple of ounces of gum arabic to thicken the mixture. Stirring it again, she held it to the candle to check the thickness. She selected a goose quill from the pile she had earlier prepared and settled down to write. The only place safe to write was like this: alone in her solitary cell in the small hours of the night, while the other nuns were sleeping in theirs. Fear skittered deep inside like the skuttling of beetles, that one night, perhaps this night, she would be discovered. And then what? Her writings would surely be worthy of excommunication. Or worse: heresy, treason, witchcraft. Then to be condemned to death, her soul dispatched to be burned in the everlasting fires of hell.

Lysbette shuddered involuntarily, then she pushed those

thoughts and fears away. Allowed herself instead to sink into her imagined world, her place of solace.

In her mind's eye she could see her imagined kingdom, no, not kingdom, for there was no king in this, her very own common-wealth. The place she had named *Alius*, the Latin word for *another way*, was as vivid as if she walked its towns and cities, its wooded hillsides and deep valleys on her own two feet. Being there was like a transcendence. She forgot all the worry of living through the death throes of her beautiful Barking Abbey. She blotted out physical sensations of cold and tiredness. Here, in this secret place, there was no greedy king who threatened Alius's existence.

She trod the familiar path between tall pines that grew like an army of sentinels on the steep sides of the valley. Layers of pine needles made the ground beneath her feet springy, filling the air with a fresh, tangy aroma. Sunshine filtered through the branches swaying high above her head, warming her back as she walked. Descending lower, towering trees gave way to meadows, lush with grass, fragrant with wildflowers. Bees and butterflies flitted from flower to flower, graceful as dancers in a montage. In the distance, a herd of cows, fat and content from the succulent grass, udders full of milk, grazed.

Lysbette followed the path in her mind, cutting diagonally through the meadow toward a cluster of buildings forming the edge of the town in the distance. At the halfway point, she bounded across the stream where it narrowed as it wound its way through the meadow. To the north was the waterfall that fed this stream, at its base the large bathing pool the women visited every day. She had drawn its image at the top of the page, the women tumbling into the shallow pool, floating in the healing, crystal clear waters, untarnished by any washing or wool-dyeing that would damage its health-giving properties.

In her imagination, at the edge of town, Lysbette paused, taking in the sight before her. The town was bustling with activity, for this was late morning and there was no time for idleness in Alius. In the huge town hall, at the heart of her commonwealth, they were preparing for a meeting of the ruling committee. She had only yesterday written the rules of its constitution.

Something banged, somewhere in the building and Lysbette froze, her hand poised over her work. For a few moments she sat, ears straining, heart thrumming, but there was no more movement, no more sound, other than the wind rattling the shutters. She breathed out a held breath. It must have been the wind catching an open window, a loose shutter.

Returning to her work, Lysbette wanted to do away with kings and popes, princes and lords, altogether. Her ideas were heretical, treasonous, she knew. But she lowered her pen to the paper anyway. It was as though her hand was being guided by an unstoppable force. Ideas for a better world pouring from her pen. How could she keep them to herself? Always in her mind there was Utopia, but Lysbette's Alius was different. There were inherent problems with More's world. And besides, Lysbette had experienced living a monastic life for the last nine years. There was much to admire and draw from this enclosed society of women. Further, she had read about other civilizations, far away from her own. She was especially interested in the writings of Jean Parmentier, a cartographer and poet, who traveled east and encountered the Minangkabau peoples in the hills of Aceh. He wrote of a peaceful, matrilineal society, where wealth was passed from mother to daughter rather than father to son. Where the arrival of a daughter in the family was cause for huge celebration.

Imagine that!

Lysbette had read Plato and Aristotle, she had read the new

ideas of modern writers, and she had given much thought on how to live another way. A way that worked for the many, not only the privileged few, and in a way that lifted and benefited women, and not just men.

But before she could write another word, the lauds bells clanged above the whine of the wind and the dash of the rain against the windowpanes. It was time to pray and Lysbette, would seek guidance from her silent Lord. Was this a test of her faith, she wondered, as she packed her writing things away? Was her heart now a battleground between God and the devil himself?

She supposed, as she left her room and made for the chapel, she would find out soon enough.

Although she and the others knew their doomsday was coming, when the men finally arrived in the early morning, the potent mix of fear and despair that marked the end of her abbey life filled her belly. For several days, while the abbess and the remaining nuns watched, powerless to stop them, they stamped through the echoing halls and corridors, yelling instructions in their booming voices where until now, only nuns had crept in whispering quietude for more than eight hundred years.

The men skinned their beautiful abbey, stripping lead from roofs, pulling out oak beams, and lifting bells from the towers. The harmonious peals of bells that rang out across the surrounding countryside, guiding the rhythms of the day, were to be silenced forever and melted into cannon balls. Soon they would boom out across killing fields, in the name of the King, and God. The men scoured the buildings for silver and jewels, gold vestments and valuable cloth. They took the books from the library, the braying cattle from their pastures, the chickens from their coops.

Inside Lysbette's heart grew a fireball of fury toward King Henry and his greed, and against this world of men. One by one, the nuns departed, home to their families. The older nuns were to be granted a pension, the younger expected to marry and receiving nothing at all. Just a handful remained now; those with nowhere else to go.

"Come with me," Agnes pleaded. She'd been offered a place at the Convent of the Blessed Heart in Paris. "I am sure they would take you in too."

Lysbette sat on her bed, running her rosary beads through her fingers as she watched Agnes fold her few possessions into a trunk. Her own things were packed, too, and sat beside her. But where would she go? With Sir Thomas dead, there was no Chelsea to return to. The More family, having risen so high, were now cast out, their lands taken and their name at court never mentioned. And Lysbette, a relatively newly professed nun, was not entitled to the generous pensions of the seniors.

She was penniless and homeless once more.

Her stomach churned with anxiety. What would become of her? Of her work? Hastily sewn behind a false lining of her case was her manuscript. This was her obsession. She couldn't bear to be parted from it. How could she enter another religious house with this upon her person? Perhaps those on the continent were less lenient than Dame Dorothy Barley had become, so distracted as she was by the inevitable march of destruction. And besides, the march of Protestantism, as Lutheranism was now known, across parts of the continent meant there were monasteries being destroyed there too. Perhaps they would manage another few years in an abbey there, but surrender would surely come once more. She couldn't bear to go through this again.

Lysbette reached out a hand to touch Agnes's and smiled into her friend's dear face.

"I cannot come with you, Agnes. I'm sorry. My place is here, in England."

"But why? There is nothing here for you."

"I'll make my way." She didn't mention the gold and rubies Dame Dorothy had given her before the commissioners spotted them. The abbey's wealth was what they were after, and Dorothy decided they shouldn't get all the spoils. Lysbette had also saved Chaucer's *Canterbury Tales*, *Aesop's Fables*, and works of Cicero, Aristotle, and Virgil from the library, putting those in her case too. She could sell them if she became utterly destitute. When the end of the world was nigh, one must do what one could to save oneself.

Agnes studied her face. "I see you are resolved and that nothing I say will change your mind."

They sat there in silence, hand in hand. Agnes was the closest friend Lysbette had had since John, and the thought of losing her, too, was almost too much to bear.

"You will make your mark on the world," Agnes said finally. "Of that, Lysbette Angiers, I am sure."

Chapter 24

Milly

Levittown, Long Island, New York, July 1953

I f the day is hot and humid outside, in the hairdresser's, it's a
sauna. Heat pumps from the long line of metal hairdryers, like
bulbous tin hats of the atomic age. Beneath them, cross-legged,
women sit like a gowned army awaiting their orders. In their
hands, a row of open magazines, *My Life* on many of the covers.

"Good morning to you, Mrs. Bennett! It's been such a long
time!" Janine, her stylist, runs her eyes over Milly's hair with a
growing look of disapproval.

"I know, it's a mess. I've just been so busy . . ."

"Hmm." Janine steps forward, lifts and drops a few lank locks.
"What's it to be today? Restyle? Perm?" Her own hair, a bright
orange mop, is arranged in tight curls atop her head into a poodle
style à la Lucille Ball.

"Just a simple cut and dry, Janine. It's my wedding anniversary
this evening, and my husband is taking me out."

"How lovely! Where is he taking you?"

"I don't know. It's a surprise."

Janine claps her hands in delight. "Oh! How romantic! Have
you a new dress?" Milly opens her mouth to reply *No, I've not had
the time*, but Janine is off again, "And your nails—I hope you have
booked a manicure!" Milly simply smiles.

"All right then, we'd better get you looking your best." Janine is hopping from foot to foot, hair bouncing, smile wide. She appears to be more excited than Milly at the prospect of her anniversary evening with George. "I'll go get you a gown." She walks off calling, "Be back in a moment to get you all comfy!"

Once she's in her gown and seated in front of the mirror, they discuss options for her hair. Janine is a little disappointed that Milly just wants a modest cut, curlers and dry, and not anything more daring like color and a drastic change of style.

"Any magazines?" Janine asks once Milly is back from her hair wash.

"*My Life*, if you have one."

Janine clicks her tongue. "They're all out I'm afraid. So sorry, Mrs. Bennett, it is the most popular magazine of the moment." She nods at the pile in the corner. "Plenty of *Good Housekeeping* or *Woman and Home*. No idea why they're all hooked on *My Life*."

"I think it's the series on that mysterious island, Alius."

"But it's just a silly story," Janine says, setting to work with her scissors, "isn't it?"

"I hope that one day it *will* exist," Milly says.

Janine laughs and says, "Sure, and I hope money grows on trees someday too." She moves around Milly with her comb and her scissors, expertly snipping and cutting. Milly watches Janine's quick fingers in the mirror, her mouth moving as she whitters about useless men she has dated, hair and beauty products she recommends. She flips from one subject to another with barely a breath taken between. At last, the rollers are in, and Milly is led to the line of hairdryers. She sits beneath one, and the heat blasts out.

Milly lets her eyes drift shut. She is tired. Over the course of the past six months, she's spent many long hours working on the manuscript. Now she is finished. Once her series in *My Life* is completed, she will need to reveal the truth about the source of the Alius story. She wonders what Winton would have made of it all. Indeed, what Charlotte and Lysbette would have thought. Milly's retelling of Alius has been popular beyond her wildest dreams, but how to reveal the truth, without Milly's name being attached to it, is a growing knot of anxiety deep inside. First, she will need to break it to Myra and get her and the board of *My Life* to agree to a feature on the manuscript as a source for the story. Assuming that goes to plan, there may be a furor from their readership. They're likely to want a reveal of who "Charlotte" really is. Can Milly trust the magazine to maintain her anonymity? And then what to do with the manuscript itself? Surely its value will far exceed anything Winton had originally envisaged with all the publicity and the story Milly has made from it. How on earth will she keep herself out of the media without help from anyone? And always, hanging over her head, is the question of how an ordinary housewife could have broken this unbreakable code without revealing her role at Bletchley. She cannot risk any of that being brought to light or she'll have the British authorities on her in a flash.

Through some correspondence with the history department at Cambridge University, Milly has managed to find some information on Lysbette Angiers. She had been a ward of Sir Thomas More after her parents died, leaving her an orphan. She'd been ordained as a nun at Barking Abbey and was one of just thirty nuns remaining when the abbey was dissolved on November 14, 1539, by King Henry VIII. What happened to her after that is unknown, except that Milly knows from Charlotte's note in the manuscript that she ended up in Paris where it seems she was brutally murdered. Murdered, she supposes, for daring to hold views and ideas not appreciated by the powerful of the day. Milly thinks of Susan, how she was questioned by the HUAC. How she refused to give names of others suspected of un-American activities and was fired from her beloved job at the library. The parallels with the story she is uncovering feel all too real. And she feels a twist of anxiety about the series in *My Life*, its popularity growing beyond belief.

"Darling," Myra had said, when she invited Milly to lunch at Le Coq Rouge yesterday to celebrate the success of the series. "Choose anything you like on the menu . . . Langoustine, caviar, filet steak. You name it, you *deserve* it."

Myra had been draped languidly on her chair, glass of Bollinger in one hand, cigarette in the other, peeping over the top of her sunglasses at Milly, a smile playing on her lips.

"I do?"

Myra raised her glass at Milly. "Your little contribution to *My Life* has resulted in a noticeable uptick in circulation. The board are delighted. *My Life* has a significant lead in the circulation race. Women readers—housewives in particular—are the ones everyone wants."

"But why?"

"Because middle-class man earns the salary, and his wife has the time to spend it. And wives are doing that in droves. So, the higher the circulation figures, the advertisers flood in, and our revenue goes up. And that, my dear, keeps the shareholders happy. The beauty of the circularity of capitalism."

"Surely the rise in popularity of *My Life* isn't only to do with me?"

"No, not solely. But the story has hit some sort of community nerve among our readers. It's a zeitgeist of our time." Milly smiles at the irony of that. Myra had leaned down and pulled a folded newspaper from her bag at her feet. "It's even made the national press," she said, handing the copy of *The New York Times* to Milly. The op-ed article was on page 9, entitled "The Tall Tale That's the Talk of the Town." Milly skimmed it, her heart beating faster, her body heating up as she read.

> . . . It was my wife who first alerted me to a serialized story in the popular women's magazine *My Life*. Now, it is not a rag I would usually pay attention to. But, she informed me, this story is fast becoming the talk of the town. And she wanted me to find out if there was any truth behind it. The story, in case you have no idea to what I'm referring, is about a fictionalized island called Alius (for those who don't understand Latin, *alius* means "another" or "different") which, according to the story, has just become annexed to the United States as state number forty-nine. Now the reason for all this excitement over this fictional new state, and I summarize in a nutshell, is that Alius is firmly in the hands and control of its female citizens. Alius is a matrilineal society. The story goes into much greater detail than I have room for here, but suffice to say, it is making the women of America reconsider their position in society. It has certainly generated some interesting discussions in our household. If you haven't heard of it yet, men of America, I suggest you take a look. It might prepare you for some interesting conversations with the women in your life . . .

Milly looked up at Myra, the ball of fear unwinding, thrashing inside as the implications of what she had read sunk in. "But . . .

This isn't good, Myra. You said nobody serious would pay attention."

"And I still hold to that. This is fiction. One rogue journalist picking up the story is nothing. Don't stress, Milly. The board are over the moon with our sales figures. So, I say, here's to you." Myra had winked and raised her glass of champagne.

Now, Milly ignores the uncomfortable twist of anxiety and instead sketches out in her head the article that will reveal how her pseudonym, Charlotte, is named after the real Charlotte Guillard, and that the original *Alius* was written by a four-hundred-year-old ex-nun, Lysbette Angiers. She will say that, like so many women from the past, Lysbette and Charlotte are long forgotten, nameless, unimportant. These women were educated, well-traveled, and clever. Lysbette herself was so wise, so insightful, that her ideas are still relevant and resonant in the here and now. Her voice is urgent and clear, rising as it does from the pages of Charlotte's manuscript with warmth, character, and humor. How magical that this was preserved in the pages of this book, so cleverly concealed by her dear friend Charlotte Guillard. History, until now, has been about wars and kings and empires rising and falling. The realms of men. Women, bar a handful, have been absent from the story. But here, in full Technicolor, is the mind of a woman so ahead of her time that the whole country now has been swept along with it.

There is a tap on Milly's shoulder, and she jumps, opening her eyes to find herself back in the hairdressers, with the hum of the dryers and background rumble of conversation.

"I found you a copy!" Janine presents her with the latest edition of *My Life* with a flourish.

"Thank you, Janine!"

Milly opens it, straight to the middle pages. Like Lysbette, she has structured the story such that as she travels around Alius, encountering different fictional people as she goes, with whom she discusses all manner of topics from education to religious tolerance; from nature and how it will be bountiful, if man does not abuse it, to living modestly and not being driven by greed; from equality of sex, race, and class, to the vesting of all property into the hands of women.

In today's story, Charlotte was in a house discussing the physical abuse of women.

Why is it that women are blamed for the desires of men? They are seen as the temptresses who lure men and cause them to be violent and ungallant toward them. Almost always, however badly the man behaves, it seems to be the woman who is at fault. Her manner, her dress, her ways. In Alius, they do not see things that way. When I explained how it works in America, they were shocked. Do you blame the silver for the robber's desire to snatch it? they asked, or the victim of a murder for the stab to his back? Is it the hare's fault that the poacher traps him? Surely it can be no more the woman's fault for her existence on this earth than it is for every man's lewd desire of her.

In Alius, there is no prostitution, for women have all the financial security they need, wealth being passed from mother to daughter, not from father to son. When a daughter is born, there is celebration. A daughter is a gift, because woman is the giver of life, she is the one to nurture and create, and that is to be treasured by society. When boys reach maturity, they must leave the family home and live in a central community where they continue their education and work until a wife chooses them and they will be permitted to live in her home for so long as she is happy with that arrangement. But should he mistreat her or not fulfill his duties as a father and husband, she is within her rights to send him away, and he must return to the community home. Bad behavior is not tolerated in men or women, and the ruling committee will decide if a person must be banished or punished. All government, local and central, is by committee, so that no one individual can become corrupted by power.

Should a man physically abuse a woman, an act the women of Alius say is highly unusual, as boys are raised to understand respect, the punishment would be banishment to a barren and isolated part of the island where hard physical labor is imposed, and the chances of returning to society, remote.

Milly feels the familiar leap inside at the thrill of seeing her words in print, then looks at the selection of letters that have been printed beneath the article, and her heart fills when she reads what is there.

Dear Editor,

I am a middle-aged housewife, and my children are all teenagers and will soon be fleeing the nest. Until I read the story about Alius, I thought I was satisfied with my own life. I had everything I needed—a comfortable home, a husband who treats me well and four healthy children. I had nothing at all to complain about.

But I have come to acknowledge that I have long buried a deep dissatisfaction with my life. For years I have been at everyone's service, my husband's, my children's, my parents', and my parents-in-law. My own needs and desires I have squashed as theirs have been my priority. Your story has made me think, perhaps I don't have to do that. Perhaps it is okay for me to think that my desires are as important as everyone else's.

My husband thinks I am having something called a midlife crisis. I know it is something else, which I'm calling, Putting Myself First, At Last.

Thank you,
J. E. McKnight, Nevada

Dear Editor,

I know that Charlotte's story of Alius is supposed to be a fiction, but I am absolutely sure it is the truth. I am desperate to know. How can I visit Alius? I would like to move there, just as soon as I can . . .

A movement causes Milly to look up. It is Doris, her hair in curlers, hairnet in place.

"Hello, Milly," she says. Milly snaps the magazine shut as though she is reading something she shouldn't, which is quite ridiculous. She feels her cheeks flush and hopes Doris will put it down to the heat of the hairdryer. "It's been a long time since I've seen you out and about."

Milly can't move her head much, on account of the hairdryer, and she is captive, since she can't find an excuse to run away, like she usually does.

Milly smiles and makes a rambling excuse about still doing work for her English relative and the children and the housework.

Doris looks rather downcast, Milly thinks, giving her a proper look. It's hard to hear everything she is saying, on account of the hairdryer.

"Look, Milly," she says finally, "now isn't the time or place, but I fear perhaps I might have said something to upset you."

"Oh no, you haven't—" Milly feels a rush of shame. She *has* been avoiding Doris.

"Well, whatever it was, I don't want us to be on bad terms. Now Betty is asking every day if she can see your Olive. What say you to a picnic in the park with the kids? How about tomorrow?"

"That would be very nice, Doris."

"Great!" Doris beams. "I'll come by in the car at noon."

"Lovely," Milly murmurs, feeling oddly disturbed by Doris's invitation. She watches her being led away to sit beneath one of the dryers, just as Janine comes to fetch her to take out her curlers.

Later, after a wonderful seafood meal in a quaint little restaurant overlooking the sound in Massapequa, Milly and George stroll hand in hand along the wet sand on Alhambra Beach. It is lovely to be just the two of them for a change, the children being tucked up at home with Mrs. Humphries babysitting.

The sun is setting, dipping low in the sky, tinging the clouds blush, and turning the ocean to liquid fire. A cool evening breeze drifts off the water, lifting Milly's new curls and teasing the skirt of her dress.

They stop a moment to admire the glory of the sunset.

George clasps her hand tight. "Look at that, Milly. Sometimes I really have to pinch myself that we are actually here."

"Exactly a year next week."

She leans her head against his shoulder.

"We're doing all right, aren't we, George?"

"We are. We're a great team, you and I," George says, kissing the top of her head. "Together, we can face anything. I think we've proved that, don't you?"

And Milly leans a little closer still, enjoying the solid warmth of her husband, as together they watch the great orb of the sun sink with surprising speed below the horizon, leaving behind streaks of burnished copper across a rapidly darkening sky.

Chapter 25

Milly

Levittown, Long Island, New York, July 1953

A t the sound of a horn outside in the street, Edward flings open the front door and runs out to greet Doris and the children in their car. Milly gathers the picnic blanket, closes the basket, and is about to leave the house when the telephone rings.

"I can get the kids settled in the car if you want to get that," Doris calls from outside the open front door. She lifts the picnic basket Milly had prepared and balances the rolled-up blanket on top. Milly picks up the receiver.

"They've taken her." Myra's voice is thick and choking down the line. She's speaking so fast, so garbled, Milly can't follow.

"Wait, Myra, slow down. I don't understand. What's happened?"

"It was so early this morning; we were still sleeping and oh god, Milly, it was awful . . ." She begins to cry and Milly's stomach plummets. This is not the powerful, supremely cool Myra she has come to know and admire.

"Susan? No . . . It's not Susan?"

"Yes. Oh, Milly, they've taken her . . ."

"Who? Who took her?"

A few more sobs. "The FBI."

"What . . . Why? Because she lent a few illicit books? I thought she'd been questioned already over that by HUAC."

"They considered her to be obstructive because she wouldn't give up any names. She's so stubborn . . ." There is a sigh down the phone. "Besides, it isn't just about the books."

Myra doesn't need to explain. *Fellow travelers. Communists. Liberal leftists. Two women living together.* The words of the Minute Women reverberate through her mind.

"What happens now?" She runs her fingers through her hair, swallows down a lump of cold fear. *Oh Susan!*

Myra says something about lawyers and the Fifth Amendment but Milly doesn't hear much of it because Myra's voice is choked with tears and Milly realizes Doris is back, staring at her from the doorstep.

"Milly, I need to talk to you. Can you meet me—"

"I'm sorry, I can't talk right now. I'm with a friend. Could I call you later perhaps?"

"Oh. But it's urgent, see—"

"I really do have to go. I'll call you just as soon as I can."

Milly puts the phone down, gives Doris a bright smile.

"Everything all right?" Doris asks, leaning one hip against the doorframe, head tilted to one side.

"Oh. Yes. Just, um, a friend. She's having a bit of a hard time."

Doris gives her a long stare, then pushes herself off the doorframe.

"Okay then, let's go."

They walk to the car, but the desperation in Myra's voice is still ringing in Milly's ears. Her feet are on the ground but it's as though she is floating somewhere above it on a turbulent sea of unreality that is making her head swirl. She thinks of Susan being carted off for questioning. Where will they take her? What will they ask her? How much trouble can she really be in? Milly thinks of the loyal friendship and support both Susan and Myra have given her these past months and how she put the phone down on Myra and she thinks, *What a wretched coward you are, Milly Bennett. Your friends need help, and you have turned your back.*

Just as soon as it isn't rude to abandon the picnic, she'll leave Doris and do what she can to help Myra.

In the park they lay out the blankets beneath the spreading branches of the oak tree just beyond the playground, and Doris produces a beach ball. The children run off with it to play, their shouts of delight and laughter peeling out across the village green. Milly sits on the rug beside Doris as the clouds begin to dissipate and the sun breaks through, bathing them in dappled light. Doris reaches into her bag and pulls out a flask.

"Oh," Milly says, "that was clever. I didn't think to bring coffee."

Doris laughs and gives the flask a little shake. "I've gone one better than that. It's gin fizz!" She reaches back into her bag a second time and pulls out glasses. "Not too early for you, I hope?"

Milly looks over at the children playing some sort of chase and catch with the ball, Ronald taking charge. She thinks of Myra alone and anguished, Susan heaven knows where.

"It is rather. I'm sorry, Doris. I don't think I'm quite in the right mood for drinking."

"Come along, Milly. A little snifter won't hurt. Might even cheer you up. You've barely uttered a word since we left your house." Doris pours a small measure into a glass and pushes it into Milly's hands. She pours a larger glass for herself. She takes a mouthful, sighs, and fixes her eyes on Milly. "Now come on. What's bothering you? Maybe I can help?"

Milly's throat tightens and she takes a drink. The gin is strong. It does help, a little. "Honestly, Doris, this isn't really something a chat will make any better. Truth is . . . I am worried about my friend. The one who just called . . ."

"What's happened to her? Do tell me Milly. We're friends, aren't we?"

Milly is silent. The urge to tell someone, to seek their advice, to find a way to help Myra and Susan is so strong.

She shakes her head. Of all the people in the world she would confide in, Doris would be the last. "I can't," she says finally.

Doris sighs. Gives her head a small shake, as though Milly is as tiresome as one of her offspring not behaving. She leans back on one elbow and watches the children.

"Doris," Milly says, as the idea occurs to her, "look, this is an imposition, I know, and I promise I'll make it up to you, but would you mind awfully if I went home and called my friend? I did rather put the phone down on her and I feel bad about that. If you could watch the children, just for a bit?"

"Well," Doris says in a resigned drawl. "Go on then. They're having a ball, so I should take advantage while you can. If you aren't back when they've finished eating the picnic lunch, I'll bring them home."

Milly is already on her feet, scrambling to put her shoes back on.

"Oh, Doris, *thank* you. I'll happily watch yours in return some time."

Doris smiles. "I will hold you to that," she says and raises her glass.

Perhaps Doris is a nicer person than Milly has given her credit for.

Milly leans over, wondering if she should give Doris a kiss on the cheek, but settling for a pat on the shoulder instead. Perhaps she *has* been too harsh on her, and she did reach out the hand of friendship to invite her to this picnic today. Milly vows to be kinder in her thoughts toward her from now on.

"Thank you," she says again.

Edward and Olive barely acknowledge that she is leaving when she tells them she must go and help a friend, and after a final wave to Doris, she sets off at a brisk walk for home.

Milly telephones Myra as soon as she steps inside the front door. Myra picks up at the first ring as though she is waiting by the phone.

"I need to see you in person," Myra says. "I'll drive over." Fifteen minutes later, Milly stands as arranged, at the end of Old Oak Lane, hoping none of the neighbors will pass by, waiting for Myra. Her navy-blue Studebaker pulls up at the curb and Milly climbs in beside her. A pair of large sunglasses hide Myra's eyes, but Milly can see from her rumpled hair and puffed red cheeks that Myra is in a state of distress. She pulls away from the curb and they drive for a few minutes in silence.

"How is Susan?" Milly asks, "Do you know where they have taken her?"

Myra shakes her head. "I've hired the best lawyer I can find," she says. "He's handling things from here. He thinks they don't have much to pin on her. She's never been a member of any communist organizations. But he thinks there is no chance she'll ever work again as a librarian. She can't deny lending banned books. And then there is the thorny issue of us living together," Myra adds. "But the lawyer is confident he can get around that, too, somehow. Much easier for women than men, apparently. You know, two women living together for safety, or some such. And I can prove I've had boyfriends in the past."

Myra turns onto the highway in the direction of Hicksville, where she and Susan live.

"So perhaps it's not as bad as you first thought?"

"He says they may be more lenient if she will finally agree to name and shame others with communist leanings."

"My god . . ."

"She would never do that. I know Susan." Her mouth curls into a sad smile. "She'd rather die than give up her friends." Myra pauses. "But there is something I need to tell you."

That sense of unreality hits Milly again. The floating sensation, as though she isn't really here. A twist of anxiety in her guts, like a portent of doom.

Myra turns off the highway onto a quiet side street. She pulls up beside a patch of open ground that has a sign, Prime Real Estate for Sale. They sit side by side, staring out over the scrubby grass toward a line of distant trees.

Myra's fingers twist in her lap. She runs her tongue across her lips. "The FBI raided the offices of the magazine. Susan isn't the only one to lose her job." She gives a throaty, ironic laugh. "At least, I haven't quite lost my job *yet*. I've been suspended, pending an investigation. It's the Alius story, Milly. They are saying it's subversive. That, through the story, the magazine is spreading communist ideals. The fact this story has become so popular . . . It's not good, Milly."

Milly stares at Myra, the implications of what she is saying slowly sinking in. She pinches her forehead, trying to align her wildly jumping thoughts.

"But . . . I *asked* you, more than once, if this would be okay."

"I know. I thought it would be. I was wrong."

Milly shakes her head, trying to clear it. "Charlotte isn't advocating communism," she says. "She is simply telling women their thoughts and ideas, their value, isn't less than any man. It's just equality she is asking for. Not an end to democracy!"

"I know, Milly." Myra raises a hand to stop her words. "But the way you have portrayed it, this fantasy place, this society, the ideas . . . Every person who reads it comes to it from a different angle. Some see it as inspirational, and it will change their lives. Others see it as entertainment. But some see it as subversive. It doesn't matter what a writer's intentions are before they put words on a page. It's what the *reader* makes of it that counts, especially in these dystopian times in which we find ourselves."

Milly shakes her head. "But isn't freedom of speech something that is hallowed and upheld in this country?"

"Well, that's the theory. But the reality? Freedom of speech has become as much of a fiction in some quarters as Charlotte and her Alius. In retrospect, I was stupidly naive. I should have seen how all this could be misconstrued. But I guess we were all swept along by your popularity and the money flowing in."

They sit in silence.

Then Myra speaks again. "I made a promise to you, Milly, a promise I have broken. I'm more ashamed than I've ever been in my life. But when they took Susan . . . It was the last straw. She's a better person than me. You are both better people than me."

Milly is frozen. She senses Myra's discomfort beside her. She knows what's coming, but she is numb.

"The FBI think Charlotte is a pseudonym for the Communist Party." She pauses. "I had to tell them, Milly. I had to do what I could to save Susan—she sure as hell won't tell them herself." She takes a breath. "I told them there *are* no communists behind this. Just a bored, lonely housewife."

She removes her sunglasses, wipes tears from her eyes, and looks at Milly. "I'm sorry," she says, "but I had to give you up."

Later, Milly goes through the motions of bathing the children, preparing the evening meal, and tidying the house as though she is an automaton. Her mind is elsewhere, planning what to say to George when he is home and the children are in bed.

How long might it take until the FBI come knocking on her door too?

The nightmare has gone round and round in her mind so much that by the time she hears George come in, the prospect of the authorities coming to take her feels like some crazy dream she has made up in her head.

When George appears in the kitchen, Milly throws herself into his arms. The relief of having him home makes her want to weep. He will know what to do, the right people to contact. Together they can plan a way to make them see that she, Milly Bennett, and her story are no threat to the nation.

"Hey there, Milly-Moo," George says, caught off-balance by the force of her affection, and stumbles backward. "What's all this for?"

"Oh, George," she says, pressing her cheek to his chest, taking comfort from the steady beat of his heart. "It's been quite a day. I need to talk to you about something, once the children are in bed."

George begins to say something, but his voice is drowned by a commotion outside the house, followed by a hammering on the door. Milly's heart hammers in response, but her mind is frozen as she and George stare at each other. Only the children are oblivious, their laughter and high-pitched voices drifting in through the open back door from where they are playing in the garden.

No, no, not yet!

"Who the heck is that?" George moves first. The banging on the front door comes again.

"All right, all right," George mutters.

"Wait!" Milly cries, her breath coming short and fast.

"Someone is impatient," George says, as Milly stumbles down the hallway behind him.

"George, please, I need to—"

But it's too late, George is opening the door, and two men are on the doorstep. With a sickening jolt she hears, "We are looking for Mrs. Millicent Bennett" and she is running, back down the hallway and into the kitchen, out into the garden where the children stop and stare at her, big-eyed in surprise.

She gathers Edward and Olive to her. "My darlings!" She crumples to the ground, the dry grass rough against the skin of her legs. Behind her, as though from a great distance she is vaguely aware of men's voices, muffled from the house. Milly hugs her children tight, kisses the tops of their heads. They smell of fresh earth. Of butter, sugar, soap. She closes her eyes and breathes them in, savoring their small, hot bodies pressed against her own. "Edward, Olive, listen to me," she says, as they begin to wriggle out of her arms.

She releases them and they turn to look at her, confusion in their eyes. The voices reaching her are raised now.

"There are two men here," she tells them. "From the government. They are going to take me away for a short time, to ask me some questions."

"How long?" asks Olive.

"I don't know. Hopefully only a few hours. Maybe days, at most."

"I don't want you to go, Mummy." Edward's face begins to

pucker.

"I don't want to go either, Edward. And trust me, I will do everything to be back with you both just as soon as I can."

"But why?" asks Olive. "Why are they taking you? Can't they take Daddy instead?"

"Not Daddy either," Edward wails. "I don't want them to take any of us!"

Milly smiles at them as tears begin to prick at the back of her eyes. "They won't take Daddy." She takes a breath. From the house, George calls for her.

"They are taking me," she tells them, "because I wrote some stories in a magazine. They didn't like the messages in the stories. They thought I meant things that I didn't. I'll explain it all to you properly when I'm home again. But I want you to know three things. First, I love you both, and Daddy, so very, very much. You are the most important things to me in all the world. Second, don't let anyone tell you what you can or can't think, or do, or write, or say. And third, there may be people who say things about me at school or around town. Almost all of it will be wrong. Don't let yourselves be hurt by any of it. We Bennetts are stronger than anyone's mean words, so we rise above it, yes? Whatever happens, we love and support each other, okay?"

They both nod. Edward starts to cry again, and Olive follows suit. Milly gives each of them one last, fierce hug. George is calling her again. "Stay here," she tells them. "Daddy will take care of you until I'm back."

Then she goes inside the house.

In the hallway, George is gesticulating, his hair mussed where he's run his hands through it. The two men are still on the doorstep, George having barred their entrance into the house.

"Oh, Milly," he says, relief flooding his voice. "Please tell these

FBI gentlemen they've made a mistake. They are causing quite a scene, something about you spreading communist propaganda. It's ridiculous!" He lets out a nervous laugh.

Milly swallows, looks at George, and shakes her head.

"I know why they are here," she says quietly, and George splutters something unintelligible.

Outside, beyond the spread-legged strangers, Milly can see a steadily growing crowd of neighbors is forming to see what is happening at the Bennett house.

"Let them in," she says, "we are causing a spectacle."

George reluctantly steps aside, and they shuffle awkwardly into the sitting room.

"What's going on?" George hisses. His face is ghostly white.

"I'm sorry, George. I've been a fool. But I'm sure we can clear this all up. It really is a giant misunderstanding and—"

"Lady," one of the agents interrupts, "sir, I need to hurry you along. Mrs. Bennett is wanted for questioning by the Immigration and Naturalization Service. I'll give you five minutes to collect anything you might need for a few days."

"The Immigration and Naturalization Service?" George repeats. "But Milly is married to me, and I'm an American. She has every right to be here."

"Sir, the INS investigate cases where foreign-born nationals are accused of behaving in a subversive manner. And that is what your wife is accused of."

George's mouth hangs open. He clasps both hands behind his head, shaking it as though trying to dislodge a bad dream stuck inside.

"This has to be a mistake," he mutters. He glances at Milly, his face a mixture of confusion and helplessness. "What *exactly* is she accused of?"

"I'm afraid we can't tell you anything, sir."

Milly begins to shake, tremors starting in her belly and fanning out to her limbs. George can't save her. Nobody can, except, possibly, herself.

"Mrs. Bennett," the man who appears to be in charge says, "we really don't have much time. Collect your things or you'll have to come without."

Wordlessly, Milly climbs the stairs, George following behind. One of the agents stations himself at the bottom of the stairs.

"*What* is it that you've done?" George asks.

"I wrote some stories," she begins. "It was Susan, at the library, Susan, well, not her, but *through* her. It was Myra, the editor at *My Life* . . ." She is so nervous the story is coming out muddled and she trips over her words. "I was lonely, you see, and bored. It seemed a good idea at the time . . ."

"But I thought we agreed you wouldn't do this?" There is a note of frustration in George's voice. He sits heavily on the bed while Milly stuffs a couple of changes of clothes into a small bag with shaking hands, fetches her toothbrush and washcloth from the bathroom. What else might she need? She can't think straight. She doesn't know where she is going so how can she know what to bring? She sits next to George.

"I wrote a story under a pseudonym, and *My Life* serialized it. Myra promised never to reveal my name. But she did. Myra betrayed me . . ." Milly begins to cry.

"Why didn't you tell me what you were doing?"

Milly shakes her head. "I don't know . . ." George fishes his handkerchief from his pocket and she accepts it gratefully, wiping her eyes and nose. "Because you said not to do it."

George puffs out a breath. "For good reason, it seems . . . What on earth *was* this story?"

Milly twists the handkerchief around her fingers. "The idea wasn't even mine. I took it from a four-hundred-year-old manuscript. Do you remember that man who came to see me, at the end of last year? Winton Harvey-Jones?"

George shakes his head. He looks so uncomprehending, as if the world around him has shifted on its axis, so that nothing he thought he knew about it is true.

"I told you he was a distant relative. He wasn't, as it happens. He was my boss, during the war."

"At the asylum?"

"Sort of . . . The important thing is, he brought me the manuscript. He thought I might be able to help with it."

"Why?"

"That's complicated . . ." She glances toward the door. "I've not time to explain. There were some things I worked on, during the war I can't talk of. But I learned about coding."

"For pity's sake, Milly! What else have you been lying to me about?"

"I've not been lying, George . . ."

"Not telling me the truth then. Same difference."

"Mrs. Bennett?" A voice from downstairs. "We must ask you to hurry now."

"The point is," she says quickly, "Winton had a hunch I might be able to decode this old book he had. Lots of writing was encrypted in the early sixteenth century. They were dangerous times . . ." Her words hang between them for a moment. "But then Winton died, and his widow said she didn't want it." George now has his head in his hands and is shaking it. Milly hurries to the wardrobe. "I worked out the key to decipher it, and I used the ideas in it for the story in *My Life* about an imaginary place called Alius . . ."

Milly stands on tiptoe and reaches for the shoebox. She **feels** it with the tips of her fingers and edges it forward. "What st**ruck** me was just how relevant those ideas were for today's America. **It** seemed so intensely sad that those women were too afraid to **write** what they wanted, that they were compelled to encrypt a wh**ole** book to keep it safe. I thought, if only I could breathe life into **it,** just as they would have wanted. It felt like the right thing to **do.** Please believe me, George, I never meant any of this to happ**en."**

She turns to look at him while inching the box toward her. **He** stares at her dumbstruck, as though she is a stranger in his home.

"I promise, it will all make sense once you see it. And the **notes** I've made showing the key to the encryption method. When **the** FBI see, they will *know* this is just one huge mistake. They'**ll let** me come home, and *My Life* can print an explanation, Myra **can** get her job back, and Susan will be fine too. Everything will **be** back to normal and—".

But she has pushed too hard on the shoebox and it tum**bles** down from the shelf, landing on its side with a soft thump, the **lid** skittering across the carpet.

Milly's heart stops, panic rising like a scream in her throat.

The box is empty.

The manuscript and her notebook are gone.

Chapter 26

Charlotte

Paris, October 1552

Charlotte thought she knew darkness.

But inside the cell at the Palais de la Cité, this dark was the blackest of dark, thick as treacle; it draped itself over her, weighing her down so she couldn't move her limbs, clogging her throat and lungs until she was certain she would choke. She was entombed behind locked iron bars, between feet-thick stone walls, and she wondered if she would ever see the light of day again. Her throat was tight with terror, and it made no difference whether her eyes were squeezed shut or wide open, the frigid, inky air pressed down like six feet of solid earth.

Ah, Lotte! What did you do? Claude's voice suddenly, incongruously, inside her head. *I know you meant well, but really, printing that woman's work? Not your finest moment, hmm?*

My dear Charlotte, I explained the importance of reputation, did I not? Berthold now, his tone, patient and kind, just like it always was. *What are we to do with you?*

Dear god! Were these two dead husbands together, right now, in heaven? Had they compared notes? Could they be friends? She hoped so. The thought was something of a comfort, especially now.

Charlotte lay curled in a ball on a hard wooden pallet. The guards had, on account of her advanced years, granted her this small comfort. Most prisoners had nothing but the stone floor to sit or lie upon. The guard had even tossed her a rough woolen blanket.

"Wouldn't want you to die of cold before morning, would we?" he'd said, shutting the door with a clang and sliding his key in the lock.

"This has more holes in it than a sieve!" she'd called out to him. "If you want me alive, can you find another, less threadbare?"

But the guard had ignored her, his footsteps echoing off the walls as he retreated. She'd felt her way along the cell wall, the rough stone damp beneath her fingers, to the pallet where she had lain ever since. She shivered beneath the thin, musty blanket, curling her knees to her chest, resting her head on her folded arms, every part of her body complaining at the unforgiving wood when she was used to a soft featherbed. The silence was punctuated at intervals by a cry here, a hacking cough there. Somewhere, a long way off, someone was singing or chanting some strange incantation, broken every now and again by a shout and the rattling of locked gates. She wondered if Frédéric was here, too, and whether, if she called out, he would answer her.

"Frédéric?" she tried, but her voice was as thin as the blanket. "Frédéric?" Louder this time, but there was no answer. She supposed the guards would have separated them so they couldn't communicate and agree on a narrative between them.

The hours ticked so slowly by it was as though the sun would never rise again. Exhaustion finally must have made her sleep because a sudden clanging at the gate to her cell jerked her awake. A guard and the bouncing light of a lantern appeared with a bowl of thin, cold oatmeal and a bucket for her slops. She was glad of that, at least, for her bladder was full to bursting.

"What is happening?" she asked, but the guard merely

shrugged. He hung a lantern on a hook outside her cell, the flickering light pushing the suffocating darkness away to the edges of the lit circle.

"I want to get a message to my lawyer, Monsieur Riant . . ." she called. But the guard was already locking her in and moving on. Farther along the passageway, the shouts and cries from other prisoners intensified. Tortured, tormenting sounds.

After awkwardly, painfully, relieving herself over the bucket, Charlotte peered at the bowl of oatmeal with distaste. She missed her eggs and cup of wine. She missed Sophie, the creature comforts of her home, the printworks. Her stomach churned with the thought she may never see any of it again. And then there was the prospect of burning at the stake. Here, in the rank, frigid air surrounded by inhuman, echoing howls, it was almost impossible to imagine the violent red heat of a fire, licking its way toward her, the beginning of all eternity burning in hell. She forced that image away. Forced herself to ignore the awful sounds and to eat the disgusting gruel that turned her stomach and made her gag. She had no idea when her next meal may come, and she needed to stay strong.

Engulfed in perpetual darkness, it could have been hours or days that had passed by the time the guard returned. Charlotte was weak with exhaustion, numb with cold. Her limbs were heavy, her head swam, her back plagued her with spasms of pain.

"Come," the guard said, opening the gate wide to let her through. He said nothing as he led her along the passage, up the narrow spiral stairs to ground level where there was blessed daylight and normal life proceeding without heed to the horrors that lay beneath their feet in the cells below.

After the chill of the prison, a wall of heat in the small interview room from a roaring fire hit Charlotte like the searing rays of a midday sun. Monsieur Riant rose from a chair. His familiar face made her cry out in relief, and she clasped his hands as though he'd saved her from drowning.

"Monsieur Riant! I'm so relieved . . . Whatever is to be done! Have you seen Frédéric? Can you help us? What is this about? Nobody will tell me a thing!"

"Madame . . ." Riant's tone was low and calm. "One matter at a time, if you please. I imagine there is some terrible misunderstanding. I will clear this up as soon as possible. I have requested the urgent presence of Antoine de Mouchy, who ordered your arrest. Now, sit. You look . . . wretched."

"I feel it." The lawyer's nose twitched. "No doubt I smell it too," Charlotte said.

"How have you been treated?" He searched her face, his brow wrinkled in concern. They both knew, however highborn, however good one's reputation, this was no protection against an allegation of heresy or sedition.

Charlotte glanced at the guard who had stationed himself in front of the closed door, and another man standing with his back to the fire who she recognized now as one of the *mouchards*, the informers, who had been at the printworks last night, hovering in the background while the *officiers de police* arrested her and Frédéric. She'd seen that man before last night . . . But where? Her brain was too foggy to recall.

Charlotte sat, grateful for the comfortable chair, wary of the listening ears. She edged closer to Monsieur Riant and whispered close to his ear.

"What evidence do they have against us? Was it Nicolas? Or

Jean?" Her blood ran hot at the thought of the breach of the trust she had put in them. What did they hope to gain from their treachery?

But Riant was shaking his head, his lips pursed. "No, I have my suspicions who is behind this. I have my own informants who I hope will confirm. I await news . . ."

"But who would do such a thing. And why?" The only people who knew about the secret printing project were those recruited to help. Even Riant does not know.

"We will find out just as soon as de Mouchy gets here."

"And Frédéric? Where is he? He should be here, with us."

Riant leaned in closer. "I asked for him to be brought. But I was told he was currently unavailable. I am afraid for him . . ."

Charlotte gasped. *Currently unavailable.* She thought of the tortured cries from the occupants of other cells in the prison. Cries that spoke of broken bones, pulled teeth, crushed knuckles, and rope-whipped, bleeding skin. If Frédéric refused to answer their questions, refused to tell them what they wanted to know . . . Please God, it should be her on the torturer's rack, not him. This was her enterprise. She should be the only one to suffer.

She clasped Monsieur Riant's arm. "You *must* find him. Tell them I will confess if only they release Frédéric. I will repent, I'll do anything."

But before Riant could reply, the door banged open again, admitting Antoine de Mouchy. The sight of him made her skin crawl.

"I am a busy man, Riant," he began. "And I don't take kindly to being called from my *dejeuner.* There had better be a good reason for this intrusion."

"Thank you for coming, Antoine," replied Riant in soothing, respectful tones. "I apologize for inconveniencing you . . ." De

Mouchy grunted. "You see," the lawyer continued, "I think there must be an unfortunate mistake. My client, Madame Guillard, has been brought and held here under false pretenses. What evidence is there behind this arrest? Madame Guillard is a woman of impeccable reputation. Not only does she print legal and religious texts of excellent quality, but countless other works of antiquity. There can be no question of her loyalty and devotion to the faith."

De Mouchy bristled. "The evidence is clear. That is why I do not appreciate being dragged from home when the circumstances do not warrant it." He reached for his pouch and withdrew a folio. He laid it in front of Monsieur Riant. It was the first printed page of Lysbette's manuscript. Charlotte's blood ran cold.

"Madame Guillard was acquainted with a woman named Lysbette Angiers . . ." The room dipped. She could feel the weight of all the men's eyes on her, accusing, judging, deciding. "That woman was, we understand from our informers, a woman who, despite once being a nun, had strayed into the realms of witchcraft and sorcery. We believe she almost certainly was in possession of a work of heresy by her own hand. And I believe that woman had taken this work to Madame Guillard for printing, although why she should consider such a project, I cannot imagine." Nor, in that moment, could Charlotte. "But printing such a text . . . Well!" He did not need to finish his sentence.

He moved closer to Charlotte, leaning over her until she caught a whiff of fish and ale on his breath. She turned her head away. "Perhaps you can enlighten us, Madame . . . Perhaps she heard you were sympathetic, given your past publication of other heretical works . . ."

Charlotte met de Mouchy's rodent eyes as a tremor of fury rose up inside her.

"What preposterous nonsense is this! I do not know of any such work. Indeed, I was barely acquainted with this woman of whom you speak. As I told the commissioner, she came into my shop—"

"Which was a lie, Madame. Lysbette Angiers was being followed that day. She was admitted to your home, where she remained all afternoon . . ."

Charlotte swallowed. *Dear God.*

It is never a good idea to lie, Lotte!

Thank you, Claude. But sometimes it is necessary.

"I am an old woman, Monsieur de Mouchy." Charlotte allowed her voice to tremble. "I did not realize it was important to specify that I took Madame Angiers into my home as she was tired and thirsty and wished to discuss French poetry. The woman was murdered, violently, and I was in shock when I spoke to the commissioner. It was a terrible sight—all that blood, the gaping wound." She shuddered.

"Antoine"—Riant placed himself at Charlotte's side—"the commissioner was satisfied with Madame's explanation. Please, can we stick to the matters at hand?"

"Of course," Monsieur de Mouchy replied, nodding to the folio. "I suggest you read this. We found it on the printing press at Soleil d'Or on the night of the arrest. My belief is that it is a printed folio from the work of Madame Angiers, which your client planned to distribute. An act of heresy that would see her burn. I believe Madame Guillard has hidden the actual work somewhere in her home, and we intend to find it." He shoved the folio at Monsieur Riant.

Charlotte said a quick prayer for Sophie and watched her lawyer's impassive expression as he read, her mind racing for an explanation of the words he was reading.

My name is Prima, and, although I am not old—I am in my

thirty-second year—I fear I am close to the end of my life. For this reason, I am compelled to put into writing this, my true and honest account of what I have learned during my unique adventures.

But most of all, I hope you will come to understand the innate power of words. For words must be chosen with care. It's words that swell the heart to love and tolerance and words that lead to hate and persecution. Words that, spread by priest or paper, written into law or decree, spoken in private rooms or amplified to the thousands, have the force to spawn adoration and adherence, defiance and revolution, destruction and death. I hope further that whoever reads my words—the last I shall ever write—will take some heed of them. Enough at least to talk them over and think on them.

The below account, dear reader, is all truth. The only fiction, I venture, that exists in this world, is that which men of influence would have you believe for their benefit. If you seek the truth, look behind their false words at their deeds and their motivations.

Monsieur Riant glanced at Charlotte. They had known each other for many years. She saw the questioning look in his eyes and she raised her eyebrows at him, hoping he could read her thoughts in the look she returned.

Her lawyer turned back to de Mouchy. "I can understand your concern," he said smoothly, "But please allow Madame Guillard to explain . . ." Thank heavens he understood.

De Mouchy gave Charlotte a look of disdain. "It is for the court—the Parlemont—not I, to decide if we have a heretic among us. My job is simply to gather the evidence."

"But you have the power to decide who goes before that court,"

Riant reminded him.

"True . . . Fine." De Mouchy waved a dismissive hand. "Let the woman speak if she wishes, but take care, woman, for anything you say in this room may well incriminate you." He folded his arms and stared down at her.

Charlotte swallowed hard. Took a moment to pick her words.

"You understand ancient Greek, Monsieur de Mouchy?" she asked, conjuring a pleasant smile. She had a hunch de Mouchy could not understand a word of what was on that page.

"Get your client to stick to the matters in hand, Riant," he snapped.

"This is relevant, *Antoine*, I assure you."

Charlotte stood stiffly and leaned over the folio. "*Sir*, I am one of the few Parisian printers in possession of ancient Greek typeface. We are so overrun with commissions, I had to fit it in late at night to please my good client. This was a small print run of a rather obscure ancient text, *Apataó*. Do you know it? It was written by the less well known of the philosophers, Apomimisi."

The made-up names sounded good, even to her. Men never liked to be made to look foolish. Especially men like de Mouchy. *Apataó* meant to cheat or deceive, and its author, *Apomimisi*, a fake. She hoped her own fakery would work.

De Mouchy shook his head, shifted as though in discomfort. "Not well, but what of it?"

"Then the explanation of the contents of this folio will be a mystery to you. My client is a Carthusian monastery. You may check with the monk, Godefroi, if you wish. This is good, legitimate, and worthy work. This text is more than one thousand five hundred years old. There is nothing heretical in what I do. I am deeply faithful to the church, as Monsieur Riant has attested. As anyone who knows me will attest."

De Mouchy grunted.

Charlotte plowed on. "The monastery came across this obscure manuscript and wished to print more copies, should it be lost. It is not unheard of for Greek scholars to write in this way—putting themselves into the story in order to make the audience more convinced of the authenticity of the tale. It is an old literary device that goes back more than a thousand years . . ."

De Mouchy unfolded his arms and leaned forward, poking out his chin, curling his lip. "Then where is this ancient manuscript? It would be easy enough to check your story, woman, but despite searching your premises, my men were unable to locate it. All we have to go on is this . . . *dubious* paper and your word. Besides, I can find myself a Greek expert and verify your claims . . ."

"Are you doubting the word of one of the most reputable printers in Paris?" Riant interjected as though astonished.

"One who has also printed works by Erasmus," de Mouchy muttered, his jaw set.

"Are you telling me that a priceless manuscript is now missing?" Charlotte was beginning to warm to her act. She looked from one man to the other in shocked exasperation. "It must have been the *thugs* you sent to search my premises. They—"

But their discourse was interrupted by a knock. Monsieur Riant's clerk entered, breathing heavily. There was urgent whispering between the two men. Finally, they broke apart and Riant faced de Mouchy, a look of triumph flashing across his face. He swung a finger and pointed it at the *mouchard* who stood silently in the corner of the room.

"I suspected as much, but now my clerk has confirmed it. Monsieur *Faivre*, there, is in the pay of Monsieur Baubigny, head of the Paper Guild. He has been instructed to use any means he can to discredit my client's good reputation ahead of the litigation she has brought against the guild over poor paper quality. Faivre has falsely reported to Monsieur de Mouchy that my client was printing work of a heretical nature. Clearly, Monsieur Baubigny is afraid she has good cause since he is resorting to such tactics. It is a low stunt for the papermakers, and these false allegations must be withdrawn at once."

Charlotte turned to look at the *mouchard* in the corner and all at once, she remembered him. *Faivre.* Of course, *this* man was the one who had visited her printworks back in the summer, nosing around, pretending to look at her paper quality, instead trying to find information on which to report her to the Inquisitor Fidei, de Mouchy. Faivre had also been in her shop a few days ago, scouring her shelves, she recalled. He ran one of the largest paper suppliers in Paris. The man with the limp. It all began to make sense.

Some men, it seemed, would do anything, from banning and destroying books, to torture, murder, execution, or even burning a person alive, if it best served their interests.

It had happened to Lysbette, and by a whisker, thanks be to God, Charlotte would avoid the same fate, albeit for different reasons. And she knew in that moment, she would do everything in her power to preserve Lysbette's words for prosperity.

Chapter 27

Lysbette

The ruby, gold, and books were long gone, and Lysbette was down to the last of her money. She hadn't realized how expensive life outside the abbey would be. She had had to go, cap in hand, to Mercy. Alice had been there, scowling at her, as unfriendly as ever. Mercy had invited her to stay, out of politeness, but with each day that went by, she knew they wanted her gone. She'd heard them whispering, discussing options. Possible husbands who may be willing to take her on. The only maid they had been able to afford to keep was Mary. It was a joy, at least, to see her again. In her desperation she had written a letter to John Haydon, with whom she had had no contact for nigh on to ten years, with Mary's help once more to deliver it. He was her last hope.

And now, finally, her heart dancing like a skittish pony, she was on her way to meet him.

Lysbette crossed Holborn Bridge, the brook beneath dry and cracked as hard-baked bones, heading west along Holborn, a handkerchief pressed against her nose and mouth, a vain attempt to keep the ghastly smells carrying heaven knows what in the manner of bad miasmas from clogging her airways. For nine straight months there had barely been a drop of rain. Crops wilted in the fields, animals dropped dead where they stood, the mighty rivers of the Rhine and the Seine had all but dried up. Across

Europe, fires broke out in tinder-dry cities and people died of the ague from the resulting bad air.

Lysbette thought of Sir Thomas, who must once have walked this street as he went about his legal business. If only he had remained a simple lawyer and hadn't given his service to King Henry. She remembered Alice's blind ambition pushing him, always pushing him, to get closer to the King. To advance the family no matter what. Now thanks to her ambition, not only had she lost her husband, but all her wealth and social standing too.

Sir Thomas, often in Lysbette's thoughts, was all the more so on this, the twenty-eighth day of July. Today, another Thomas who had fallen from favor, Thomas Cromwell, was to lose his head, too, for treason. And today, the very same day, King Henry, was to marry for a fifth time.

She thought of the fair prince in Sir Thomas's *Utopia* and sent a silent prayer to God that the new queen, Catherine Howard, should remain united with *her* head, when the unfortunate Anne Boleyn had lost hers. She pondered the unjustness of the arrangement. These women had no choice but to marry the King. Then, once he tired of them, he would find a way to rid himself of them. A pattern, she supposed, reflected through wider society, albeit less dramatically.

She dodged a group of street hawkers and a town crier, his clanging bell and shouts of *Oyez! Oyez! Oyez!* resonating off the walls of the surrounding buildings. Stepping out into the road, she took care to avoid the baked-dry clods of manure, and a heavily laden wagon pulled by a donkey. As the crier's shouts announcing the King's happy nuptials receded, she pondered Sir Thomas's predictions that Luther's arrival marked the beginning of the end of the world. As a gust of hot wind blew dust and debris into swirling coils making her eyes smart and her throat sore, it was hard not to think he might have been right.

Lysbette pushed open the door to the public bar at Furnival's Inn, shutting the hateful wind outside. Blinking out the dust, allowing her eyes to adjust to the darkness after the bright light from the street, she glanced around the room. Several pairs of male eyes watched her in silence. She was, she supposed, as a lone woman entering the dominion of lawyers at the inn, an oddity. She missed the protection of the habit she had been forced to give up a year ago. Her life was so different now. She mourned the safety and security she had had in the abbey. The loss of it, and her friends there, had cast her adrift into a cruel and uncaring sea where she was nothing but a nondescript woman, down on her luck, clinging to the flotsam of her previous life, hoping to be saved.

John was leaning his elbow on the bar, a jar of ale held in one hand. He was elegantly dressed in lawyer's robes, a luxurious ruff, woolen cap at a rakish angle. He turned as though he felt her eyes on him and his face broke into a warm smile as he beckoned her over. Ten years melted away, and Lysbette's breath came shallow as she floated across the floor toward him. The years had been kind. A sprinkling of gray hair at his temples, gentle lines crawling outward from the corners of his eyes.

But John was a long-married man, with children. She dropped her gaze. No doubt he would see her, an almost middle-aged woman at the age of twenty-six, in a very different light.

"Lysbette Angiers," he said, his voice making her lift her eyes once more to his. John sought her hand, lifted it to his mouth, his lips brushing her skin. "You have barely changed . . ." He stared at her as though in wonder.

A flush rose from her neck to her cheeks, and her heart beat a little faster. After all this time, those feelings she had felt for him so long ago unfurled once more. Dormant, it seemed, not dead.

"You said in your letter you were in need of help . . . I cannot imagine what you must have been through, with the abbey gone."

She nodded, spoke purposefully in a bland voice. "But the King, in his holy wisdom, did what was right."

John huffed. Looked about him. "You need not worry about speaking your mind in present company," he murmured.

"Let's not talk of such things. How is your wife, the children?"

John's face relaxed. "They are well. We have been lucky. Of seven children, five still live and thrive." His eyes shone with pride.

He is happy, she thought. *And I should be glad for him.*

"You must be in need of refreshment." He waved the barman over.

"I am," she said, nodding. "The street is like the desert. Our prayers for rain go unanswered."

John ordered her an ale and shook his head, his lips a grim line. "These are trying times," he said. "So much has happened since we last saw each other."

An hour passed while they spoke of the tragedy of Sir Thomas's cruel end, of her life in the abbey, of his in the law. They spoke of their shifting fortunes, of how they were all but flecks of dust tossed upon the winds of change.

"But tell me, how is it I can help you?"

Lysbette took a deep breath. It pained her to beg, for that was what she was doing, from the man she had once hoped would be her husband.

"I need work, John," she said. "I thought I could make my own way in this world, after Barking. But it seems I was wrong. A lone woman does not fare well in this world. I was invited by a fellow nun—Agnes—to join her in Paris. But I didn't want to go. I was a fool. A stubborn one, at that."

"Can't you change your mind, go now?"

Lysbette shook her head. "The continent is overrun with Catholic refugees from England. I thought, perhaps, I could be a tutor or find work using my learning. But it seems women are not valued in those spheres. Unless it is work of a manual kind, I am never suitable for any position."

John looked at her steadily. She took a long drink from her tankard, the ale pleasingly cool and refreshing as it slid down her parched throat.

"I thought, perhaps, as you knew me, I could become tutor to your children? Or I would even work as a maid in your home. I'm happy to do anything. What do you say?"

John looked aghast. His lips moved, but no sound came out.

"John?"

"Lysbette . . . I don't know what to say . . ."

"How about *yes*, or *perhaps* . . ." She laughed. "I know you would need to speak with your wife, and I would have to meet her, and perhaps the children. I can wait . . ."

It was John's turn to avert his gaze from hers. Silence hung between them, heavy with the unsaid.

Finally, he cleared his throat. "Of course you have no money. I don't know why I hadn't thought of it. I'm so sorry, Lysbette."

"I don't want your pity."

"I know that. You were always proud. And I know what it must have cost you to come here, to ask me this . . . But surely you can see, I can't have you in my house as a *servant*. How could I?" He looked at her with pleading eyes. "Once we hoped to be married. Now . . . It's impossible."

"But that was a long time ago. So much has changed. And if I don't mind it, nor shall you."

"But my wife will mind it."

A beat more silence.

"Why? Why would she mind it?"

"Because she knows how once I loved you. How I had hoped we would marry."

"Why would you tell her that?"

"Oh Lord, I don't know! Because I wanted to be honest. Because losing you broke my heart. Because she was kind and good and she stitched me back together."

Lysbette's jaw tightened.

"Then if she is good and kind, she will have no problem taking me in . . . I mean, that was all long in the past. You are happily married now."

John shook his head. "It's impossible. Look at you. You are a beauty. It wouldn't be fair . . . I can help in other ways. I can give you money."

"I want to work for money, not receive your charity. Your wife wouldn't like that, either, I am sure."

"No."

Lysbette slumped.

"She doesn't trust you? Don't you trust yourself?"

John looked at her, his eyes full of hurt.

"You cannot ask this of me," he said finally. "You simply cannot."

The weather finally broke in late August.

Children ran out into the street, arms out, faces raised to the sky to catch the precious drops of rain on their parched tongues.

Church bells rang, strangers laughed and danced together in their joy at God's grace for sending rain. The drought, for this year at least, was over.

Lysbette stood in the parlor window of Mercy's house on Cow Lane, watching the rain fall, lazy and languorous at first, then with intent, fast and furious, thunderously loud, bouncing off the baked hard earth. Three young men in tradesmen's clothes gripped arms, lurching and jumping in the fast-forming puddles like children, soaked to the skin, faces broad with laughter, rain tumbling into their eyes. She gripped the sill, half wishing she could run outside and join the revelers, abandoning all decorum, and dance with them in the rain.

After her disastrous meeting with John, Lysbette's options ran out. She had to marry or face destitution. Alice, although in her own mind almost a pauper now, living off £20 a year and devoid of the power or influence she had once reveled in, still had some friends and connections. Needing to be rid of the burden of Lysbette, an extra mouth to feed, she began to search for a husband for her in earnest. For a twenty-six-year-old ex-nun with no means, the choices were limited. Now, Lysbette awaited a visit from one of the few prospects.

Alice entered the parlor to cast a critical eye over Lysbette's attire, tweaking the lace at her wrists, rearranging the folds of her one decent skirt.

"At least," she said looking Lysbette up and down, "God granted you good looks that have yet to fade. Men are shallow beasts, so I'm sure we can find someone who will overlook your other flaws. Remember, men like Matthew Hatt do not like women to be smarter than them. He is a merchant, poorly educated by all accounts, but did well as an apprentice and is now successful in his own trade. He has amassed some money and wants a wife and family."

"Why has he not married before?"

"Couldn't afford to, so I'm told. He spent many years traveling across Europe learning the trade, making connections. They say he is good at mingling with other traders, suppliers, buyers. An essential skill in his business. His background is not something to be proud of, so do not dwell on that. Congratulate him on his excellent business acumen. Men like to be flattered. And do not discuss books, learning, languages, or anything that may make him look a fool. Do you understand?"

"Yes, mistress," Lysbette replied.

There was a knock at the door, and Mary announced the gentleman had arrived.

"Good. Please bring him into the parlor. And wine. Bring wine . . . No, ale. I expect he is an ale drinker."

Moments later the maid returned with a tall, powerful-looking man on her heels. Rain dripped from his hat, rolling off his shoulders and the edges of his coat onto the rug.

He removed his sodden hat and coat, handing them to the maid.

"Thank the good Lord for the end of the drought," Alice said, smiling and waving him to a chair. She took Lysbette by the arm, and they sat side by side facing him, rigid backed. Lysbette kept her head down, glancing up at him a few times, surreptitiously so he did not notice, while he spoke to Alice about the journey, how good his business was faring, despite the state of things in Europe.

He was a good-looking man, by all accounts. He was neither old nor fat, his teeth looked in good order, his features regular, his face pleasant, if a little ruddy cheeked. Probably weathered from all the traveling. He had thick fair hair and eyes the speckled light blue of a blackbird egg.

The maid returned with jugs of ale and wine, bread and cheese. The days of tables staggering beneath roasted hares, beef, mutton, and pork were long gone. The family were lucky to eat wood pigeon once a week. Lysbette kept her hands folded in her lap, her demeanor serene. Hoping the man couldn't hear her heart thudding so violently she was certain it would jump right out of her chest. Finally, Matthew Hatt turned to look at her. His eyes roamed her face, and she wondered what Alice had told him about her. The fact she was so old and unmarried must have been explained. She felt herself redden beneath his gaze. She met his eyes and tried to read his thoughts. He was much more handsome than she had expected, having prepared herself for the worst. Other than her father, she had only really known two men in her whole life, Thomas and John. Good men. She had spent so much time in the company of women, she realized as they stared at each other, that a man was like a foreign creature. She couldn't read anything in his eyes. He was entirely blank to her. But not unkind, she thought, smiling at him uncertainly.

He cleared his throat.

"Mistress Angiers, it is good to meet you at last. I've heard much about you from Mistress More." A trickle of sweat ran slowly down Lysbette's back.

"Oh, I . . ."

"How do you find life outside the abbey? I'm sure it is, er, . . . an adjustment?" Lysbette nodded, and he plowed on. "You look very well. I'm not sure what I expected. Someone . . . plainer, I suppose. I thought nuns to be elderly and plain. In my head. I never met one, before you, that is."

He must be as nervous as her, his thoughts tumbling straight from his mouth. She smiled again to soothe his nerves.

"I am adjusting fine, thank you," she said. "I am indebted to this family for taking me in after Barking was surrendered." *Indebted to Mercy, at least.* She bit her lip. "I suppose not knowing what the future holds is a little unsettling, if I'm honest, Mr. Hatt."

He gave her a lopsided smile. "Well, that is why I am here. But you know that, Miss Angiers?" He laughed, a little too loudly, but the poor man was a bag of nerves. His leg was twitching, one foot bouncing up and down, up and down. "It seems that you are in need of a husband, and I a wife." He laughed again, and this time Alice joined in.

"Now isn't that fortuitous," Alice said. She bore a look of great indulgence, as though making this a happy marriage match brought her great contentment.

"What are your interests, Miss Angiers?" Matthew Hatt asked, crossing his legs, the foot continuing to bounce. He poured more ale into his cup and drank it fast.

"I like to read," she began, glancing at Alice who gave her a hard stare. "The Bible, of course," she added swiftly. "Needlework, keeping house . . ." Her mind went blank. What did ordinary women do with their time if they didn't read, write, translate, expand their minds?

"Good, good. And children?" Mr. Hatt offered.

"I'm sorry?"

"You must be interested in children."

"Yes, of course."

"Excellent. I would like a big family. I'm one of twelve. A family isn't a family without God blessing it with many children."

"No. Indeed not."

Something twisted inside. She knew marrying would result in children, of course it would. But she couldn't envisage herself as a mother. All those years thinking she never would be one, she supposed. And yet, with Mercy's children, with the children who were wards of the abbess . . . She didn't feel any affinity with them. Or fondness, particularly. Indeed, she felt nothing. Perhaps that would come once she gave birth to her own.

"Well, Mr. Hatt . . ." Alice clapped her hands together. "I do hope you are happy with what you see in Mistress Angiers?"

Looking at Lysbette, he nodded dumbly.

Alice leaned closer to him and lowered her voice as though imparting some salacious gossip. "I believe you *may* also find her useful in your work. Having been in the monastery, she writes well. A childhood in Bruges means she speaks French, Latin, too, of course."

"I am perfectly capable of making my own business negotiations." He regarded Lysbette with his face tilted to one side. "But I admit, I am not good with foreign tongues. Nor with the pen. I never was any good at school. Perhaps she will prove useful in that regard . . ."

"I'm sure she will." Alice beamed. They spoke as though Lysbette wasn't in the room. "Let us retire to the study to discuss the terms, shall we?"

Lysbette sat, frozen and mute, as, without a backward glance the two left the room.

Chapter 28

Milly

New York City, July 1953

The interview room stinks of stale cigarette smoke and old sweat. Fear is ground like dirt into the vomit-hued carpet and mustard walls.

Milly has lost all track of time and feels as though she has been suspended in an alternate reality. The thought of Olive and Edward without her fills her with such overwhelming panic, she cannot think straight. What if she never sees them again? What will George be telling them? *George!* Poor, darling George. The memory of the look in his eyes as she was led away from the house sends a fresh wave of guilt and desperation through her body. Desolation. Betrayal. And worst of all, she knows he didn't believe her about the manuscript. There is no sign of it ever having existed. It has simply vanished. The loss of it tugs at her, fills her with liquid dread that pulses through her veins like fetid water.

Nobody but she knew about the manuscript. So who the hell could have taken it?

She fingers the polystyrene cup of coffee she was handed by a woman officer who must have taken pity when she glimpsed Milly's tearstained face. The coffee is strong and dark and should help clear the fog in her brain, but she feels so sick she can't bring herself to drink it. If George doesn't believe her, then how is she going to convince the men about to interview her? She wonders if Susan is here too. The thought is somehow comforting that her friend might be just down the corridor.

The door bangs open, and three men enter the room. They introduce themselves as Special Agent Ford, Agent Kaminsky, and Agent Herbert. They carry a tape-recording machine and notepads. If Milly hadn't grasped the seriousness of her situation before, she does now. Dimly she thinks she should have a lawyer. Should she claim the First Amendment, or is it the Third? No, it's the Fifth. A rush of panic again. She knows nothing of American law or her rights or what she should or shouldn't say to protect herself. Milly has never felt more alone in her thirty-two years of life. She thinks of Ethel Rosenberg, and she begins to tremble, uncontrollably.

The men settle themselves around her, spreading their bulk, scraping chairs, clearing throats, slapping notebooks on the table. They regard her with serious expressions.

She tells herself these are just men. Fair, reasonable men. Husbands, fathers, sons. She takes long, deep breaths, feels her heart rate slow, the panic subside. It will be fine, if she can only get them to understand the truth.

Kaminsky plugs in the tape recorder, switches it on.

"Millicent Anne Bennett," begins Special Agent Ford, "I hope you know why you are here." Ford, she assumes, is the senior of the three men. He has a mane of silver hair and a heavily lined face. A pair of intense, dark eyes lock onto hers. Intelligent, she thinks, but reasonable. She can trust this man. She must.

"Not really," she says, looking from man to man. She feels small and female in this room of males. They will be kind to her because of this. She is a young mother. A housewife. They will see she is no threat; how can she be? "I just want to go home to be with my husband and children."

Agent Herbert begins to take notes.

Ford sighs. "Mrs. Bennett, if you cooperate, you will make things a good deal easier for yourself."

"Of course. I want to help. Please tell me why I'm here."

"We don't have to do that."

"I'm sorry?" She laughs. Is this some kind of twisted joke? She has never quite understood the American sense of humor.

"This is no laughing matter," barks Ford. He isn't smiling.

"Am I entitled to a lawyer?"

"I'm afraid not," Ford says. "And before you go bleating about your rights or claiming the Fifth, as an alien who is a danger to national security, you *have* no rights." He shifts in his chair. "Mrs. Bennett, you are in very serious trouble. You are facing deportation, and I strongly suggest you answer our questions honestly and openly, understand?"

Milly's chest is heavy, as though her lungs are filling up with concrete. There is not enough air in the room to breathe. She swallows hard, trying to quell the panic as Ford's words pound inside her head. She nods, slowly.

"Good. Then let's begin." He nods at Herbert to start writing.

"Mrs. Bennett, are you, or have you ever been, a member of the Communist Party, or other affiliated organizations, at home or abroad?"

"No!"

"Do you admit to writing a series of accounts, published in the magazine *My Life*, about a fictional forty-ninth state of America?"

"Well," she begins, her voice sounding, even to herself, tremulous and weak, "I mean, I did, but it was just a story, and it wasn't pro-communist or anti-American."

"That's for us to judge, ma'am. Do you accept those stories were written by you with the intention of influencing readers into thinking they were true? And for women to compare them to their own lives and feel dissatisfied?"

"Well, yes, but not in the way you're suggesting. You see, the basic story was inspired by another written by a woman who lived hundreds of years ago. In retrospect I was foolish and shouldn't have presented it as my own work. I love America. I really do." She stifles a sob. The men exchange a glance.

Ford's mouth is turned down as though in distaste. She feels the eyes of the other men, too, heavy with distrust. She pulls a handkerchief from her handbag and blows her nose, balling it in her hand. But despite her efforts not to cry, her eyes swim with tears.

Ford leans back in his chair, watching her. Is he trying to work out what to do with her? Perhaps he thinks she is insane. Or maybe he is just awaiting her confession. Whatever it is she is meant to be confessing to. They continue to observe her in silence as she withers beneath their gaze.

"Look, I know you will find this all hard to believe," she says to fill the silence. "But here is the truth. I was lonely. I admit, a little bored too. I didn't really fit in with the other mothers at school. It was hard moving countries. And America and England . . . Well, we might speak the same language, but . . . We aren't really the same at all. I had the opportunity to write for the magazine, so—"

Ford straightens. "How did you find this opportunity?"

"Through my friend, who worked at the library."

Ford consults his notes. "Susan Leeson?"

"Yes. But I promise you, Mr. Ford, Susan knew absolutely nothing about what I was going to write about. She is entirely innocent of anything. She is a good—"

"Did you know," cuts in Agent Kaminsky, leaning his bulk across the table, arms and hands spread, "that Susan Leeson and

Myra Bougas are sexual perverts?" Milly stares at him open-mouthed.

"I . . . I don't see how any of that, if it is even true, which it isn't, is relevant?"

"Sexual perverts and the reds are one and the same thing," Kaminsky says, with a wave of his hand.

"The point is," Ford cuts across Kaminsky, "you are friends with two women, also suspected of subversive activities, through whom you were given work as a contributor to this magazine."

"That's not what I said—"

"Tell me about the content. You could have written about anything, Mrs. Bennett. I've read your columns closely and carefully. It is very clear to anyone who reads them that they are a thinly veiled attempt to undermine core American values."

"That's nonsense! I didn't! You are framing this all wrong—"

Ford slams his hands on the table, making Milly jump. "Tell me the name of your Soviet bosses, Mrs. Bennett."

"What!" Milly exclaims. "This is ridiculous! I don't have Soviet bosses!"

Ford glances again at his notebook. "Then who is the mystery male visitor neighbors say came to your house over a period of time late last year?"

"You've been speaking to my *neighbors*?" Milly chokes.

Ford opens his hands in a gesture that says, *so what.* She forces a few deep breaths. She needs to stay composed.

"That man," she says "came to visit twice. He was an old friend of mine from England. He collected rare books and manuscripts and had in his possession an old, encrypted manuscript that he was unable to decipher. It is called the Van Hal manuscript, and you can check that out. There must be records of it somewhere. He suspected it had been written by women, because of the illustrations. As a woman, he thought I might be better able to work out the key."

"Why would he travel all the way to New York to give it to *you?* Are there no women in England?"

Milly stares at her hands, heat blooming inside. She cannot reveal the truth about Bletchley Park. Its existence must remain utterly secret, as must her role in it. In the end, she simply shrugs.

"He thought me intelligent, I suppose. And assumed I had time on my hands."

Ford nods for her to continue.

"Well, I worked on the manuscript, and I *did* work out the key. I did lots of research into sixteenth-century encryption techniques and the history of the period. First, I worked out the base language, which was ancient Greek. I had studied Greek and Latin at Oxford before the war—"

"What was this man's name?"

"Winton Harvey-Jones."

Herbert writes it down.

"Winton Harvey-Jones can verify all this?"

Milly shakes her head. "He died, I'm afraid."

"How convenient."

"No, actually, it wasn't. I was very sad to hear of it. Anyway, it took weeks of work, but I found the key hidden in the book itself. I simply used the contents of this book, reworked it a little to make it more up-to-date, and put all the ideas into the series for *My Life*."

"If your story is true," Ford says in measured tones, "which I find hard to believe since there *is* no evidence of any manuscript, tell me, why would an ordinary housewife have such intimate knowledge of coding techniques?" He pauses and Milly can think of nothing to say to that.

"And where is this manuscript now?" Ford asks.

"It's been stolen. Gone from where I was keeping it in my house. Perhaps you can help me find it . . ."

"All right"—Ford leans forward, hands planted on the table—"let's get to the point here. You have published subversive material and—"

"*Please*, Mr. Ford, I accept what I did was, in hindsight, stupid and naive, but truly, I never had bad intentions, and all those ideas really were in the stolen manuscript. Mr. Harvey-Jones's widow can attest to its existence—I have her telephone number."

"Whether or not this manuscript exists"—Ford gives a pained expression of patience—"is rather beside the point. It's the end result that matters here, not the inspiration behind it. As a person who has lived in this country for less than five years, you are caught under the Immigration and Nationality Act—you might have heard of it, there was a good deal of press about it last year—the McCarran-Walter Act, for deportation back to England."

Milly begins to tremble. "You can't do that without it going to court or something, surely?"

"Here's what's going to happen. I'll hand your case over to the INS, the Immigration and Naturalization Service, who oversee enforcement of cases like yours on behalf of the Justice Department. There will be a formal hearing in front of an INS examiner. In the meantime, you will be taken to Ellis Island until your case can be heard."

"But I must be able to get bail—I'm hardly a criminal! What about my children?"

"Not my problem, Mrs. Bennett. They have a father."

"Why can't I get bail?"

Ford shakes his head and closes his notebook. "You can take that up with the INS, but in most cases it's refused. There is clear legal precedent, I'm afraid, Mrs. Bennett, that says you have no right to any due process or constitutional right as an alien engaged in subversive activities. We'll arrange for your transfer to Ellis Island right away."

"But you can't!" Bile rises in Milly's throat. She cannot be separated from Edward and Olive. From George. She told them it would only be a couple of days. How long could all this take?

"I . . . I want a lawyer. Surely, I'm entitled to a lawyer?"

"You can try," Ford says, a wry smile on his face. "Good luck finding someone to represent you with this."

"The National Lawyers' Guild are your best bet," says Kaminsky. "That twisted lot will represent anyone. Or you could try the ACPFB—The American Committee for the Protection of the Foreign Born."

This cannot be happening. She is caught in a nightmare she can't wake up from. She is so tired. She longs for her home. To be normal. To shower and sleep for a hundred hours. To wake and hug her children. Why did she not appreciate those dull days, those simple pleasures *more*? And now, she may lose everything! Lose the people she loves most in the entire world.

"Best tell the husband what is happening," Ford instructs Herbert. Kaminsky switches off the recording equipment.

The three men stand. Ford looks down at Milly. "Good luck, lady," he says, and they leave, locking the door behind them.

Milly sits in the silence, staring at the closed door. In the utter stillness of the room, there is again that sense of unreality. Her mind flits to the missing manuscript, to the women who encrypted it, and their statement that they were doing so to preserve it for prosperity. *Until such time as it would be safe to publish in a world ready to hear what was inside.*

The world, it seems, is not ready, and it is Milly, the fool, who failed to see that. Milly, and her family, who must now pay the price.

Chapter 29

Milly

M illy has been incarcerated for a month, but it's easy to lose track of time when a person is separated from the rest of the world behind a high, chain-link fence. When each day is the same bewildering confusion of regimented roll calls, canteen meals, supervised chores, yard time, mail call, library, laundry, wash call. Sleeping in a dormitory makes Milly think of *Tom Brown's School Days*, which she'd enjoyed as a child, only this dormitory with its six beds in two lines of three is filled not with exuberant, mischievous schoolboys, but worried-eyed, exhausted women, ground down by uncertainty and powerlessness.

Twice a day, Milly walks with the others in the yard, tramping up and down behind the fence, staring out across the water toward the tantalizingly close Manhattan skyline. In the other direction, the tall shape of Lady Liberty, her torch held aloft, taunts the residents of Ellis Island with false hope. Wherever they are in the detention compound, there are guards watching. As though the thousands of them kept here are going to scale the fence and swim their way over to the mainland, swarming out and infecting America with their foreign ideas, their un-American values.

Milly finds herself among a raft of Italians, Jews, Eastern Europeans, Mexicans and South Americans, French, Swedish, and other English people. Some have been here for months, even years. Many have no idea why they are even here. Several cannot be deported because the countries from which they came refuse to let them reenter, even if they wanted to return. So now, here they are, set to stay indefinitely in this purgatory, forever stateless.

The buildings are crumbling and the whole place is grimy and unkempt. In winter, it must be freezing. But Milly tells herself she won't be here to find out. She can't be. She *needs* to be back with George and the children in her comfortable little house on Old Oak Lane. She will never, ever, take anything for granted again. Sometimes, the panic of this separation, the lack of news from home, the isolation, is so overwhelming, she fears she will go mad with it.

This place was never designed to hold so many people, crammed in for want of anywhere else to put them. But there are a few creature comforts, at least. There is a chapel and a post office, and a commissary that sells cigarettes, stationery, stamps, and sweets. Inmates are allowed to receive mail. For children, there is a playroom, and families are allowed to stay together in one room. Best of all, there is a library, thanks to the Salvation Army, with an extensive selection of books, newspapers, and magazines. Whenever she can, Milly comes here, always finding sanctuary in books. Where she writes letter after letter home to George, to the children. So far, she has had no letter back. How angry must he be with her?

Each day, in the library, she sees the same, distinguished-looking gentleman already there, writing furiously for hours at a time at the same desk.

"I'm C.L.R.," he says, one day, approaching her and offering his hand. "C.L.R. James. But you can call me Nello. I've seen you in here every day." He gives her a quizzical look. "Let me guess, they found out you're a communist, and they're sending you back to Britain?"

"Milly," she says. "It's a little more complicated than that. But essentially, that's what they are claiming. How about you?"

"Well, I *am* a Leninist, so they got that right. But this"—he waves a hand around him—"this is all wrong."

"Are you English too?"

"I was born in Trinidad, lived in Britain for years. Do you like cricket? I live for it. Thinking of putting together a team, right here. We could host visiting teams. The Ellis Island cricket tour— you reckon it'd catch on?" He gives a throaty laugh.

Milly points to the voluminous notes he has on the desk.

"What are you writing, Nello?"

"It's a critical analysis of *Moby Dick*. I'm going to send it to every member of Congress to point out the allegory of Melville's novel and its relevance to this moment in American history. I'm hoping my intellectual brilliance will convince them to let me stay."

She laughs. "Seriously?"

"Oh yes, I'm deadly serious. It's almost done. My friend is organizing to publish it privately—"

"Mrs. Bennett!" A guard calls to her from his position at the door. "You have a visitor. I'll take you down now."

"Oh!" A visitor! Could it be George? *Please let it be George.* She turns back to Nello. "Well, good luck, Mr. James. It sounds most interesting—I hope it works for you."

And then she is out, following the guard across the yard to the main building where the interview rooms are.

George is already seated at a table when Milly enters the room. The first thing she notices is that his hands are trembling. More than anything, Milly wants to take them into hers and stem the tremor. She aches to make everything okay for him. This man, who has always been a tower of strength, who now sits here, pale and defeated, as though the very core of him, his spirit, has been scooped out and only the outer husk remains.

Milly is seated opposite George and told they are not allowed to touch. There is so much to say but not enough words in the dictionary to express the love and regret, and so they sit, staring into each other's eyes, a desert of table between them. There is nothing like a spell on Ellis Island to force a person to count their blessings.

What she means to say is, *I love you. I miss you all so much I think I might die.* Instead, *"Why didn't you reply to my letters?"* falls from her mouth, her words spiked with accusation and hurt.

He shrugs. "I'm sorry," he says. "I didn't know what to say." George rubs a hand across his face. His skin is gray, and his eyes are rimmed red. What has she done to him?

He glances across at the guard standing by the door. "How are they treating you?" George asks, searching her face.

"Oh . . . Not bad."

"It was the ACPFB. They managed to get me this visit."

"I'm so grateful."

"Well . . ." He shifts in his seat. "I didn't write because I didn't know what to think. And then so much was happening, I . . . It's been hard." A tear rolls down his cheek and her throat tightens.

"What about the children?"

"They miss you so bad. But they're fine. Confused, but fine. They ask all the time when you will be coming home. My mother had to drop everything and come and help for a while. She wasn't happy. But she's gone now, there was no need for her to stay."

"What do you mean?" Milly's heart hops. Does he know something? Are they letting her go?

George's shoulders slump. "I've been fired, Milly."

"*What?* But why?"

"Because of *you.*" George waves his hands at their surroundings. This dingy little room with its hateful Formica table that divides them. The guard that stands by the door watching their every move. The filthy walls and high, barred window. The locked door, reminding her she isn't free to leave. "What did you expect, writing that series in *My Life*? I've read all of the stories." The first note of anger in George's voice. "They will deport you, Milly. Our family will be broken up. I don't know how I'll ever get another job. We'll lose the house. *Why*, Milly, that is the question I keep asking myself. I just don't understand. Why you would risk all we had . . ."

"Oh god. Surely it won't be that bad. Of course, if I'd known . . . George, please. You *know* this person they are painting me to be isn't me. Look, I was unhappy, lonely. I didn't fit in. Then, when Winton visited with his manuscript, and Susan suggested I write the column . . . It all fitted into place. I never expected I'd unlock the manuscript, but I did."

"*Stop* this madness!" A muscle flexes in George's jaw, a vein throbs in his neck. "There *is* no manuscript. This Winton . . . Is he your controller or something, are you some kind of spy?"

There is a wild look in George's eyes. One she has never seen before. A look of mistrust, confusion. As though his entire world has been blown into tiny fragments and he is fighting for survival among the dregs of it. He trusts no one, least of all her.

"No! Of course not. George . . . You *know* I'm not a spy! Someone has stolen the manuscript. If you find out who, or why, then I can clear my name—"

But George just sits there, staring at her as though he has never seen her before, lips tight, shaking his head, eyes full of hurt and disbelief.

"This is *me*," she says weakly. Tears begin to fall.

"I don't *know* you anymore, Milly," George says finally. "Perhaps I never did. You were cagey about aspects of your life when we met. What you really did during the war. And now I think, perhaps there was a reason for that."

Milly shakes her head. "You have to trust me, George. You have to."

"I can't tell you how awful it's been." George's voice cracks, and his eyes suddenly fill with tears. "The whole neighborhood treats me and the children like pariahs. Even Mrs. Humphries pretends she doesn't see us, putting her head down and crossing the road if she encounters us. . . . Milly," he says, staring straight into her eyes as though trying to reach into her soul, "Milly, I need your honest answer. Are you, or have you ever been, a communist?"

Milly leans forward; before she can stop herself, she has his hands in hers. "No. I have never been a communist. I am not even very political. You *know* I'm more interested in antiquity. Please, George, if we can only find this manuscript, I can prove all of it to you. I've been stupid, yes, but dangerous, absolutely not."

George continues to stare into her eyes for a few moments, then nods. For the first time, he looks relieved.

"No touching!" the guard shouts and they spring apart.

"Why did they fire you from the bank?" she asks finally. "I still don't understand. I've not been convicted of anything."

"Because a wife is assumed to hold the same political opinions as her husband." George's voice is bitter. "My only saving grace is that I fought for America during the war and haven't been a member of any questionable organizations. Otherwise, I'd be hauled in too."

"Oh dear god . . ." Milly thinks about how proud George was to have fought for his country, for freedom. How hard he's been working to provide for his family. How bright his future had looked. She really has ruined everything. "What will you do?"

He shrugs, the anger gone, the defeated look back. "I've put the house up for sale. With no job prospects, I'll have to take the children back to Kentucky and live with my parents. And besides, there's the legal fees. We've found a lawyer to represent you."

Milly buries her face in her hands. How had it all come to this? "We could go back to England, together," she says, the idea occurring. "Even if they *don't* throw me out . . ."

There is so much hurt in his eyes. A knife twists in her heart.

"How could we ever get past *this*?"

She nods and stares down at her hands, folded on the table. Trust. She has never appreciated how fragile, how central that is to everything.

"Time's up, sir," the guard calls out from his position at the door.

Fresh tears spring into her eyes.

"I wish you would believe me, George."

"I don't know what to believe."

"Write to me, please."

Grim-faced, he turns away and leaves.

Mr. Gordon O'Malley is fresh-faced and young. So young, he must have finished law school only this past summer. Milly's heart sinks. She had hoped for a gray-haired, wily solicitor who knew the system and would reassure her everything would be okay. This man is barely a man at all.

"Mrs. Bennett," he greets her with an outstretched hand, which, at least, is warm and firm.

"I'm afraid your chances of not being deported are slim," he begins right off, squirming a little in his chair as he delivers the bad news. "The material you have been publishing is . . . Let's say, damning."

"And what if I can prove what I published was actually written four hundred years ago? That it wasn't written by me at all, but by other women, long dead, equally persecuted, long before communism?"

The center of Mr. O'Malley's cheeks become perfect circles of red. "That may change things, I suppose, except . . . Why the subterfuge?"

"I don't know," Milly replies, her insides churning. "Have you ever made a stupid decision, Mr. O'Malley, that seemed like a good idea at the time, only you never foresaw the consequences?"

He laughs awkwardly, squirms a little more.

"Your husband told me there is no actual manuscript for us to produce as evidence."

"It was stolen."

"By whom?"

"I've no idea. Nobody knew about it. I know it sounds farfetched, but might the FBI have broken in and found it, looking for evidence?"

He nods. "That's not so preposterous as you might think, Mrs. Bennett. The INS and the FBI have broken into our offices multiple times and stolen files. . . . But, anyway, without the manuscript it will be hard to prove anything."

"It's ironic, don't you think, Mr. O'Malley, that manuscript or no manuscript, we seem to be no freer than we were four hundred years ago?"

He stares at her for a moment. A serious look falls over his features, transforming his face to one of a man a decade older, wiser.

"I do think, Mrs. Bennett. And that is precisely why I do the work I do. I could be earning four times as much if I got a job in the city, but I want to do something that makes a difference. Which is why I'm here."

Thank god for people like Gordon O'Malley.

They smile at each other as a wave of understanding passes between them. Milly is warming to this young man and is reminded, not for the first time, never to judge people by first appearances.

Mr. O'Malley clears his throat. "Well," he says, "manuscript or no manuscript, you are in trouble. There will be a hearing before the INS examiner. Should the decision go against you, you can appeal, but there must be good grounds for overturning an exclusion order. Further, you have no right to bail until the hearing, I'm afraid. You can apply for a writ of habeas corpus, where a court would hear whether your detention is lawful, but in most instances, the court rules in favor of the Justice Department and the INS. Where national security is at risk, there are very few rights to fall back on. Foreign-born radicals are detained here for months, even years, without trial, Mrs. Bennett. In your case, the country from which you came won't likely refuse you entry, so your case shouldn't be delayed. I'm laying it out to you straight, so if there is anything, anything at all you can think of that might help, then please, tell me now."

As Mr. O'Malley's words sink in, Milly's blood turns to ice. She takes a deep breath. She is about to break a law, one that, should she get out of this, might land her right back in jail in Britain, but right now she would do anything, anything at all if it meant she could be reunited with her family.

"Mr. O'Malley, can I tell you something in the strictest of confidence? It might make a difference to my case."

He nods. "Please do." He pulls out his notebook.

"The reason I was able to decipher the manuscript was because during the war, I worked for a secret organization set up by Mr. Churchill and the British government. Its purpose was to decode intercepted German and Japanese messages. The organization remains top secret to this day, and I signed the Official Secrets Act where I promised never to speak of it, under any circumstances whatsoever, even those such as these." Mr. O'Malley is staring at her, his pen unmoving in his fingers.

"Even my husband knows nothing of my work during the war. He thinks I did secretarial work at a local mental asylum. Nobody knows, apart from the people I worked with, who are similarly sworn to secrecy. It was my superior at that organization who came to me with the manuscript, knowing my skills at decoding. Mr. Harvey Winton-Jones is sadly now dead, but perhaps you could have some luck with the War Office? If they can confirm, then it might show something of my good character, and how I, too, did my bit for my country."

Mr. O'Malley hesitates, tapping his pencil on his notebook. "Do you know if there were any Americans involved in this secret organization?"

Milly nods. "I believe so, but I couldn't tell you who, or what they did. We really only knew what was happening in our hut. There were thousands of us who worked at Bletchley Park. But at some of the social events, I did hear a few American voices . . . That's as much as I know."

"Well," Mr. O'Malley says, jotting down two words, *Bletchley Park*, and then closing his otherwise empty notebook. "I can't promise, and I still think your chances, in this current climate, are slim . . . But it's worth a try. Finding that manuscript would help too. I know someone who works at the CIA. Perhaps they can help . . . I'll go and start digging. In the meantime, if you think of anything else, Mrs. Bennett, you let me know." He slid his card with his telephone number stamped beneath his name toward Milly.

As Milly is led back to her living quarters, for the first time since this nightmarish train of events began, hope begins to unfurl.

Chapter 30

Charlotte

Paris, November 1552

Charlotte was in a deep and dreamless sleep when Sophie woke her.

"Madame, you have slept too late," Sophie cried, shaking Charlotte by the shoulder. Her eyes were huge and round, full of fear, Charlotte saw, as she stirred.

"Thank goodness." Sophie sat heavily on the bed, one hand upon her chest. "I thought—"

"That death had claimed me in the night?" Charlotte finished, pushing herself upright. Her body throbbed and ached as though her one night in the prison cell at the Palais de la Cité had aged her ten years more. A month had passed since her release, but the shock of it was still raw and visceral inside. She smiled and patted her maid on the arm. "Oh, I've a bit more to get done in this life before I move to the next."

Sophie herself was no longer in the flush of youth. "There's plenty of life left in the both of us yet," she added, and Sophie returned the smile.

"So we had best get on with the business of the day," Charlotte said, but neither of them moved and they sat in contemplative silence for several minutes. A new day, but one that filled Charlotte with a stirring anxiety.

Today was the day of the paper trial, and although she couldn't be there in person, due to her misfortune of having been born female, her nerves would be on edge all day until Monsieur Riant was able to bring news of the result. Given the lengths the Paper Guild had gone to discredit her, Charlotte's desire to win was higher than ever. Fortunately Yolande, her partner in this litigation, had been spared the horror of arrest that night, having kept out of the suspicious gaze of de Mouchy. Without any contrived reason to arrest her, Charlotte's friend had slept soundly in her bed that night. The guild must have hoped that without Charlotte as an ally, Yolande would have withdrawn the case from court. Of course, Monsieur Baubigny had, like most men, underestimated the pair of them.

"It's a cold day—snow on the way, I think," Sophie said now, poking at the fire, throwing on another log. "I've put out your thickest woolen skirt and bodice."

"Thank you." Charlotte climbed stiffly out of bed and stretched.

Today would be a long day, and a frustrating one, excluded as she was from the courtroom where the future prosperity of her business was to be decided.

Sophie smiled. "Here, come closer to the fire and let me help you."

Later, as Charlotte crossed the courtyard, it began to snow. Tiny flakes fluttered from a flat, pewter sky. She pulled her shawl tight across her shoulders and was grateful for the warm clothes. But still the cold managed to seep through the layers of cloth and skin until it became a dull ache in her bones, a stiffness in her joints.

The presses were in full swing when Charlotte stepped into the workroom. The sharp, metallic smell of ink, the clatter of the presses, the low hum of men at work were so familiar, so dear. It was easy to take its existence for granted, like that of Paris, of France, of life itself, until a looming threat was sent to remind one that all that seems solid is both precarious and fleeting. A stab of fear that this thriving industry of hers may be teetering on the brink of destruction if she took a wrong step seared deep in her chest. They were busier than ever, despite all that had happened, with a commission to print all the works of St. Augustine and a joint commission with Yolande to print the complete canon law. Charlotte prayed for a good result, so that at least they may have decent paper on which to print it.

Charlotte watched her men work with raw, painful affection. Poor Frédéric, who had endured a night of hell as a "guest" of the Palais de la Cité, bore the pain and scars he had sustained that night with fortitude. But she could see them in the limp he tried to hide, in the wince as he used his damaged fingers, as well as in the subtle change in him. She could never repay his sacrifice or lose the guilt she bore for what happened to him. She had softened, however, toward the cantankerous typesetter, Nicolas, and his impressionable apprentice. Following the shock of the arrest and Frédéric's torture by the inquisitors, there had been a perceptible shift in her workers. They drew together, like a family looking out for one another in a cruel and dangerous world. The thought of their loyalty brought a lump to her throat.

Charlotte's stomach rumbled, reminding her she was yet to break her fast. The men, too, must eat. Friday meant salt fish and rice, eel and bread, livened by a plate of almonds, figs, and spiced wine.

She let the chatter during the meal flow over her. She was only half present. The talk of engagements and babies born, of ailments and cures, of gossip and scandal carried on around her as it had always done, and no doubt always would. She thought of the courtroom, of the hateful Monsieur Baubigny and hoped Monsieur Riant would get the better of him and his lawyers. She thought of Antoine de Mouchy and his band of heretic hunters, and of the poor dead woman.

The idea had come to her when she lay in the dark in her cell in the Palais de la Cité. She had made a vague promise with herself that she would think on it if she ever got out of the place alive. She had, for which she thanked the good Lord, and now that idea had evolved and solidified over the past days into something tangible, possible.

It had all begun last summer when the noonday bells rang out through the shimmering heat and brought Lysbette Angiers to her door. And now, as Lysbette herself lay beneath the snow-covered ground, Charlotte saw as clear as a vision sent by God himself, what it was her destiny to do.

The warm, spiced wine spread heat through her veins, and she smiled at her men seated around her. For whatever happened hereafter, she would have this memory, and it mattered, she realized, as much as anything else she had achieved in her long life.

Charlotte was in her study, working through that month's ledgers, when Monsieur Riant, Yolande on his heels, burst through the door.

"I wanted you both to know at once," Riant announced breathlessly, slapping his court papers on the desk between them.

Yolande sank into a chair. "Put us out of our misery, Monsieur, please. And after all dear Charlotte has been through, I trust the news will be good."

They both turned to look at the lawyer. "Heavens, yes," Charlotte urged. "Did we succeed?"

Monsieur Riant shook his head. "I am very sorry, Mesdames, I bring only bad news." He was not one to attempt to cushion a blow. "It seems the guild's hold over Paris is too strong. I fear the judge himself had been *influenced*. He was prejudiced against our claim from the very outset. I am afraid we never stood a chance."

The lawyer proceeded to lead them through the events of the day, but Charlotte barely heard. None of the explanations mattered. Just the result: The trial was lost. Yolande looked as though she wanted to weep, but inside Charlotte grew a ball of anger and resolve. Baubigny, de Mouchy, and all the other men who had in her long life tried to intimidate her, stop her, frighten her into submission—she would not, ever, give in to any of them.

This was the final push she needed.

Later, Charlotte gathered together Yolande, Sophie, and two of her other most trusted female illustrators in her study. With cups of wine in hand, they sat around a cheerful fire.

"My dears," Charlotte began, and the room fell silent. "I have a very special project I need help with. I have chosen all of you because you are wise and faithful, trustworthy and talented. I have also chosen you because you are women. And I believe this is a job only a woman can do."

They listened in silence as she explained about Lysbette Angiers, her suspicion that Antoine de Mouchy was behind her death, her plan as to how they could preserve her work for posterity. The danger it would put them all in should they be found out. There was no sound in the room bar the crackle and spit of the fire.

Charlotte took a gulp of wine, the hot, sweet, spicy liquid warming, calming. "You are also here because between you, you possess all the skills I need to complete this project. My friends,

I hope you will help me to translate Lysbette's work into code." She showed them the cipher given to her by her husband Claude. They would have to disguise the key within the manuscript itself in the hope that someone in the future, preferably a woman, could transcribe it. She had given much thought as to how this might be achieved. A woman's mind paid attention to different things, and Charlotte had an idea of how to make her code more accessible to a female reader than a male. "You, my talented and wonderful women, will grace the work with your drawings and illustrations of the strange and wonderful land that Lysbette has imagined. And within the illustrations will be the hidden clues to the key for the code." She looked from each set of watchful eyes to the next then continued. "Given the dreadful outcome of the paper trial today, I have also decided instead of paper we will use the best-quality vellum I can find. The paper we are forced to print on is such poor quality it will disintegrate in just a few short years. I want this to last the test of time."

The women looked from one to the other. There were a few urgent whisperings and then, after a brief pause, Yolande was the first to speak.

"I am on board your ship, dear Charlotte," she said, and the others quickly chorused their agreement. Relief washed through Charlotte, and she smiled at them all.

"Once we have completed the encrypted work, we will take it to a place of safety until such time as it will be safe for Lysbette's work to be revealed in all its glory. I hope with all my heart that a time will soon come when the world is ready for Lysbette's wisdom, and a new order of things besides."

Later that same evening, after darkness had fallen, a tall, distinguished-looking man swathed in a fur-trimmed cape stood in Charlotte's entrance hall, waiting for her. Charlotte's pulse fluttered. The man cut an imposing figure. Surely not another inquisitor?

"Monsieur?"

He turned to face her, towering over her as he pulled off his gloves, one finger at a time. "Madame Guillard?" he asked, his voice resonant with authority. She nodded.

"My name," he said, "is John Haydon."

Charlotte's knees went from beneath her, and she lurched sideways. He sprang forward and grabbed her elbow to save her from falling.

"Madame? Are you unwell?"

She took a breath and steadied herself, moving away from him so that his hand slid from her arm. She looked at him with suspicion. "What is your business, sir?"

The man wore his cap low over one eye. A plumed, brilliant white feather quivered beside it, giving him a jaunty, playful look, at odds with the serious expression in his dark eyes. His neat mustache and sharp little beard were trimmed to perfection. He wore his clothes well. This was a wealthy, confident man dressed in silk and leather, an exquisite ruff setting off an elegant jaw. His presence changed the air in the room, charging it with something that made Charlotte's skin prickle.

Was this man the lover Monsieur Hatt had alluded to? Could he really be Lysbette's murderer? Was her death a crime of passion and nothing to do with Antoine de Mouchy at all?

"Is there," he said finally, as a maid walked through the entrance hall, "somewhere private we may talk?"

She hesitated, her mind racing with possibilities. What if he had come for the manuscript? Was this the man Lysbette had feared so much? But why? Was he a heretic or a defender of the faith? Perhaps it would be in her best interests to find out.

"This way," she said, leading the man toward the old library. She left the door ajar, in case she needed to shout for help, and gestured him toward the visitor's chair. She seated herself on the other side of the fireplace.

"Please," he said, lowering his voice and extending his hands in a gesture of friendship. "I'm sorry if I cause you alarm. I was a friend of Lysbette Angiers, with whom I know you were briefly acquainted. Given the circumstances, I could not give you advance warning of my visit. But I assure you, you have nothing to fear from me. Once, Lysbette and I were . . . close. We grew up together, both wards of Sir Thomas More. Later"—he cleared his throat, checked over his shoulder, as voices reached them from the hall—"we fell in love. I wanted to propose, but my father had already promised me to another. Lysbette was an orphan. She had no money and no connections. I have been married to Isabelle these past twenty years, and we are happy. She has given me three sons and two daughters. I love my wife and would not seek to harm her. But, between you and me, there will always be a slice of my heart devoted to Lysbette. She was a very special, clever woman, and she didn't deserve . . ." His jaw clenched and his fists bunched at his sides. ". . . what happened to her."

"Mr. Haydon," Charlotte interrupted, "I am sorry indeed about what happened to your friend. But I cannot think what any of this has to do with me. I met the woman once. She made a good impression upon me, and it was a terrible thing that her life should have been stolen so violently. That tragedy is some months old now, and I have put it behind me. I have nothing further to tell you or anyone else. Was it the commissioner who directed you here?"

"It was not the commissioner. I am trying to avoid him. I understand I am implicated because of letters I exchanged with Lysbette and the commissioner concluded my guilt as a result. No, Madame, it was Lysbette herself who directed me here. She wrote to me before she died. She must have had a premonition, for her letter bade me come to you, should the worst happen."

Charlotte looked at him with wide eyes.

"You have to understand," he said, his voice grave, "England has been in turmoil for the past fifteen years—ever since the dead King Henry, God rest his soul, split from Rome. But our new King, Edward, although young, is determined to distance himself even further from the Catholic faith. There is no more Mass, no celibacy among the clergy, no more Latin in church services." He sighed. "England has become a dangerous place for those who follow the old faith." He paused a moment to take a slug of wine. "Lysbette, as you probably know, had been a nun at Barking Abbey for almost ten years. But, after all that happened, I think she underwent a transformation." He sat in silence for a few minutes, a morose look upon his face. Then, with a visible shake, he was back in the room.

"When the abbey was closed, Lysbette had nowhere to go. She came to me in a terrible state, asking me to take her into my home as a tutor or servant. But what could I do? I was married with small children." He shifted uncomfortably in his seat. "Isabelle has a good heart, but taking Lysbette into our household . . . It was too much to ask of her. She knew about our history—I had not wished to lie to her—and Lysbette was an uncommonly beautiful woman." A shadow passed over his face.

"I will forever feel guilt for my actions, but I turned her away. The next I heard, she was married to a cloth merchant, a match arranged by Alice More, a woman who never liked Lysbette, although I never really understood why. I hoped Lysbette would be happy—I knew nothing of the man—but I fear the marriage brought her sadness. There were no children from the marriage. She occasionally wrote to me. It was never anything more than correspondence between friends. I thought if I could offer her some form of comfort, show her that at least one person in the world cared for her, that would be something. Then, this summer, I received this."

He took an unsealed letter from his pocket and handed it to Charlotte. She read,

My dear John,

I fear it is likely that by the time you read this, I may be dead. I believe my life to be in grave danger from the very person who should protect me from harm. I want you to know that I have always been grateful for your gentle and generous friendship.

When we were children, you encouraged me to read Sir Thomas's book, Utopia. That book had a profound effect on me, in a way no other has, before or since. It lit a spark in me, making me realize that where there is destruction, there can be new beginnings and a whole different world, better than the last.

Over the years, driven by a passion derived from my own experiences, I have worked on my own vision of a new order. One radically different from the one we currently inhabit. I live in hope that one day, something of this imagined world might come to be, and for that reason I desire my work to be kept safe from those who want it destroyed.

John, once you asked me to contact you if there was ever anything I needed. I have thought of coming to you so many times, but I have held back, never wanting to burden you.

Now, in light of my impending death, I ask one thing of you. I am shortly to depart for Paris where I hope to leave my life's work in the care of esteemed printer Charlotte Guillard, whose printing presses lie beneath the sign of the golden sun on La Grande Rue St.-Jacques. I will ask her to print some copies so that it may be preserved in perpetuity. I need these copies delivered anonymously to the addresses of the people I will leave with the manuscript, and that I copy here in this letter. But this is a dangerous task in this, our present, and it is unfair of me to place that burden in her hands alone. So I ask you to offer whatever assistance she may need to carry out my wishes. Indeed, if she is of the opinion that it is of too great a risk to her reputation, then please take the manuscript from her and deliver it to Sister Agnes at the Convent of the Blessed Heart by the church of Notre-Dame. As an old friend, I hope Agnes will store the work in the library there where I must hope it will remain safe until some future, more enlightened, time.

John, I thank you, you will always be in my heart, dearest.

Yours,
Lysbette

Charlotte looked up to meet John's eyes, which gleamed moist in the firelight. Her own, she found in surprise, were also awash with tears. A lump had formed, hard, in her throat. Lysbette Angiers had found a way to speak to her from beyond the grave, to weave her way into her heart, and to become as dear to her as though she had been a real, lifelong friend.

She swallowed.

"You may wonder," John continued, "why I visit you only now . . . I came to Paris as soon as I received this letter," he said, "in the hopes I might be able to save Lysbette from her fate. But of course, by then, it was too late. The commissioner, it seemed, had made up his mind that I was responsible for her murder. So, before he could catch me, I left for Calais to make some inquiries of my own."

Charlotte regarded him, his face illuminated by the bright light of the fire. Lysbette had trusted this man, and she felt in her bones he was worthy of that trust. She breathed deeply.

"Well, Mister John Haydon," she said finally, "it seems you and I have the same wish to help Lysbette Angiers. And I have just the notion how."

Chapter 31

Lysbette

Paris, July 1552

For some, the deepest, darkest hours of the night were to be feared. It was the time when demons and ghouls roamed the earth. When the grim reaper visited. Some would say when the devil danced brazenly on the earthly realm. But for Lysbette, those hours between midnight and dawn were her sweet friend.

She didn't waste them on sleep. After years of conditioning, her body and mind were alert during those hours. Years ago, at Barking, it had been for prayer, chanting, or divine contemplation. But even now, she still woke at 2 a.m. as though an internal bell rang inside her for matins. If Matthew was in an ale-induced stupor, she would take the opportunity to slip out of bed, pick up her shawl from the chair beside the bed, and steal from their room to work in glorious solitude and freedom on her manuscript.

Now, inching the door open, she slunk through as silent as a cat on velvet paws. She stood for a moment, listening to her husband's rumbling snores muted by the door between them. She crept along the corridor of their modest Paris lodgings through the dense dark, feeling her way along the wall with both hands, eyes seeking out any pinprick of light. The wall was cold against her palms as she felt for the wooden doorframe of the room next door to theirs.

When they arrived from Calais the evening before last, the

landlady had lamented they were her only guests. But this **had** given Lysbette the opportunity she didn't know she would **have.** Her fingers found the ridge of the door. She ran her hand down until she found the door handle. A floorboard creaked beneath her feet, and she froze, ears straining. But all was silent, and she inched the door open, praying its hinges were well oiled.

Closing the door quietly behind her, she edged her way toward the desk that stood before the window looking out over the street.

The room contained very little. A bed, wardrobe, desk, and rug. The air was still and stale, the walls pressing in. She shivered, even though the night was warm. With luck and God's good grace, she would return before Matthew woke and he would never know she'd been gone.

Turning to the bed, she knelt and felt beneath. After her meeting with Charlotte Guillard this afternoon, when they had returned to the lodgings earlier this evening, she had stolen in while Matthew visited the privy. Her fingers brushed the slippers and neatly folded cloak, then found the paper she'd left there, together with a pot of ink and quill, a candle and tinderbox. As quietly as she could, Lysbette struck the flint against the striker, breathing a sigh of relief when the sparks flew and ignited the hemp. She lit her candle and placed it on the desk, senses on high alert for any noise or movement.

It felt strange not to be working on the manuscript. Now it was no longer with her, she felt a tug of loss. Then she sat for a moment, letting her nerves and her thoughts settle before she began. Matthew was getting worse. His behavior was more volatile than ever, and with each passing day his loathing for her grew. The harder she tried to ingratiate herself, the more resentful he seemed to become. Had he found the manuscript before she'd been able to take it this morning to her friend Agnes at the Convent of the Blessed Heart, she shuddered to think what may have happened.

But leaving the manuscript there wasn't enough. It would soon be forgotten, left to crumble into dust on a shelf, if by some miracle it wasn't first found and destroyed as a work of heresy. That was why she needed to convince Charlotte Guillard to take the manuscript and print as many copies as Lysbette could afford. She had considered carefully the people who should be recipients of her book. Certain of the nuns she had once lived with at Barking; Sir Thomas's daughters; the maid, Mary; and a few other trusted women she had met over the years. In the hope Charlotte would agree to her commission, Lysbette had, before they left Calais for Paris, already taken the precaution of sending their names to John, with a letter of explanation, asking him to oversee their delivery in case anything should happen to her.

Now there was one last thing to write. A preface to the book she fervently hoped Charlotte will agree to print. She will take this preface with her when she goes to meet Charlotte outside the convent in just a few short hours. In it, readers will find an explanation, an expression of hope for a better future world.

In the world of men and women, nothing would ever be perfect. And that is why power should not be placed in few hands. More minds in control were better than one mind, and people must be replaced if they abused their power, or performed badly.

She picked up her quill, dipped it into the inkpot, and began to write her closing thoughts on *Alius*.

In writing this, my imagined commonwealth, I hope that you, the reader, will dwell on all it contains. I hope and pray it will not bring repression and punishment. God, in his kingdom of heaven, cannot be at fault. But man is flawed and full of sin. And so. I wonder. what if man has been wrong all along? We know the world is populated by many peoples—savages, as we from "enlightened" Europe understand them to be—peoples of very different faiths and beliefs and ways of life. We are so certain that we have right and God on our side. but so are they. And it makes me wonder—who can be right. and who wrong?

Perhaps all of us are wrong.

Perhaps it doesn't even matter. for what matters most is the way we live our lives in the here and now. before we ascend to the kingdom of heaven. And what if it is us. fallible mankind. who has made the biggest mistake of all. What if God is not a he?

I have read of a place in the East where the female is not only revered. but holds the power. as they are acknowledged to be at the heart of it all. But here. in our patriarchal world. the female is reduced. shamed. battered into acquiescence. Women are desired by men. yet resented for the desire men feel. I believe it is because men discern in women a quiet power men are afraid of. so they repress it to raise themselves up.

I do not believe this is how we are intended to live.

I believe that men and women were intended to be equals.

Perhaps God is without sex at all—

A crash and an angry yell sounded from down the hall. She froze, quill held aloft, heart thundering in her chest. Matthew's voice, "Lysbette, where in hell's name . . ." Her breath stopped. She shoved the paper, ink still wet, knowing it would smudge but that couldn't be helped, together with the quill and ink into the desk drawer and pushed it shut. Matthew's voice grew closer. He must have seen the chink of candlelight beneath the door. She stood, trembling violently.

"Lysbette!" Matthew was outside the door now. White hot fear gripped her like a giant iron fist. She prayed the landlady would hear and come to see what the commotion was. She prayed the woman was a light sleeper.

"In here," she called, attempting to keep her voice light, but it was cracked and reedy in her terror.

The door banged open, and Matthew stood, a devilish apparition in the light of his lantern, swaying on the threshold. Looking at her husband now, his hair on end, his cheeks flaccid and eyes red-rimmed, Lysbette wondered that she ever thought him handsome.

"The plague upon you, *woman*, what in God's name are you doing here?"

"I couldn't sleep, sir. I didn't want to disturb you so—"

"Well, damn you, you have!"

"Hush now. I'm sorry." She approached him to take him by the arm. "Come, let's return to bed."

Matthew shook himself free of her hand, recoiling from her.

"Don't speak to me as a *child*, you twisted, barren fool." His words, always, a stab to her heart. She'd failed him in the one wifely duty expected of all women. Her lack of offspring earned her his derision. A contempt that over the years had bloomed to mistrust and loathing.

He shoved past her and over to the desk where the candle still burned, illuminating the scratched and worn wood. Instinctively she followed him, willing him not to pull open the drawer. He stared at the desk as though able to see through the wood to her writing below.

"What were you doing here?"

"Nothing, I told you. Walking about . . ."

"I'm not a fool, you devil's whore. Who were you writing to?"

"Nobody." That, at least, was the truth.

Matthew studied her face for a moment, and she felt her cheeks grow hot. In a show of extreme self-control, he turned, brought his face low to the desk, ran his finger across it, held it up to the light of the candle. Wordlessly, he held his forefinger out toward her, skin stained with wet ink.

His lunge for her was so sudden and unexpected, Lysbette had no time to react, and the force caught her off-balance. His big hands clasped around her upper arms stopped her falling, but he shook her so hard her head snapped back and forth, rattling her teeth in her skull. "Stop! Stop! Please!"

The back of her head smashed against the wall. Blood trickled down her neck, and her knees gave way. The room spun as Matthew grasped her by the throat, tightening his grip until she choked and heaved for breath.

"Tell. Me. What. You. Were. *Doing*," he yelled, through gritted teeth. Matthew loathed being lied to, loathed being made a fool of. Probably because deep down, he knew he *was* a fool. His grip intensified and she spluttered and choked, scratching his hands and her own neck in her desperation. Just as she began to lose consciousness, he loosened his grip, letting go and she crashed to the ground, heaving in precious air, her neck and throat on fire. Pain pulsed from the back of her head. His foot landed with a thump against her useless, empty womb, and she curled into a ball.

It seemed the landlady was a deep sleeper after all. There were no running feet down the hallway to save her.

"*Tell me!* Or have you hidden it by sorcery, you *witch*?" He hauled Lysbette to her feet, grabbed at her shift, tearing it to see if she had something concealed beneath. The lack of any letter or other evidence of her cuckoldry seemed to infuriate him even more. "You have a lover, don't you?" His voice ignited in fury.

"No! *No.*"

"It's that John Haydon, isn't it? Don't think I don't know about you writing to him." *How? How can he know?* Her brain struggled for an explanation, but her terror made thought impossible. "I must have been a *fool* to take you on, you harlot. All those years in an abbey should have made you pure of heart. Instead, you are rotten inside, putrid and stinking. I just need proof of your wily, lustful nature and then I'll be rid of you. It's not the first time you've stolen about in the dead of night. I've woken before to find you gone. It's mischief you make, I know it. And once I've found what it is, I'll have you on the pyre, burning in everlasting hellfire."

Matthew had her arm pinned painfully behind her back. Of course he wanted her gone. Then he would be free to make an honest woman of Amy Monkford, daughter of the innkeeper at the Sow, who he forced himself upon. The girl who now bears the fruit of his attentions in her hard round belly. Where Lysbette failed, Amy succeeded. She is welcome to him, if only Lysbette didn't have to die first so he could be free.

He pushed her before him, walking in a circle around the room.

"I know you've been writing to him, meeting him. Doing filthy things with him. Making me a fool. Beguiling me, forcing me to marry you with your bewitching ways. How did you do it, eh? A love potion, was it? Or some pact you made with the devil?" He pushed her arm farther up her back making her screech with pain. *How can he know about the letters?*

"Please, Matthew, let me go . . ."

Lysbette let out a sob as pain seared through her shoulder. Her throat was so swollen and tender, she struggled for breath. They arrived back at the desk, and with a little gasp of understanding, Matthew spotted the drawer and wrenched it open, revealing the half-written preface, inkpot, and quill.

"I *knew* it," he said through gritted teeth. He pulled out her writing and set it on the desk, edging the candle closer. He was silent as he stared at it.

"What in God's name is this?" He peered at the words.

Panic flared inside. He would surely kill her now. He jerked her, but she could not form words. He stared at the text and then the thought penetrated, *He couldn't understand it!* Matthew could barely read English let alone Latin.

But he knew people who could.

He let out a laugh. "Just wait till I get this home and present it to the magistrate. Proof you are in league with the devil! I knew it. *I knew it!*"

He released her arm as though now her fate was sealed, he no longer needed to keep hold of her. Her heart slowed, her panic subsiding. He really was a fool, this man.

She swallowed, painfully.

"It won't do you any good," she gasped, her voice hoarse. "The King repealed the Witchcraft Act five years ago. Your accusations are not only wrong, but pointless. The magistrate will laugh you out of court."

Although any magistrate would consider her writing heretical, unless she recanted, so she would be for the pyre anyway. But Matthew needn't know that.

"Shut *up*, *whore!*" He leaned toward her, his face inches from hers, his breath rank. "If I can't be rid of you in England, I'll do it here, in France. They still burn their witches."

Matthew tucked the preface beneath his arm and dragged her

back to their room with his other hand. Holding the candle aloft he grabbed her traveling case, the same one she had left Barking with thirteen years before, with its false lining, from where it stood in the corner of the room. He flung it on the bed and tore open the buckles. He rummaged inside and, with a yell of triumph, held a bunch of letters aloft. Her stomach dropped. Dear god, she had forgotten those letters were in there. Letters from John from over the years since she had been married. Of course there was nothing between them. Simply his acknowledgment of her misery in the spaces between his words. Matthew would never pick up on those unsaid sentiments, but the existence of those letters would be enough evidence to him of her unfaithfulness.

And it was those letters, not the manuscript or the preface, Lysbette realized in that chilling moment of clarity, that just sealed her death warrant.

Before another word could be said, the door swung open and the landlady stood on the threshold, lantern held out before her like a shield. Thank heavens she woke after all.

"What is happening in here?" Her voice was shrill. "I heard a most dreadful commotion that nearly stopped my poor heart." She rested her palm across her chest in a demonstration of her distress at being woken in the night. She held her lantern out farther and squinted at Lysbette. Matthew dropped her arm like a stone. The woman was silent as she took in the scene. "I run a reputable establishment here, sir," she said finally. "I do not want anything to tarnish that during your stay. It could be very expensive for you, and my brother is rather good at ensuring those indebted to me pay up. Understand, sir?"

Matthew grunted and the woman left. He swore under his breath.

"We will finish with this business in the morning," he said.

"Do not entertain any notion of getting out of this bed until then."

Not another word was said as they both climbed back into bed. Lysbette lay curled in a ball, every part of her throbbing with pain as slowly, Matthew's breathing steadied, and the snores began once more.

She was saved, this time, but for how long?

It was imperative she was there to meet Charlotte at the gates of the convent by the time the lauds bells rang out.

Soon she must creep from this room once more, only this time, she hoped, she would be safely in the Convent of the Blessed Heart before Matthew noticed she was gone.

Chapter 32

Milly

Ellis Island, August 1953

Sweltering August hours flow like a river of sweat into seem-ingly endless days and weeks. The creaking infrastructure of Ellis Island swells and throbs under a baking sun as its inmates and guards alike, hot and irritable, languish behind their steel enclosure.

Milly spends more and more time with Nello in the library. His intellect is astonishing, and despite bouts of despair, he is excellent and amusing company. They discuss class struggles, the evils of capitalism, and ancient Rome. They talk about inevitable tensions between men and women and civil liberties and racism. After they put the world to rights, they talk about their favorite food and Nello tries to convince Milly that cricket is the most beautiful game in the world.

When the news comes that Nello is to be deported and sent back to Britain despite his tome on Melville and *Moby Dick*, Milly cries. He has been the only distraction, the only thing that makes a few of these endless hours bearable.

"Good luck, my dear," he says on the day of his departure. "Do not give up hope. Never. Give. Up. You promise?"

"Choose rather to be strong of soul than strong of body," she says, by way of agreement. "Pythagoras," she adds, in case he should think it her own wisdom. "It's something I remind myself of each day."

She waves goodbye and after the mail call later that morning brings her letters from home, she adopts his desk as her own, settling down to read. She opens Edward's first.

Dear Mum,

I miss you so much it hurts in my tummy. Daddy says we have to move to Kentucky, and we must tidy our toys away because people keep coming to look at our house as they are going to buy it. He says Grandma will take care of us while you are gone. I don't want Grandma. I want you. Yesterday I rode my bike all by myself to the end of our road and back. I'm getting really fast. I wish you could watch me.

  Please come home as soon as you can.

                                          Love from,
                                          Edward

Milly wipes the tears from her eyes and opens Olive's letter. George has penciled thick lines so her writing doesn't drift and he has helped her write some of the harder words.

Dear Mummy,

I wish you were here to cuddle me. I miss cuddling you. I have Teddy but he isn't as good as you. I'm trying to be strong like Daddy says, but I cry sometimes like when Betty said she didn't want to be my friend anymore. I'm sorry for telling Mrs.

Humphries about your special address book. Daddy said it would
be okay though.

Love from Olive
(age 5 and 2 months)

Milly frowns. Address book? What does Olive mean? She has
her address book, right here in her handbag, where it always is.
Olive must be confused. Inside the envelope there is one more
letter. *George*. Finally, he has written. Tears well and her fingers
shake as she unfolds it. Perhaps he has found a way to forgive her.

Dear Milly,

I'm writing this in haste, and the letter is short, I'm afraid, but
I will write a longer one when I have more time. I'm meeting
with Gordon O'Malley shortly and he will brief you when he sees
you. I heard just this morning that your hearing before the INS
examiner will be on Tuesday next week.

You should know that there has been a development, which
will explain the contents of Olive's letter. I'm not saying I am
happy about any of this given the mess we all find ourselves in,
thanks to you, but it seems I at least owe you an apology for one
part. It concerns the manuscript (which Olive calls your address
book). It turns out you were at least telling the truth about that,
and Olive knew about it all along. She started talking one day
about how you might need the address book while you are "On
the Island" (as we call it, like it's some vacation camp) so you can
send postcards to your friends, and how we must get it back from
Mrs. Humphries.

Yes, you read that right. The culprit who stole your "address book" was Mrs. H. She, too, confessed after Olive spilled the beans to me, and I confronted her. Here, I think, is the full story.

Mrs. Humphries had been attending meetings of some group called the Minute Women, whose purpose I don't fully understand, but Mrs. Humphries explained it was a local charity or something that Doris from the school runs. It turns out that Doris had been urging everyone to keep their eyes on neighbors, colleagues, friends, even, for potentially subversive behavior. Mrs. Humphries remembered you had had a strange gentleman visitor late last year and since that time had been unaccountably busy on some mysterious project. Mrs. Humphries's husband, as you know, is in Korea, and she takes her patriotic duties very seriously. When you asked her to babysit because you were working on a project for your "relative" she became suspicious. She also watched you regularly going to the library and meeting with Susan who had also been accused of un-American activities.

So she spoke to Doris about you and Doris said she would need some sort of evidence. When Mrs. Humphries was babysitting that night we went out for our anniversary, she questioned Olive about whether she had seen you meeting people she didn't know, or writing messages, or collecting envelopes. That was when Olive talked about your "address book" and how it was in strange writing that didn't look like English. Olive knew exactly where the book was kept because she'd seen you take it out of a shoebox on the shelf in your wardrobe one day when she was hiding beneath the bed during a game of hide-and-seek. She showed Mrs. Humphries where you kept it. She must have gone into our bedroom when the children were asleep and taken it.

She showed it to Doris, who obviously had no idea what it was, so she confided in Frank that evening, because this was his

area. Frank is desperate for a promotion and finding a commu-
nist, particularly a foreign-born one, would be quite the coup.
Well, to cut a long story short, Frank couldn't understand any
of it, either, but decided the manuscript was ancient, and there-
fore irrelevant. Doris gave it back to Mrs. Humphries the morn-
ing before she met you for the picnic. Mrs. Humphries said she
planned to return it when she next babysat, hopefully before you
noticed it was missing.

Then of course the FBI arrested you that same day and took you
to Ellis Island, guilty of much more than even Mrs. Humphries
had imagined. So, thinking what she had was an irrelevance,
and embarrassed that she had stolen the book and notebook, she
simply hid them away in her own home. It was only because of
what Olive told me that the whole matter came to light.

I have retrieved both and handed them over to Mr. O'Malley
to do with what he can.

I hope for your sake and the children's that this awful matter
can be cleared up. As for our life together, and my future career,
those remain in tatters, whatever the outcome. I won't be allowed
into the hearing, but I shall see you afterward.

Good luck,
George

Milly reads the letters through three times. Mrs. Humphries . . .
Mrs. Humphries! She paces the library, anger and resentment bub-
bling and boiling inside. She trusted the woman! She'd let her
take care of the most precious people in her life, Olive and Edward, when Humphries had been suspicious of Milly, spying on
her, all this time! *How could she.* She shakes her head in disbelief.
If it had been Doris who had done this, she might have believed

it. But not kind, sweet-natured, lonely Mrs. Humphries. How could she misjudge a person so badly?

There is good reason, after all, why books, and dogs, are preferable to people.

This whole thing is like some mad, unhinged nightmare. But live through it she must. She just hopes she can come out of it on the other side with her family, and herself, intact. And maybe now the manuscript is found, now that Mr. O'Malley knows about her role at Bletchley Park, things will, after all, turn out okay.

The INS hearing takes place in a stuffy little room in the offices of the Immigration and Naturalization Service in New York.

Mr. O'Malley explains the process before they go in.

"They have a full list today," he says, wiping sweat from his brow with a crumpled handkerchief. "So I don't suppose this will take too long."

"Do you have the manuscript, and my notebook?" Milly asks.

He taps the side of his briefcase. "All in here."

"What about Mrs. Humphries? Is she going to be here? I'd like to give her a piece of my mind . . ."

Mr. O'Malley shakes his head. "That probably wouldn't be the best idea. I doubt she will be here. The INS can call witnesses . . . But this isn't like a normal court proceeding, Mrs. Bennett, you need to understand. *We* don't have the same right to call witnesses." He sighs. "The best we can do is hope the judge thinks this is nothing serious and that you look like a nice lady, a good mother, and a decent wife. He might take kindly to you then."

Milly stares at him. He is trying to manage her expectations. She knows that, but still, she has faith in the justice system.

Surely it can't be as bad as O'Malley is saying. The INS examiner will look at the evidence. He will see she is no communist. That she has never been anything other than a law-abiding, politically moderate person who may have been misguided but never meant any harm. Perhaps he will have heard through quiet and confidential channels about the work she did during the war. He will see she is no threat to the national security of America.

In the end, it is all over in thirty minutes. Mr. O'Malley speaks eloquently and enthusiastically for Milly, setting out all the detail they had gone over beforehand. The examiner, an elderly white-haired gentleman, looks utterly bored by the proceedings and flicks through her file. He dismisses the matter of the manuscript with a wave of his hand, calling it an irrelevance. He is also disinterested in Milly's wartime work. Then he calls an expert witness, by the name of William Odell Nowell, who proceeds to talk at some length about the insidious content of Milly's articles and the effect they are having on women across America.

Milly turns to Mr. O'Malley and hisses, "Who is this guy? I've never seen or heard of him in my life before!"

Mr. O'Malley mouths for her to be quiet. When he finally gets the opportunity to ask the witness some questions, the man says he is a government employee, with expertise in the areas of print, radio, and television, whose task it is to monitor program, news, and commentary content. Later, Mr. O'Malley explains this man, along with several others he has encountered at hearings, is a professional expert witnesses who makes a good steady income from appearing regularly at these deportation hearings.

All of Milly's faith in the system evaporates as fast as spilled water in the midday sun.

The examiner makes his conclusions swiftly. Milly is to be permanently excluded from the United States and will be sent back to Britain on the next available transport. He stamps his gavel and it's on to the next case. The waiting guard takes Milly by the arm and leads her, numb with disbelief, into the waiting area.

George is outside, face pinched. He takes one look Milly's face, glances at O'Malley who shakes his head. He gasps and lurches forward. Takes Milly in his arms and hugs her fiercely.

She has held it together until that moment, but now, in the face of George's show of affection, she loses all control, clinging to him, her tears an unstoppable flow.

"I'm sorry, I'm sorry," she sobs, over and over.

"Shh." George rubs her back. "There must be something more we can do."

Mr. O'Malley ushers them into a small interview room, away from the haunting stares of the other people waiting outside to find out their own fate, or that of their loved ones.

"One of the dissenting judges in a recent case that went before the Supreme Court said," Mr. O'Malley speaks gravely, "and I quote: *Security is like liberty in that many are the crimes committed in its name.* I'm afraid you are a victim of such a crime, Mrs. Bennett. We can appeal to the attorney general, but I wouldn't get your hopes up." Milly thinks of Nello and how he made her promise never to give up hope.

"Do whatever you can, Mr. O'Malley. Please," Milly says, holding George's hand.

"I will." Mr. O'Malley gives them both a look. "I've a phone call to make. I'll leave the both of you in here for a few minutes. He glances at the guard who stands impassively by the door. "Give these folks some privacy, will you?" he says, irritation in his voice. "They are not going to leap four stories from the window if you wait outside the door."

The guard grunts but does as he is bid and closes the door behind him.

"Do you forgive me, George?" Milly asks, looking into his eyes. There is so much distance, so much hurt and exhaustion, she knows for certain, before he even answers, that things will never be the same between them again.

He runs a hand through his hair. Swallows back emotion. "Oh, Milly. I don't know. Everything has changed, the future so uncertain. I have to think of the children. Put their needs first. I have nothing—no money, no career. No wife. And I keep going over and over in my head, *why, why, why?* I never really knew you at all. The fact you had to keep all this from me. I don't know where it all went wrong. Look, I need some time, there is a lot to do. I've sold the house; we move to Kentucky next week.

"Oh, George . . ."

"I'll write to you from there. Once I've got my head straight and figured out what I'm going to do. Once we know more from Mr. O'Malley and the attorney general's office."

She nods. What else can she say?

Just before George leaves, he turns to her and says, "Susan sends her love. She's been released. They had nothing on her. Myra's out of work too. Not sure what they'll do next. They both are dreadfully sorry for what has happened to you. They said they would write."

Milly nods, and then George is gone. Back to the children, back to the home that soon will no longer be theirs. Panic flutters inside. Unless the attorney general takes pity on her, she won't be able to picture where they are, won't be able to see them grow, won't know them in any way at all.

It is less than a month later when Mr. O'Malley brings the news that Milly's appeal has been refused. She is to join a ship back to Britain in two days.

She sends a telegram to Aunt Tabatha, the only person who can help her now, and another to George.

Aunt Tabatha replies straight away.

RECEIVED THE AWFUL NEWS. CANT IMAGINE YOUR
DISTRESS. TRY NOT TO WORRY. I'LL TRAVEL DOWN TO
SOUTHAMPTON TO MEET YOU. WE'LL WORK SOMETHING
OUT. LOVE AUNT T

From George, there is only silence.

Chapter 33

Charlotte

Paris, May 1557

It was a glorious morning. Charlotte sat up in her bed, propped against many pillows. From her position, she could look out of her open window into her garden. The cherry trees were in full bloom, their branches heavy with pink and white blossom. She wondered if she might have enough strength today to leave her bed and sit on the bench beneath the largest of them.

But the thought of getting down all the stairs, maneuvering herself through the house and out into the garden was too much. And then there would be the pull of the printing works across the courtyard. Going there, if she even had the strength, would only upset her. It was the thought of her six printing presses going on without her. She would leave all her enterprise to Frédéric. After what he had endured, because of her, and for his loyalty, for his dedication to the printed word, it was the least she could do. And she knew the business would be in the best of hands.

Intellectually, that was exactly what she had always wanted and planned for. But emotionally, it was a stab to the heart. She knew her end was near, and she was at peace with it. Best to stay up here. She would get Sophie to move her comfortable armchair into the patch of sunlight beside the window. Sitting there, with the window open, the fresh spring air in her lungs, well, she could close her eyes and imagine she were twenty again, a young bride with Berthold at her side exploring their garden for the first time.

A moment later, Sophie appeared as though summoned by Charlotte's thoughts.

"Madame," she beamed when she saw her already sitting up in bed. "You are looking well!"

Charlotte laughed at that, her laughter quickly turning to a coughing fit. When it was over, she was breathless, as she often was these days, her old heart beating too fast behind her breastbone. Sophie, used to these episodes, brought Charlotte a cup of warm ale and a clean handkerchief. Dipping a linen cloth in a bowl of cool water, Sophie placed it gently against Charlotte's hot forehead. "Might you manage a little buttered bread dipped in milk? You need to keep your strength up—you have a visitor this afternoon, remember?"

She did remember. This was to be her final act in the strange turn her life took the day those noonday bells brought Lysbette Angiers to her door.

She had fulfilled her part in God's grand plan, and in some ways, these last five years, when she and her closest group of women had worked together in one great collaboration of transcription, translation, illustration, and encryption, had been the happiest of her life. The sense of purpose, the knowledge she was to leave behind something of true value and beauty, had, she was sure, kept her alive. She hoped, in ensuring Lysbette's masterpiece was preserved for future generations, she had done it justice. Not only in disguising its contents from this ever more intolerant and violent world in which they lived, but in the workmanship she and the other women had devoted to it. And that one day, a future generation of enlightened men and women may take inspiration from Lysbette's glorious ideas.

The work had had to be completed around the household's other commitments, but it was a collaboration that made Charlotte's heart swell with pride and pleasure. She, Yolande, Sophie, and two of her best illustrators, Anne and Clara, had brought the images on the pages to exquisite life. Between them, these talented women had worked so many hours together, talking, laughing, arguing at times, to produce a piece of art and literature of such breathtaking, intricate beauty that she knew it would have made Lysbette proud. She had not been able to resist designing a few touches of her own into the encryption key that her illustrators had so skillfully worked into the illustrations in the manuscript. Charlotte's own printing mark and initials had been included. So tiny, so well concealed, that the uninitiated would miss the references entirely. She just hoped they had done enough to keep the contents of the manuscript secret, but accessible at some future date to those who will one day be deserving of its contents.

Charlotte had thought long and hard about the best method of encrypting the work. Whoever was able to decipher it would never be known to her. That someone, she decided, should be a woman, or a group of women. It would have to be women of good education who had the ability to decode the work and read ancient Greek. They were women who would need to know astronomy, botany, and legend. They would need to understand the principles of applying a sophisticated cipher. It was a good deal to ask, but she felt certain that, one day, such a woman or women, would exist and find a way to crack the code.

It was, after all, God's plan.

And she had done all she could to conceal the keys to the encryption method. Few would imagine she'd have been fool enough to place the key in the document itself. And if she hid the manuscript among men, she felt sure it would be safer still. Which was why the encrypted manuscript would be taken this very afternoon to her old friend, the monk Godefroi Tilmann, who would hide it among other manuscripts in his well-stocked library at the monastery deep in the French countryside.

"Bring me the manuscript, Sophie," Charlotte said once dressed and helped into her armchair by the window. "I must part with it this afternoon, and I should like to spend an hour or two alone with it before I must say goodbye."

Sophie nodded, a sad smile on her face, and left the room. When she returned, a crease of worry had appeared on her forehead, the leather-bound manuscript heavy in her hands.

"What bothers you, Sophie?" Charlotte asked as the maid laid the book carefully in her lap.

Sophie straightened. She hesitated a moment before replying. Her kind gray eyes searched Charlotte's. "I fear this project, this manuscript, has become so much part of your life, that without it . . ." Her voice faded and she bit her lip.

"Without it I shall have nothing left to live for?"

Sophie nodded once, tears filling her eyes.

"Tsk, Sophie," Charlotte scolded. "I have lived a full life . . . Do not worry yourself so." She patted her dear maid's hand. "And when I am ready to go, I'll be sure to let you know."

She chuckled to lighten the mood and waved Sophie away.

John Haydon arrived shortly after the noonday bells. He filled the space in Charlotte's room, his tall frame, his stance, his masculinity charging the atmosphere so differently. She had grown used to having only women in her private quarters. But having worked all her life predominantly with men, she realized she missed them. Missed their jesting, the way they carried themselves. She missed their different way of looking at the world. Lysbette had been right. Society needed men *and* women. But like everything in life, they should be in balance. Not only nature and nations, but the sexes, too, must find equilibrium with each other if there is ever to be harmony in this world.

She held out both hands in welcome. John strode over to her and took her hands in his, bending forward to place a gentle kiss on each. His dark hair was graying even more than when she last saw him, and the lines of age around his eyes and mouth had deepened. Age, she noted, came for everyone in the end. But his eyes were still the warm, intelligent brown she remembered. *How good he and Lysbette would have been together,* she thought, *if only that had come to pass.* He was a good man. Charlotte could see that. Like her own Berthold and Claude had been. Like Frédéric, Monsieur Riant, and, come to think of it, most men she knew. Not the cartel at the papermakers guild who only cared for their profits, or Antoine de Mouchy and his vile heretic hunters.

"It's good to see you, John," she said as he pulled up a chair to sit beside her. "How is your family?"

"Growing up fast," he said. He rubbed his eyes as though trying to rid them of exhaustion. "Truthfully, I don't see as much of them as I would like. I am so often traveling these days."

"And how is it . . . Out there, on the road?" She inclined her head to the open window. Shut up here, in her bedroom away from the world, it was easy to ignore all the troubles.

John sighed. "Our Queen Mary now wishes to restore the Catholic faith in England, so the wheels turn once more. It is Protestants who are now to be burned at the stake. I fear that unless Catholics and Protestants can learn to live with each other in peace, there will be many more deaths. Besides, we will be at war again with France, too, before the summer is out. So, this may be my last opportunity to visit, for who knows how long."

Charlotte looked down at the manuscript. It felt more urgent than ever that it be taken to safety.

John followed the direction of her eyes. He sucked in a breath. "Is this it?"

"It is."

"May I?"

He took it from her as gently as a babe in arms.

Carefully, he opened the leather cover and, sheet by vellum sheet, he leafed through, pausing to look at the illustrations.

"Of course, I cannot read a word," he said, "but the illustrations are exquisite. As is the calligraphy. The whole thing . . ." He shook his head as though in wonder. "It is a work of art."

"Thank you. I hope Lysbette would approve."

"I know she would. What have you done with her original work?"

Charlotte sighed heavily. "Although it pained me to do it, I had Frédéric bury it deep beneath that cherry tree." She nodded toward the window. "I suppose it will disintegrate soon enough, especially if the quality of the paper on which it is written is as bad as it is in Paris. I couldn't bear to burn it. Somehow, burying it in my garden felt right."

John nodded. "That does seem fitting."

"John . . ." Charlotte hesitated. She needed to know the answer to the question that had pained her all these years. "When you first visited me after Lysbette's death, you said you had traveled to Calais to make inquiries about her husband. Tell me, did you find him?"

"Ah . . . You may recall," he said, leaning back into his chair, his eyes settling upon the cherry blossom, "that after his wife's death, Hatt fled Paris rather fast. It turned out there was a woman in Calais he was keen to get back to. She was expecting his child, and now that he was free, he planned to make an honest woman of her. But, it seems, the road between Paris and Calais can be treacherous. As he reached the marshlands about twenty miles outside Calais, he met an untimely end himself . . . The local magistrate concluded, as there was no evidence to the contrary, that he was set upon by robbers. Cloth merchants are good prey, carrying either valuable merchandise, or, better still, money. And our foolish Matthew was traveling alone." He glanced briefly at Charlotte, then back at the cherry blossom. "His body was found the following day beside the road, run through by a sword, his belongings and horse long gone." Charlotte remembered how John had learned of Lysbette's unhappiness in her marriage from her letters. Unhappiness, or worse?

Charlotte watched John as she let this news sink in. Birdsong drifted in through the window. The coo of a dove, the pretty trill of blue tits calling to each other across the garden. A sense of peace settled over her.

"How tragic," she said finally.

John turned back to look at her. "Indeed," he said. Was that a wink he gave just then? Or were her old eyes failing her?

An eye for an eye, John mouthed, or so she thought.

They sat in silence for a few minutes, Charlotte remembering how John told her he had ridden from Paris *posthaste* toward Calais only a few hours after the husband had disappeared. Time enough perhaps, to have caught up with him twenty miles outside the city.

She would not ask him if those events were connected. Instead, she said, "Well, John, you have a lengthy journey ahead to Godefroi at Grande Chartreuse"—she nodded at the manuscript—"so you will need some sustenance. I'll have Sophie bring refreshments and we will toast the memory of Lysbette."

As they waited for the food and drink, Charlotte felt a deep sense of calm and release. All was now in order. Lysbette had helped her to open her eyes and see the potential of this world in full illumination. Charlotte had played her part in preserving and, hopefully, saving Lysbette's work until a time when such words were no longer forbidden. And the man responsible for Lysbette's death had met his own untimely end.

All was fair and well.

Whether this was God's grand plan, whoever God really was, she supposed she would never know. But Charlotte did know she was ready to move now, peacefully, from this world to the next.

And for that, she was deeply grateful.

Chapter 34

Milly

Oxfordshire, October 1953

Aunt Tabatha slides the plate of scrambled eggs and toast in front of Milly.

"Careful, it's hot."

Milly stares at it. The idea of pushing that much food into her mouth and swallowing it makes her stomach turn.

"Ach, c'mon, love. You can't live on air. You're fading away before my very eyes."

She sits opposite Milly, concern etched into the contours of her face. Milly picks up her fork, pokes at the egg.

"I don't want you to think I'm ungrateful," she says, a tear escaping from her eye. She wipes it away roughly. Stupid, pointless tears. She's shed buckets of them these last three weeks and fat lot of good they've done.

"I know it's hard," Aunt Tabatha says, "but try and eat just a little. You need to keep your strength up. You'll see. In time, it will get easier. And somehow, someway, you'll get to see that family of yours again. I feel it in my bones."

"Then why hasn't he telephoned? Or answered my letters?" The question she asks about a thousand times a day. She has sent letter after letter, including her private confession about Bletchley Park, and why she has been unable to speak of it, although she doesn't name it, of course.

Aunt Tabatha sighs. Munches on some toast. Just like everything else she does in life, Aunt Tabatha chews in quick, efficient little movements. No fuss. Get the job done.

"Listen. George isn't a bad man. He's probably just working things out. His world has gone topsy-turvy. Maybe he wants to sort things out before he gets in touch? So that when he does, he has some good news."

"But what good news? There can't *be* any good news. I've made an unholy mess of things, but honestly, Auntie T, the more I go over it in my mind, the angrier I become. What sort of country separates a mother from her children? What sort of country *executes* another mother, whether she really was a spy or not, because society thinks a wife cannot have thoughts and opinions different from her husband? What sort of country urges its citizens to spy on one another, make heaven knows how many lose their jobs, throws them out, locks them up? And for what? For daring to think, or speak or write something, that someone, somewhere, might think is wrong?" She screeches in frustration.

"Shh," Aunt Tabatha soothes. "This won't do you any good at all. Now, I've been thinking. What do you say to making that trip this morning to the Bodleian to see if they might be interested in taking in the manuscript you said you might like to donate?"

Milly breathes out, long and slow. She nods. It's time to let it go. And it will be much better that it's kept and preserved in a library than here, shoved inside her small suitcase in their temporary lodgings.

Aunt Tabatha hesitates. "It also occurred to me," she says slowly, "that it might be worth popping into your old college. Seeing if they will let you finish that degree of yours? It was always something you wanted to do, and you never know where it might lead . . ."

Milly looks up at her. For the first time since she arrived back in England, there is a shift inside. Like the tiniest seed buried deep in frozen winter soil opening, a fragile shoot of something like hope, emerging. A way forward where before there had only been solid black hopelessness. And besides, she owes it to Aunt Tabatha to try. How will she ever repay her kindness? For dropping everything to come down here from Scotland to pick Milly up from her despair in Southampton; finding lodgings in Oxford where Milly asked to be, close to where she grew up and the only place in England she has ever called home; paying for everything and looking after Milly like she's her own mother.

"You were always such a funny little thing," Auntie T is saying, between mouthfuls, "with your head buried in those books about the ancient myths. You knew all the gods and philosophers and what-not by heart. Then, when you started on the Latin . . . *Well*, I said to your father, *she'll be bound for a life in academia, mark my words. Before you know it, she'll be writing books and giving lectures.*" She chuckles at the memory. "Anyway, I was thinking, what about teaching when you've finished the degree?" she asks. "I never really had you down as the type to stay home. And besides, it'd take your mind off all your troubles."

"Thank you, Auntie T," Milly says, taking a tiny bite of toast. "I really will give it some thought."

Two hours later, after several explanations to three different but equally circumspect-looking librarians at the Bodleian, Milly is taken through to a little side room where Mr. Tompkins, the curator of rare manuscripts and books, has agreed to meet her and look over the Van Hal manuscript and her decryption notes. She explained for a fourth time about her correspondence, almost a year ago now, with a Mr. C. G. Clarke, archivist, at the library, about Winton Harvey-Jones and his collection and her work in solving the puzzle of the book. She has repeated the story that Winton taught her all about coding and encryption as a hobby so many times that she almost believes it herself.

When Milly hands him the manuscript with her bare hands, Mr. Tompkins winces and leads her through to the restricted area of the library.

"Only academics and those with special permission can come here to examine the rare and fragile work we keep," he explains. He carefully lifts and places her manuscript in one of the specially designed cradles. "The less they're handled, the longer they will keep in good condition."

Milly cringes inside when she thinks of her own handling of this precious book. The way she kept it in a shoebox and worked on it at the kitchen table, turning the pages with her grubby, un-gloved fingers. Mr. Tompkins hands her a pair of silk gloves and puts on his own.

As Milly carefully turns the pages to show Mr. Tompkins the work, as though seeing the book with fresh eyes, she feels goose bumps rise across her skin at the beauty of the illustrations, the intricacy of the encryption, and the power of the words concealed within. She shows him the glorious sun with Charlotte Guillard's printing mark, its rays and spray of stars spreading out across the page, hears Mr. Tompkins's sharp intake of breath as she talks him through the zodiac illustrations that conceal the key to the code.

"Well, Mrs. Bennett," he says finally, turning to look at her over his reading spectacles. "You have done the most remarkable work. Indeed, I am quite astonished. Speechless." He pauses. "I would be honored to take this manuscript into our collection. It is unique . . . Priceless. Well, I needn't tell you that. Once it is unveiled to the public, it is likely to garner a great deal of interest. How would you feel about speaking to the press about it, and how you came to decode it?"

A thousand thoughts crowd Milly's mind. She can't do publicity. Not after all that happened with *My Life*. That episode has cost her George and the children. The trauma of these past weeks has left her barely able to function, let alone handle interviews with the press. And she hardly wants to risk, now, any more question marks over her ability to decode and come under suspicion of the British authorities.

"Look," she says finally. "Mr. Tompkins, I'd rather you told the press the manuscript and notebook have been donated anonymously. I have no wish for any publicity in connection with this at all, I'm afraid."

Mr. Tompkins gives her a long look, then nods firmly. "As you wish. I understand." *You really don't.* "Leave it all to me. I will ensure there is no connection with your name. And, Mrs. Bennett, thank you. We'll take good care of this extraordinary book for posterity."

Milly takes one last look at Charlotte's tiny initials *CG* and the sun from her printing mark, and she smiles. *I might have caused a storm in America, thanks to you, my friend, but here we are, and I've done my best for you and Lysbette Angiers. I'm sorry to say that even now, the world isn't quite ready to hear what you both have to say, but we must hope that one day, the next generation, or the next, or the one after that, will be. Your words are out there now, and always will be. I hope you would be pleased about that.*

Milly checks her watch. She really must go. Aunt Tabatha will wonder what's become of her. After saying her goodbyes to Mr.

Tompkins, she winds her way through the college grounds toward the bus stop and thinks perhaps this afternoon she will write a letter to Somerville and inquire about finishing her degree. She will need to do something and find a way to earn a living. She can't rely on Auntie T forever. At some point in the not-too-distant future, she'll need to return to Scotland and her life there.

Milly pops into the bakers and the grocers on her way home to pick up some bread, cheese, and a few tomatoes for their lunch.

"I'm home," she calls, as she pushes open the door to the tiny sitting room with her foot, her arms being full of the lunch provisions.

Milly senses their presence before she sees them. Something in the air is different, but so familiar it stops her in her tracks. The shopping crashes to the floor as her hands fly to her face.

Her family!

"Mummy!"

Milly is on the floor, the room blurred by a wash of tears, and the children, oh, her darling Edward and Olive, are suddenly in her arms real and alive and solid. The feel of them, after she has dreamed over and over of such a moment, is too much and she cannot speak, only bury her sobs in their hair, cling to their sweet, hot bodies.

"We missed you so very much, Mummy," Edward cries.

"Can we stay here?" Olive asks, "In England, with you?"

Yes, yes. Now she has them, she will never, ever risk letting go of them again.

"Mummy, you are squeezing me too tight. I can't breathe." Olive again.

And she releases them and then they are all laughing and crying at once and Milly is on her feet and in George's arms and dimly she hears Aunt Tabatha say she will get the kettle on and something about squashed tomatoes but she doesn't care because they are here and her cheek is pressed against George's chest and beneath his sweater, his shirt, his skin, she can hear his heart beat strong and true against her ear.

Later, when they are all sat around the small kitchen table—they will have to find somewhere bigger—George tells her that he *did* write to say he was coming, and he couldn't call on account of his own lodgings not having a telephone. It's possible they beat the letter because he wasn't sure if he used the right stamps, and anyway, it doesn't matter because they're here. He explained once he'd decided they should move to England, his mother had taken it badly, and their continued stay in Kentucky became impossible. So they moved temporarily back to New York, and he never received most of her letters.

"We found we couldn't live without you," George explains. "I'm hopeless without you, Milly, and besides, how could I deprive my children of their mother? I used the small amount of equity in the house after the mortgage was paid off to get us back here. I'm utterly broke."

"What's broke?" asks Edward.

"It means having no money," Milly explains.

"Do we have enough for a tortoise? Or a snake?" Olive asks. "Daddy promised me a pet."

"I'd rather have a dog," Edward says, wrinkling his nose at Olive.

"One day," George says, "when we are back on our feet, Edward may have his dog, and Olive a tortoise. But no snakes."

"Perhaps Hinchcliffe might still be willing to give you a reference and you can find work with a bank here, George?"

"I've had plenty of time to think about all that, Milly. Truth is, I hated that job. But I never wanted to admit it. I thought working hard and earning good money was making you and the children happy. I had no idea you were so lonely and unfulfilled too."

"We were both unhappy, but we hid it from each other."

"So it seems."

"No more secrets?"

"No more secrets."

They smile at each other and clasp hands across the table.

"Anyway, I have a plan. I wrote a letter to British Overseas Airways Corporation, but I probably put the wrong stamps on that, too, now I think of it, so I will write again. You see, Milly, the only thing I really understand, can do well, is up there." He points toward the ceiling. "Flying planes. So, I figure, why not convert to being a commercial pilot? If I can fly planes over the Channel to take on the Germans, I can fly tourists and businessmen back and forth across the Atlantic. What do you think?"

"I think it's a wonderful idea!"

"And," chips in Aunt Tabatha, "Milly has some plans of your own. Don't you?"

George looks at her.

"It was about finishing my degree, but I needn't do that now. Not now you are all here."

"I know it was always your dream. Once we are back on our feet and the children in school, you must." George smiles at her and heat spreads through her body.

"I've no idea how we shall manage," he adds, "with not a dime between us."

"It's lucky, then, isn't it," Milly says, unable to hold back her own smile, "that today I donated the manuscript to the Bodleian Library."

"How is that lucky exactly?" George's forehead creases in confusion.

"Because," Milly explains, "it turns out there is a monetary award for outstanding work in preserving and understanding items of exceptional historical merit given by the University of Oxford each year. Although there is no guarantee, Mr. Tompkins at the library, who is the chair for the awards committee, will put my work forward. Entries for this year's award must be received by the end of this month, and the award will be made on the second of January. He says there is nothing even close in terms of historical merit and thinks I have an excellent chance of winning. It's not a fortune, but it will be enough to get us set up until you have a job, George."

"Well, I never!" Aunt Tabatha exclaims.

"My clever wife," George says, kissing her hand. "This is wonderful news. Finally, something good to come from this whole fiasco." Aunt Tabatha stifles a sob and leaves the room.

Milly looks around the table, her heart full. Olive and Edward discuss suitable dog and tortoise names and George, lovely George, is sitting right here beside her, his hand in hers. The last year has been full of twists and turns she never could have predicted, and it will take some time for the trauma of the previous few months to settle. Who knows what the future will bring, and for sure there will be bumps and hurdles along the way. But they are here, together, and suddenly that is all that matters.

She looks around at her precious family. She will never take them, or her liberty, for granted again. They will build a new life here; it won't be a perfect, utopian one, but it will be honest and real, and filled with love.

And for all of that, she will be forever grateful.

Behind the Book

The Manuscript

The inspiration for this novel was sparked when I stumbled across an article about a famous six-hundred-year-old manuscript known as the Voynich manuscript, which is kept in the Beinecke Rare Book & Manuscript Library at Yale University. The manuscript, written by hand on vellum pages, is encoded, and, at least at the time of writing this book, remains unencrypted despite multiple efforts to unlock its secrets over the past hundred years. It is possible that by the time this book is published, AI might have solved the puzzle. Recent research suggests the underlying language of the Voynich manuscript is Hebrew, but Latin text has been detected and there are also suggestions it could be Arabic or Malay. In short, the experts simply don't know. There are some theories that the book was written by women. The idea of what might be in this manuscript is fascinating, and I found myself imagining what the contents might be, and how it might have been encrypted.

Although my manuscript is set over one hundred years later than the real Voynich manuscript, I used it as a model for my own version. I had some fun weeks inventing what might plausibly be considered so dangerous at the time that such a book would need to be encrypted, while remaining faithful to the theory that it was indeed written by women. I also had to research early modern encryption methods to come up with something plausible. For the content of the manuscript, I gained inspiration from various sources. Thomas More's famous *Utopia*, which had such an effect on my character Lysbette, together with some of the ideas of Desiderius Erasmus were useful in this regard, as well as some of the very early feminist writing that began to emerge in the sixteenth century. In particular, a pamphlet entitled *Jane Anger, For the Protection of Women*, published in 1589. Jane Anger was probably a pseudonym, but it was one of the first pieces of writing published by a woman on a nonreligious theme arguing against male misogyny. It was addressed to "All the Women of England."

Charlotte Guillard and Sixteenth-Century Paris

While researching the history of printing, I came across the figure of Charlotte Guillard, a female printer of high regard in Paris in the first half of the sixteenth century. At that time, Paris and Venice were the two biggest centers of printing in Europe. Due to the way the guild system worked in France at that time, women who were wives or daughters of deceased printers and who had learned the art of printing by working with their husbands or fathers, were permitted to carry on the business alone after they had died. There were several prominent women printers at that time, including Charlotte Guillard and Yolande Bonhomme. The two women collaborated on large projects, including taking the Paper Guild to court over the terrible quality of paper available in Paris at the time, although the case in question was brought a few years earlier than it took place in my book. They wanted to be able to source direct from the paper mills so they could control the quality, but they lost the case. It is possible that more of their books would have survived the ages had the paper quality been better. The actions in the book of the fictional leader of the guild, however, to win the case were entirely my invention. Antoine de Mouchy was a real heretic hunter in Paris.

Charlotte was a fascinating woman. While she did print mainly religious texts, she also printed scientific and humanist works, most notably those of Erasmus who was declared a heretic and whose books were banned and ordered to be burned. She also printed some anti-Protestant titles in which the heretic hunter Antoine de Mouchy wrote a preface. There is conjecture she may have done this as a precaution. So what she really thought and believed is something of a mystery. Although Charlotte's storyline is entirely invented, I felt able to bring her into my story and give her a role that *might* have been within her character had she really encountered the fictional Lysbette Angiers.

The only words of her own ever put into print are those in the Latin/Greek dictionaries as mentioned in this novel in 1552.

Lysbette Angiers and Sixteenth-Century England

Lysbette Angiers is entirely my own invention. Although she isn't based on a real person, Thomas More did take in various wards and adopted a couple of girls too. He very much believed in educating girls and did set up a school in his grand Chelsea house where he hired a tutor to educate mainly local girls. His own daughters were highly educated and intelligent. I have been a little unkind to Alice More, and all references to her attitudes and character are from my own imagination. Thomas More himself was a deeply devout man and a product of his time. He reacted to the threat of a new age and the unprecedented attack on the

Catholic Church within the context of his faith and what was expected of him by King Henry VIII, the violent turmoil in Europe, and some truly extreme weather events that led to famine and sickness in the early sixteenth century. From More's perspective, the only explanation for the crumbling of the known order and structures all around Europe was that this was the beginning of the end of the world and God's punishment for the sins of man.

Once again, I find his character full of interesting inconsistencies. He was great friends with Desiderius Erasmus. Erasmus was a vocal proponent of peace and liberty, and being against violence, the tyranny of princes, and the power of the state, while More was deeply conservative. Erasmus was labeled the worst of all heretics. And yet in *Utopia*, sometimes framed as the first communist writing, More suggests the perfect nation would see all power and wealth vested in the state, under a "fair prince." Erasmus was outspoken against the burning of books and heretics, yet More was responsible, under the orders of the King, for both. In the end, More died for his faith, and for not accepting the changed world around him. How the fortunes of his entire family must have altered after his death.

While Lysbette is fictional, I was most interested to understand the lives of nuns before and after the dissolution of the monasteries. The nuns led quite extraordinary lives within the patriarchal organization that was the Catholic Church. They were educated, and, at least within the abbeys themselves, they held responsible positions managing huge estates that generated vast sums of money, hence the King's interest in adding their wealth to his coffers. After the dissolution of the monasteries by Henry VIII, I wondered how, after such a life, the nuns adjusted to their vastly changed circumstances in the secular world.

Another influence on my character Lysbette and her writings

are the Minangkabau people of central Sumatra. It was a place that has stayed in my mind since I visited Bukittinggi and surrounding villages of the highlands of Sumatra myself as a backpacker in the early 1990s. Apart from the beauty of the place and the fertile land, these highlands are home to a matrilineal society (which predates its Muslim religion). Property and inheritance pass down the female line. It was a place unlike any I had ever visited, before or since. I was welcomed into a woman's home where I was offered sprinkles on toast (courtesy of the Dutch influence). I learned that boys live at home until around the age of twelve when they go to live in the local mosque. When they marry, the husband is permitted to live with his wife as a guest in her house. If the husband does not behave well, she can simply kick him out. Women and girls are cherished, and men and women share power. It was eye-opening for me in the twentieth century and must have been more so in the early sixteenth century. Contact was first made by French explorer Jean Parmentier in 1529, before the island converted to Islam. I therefore like to think it is perfectly possible that Lysbette could have read about this fascinating place after his return to France.

The Convent of the Blessed Heart in Paris is my own invention.

Milly Bennett and Twentieth-Century America

Milly and her family are invented characters, but the setting and atmosphere of that time in early 1950s America is inspired by the real history. I was particularly interested in the role of women during this, the second Red Scare. While working-class women had no choice but to work and raise their families, middle-class women were expected to stay home, raise their children, and look after their husbands. They were considered the bastion of the home, the family, and, in that respect, the very foundation of the American way of life, which in itself, of course, was a fiction created after the war. A yearning for some sort of utopian ideal. The perception in those years that democracy, the church, and American values were under unprecedented threat from communists was real and widespread. They were thought to be infiltrating the very heart of America, its government, its entertainment industry, its schools. Communist spies and infiltrators were thought to be hiding in plain sight (and of course some were), potentially in every neighborhood in every town. The prospect was terrifying, and, whipped up by prominent politicians such as Joseph McCarthy and figures such as J. Edgar Hoover, the then head of the FBI, so began an era of anti-communist hysteria.

Countless people, from politicians to teachers and librarians, lost their jobs and livelihoods for coming under suspicion for not only belonging to so-called suspicious organizations, but also for having any liberal or left-wing attitudes, for supporting the New Deal or any Social Security program, feminism, or for being gay or foreign or a multitude of other reasons. Others, particularly those born outside of the United States, faced deportation, including those from supposedly friendly countries such as Britain. An alien was unable to claim any of the usual rights afforded to US citizens to due process. William Odell Nowell, who gives evidence against Milly in the novel, and several like him, really did make a living from giving "evidence" as paid witnesses in deportation cases, having never encountered the accused before. The man Milly meets on Ellis Island was the celebrated intellectual C.L.R Lewis who really did send a copy of his interpretation of

Moby Dick to every member of Congress, and who was deported back to Britain.

The Minute Women was one of the largest anti-communist women's groups that operated during the 1950s, predominantly by suburban, white, middle-class women. In 1952, they had over fifty thousand members. They operated in a semiunderground fashion, rather than overtly being political, keeping their membership and activities secret. Their remit was to protect what they saw to be the heart of America—the home and local community—from the threat of communism. They were right wing, rooting themselves in traditional values and not in any way feminist. They undertook letter-writing campaigns, harassment and heckling, targeting anyone from school boards to librarians.

Levittown, Long Island, was one of several new suburban towns built rapidly after WWII for returning troops by Levitt & Sons, the building company owned by Abraham Levitt. Although I found no evidence of any involvement of Levittown residents being part of the Minute Women organization or hot on routing out communists, since Levittown was built with the vision of it being a modern-day Utopia for middle-class war heroes and their families, it seemed like an apt setting for my story.

Milly's reluctance to disclose her time at Bletchley was based on reality. The existence of Bletchley Park was kept top secret during and after WWII. It wasn't until 1974 that any of those who had been there spoke of its existence.

Acknowledgments

My heartfelt thanks to the whole publishing team at William Morrow who, I hope, will continue to publish a wide array of thought-provoking books written by an equally wide variety of authors with full freedom, for a very long time to come. My special thanks to my editor, Liz Stein, who is a joy to work with and who, as always, brings great wisdom and elevation to my work. Huge thanks too, to copy editor Laurie McGee for her careful checking of this novel and spotting my many errors. I am most grateful to [artwork designer TK] for bringing to life the zodiac page of my fictional manuscript which hid the key to the cipher. It is such a thrill to see this imagined illustration take shape, as well as to [cover designer TK] for the wonderful cover of this book.

Thank you to my fabulous literary agent, Caroline Hardman, and the team at Hardman & Swainson for championing my work. My gratitude, also, to my wonderful circle of author friends without whom life would be much less fun. My especial thanks, though, must go to Frances Quinn and Zoë Sommerville who read early versions of this novel and whose valuable feedback means their names should almost be on the front cover alongside mine. I am very grateful to Nikki Smith for brainstorming the original idea, to Polly Crosby for feedback, general good advice, and for arranging the best, life-enhancing writing retreats. Thanks to Eleni Kyriakou, Nicola Gill, and Charlotte Levin for the help and chats. Thank you to Gill Paul, Kate Thompson, and the historical novelists' gang for the fabulous lunches and mutual support network.

I particularly want to mention and acknowledge the enormous efforts and dedicated hard work put in by booksellers, librarians, reviewers, and book bloggers to ensure books find readers and readers find books. In an ever-more-crowded marketplace, this is harder than it sounds. Freedom to read and freedom to publish should never be taken for granted and we must guard these closely.

Finally, my grateful thanks to my wonderful, patient husband and family who walk the walk with me through the highs and lows of every book. I could not do this without you.

Discussion Questions

1. Imagine you are writing a work like *Alius*. What would your "different way" look like? Which aspects of society in your Alius would differ from the reality in which you live currently?

2. Lysbette sees monasteries as matriarchal communities. What other communities, industries, or other collectives can you think of as matriarchies?

3. *Utopia* had a lasting, almost revolutionary, impact on political and critical thought. What other written works have had a similar political and social effect?

4. Milly and her sister-in-law Ida consider their husbands "reasonable" men. What does this mean? Is it enough for a man to be "reasonable?" How can men be active in the struggle for the rights of women?

5. Who decides which words are "forbidden?" How does the book banning of today compare to the censorship Lysbette, Charlotte, and Milly experienced in their respective decades?

6. The Minute Women were a real collective that used fearmongering to justify reporting peers to authorities with little to no evidence. How can people protect themselves from fearmongering rhetoric?

7. What do you think of John Haydon's decision when Lysbette comes to him for help? Should he have decided differently? If so, how?

8. Milly is given the manuscript to decode in part because she

"thinks like a woman." What does this mean? In what ways does Milly's lived experience make her the perfect person to decode the manuscript?

9. At the time of your reading this, is the world ready to hear what Lysbette has to say?

10. Without the printing press, in all likelihood, the Protestant Reformation, the years of violent religious wars and the enlightenment that followed, would not have happened. We are now living through a digital revolution with the advent of artificial intelligence, the likes of which we have never seen before. What consequences of this can you foresee? Do you feel optimistic or pessimistic about the changes it will bring?

About the Author

Louise Fein is the author of *Daughter of the Reich*, which has been published in thirteen territories, the international bestseller *The Hidden Child*, and *The London Bookshop Affair*. She holds an MA in Creative Writing from St. Mary's University. She lives in Surrey, UK, with her family.